HOOKED ON
DEATH

HOOKED ON DEATH

A Max Addams
Fly Fishing Mystery

David Leitz

PRAISE FOR DAVID LEITZ'S
MAX ADDAMS SERIES

"To my delight . . . there are delightful characters, and humor and sex and terror and an obvious knowledge of fly fishing."

Steven Bodio, FLY, ROD & REEL

"Not only does Leitz clearly know fly fishing, he is inventive in making that knowledge integral to a fast moving plot."

OUTDOOR LIFE

"Fortunately you don't have to go far to satisfy your craving for good fishing and rip-roaring good murder mysteries. In fact, if you're planning to learn to fly fish (or teach someone else to do so), you could do worse than to buy Leitz's books as primers before taking one cast. Unlike the trout in Leitz's stories, once he catches you, you won't be released."

Hank Nuwer, MUNCIE STAR PRESS

"David Leitz has done it again! He writes intelligent, full-of-surprises myster- ies . . . a highly entertaining mix of quirky characters, great sense of place and a tense plot with lots of twist along the way."

Rae Francoeur, NORTH SHORE MAGAZINE

". . . not one page leaves you yawning.
Leitz's simple and creative style provides great entertainment for anyone."
Mark Quarantiello, ANGLER'S UPDATE

". . . a thumping good read . . ."
Gary LaFontaine

OTHER BOOKS BY DAVID LEITZ:
The Fly Fishing Corpse
Casting In Dead Water
Dying To Fly Fish
Fly Fishing Can Be Fatal

FOR MY BROTHER JIM.

CHAPTER ONE

On the list of twenty-five irreconcilable differences my wife's lawyer presented to the judge at the alimony hearing, "Urinates in the yard" was number sixteen.

Numbers one through fifteen had to do with fly fishing.

The other nine were lies.

As a result, I know she's still convinced that peeing off the porch is one of the reasons why, once we were divorced and I'd been canned from my job in the New York City ad agency, I moved all the way up here to northern Vermont and now own and run this fly fishing lodge. My daughter, Sabrina who is now in her late twenties and visits the lodge occasionally with her husband and daughter tells me her mother is positive I sit around all summer long in old, patched fishing waders drinking cheap beer, smoking bad cigars and telling dirty jokes to one bunch of male misfits after another.

To be honest, there are times I wish it were like that. But it's not. And far from it.

Running a fishing lodge is a pain in the ass. Every year, something happens to make me want to stick a "For Sale" sign up at the top of our access road, aim my Jeep west and keep driving.

This past spring is a good example. What should have been a simple visit by Sabrina and couple of friends from New York City turned into a nightmare of ancient Native American curses, betrayal and senseless murder.

* * *

It started with a haircut.

There are only two barbershops in the town of Loon. Drome's is neither the best nor worst . . . it's just the one I've been going to since I first moved up here ten years ago. It's two doors in from Main Street, just around the corner from Sam's Sporting Goods store. An electrified three foot high, red and white barber pole that lights up and turns slowly when the shop is open, hangs head height between the entrance and the terminally fogged plate glass window with "DROME'S" stenciled on it in big goldleaf letters. Inside, through a door with a bell at the top that tinkles when it opens, Drome's is one deep rectangular room. The floor is large black and yellowed-white squares of cracked ceramic tile under a ceiling of buzzing fluorescent lights. The top half of both long walls are mirrored. Three barber chairs and three sinks are on the left. Along the facing wall several metal-legged chairs with torn plastic covers on their padded seats flank a low table piled high with mostly out-of-date magazines. At the very back of the room, an old Zenith color television set hangs precariously from the wall. I've never seen it turned on. Instead an old tube table radio, always tuned to one of the many Canadian stations we get way up here, fills the shop with static-y American music with French lyrics.

Stormy's brother, Rayleen says that back in the fifties when crewcuts were popular, Drome's owner Peter Dromeshauser had two other barbers working for him and the three of them cut hair from eight in the morning until seven at night six days a week. Now Drome's is just Pete and he only cuts hair on Tuesdays and Thursdays. The other three days he works in the Loon Lager bottling room in the new brewery building on the north end of town.

Although I trim my beard every other day, I only get two haircuts a year; Once, just before the fly fishing season starts and once, just before Thanksgiving. If I need to look neat for some reason in between, like a wedding or a meeting at the stuffy offices of Loon Cooperative Bank about all the money I owe, Stormy and a pair of my fly tying scissors do a passable job on the lodge back porch.

Since fly fishing season was to begin in a week, I was in Drome's waiting my turn. The walking cast on my lower leg was stretched out in front of me. I was reading a very old PEOPLE magazine.

Peter Dromeshauser, a cigarette hanging from the corner of his mouth, was standing behind the center barber chair cutting Loon Hotel owner, John Quinn's thick black hair. Pete is tall and big boned but so thin and gaunt that upon meeting him for the first time most people think he's terminally ill. The rapid snip snip snip of his scissors was almost a percussion counterpoint to the one note musical hum of the fluorescents. John, his florid face protruding from the hairy white sheet, had his eyes closed. He looked like he was asleep. Waiting in the sagging chairs along with me was Wabnaki chief, Danny Shortsleeves and Loon County Sheriff's deputy-in-training, Richie Norville. Richie was sniffing at a bad head cold. Danny was chewing on a smoldering cigar.

I had actually limped into Drome's first so, by rights, was next in line, but Richie, upon arriving right after me, had asked if he could take my place. "I'm on duty in forty minutes, Max," he said, hanging his smokey hat on one of the pegs by the TV. "You mind if I bump you?"

I wasn't in any hurry and was glad to be sitting. Besides I never get a chance to read PEOPLE so I said, "Be my guest."

"It won't take long," Richie said, running his hand over is carrot colored brush cut. "Right, Mr. Dromeshauser?"

The scissors never skipping a beat, Pete looked up from the top of John's head and, squinting through the cigarette smoke, nodded agreement in the mirror. "Damn straight it won't take long," he said. "You're not givin' me that cold,"

The new looking, patent leather belt full of cop gear squeaked like a horse's saddle as Richie sat two chairs away from me with a beat up copy of last October's PLAYBOY.

"How's your training coming, Richie?" John asked from under the snipping scissors.

Richie frowned but didn't look up from the magazine. "Too slow, if you ask me. Seems like the Sheriff's never around."

"I haven't seen much of Simon last couple weeks, either," Pete said and then laughed knowingly. "What's he doin'? Workin' an-other job on the side?"

Richie sighed. "I'm not supposed to say, Mr., Dromeshauser."

"Com'on, Richie. We ain't gonna tell anybody. What's he doin'?"

"He's working part time out at Red Town helping get their police force organized."

"What's to organize?" Pete said. "They only have two cops."

"Yeah, I know but, I guess they don't have shifts or patrol schedules. And they never use their computer." He looked at each of us. "Please don't say I said anything. Sheriff Perkins would fry my butt."

"We're not going to say anything, Richie," John said. "Be-sides, far as I know, there's no law that says the sheriff can't work another job to make ends meet."

"I know there isn't," Richie said. "But, well, Sheriff Perkins wants to get re-elected and . . ."

"Stop worrying about it, Richie," Pete said, leaning back to study John's head. "I already forgot what you told us."

65 year old Chief Danny Shortsleeves came in for a shave about five minutes later. One of only 1,275 full blooded Wabnakis left in the world, he's built like an oil drum. About six feet . . . in height and circumference . . . he has a broad, flat face that looks like it was fashioned from an old catcher's mitt. His dark chocolate colored eyes remind me of a crow's. Parted in the middle, his thick charcoal gray hair hangs in two long braids over the front of his shoulders. Summer or winter, I've never seen Danny in anything but green and black buffalo plaid wool shirts and heavy twill khaki trousers supported by wide leather braces. Today, the steel-toed, logger's boots, that I'm sure must lace to his knees under the kha-kis, were caked with the dried rust-colored mud that was the ac-tual . . . and originally non-racist . . . reason everyone in Loon sim-ply refer to the hundreds of acres of Wabnaki land out on Robinson Mountain as, "Red Town".

Danny pulled off his heavy tent-size, canvas coat and tossed it on the chair beside me. It smelled like cigar. "Morning, Pete,"

Danny said. "Richie. Max." His broad, gold-studded, toothy smile was bigger than ever.

"Set the date yet, Danny?" John asked.

"May 12th." Danny had finally received tribal consent and was marrying his childhood sweetheart, Rachel Arneau. The couple had waited the ten years the State of Vermont required until Danny's first wife could be declared legally dead. Although most of it happened before I moved to the Loon area, Stormy had told me how Danny's wife had one day just packed an old leather suitcase and disappeared. "Woman was a hard drinker, Max," Stormy had said. "Even for an Indian. Always wanderin' off somewhere and Danny was always goin' and gettin' her and bringin' her back." This time, Danny couldn't find her. And neither could the sheriff's department or the state police. A yellowing picture of her still hangs in the "Missing Persons" section of the Loon post office.

We each shook Danny Shortsleeves' big hand and congratulated him on his upcoming wedding.

He looked at my cast. "How's that ankle, Max? Heard you busted it."

I shrugged and tapped the cane leaning against the chair. "At least the crutches stage is over. And maybe I can drive now." I had slipped on some icy rocks back in November and broken the Calcis bone in my left foot just below the Achilles' tendon in my ankle. It had been reset twice since the but now, according to the latest x-rays, was finally knitting. Day before yesterday my doctor had soaked off the heavy, hot and itchy, calf-to-toes plaster cast and replaced it with a lighter, less bulky, but none the less hot and itchy, fiberglass model with a rubber lump set in the heel so I could finally walk without crutches. "The whole thing's a pain in the ass," I said.

Danny put his hands on his hips and looked at John Quinn's reflection in the mirror. "So, how's things at the hotel, John?"

John opened one eye. "A little muddy," he said. "What's it like in Red Town?"

"Tomato soup." Danny Shortsleeves sat heavily in the chair on my other side and pulled a large, wrapped cigar from his breast pocket and looked at me. "River clearing out by your place yet, Max?"

I nodded. "It looks a lot better today." This time of year the snow was still thawing in the higher elevations and the normally vodka-clear Whitefork River which runs by my fishing lodge is the color of cafe au lait. "We're drying out pretty well. I think run-off's just about over."

"How's those tapes coming you're making, Danny?" John asked.

Danny shrugged and began peeling the cellophane from the cigar. "Just finished recording the last one over at the radio station before coming here."

Richie looked up from the magazine and frowned. "What tapes?"

"Danny's recordin' Indian stories up at the radio station," Pete said. "All the tribal legends. Nobody can tell 'em like the Danny can." Chief Danny Shortsleeves was a regional celebrity of sorts. His dramatic one man shows were in constant demand by community organizations, regional church groups and school assemblies. I have never seen one but my housekeeper Stormy says that, to see him on stage, half naked and lit only by the light from a simulated campfire, is really an experience.

John twisted slightly in the barber chair to look at Richie. "Danny's tapes are going to be a part of that new Wabnaki Native American exhibit that Danny, Rachel and their people trying to put together at the Loon Historical Society."

Richie's frown deepened. "Where's the Historical Society?"

"Library," Pete said. "Jesus, kid, you do have a lot to learn."

"I didn't grow up here, remember?" Richie said. "How am I supposed to know there's a Historical Society in the library?"

"Good thing they haven't needed a cop over there," Pete mumbled. He turned on the blow-drier.

"Yeah," John said, with a laugh. "You ought to go over there and take a look, Richie. Might help you understand the town you've learning how to protect."

"Give the kid a break," Danny said. "Half the people in this town don't even know there's a library." He bit off the end of the cigar and spit it in an ashtray.

Danny was right. They were being a little hard on Richie. I'd lived in Loon almost ten years before I visited the little museum. And I probably wouldn't have gone then had I not been dating the Mayor. As it was, she had to practically drag me. "It's pretty interesting, Richie," I said. And it is. Five rooms of interactive displays that trace the history of the area from the French trappers to the old time loggers to the days when Loon was known as, "The Boot Capital New England". Old photographs, clothing, artifacts and life-size dioramas that depict scenes of everyday life in colonial Loon fill the rooms. Until a couple years ago, however, it was only a whiteman's exhibit. Then Chief Danny, the Wabnaki tribal council members and Rachel, who taught 12th grade history at the Red Town high school, petitioned the Loon City Council and the Loon Historical Committee for equal representation and got an enthusiastic okay from the Council to enlarge the exhibit. The Historical Committee, under the leadership of a woman named, Elizabeth Ross vetoed it with a 12-0 vote claiming inadequate space and funds. Undaunted, Rachel, Danny and tribal council marshalled Red Town elementary school children who sold magazines and cookies, collected bottles and cans, and washed pickups for the better part of two years to make the two thousand dollars needed to receive matching funds from the town to renovate the empty fourth floor of the library's north wing and put together the Native American part of the town's history. It was now just about ready to open.

Pete looked at Danny in the mirror. "They still planning to open your exhibits in June?"

Danny shrugged. "My opinion, it could open tomorrow. Everything's finished."

"Then why the delay?"

"Somethin' about not enough emergency exits up there on the fourth floor." He shook his head. "I don't know. That Ross woman at the Historical Society's been throwing in one monkey wrench after another since we started this thing."

"Gee, I wonder why?" John said, sarcastically. "The woman's the biggest bigot in New England. Don't you remember all the trouble Bryce and I had getting our liquor license? She and that bunch of homophobics they call a committee fought us for months."

I remembered that. John and his partner, Bryce Hill had been the only openly gay males in Loon when they bought and began to restore the old run down Loon Hotel. Because it was a designated historical landmark, everything they did to the ramshackle building had to be approved by Elizabeth and her committee. Whether it was the red color they wanted to paint it, the perennial gardens Bryce wanted to plant out front or the bar and restaurant they wanted to put in overlooking the gardens in the back, the Historical Committee fought them. Finally, my former girlfriend, Loon Mayor Ruth Pearlman, stepped in and, with a fancy bit of political maneuvering, got the state to remove the Loon Hotel from the list of Historical Landmarks on the grounds that its dilapidated condition required major rebuilding if it was to meet modern hostelry codes. Today, the old Victorian former ark is one of Loon's more beautiful buildings. And the small restaurant they added after Ruth's intervention, has received rave reviews from regional critics and was the weekend dinner destination for lovers of San Francisco-style cuisine from as far away as Boston.

"I sympathize with you, Chief," John said, studying his hair in the mirror. "They can be a nasty bunch."

Danny shrugged. "Actually, it doesn't make that much difference. The school's got them kids digging for homelife artifacts anyway."

Pete turned off the blow-drier again. "What kind of artifacts?"

"Pottery, eating utensils, skinning tools," Danny said.

"Where they gonna find stuff like that?" Richie asked.

"Out at Max's place," Pete said. "Don't you read the Sentinel either, kid?"

Richie blushed.

"The Loon Sentinel had a big story when they began digging last month." I said to Richie. Two ten foot square sections of the lawn at the lake's edge in front of Whitefork Lodge had been cordoned off and, with criss-crossing string, divided into one foot sections. "I've got a half dozen of Rachel's high school kids digging with spoons and little brushes from sunrise to sunset."

"School kids?"

"Seniors," Danny said. "Doin' it for credit."

"Man," Richie said. "Spending the spring digging in the dirt. Wish I'd had a teacher like your Rachel when I was in high school."

"Wasn't Rachel's idea," Danny said. "If she had her way, those kids would be in the classroom where they're supposed to be. She doesn't like tampering with sacred remains."

"Then how . . . ?"

Danny gestured at me with the cigar. "Max's girlfrien . . . er, the mayor pushed for it. Got the school board involved. One thing led to another and then the Sentinel got hold of the idea." He shrugged. "'Though Rachel still don't like it, it sure created some good publicity." He winked at me. "Right, Max?"

I nodded. When the high school kids first started digging we not only had all the major newspapers come up to the lodge for pictures and interviews, but vans and equipment trucks for every TV news magazine in New England were parked out on the lawn.

"'Though nobody up here I know of actually saw it," Danny continued, "last Sunday's New York Times supposedly even had a story about it."

"Why is Rachel so against the digging?" Richie asked.

We all looked at Danny. He sighed. "Guess you could call my wife-to-be, a bit militant," he said. "She don't mind diggin' up a few bowls and arrowheads. It's bones she's got a thing about."

Richie closed the PLAYBOY. "What if they do dig up some bones?"

Danny shrugged. "Rachel'll make sure they get put back. She don't want sacred graves disturbed."

Richie's eyes widened. "Graves?"

He nodded. "The Ancient Ones buried some of their dead where Max's lake is now."

Pete turned. "Did you know all this when you bought the place, Max?"

"Some of it," I said.

"How deep have they dug now?" John asked.

"A couple feet," I said. "Maybe three in a few places."

"Finding anything?"

"Some pottery so far," I said. "I actually haven't been paying much attention." I looked at Danny. "Rachel's out there every day." At least once a day, Rachel Arneau comes out to the lodge, walks down to the excavation and goes over what's been found. "Ask the Chief."

"She don't tell me anything." Danny frowned.

Pete laughed. "How's Stormy handlin' havin' this dig thing goin' on?"

"Stormy doesn't mind," I said. "She made the kids turn over her garden before they did anything else." Every spring, Stormy plants a vegetable/herb garden just outside the lodge back door. Even with our shorter growing season, she manages to harvest not only enough peas, onions, carrots, raddichio, peppers and tomatoes for meals, but to can and freeze for my use over the winter.

"How is my friend, Stormy?" Danny said. "I haven't been to a meeting in a few months." He was referring to Alcoholic Anonymous meetings. He and Stormy usually attend the one held in the basement of the Unitarian Church on Sunday night. Although Danny himself has never had a problem with alcohol, Stormy's told me he's still looking for answers to his wife's disappearance.

"She and Rayleen are getting the lodge ready," I said. Stormy and her brother spend the month before fly fishing season readying Whitefork Lodge for our onslaught of guests. Rayleen, with hammer, nails and fiberglass patches. Stormy, with a tank vacuum the size of an Airstream, a mop and gallons of vinegar and water cleaning solution.

"Whitefork booked opening day this year, Max?" John asked.

Most recent years, because of the mud and run-off, Whitefork Lodge has been empty not only on the opening day of fly fishing season but for the entire first week following.

"In a manner of speaking," I said. "I guess we are booked."

"In a manner of speaking?"

"My daughter's bringing a couple friends up from New York City for a few days." I shrugged. "Arriving Monday, leaving Saturday morning."

"Chicks fly fishing?" Richie said with a leer. "You need any help, Max, just call me."

Danny raised a thick, black eyebrow. "From what I remember, Max's daughter can out fish any man I ever met."

"Me included," I said and looked at Richie. "Women anglers are the fastest growing part of the sport, Richie."

"No shit?" Richie frowned.

I nodded.

"Didn't know that." Danny blew a thick wad of smoke into the air and studied it.

"You're comping them, I assume," John said.

I shook my head. "Sabrina wouldn't hear of it."

"How old are they?" Richie was now leaning forward in his chair. "Any cute ones, Max?"

I frowned.

"Sabrina bringing your grand daughter?" John asked.

I shook my head. "My ex-wife is coming up to New York from Florida to baby-sit for her."

"Florida," Richie said, "She live there?"

I nodded.

"Anywhere near Disney World?"

"Her husband works at SEAWORLD."

"Now, there's the place to meet chicks."

"Jesus, Richie." Danny looked at Pete. "You might be doin' the world a favor, Pete," he grinned, "if you snipped off this kid's balls along with his hair when you cut it."

"Hey." Richie frowned at Danny. "You taken a look at the

available women in this town lately? We single guys could use a little imported talent. Right, Max?"

Pete's scissors stopped snipping and everyone looked at me. Being a small town, it was common knowledge that Loon mayor Ruth Pearlman and I had broken off our long relationship several months ago. It was also pretty well known that she was dating, Doug Bolick, a University of Vermont professor who lived in town.

Richie had been looking from face to face and now realized what he'd said. "Oh, gee. I'm sorry, Max. I forgot . . ."

"Don't sweat it," I said and then looked at the others. "And stop looking at me like that. Richie's right. I am unattached."

Chief cleared his throat and looked away. John closed his eyes as Pete's scissors resumed snipping. We were all silent for a few minutes. Moon River in French began playing on the radio.

John was the one who finally broke the silence. "That true, Max? About women being the fastest growing part of fly fishing?"

"Second only to salt water." I said. "The magazines I read say it could replace cross country skiing."

"Could just plain replace all kinds of skiing for all I care," Pete said. "Can't get through Hooker Hill Road from November to February 'cause of those Goddam idiots waiting in line to park at Snob's Hill." Snob Hill was what most Loon old timers call Robin's Hill Ski Area, which, with it's six trails, three chairlifts and one gondola, takes up about three-quarters of the south side of Robinson Mountain just five miles north of town. "Goddam snob-asses with their big cars."

Richie laughed. "You're just bitchin' because tourists don't get haircuts."

We all chuckled.

"Screw haircuts," Pete said, glaring at the deputy in mirror. "I'd just like to be able to get over to my job at the brewery the easy way in the morning." He turned and shook the scissors at Richie. "Why the hell don't you cop bozos get up there and direct that traffic, anyway? I pay your Goddam salary." His sunken eyes darted to Danny Shortsleeves. "Or better, now that you and Rachel's gonna be multi-millionaires, why don'tcha widen the road up there? Gonna have to anyway, if she gets the state's okay for that gambling casino she wants so badly."

We all looked at Danny. It was well known that Rachel was spearheading the drive for permission from the Vermont State Gaming Commission to build an one hundred acre casino and entertainment complex on Robinson Mountain that would incorporate the Robin's Hill Ski Area. "You'll have to ask Rachel about that," he said, blowing a column of smoke at the florescents.

"From what I hear," John said with a laugh, "with the kind of money you two'll be getting, she could buy the state's okay."

"No offense, Chief," Pete said. "But I hope Montpelier tells her to stick it." Freeing him to marry wasn't the only benefit of Danny's ten year wait. It also was freeing Danny's first wife's considerable estate. Rumor was the stocks, bonds and cash her father had left her had grown to more than 10 million dollars.

"Heck, I think a casino would be great," John said. "What about you, Max?"

"I'm not so sure." I laughed. "I don't think bus loads of blue-haired gamblers crowding our country roads is what fly fisherman have in mind when they book a week or two at Whitefork Lodge."

Pete lowered the barber chair so John could climb out. "Well, gambling or no gambling," John said, dusting hair from his trousers, "I think women taking up fly fishing is great news. And I've got to believe that if as many as you say are doing it, Max," he came across the room picking hair flecks from his white shirt, "not all of them are going to want to stay in rustic fishing lodges like Whitefork." He slipped on his maroon blazer with "Loon Hotel" embroidered on the breast pocket. "I've been telling Bryce we should broaden our customer base." He squinted in the mirror above my head and straightened his tie while, behind him, Richie climbed into the barber chair. "You don't mind, Max, Bryce and I might run a couple ads for the hotel in one those fly fishing magazines. See what happens, you know?"

"Doesn't bother me." I rapped my knuckles on my cast. "I've

just got to figure out how I'm going to guide with my leg like this."

"My offer still stands, Max." Richie smiled in the mirror.

"Forget it, Richie." Pete frowned. "Max needs a fly fishing guide not a horny traffic cop." He clicked on the electric clippers and started a furrow in Richie's scalp.

"I was talking about the rest of the season anyway, Richie," I said. "I'm sure my daughter can help me with her friends. If they even want to fish at all." I looked at Danny. "Actually, one of them is quite interested in the dig."

Danny's eyes narrowed. "The dig?"

"Yeah. A college friend of Sabrina's. She now works at the Museum of Natural History in New York," I said. "Digs are their thing, I guess."

He picked a piece of cigar off of his tongue, "She ain't gonna mess around with it is she?"

"If you mean, get down in there and dig around," I said, "I doubt it. But, who knows? Maybe she'll help find something important."

Danny frowned and wiped the cigar piece on his thigh.

"Speaking of important," John said, looking at his watch and starting for the door. "I've got a dozen guests checking in about now. Bryce'll kill me if I'm late. If she's got the time, send Sabrina by, Max. I'd love for her to see what we've done to the restaurant." He gave us a wave and with a tinkle of the door bell, was gone.

The four of us who were left were quiet again for a few minutes while Pete's electric clippers hummed, the florescents buzzed and the radio played, EBB TIDE in French.

Finally Danny said, "Been thinkin', Max. Why don't I help you this season?" He smiled. "Could come over while Sabrina and her friends are there. Sort of ease me into it, you know. That way, by the time you get real busy, I'll know the river and the way you like things done."

"What about your weddin'?" Pete said. "What'll Rachel think?"

"What's to do? I been livin' with the woman for almost ten

years. It ain't like we're gonna take a honeymoon." Danny looked back at me. "I'm serious, Max. I'm not really the chief. You know that. And now with the tapes done, I got nothin' but time on my hands." Danny's position as Wabnaki chief was little more that a title. As had always been the custom of eastern Indian tribes, women were the political and spiritual leaders of the community. Rachel currently held the position. "Be nice to see little Sabrina again. What's it been? A dozen years?"

"I don't know, Danny," I said. "It's been a while. Thing is, I'm not sure I'm ready to go so far as to pay anyone."

"Pay?" He laughed. "In a couple weeks, money ain't gonna be my problem. Hell, I'll guide for you for nothin'. Long as you supply the gear. Most of my equipment's pretty dated."

"Let me think about, huh? I'll get back to you before tonight, alright?" Actually my concern wasn't money. It was his age. Wading around on slippery boulders in a fast moving river could be dangerous.

"You got my number in Red Town?"

"Stormy'll have it."

"You ask her, Max," he said. "She'll tell you I'd be a big help around that river of yours."

I laughed. "I haven't even had a chance to tell her about this weekend's guests coming yet," I said. "Sabrina only called last night."

Pete clicked off the electric clippers and smiled at me knowingly. "It was me, Max, I'd check all this with Stormy before you think about bringing in anyone else." He looked quickly at Danny and added, "Nothing personal Chief, but you know how that woman likes things just so."

Danny blew on the end of the cigar, "Ain't that the truth," he said.

* * *

Because my old cast was too bulky to work a clutch, it had been

quite a while since I'd driven. Rayleen and Stormy had been sharing the chauffeuring duty when I needed to go somewhere. Neither one of them, however, had been available this morning, so
Skip Willits, owner of the Starlight Bar & Grill, a popular road-
house just up the road from the lodge had been nice enough to
drive me into town in his new, red Dodge pickup. I'd arranged to
have Stormy pick me up at Drome's in the lodge's old CJ-5 soft-
top Jeep after her grocery shopping.

By the time she pulled up out front and honked, it was just
me, Pete and the French speaking station left in the barbershop. I
said goodbye and, still awkward with my new cane, hobbled out
to the Jeep. After two tries, I climbed in. "God, I hate this," I said,
arranging my leg and slamming the door.

"Thought you was getting a haircut," she said, putting the car
in gear and making a U-turn back toward Main Street.

"I did."

"Don't look like much of a cut to me." She stuck one of her
stumpy little unfiltered Camels in the corner of her mouth and
depressed the dashboard lighter. "Still too much in the back."

I sighed, leaned my head back against the seat and watched
her light the cigarette. Not more than an inch over five feet tall,
Stormy's once coppery red hair still has enough color left in it to
make the long, steel gray braid that hangs down her back look
permanently rusted.

"See you got the new cast okay, though," she said. "You gonna
be able to drive yourself now?"

I nodded.

Stormy unzipped a corner of the plastic side window and
flipped an ash out the crack. Today she was wearing a faded red
nylon parka over her trademark ankle-length, flowered caftan. The
sleeves of the parka were pushed up above her elbows and her
thick, freckled forearms were already slightly sunburned from hours
in the garden. Twice widowed, she lives on a side street in town in
the house she grew up in. During the fishing season, her brother

Rayleen picks her up every morning in the dark and they commute out to lodge before the guests wake up.

"Danny Shortsleeves was at Drome's," I said, once we were out of town and down shifting up the truck lane on the long hill that winds beside Gracey Gorge.

"That's 'bout the only place the man can go these days without somebody calling him names."

"I don't think it's quite that bad." Like a lot of communities where poverty and the resulting crime have become a part of daily life, the ugly face of prejudice has shown itself in Loon. The Wabnakis and the whites have squared off, blaming each other for the problems. Tension had been increasing and, although no major confrontations had taken place, there had already been a couple of racially motivated skirmishes at high school sporting events and I'd heard that one saloon north of town called, Smitty's refused to serve Indians.

"Overta the grocery store just now," she said, "the meat man wouldn't bone out a leg a lamb for little Penny Harper."

"Maybe he was busy."

"He weren't busy at all. Just another one of them damn Indian haters, is what he is." She honked at a muddy Golden Retriever just about to step off the curb. "Complained to the manager is what I did. Got that pretty little girl her boned leg, by God."

I smiled. "I'll bet you did."

"I did. Told 'em all off too. Said Whitefork Lodge'll take its business somewhere's else they keep up that kind of nonsense." She looked at me. "So, how's the Chief?"

"He ask about you," I said. "I guess he hasn't been going to meetings."

"All this hate stuff, can't rightly blamed him. Besides, that Rachel must be drivin' him nuts. She's turnin' into a real weirdo."

"Rachel?" Although I rarely talked to the woman when she came to look at the dig, when we did say hello, I thought she was quite pleasant. Even if she was a bit intense. "What did she do?"

"Chewed out them poor high school kids at the hole this mornin' just 'cause one of 'em thought he had a bone."

"Was it?"

"Hell, no." She frowned. "Just a piece of root is all. Woman went nuts. Chantin' and throwin' herself on the ground. Jumped right in the hole in that damn black cape a hers even. Started diggin' and howlin' in Wabnaki."

"Danny said she's concerned about someone maybe disturbing a grave."

"Ain't no graves in the yard. Woman's just a freak."

"Everything back to normal now?" When Skip had picked me up, three teenagers were already on their hands and knees in one of the holes.

She nodded. "She calmed down. Went to school, I guess. After that they was like little kids in a sandbox."

I shrugged. "It'll be over in a week or so."

"Not for poor Danny. Heard that now that they're marryin', she's been made the Wabnakis' high mucky-muck witch doctor . . ."

"Medicine Woman?"

"That's it."

"That's an honor."

"Is. But, I think she's turned wacko 'bout it. And not just at our place. I hear already she's been running 'round Red Town castin' spells on folks she don't like. Even at the school. Damn woman's drunk with power, is what she is. Crazy bitch's gonna hurt somebody."

"I doubt that." I laughed again. "Besides, in a couple weeks she'll be too busy counting her money to bother anyone."

"Maybe. Maybe not. But I ain't sayin' no more." She looked in the rear view mirror. "For all I know. damn woman could be listenin'."

"Jesus, Stormy . . ."

"Don't Jesus Stormy me, Max Addams. You ain't seen her the way I seen her. And this morning . . ."

It was time to change the subject. "Speaking of kids," I said, "you see my note?" I'd left a message about Sabrina coming on the hall table before I'd left this morning.

"Nope." She shook her head. "Been cleanin' the cabin all mornin'. What'd it say?"

"Sabrina called last night and wants to bring two of her friends up the Monday after opening day. They'll be staying through Friday."

"Sabrina?" She glanced at me. "She ain't bringin' that pain in butt husband of hers, is she?"

"Nope. All women."

"Little Elise comin' too?" Stormy loved my grand daughter.

I shook my head. "She'll be with Marge in New York."

"Oh well." She smiled. "Be like old times, won't it?"

"Except there will be two other women."

"Sounds like reasonably easy duty to me." She looked at my cast. "'Cept for you. How're you gonna guide like that?"

"Maybe I can rig something to keep it dry. Besides, Sabrina knows the water."

"We comping them?"

"Nope." I shook my head. "She insists on paying."

"Then, she's a payin' customer, Max. I won't allow her to do no guidin'."

I sighed.

"And, you know Rayleen ain't gonna be no help. Monday night he leaves for his church tent raisin'. He won't be back 'til Thursday at the earliest."

I nodded. Every spring, as soon after Easter as the weather allowed, Rayleen's church, The Lord's Workers, moved their fire and brimstone from the old boot heel factory they rented all winter to the chunk of land they owned out on Monday Lake. The tent raising ceremony was one of the biggest events on the church calendar. It took at least three days and was a command performance for all Lord's Workers.

"Suppose these girls'll be wantin' teachin' too." She shifted up into third as we crested the hill.

"Yeah. Sabrina told me that neither of the women have ever picked up a fly rod much less fished with one."

"Maybe you could call that new guide up in North Stoneboat." She snubbed the cigarette in the full dashboard ashtray. "What's his name?"

"Jim Lukens?"

She nodded. "Maybe he could help you out."

I shook my head. "I've heard he's expensive."

"Well, you better thinka somethin', Max Addams," she said. "I ain't gonna be no help. Havin' all women in the lodge ain't like havin' men. Even if one of 'em is your daughter."

"Chief volunteered."

"Well, whyn't you say so? That solves that." She laughed. "Hell, that crank, Beth Ross is lookin' down her long nose at us already. What's one more Indian?"

"I'm just worried he might be too old. I wouldn't want him getting hurt."

She gave me a sideways glance. "Who you callin' old?" She looked back at the road and smiled.

I sighed. "He'll sure add a little pizzazz, won't he?"

She laughed. "Prob'bly scare the be-jezzuz outta Sabrina's friends at first."

"I'll give him a call as soon as we get to the lodge and see if he still wants to do it."

"Maybe you can talk him into stayin' the season."

"I think that's what he has in mind anyway."

"Just you make sure, Max Addams," she said, "he gets the blessin' of that witch, Rachel. Can't do much about what that buncha losers at the Hysterical Committee thinks but, I sure don't wanta be on Rachel's bad side."

CHAPTER TWO

"Damn," Stormy said, pointing through the windshield at our Whitefork Lodge sign as we turned into our driveway. "There's more trash. I just cleaned up one pile on my way out this mornin'." She stopped the Jeep. Three black plastic trash bags lay broken open in the grass under the sign. Cans, chicken bones, wads of aluminum foil and all kinds of paper food packages were scattered in a twenty-foot circle.

"Looks like 'coons got into these," she said.

"This is the second pile?"

She nodded. "S'mornin' just after you left, there was four of 'em. Hadn't been broken open but looked ugly just the same."

"Someone's throwing garbage on our property?"

"'Course someone's throwin' garbage," she said. "Them diggers down there in front of lodge might be just kids, but to a lot idiots they're still Indians."

"Jesus."

She flipped her hand as if waving away a fly. "Don't worry Max, I'll get Rayleen up here to clean this up, soon's we unload the groceries." She put the Jeep in gear and we started down the gravel access road through the spruce toward the lodge.

We lurched over a boulder. "I can't believe it." I gripped the dash. "What are those kids hurting? It's their heritage they're digging for."

"Ain't the kids diggin', Max." She steered around a massive, water-filled pothole. "It's us for lettin' 'em be here that rankles folks."

There were two pickup trucks and a jacked-up, old Ford Bronco in the turn-around when Stormy and I got to the lodge, so she parked in front of the long porch. I could hear rock music coming from the direction of the dig. Two of the five teenagers kneeling in the two ten foot wide excavations by the lake waved and we waved back.

Rayleen was standing down by the lake beside the little log barn we call the workshop and Stormy yelled to him as she climbed from behind the wheel. "Rayleen. There's more a that trash up by 16. Get it, will ya, 'fore it's strewn from here to The Starlight."

He nodded and headed for his old, green International pickup parked on the shady side of the building.

As best I could, I helped unload, carry in and put away the groceries.

"Gonna have to go back to town for more things," she said, putting two, big, one gallon tubs of ice cream in the freezer. "Ain't got the right kinda things for girls."

"I see you just happened to pick up Sabrina's favorite ice cream," I said, referring to the ice cream.

"Woulda bought this anyways." It's called, *Stormy's Mysterious Maple Vanilla* and is based on a simple but delicious concoction she had invented when Sabrina was a little girl; vanilla ice cream with maple syrup stirred in. At everyone's urging, Stormy submitted the idea to the Ben & Jerry's Ice Cream Company in a statewide flavor competition and it won. Theirs tastes as good as her original and Ben & Jerry even use her name on the package. Now, every spring, during maple sugaring, it reappears in stores and she uses the lifetime coupon she received as winner to stock up. "'sides, I ain't talkin' 'bout buying more food," she said, transferring eggs from a carton to the egg-shaped recesses in the refrigerator door. "We're gonna need soft facial tissues in the bathrooms. Some nice smellin' soaps. Candles for dinner. Flavored decaf . . ."

"Jesus, Stormy. This *is* a fishing lodge . . ."

"These are women, Max. And they're from New York City. They might talk big 'bout how they're gonna be roughin' it up in the northwoods and all but, believe me, it's only talk. They like the nice stuff."

I laughed. "As long you don't put up ruffled curtains, do what you think is best."

"Intend to." She thumbed toward the pantry without looking up. "Better make sure we got enough Loon in there. Think there's only enough for you 'n Rayleen. You know how much Sabrina likes that stuff."

I looked. There were two cases. "We'll need more." Not only was Sabrina a fan but so was just about everyone else who came to the lodge.

Loon Lager is the beverage of choice all over this part of Vermont. Begun in a basement in the town of Loon by two bored college dropouts, Art Currier and Tom Davies, The Loon Lagering Company, at first, was nothing more a couple beer drinkers attempting to create a taste they couldn't find commercially available. Art and Tom's first bottling was about ten cases, of which they drank seven. The other three cases were parceled out, brown long neck by brown long neck, to friends and neighbors as gifts or barter for services they needed. The rich, clean, slightly sweet taste, unique red-amber color and whipped cream-like head was an instant success and Art and Tom's second bottling was more ambitious. The two hundred barrels' worth they produced was gone in a summer, most of it, over the bar at Skip Willits' Starlight Cafe out on Route 16. Today, only a little more than four years later, The Loon Lagering Company cranks out about twenty thousand barrels of Loon Lager from their new brewery in what had been a paper pulp mill on a bend in the Whitefork River on the northwest side of town. Success hasn't seemed to affect Art and Tom. Like the brewing business' version of Ben and Jerry, they still look like two bored college dropouts with their long hair, scraggly beards, jeans and anti-establishment tee shirts. They also still hand-make the beer and the recipe remains a secret, although Rayleen claims he's heard that a key ingredient is maple syrup taken from the first boiling of the first run of sap each spring.

Although you can find a bottle or two of Loon Lager in bars over in New Hampshire, ninety-nine percent of Art's and Tom's production is still sold only in northern Vermont. In fact, it's un-usual to walk into a bar up here and see any other beer being consumed. Nevertheless, thanks to businesses like mine, Loon La-ger can be found in front of television sets and on patios all over the United States. Most Whitefork lodge guests take several six packs of that brown bottle with its distinctive night black, orange and yellow label featuring the elegant loon silhouetted against the moon home with them. As Stormy said one day as we stood on the porch watching two of our fly fisherman load three cases in the trunk of their Volvo, "Sometimes makes you wonder whether they come for the trout or the beer, don't it, Max?"

After the groceries were put away, Stormy and Spotter—my old part black Lab, part English Setter—walked back up the ac-cess road to Route 16 to check on Rayleen's cleaning job and get the mail from our box. I took a bottle of Loon Lager from the refrigerator, opened it and went to the phone in the hallway to call Chief Danny Shortsleeves. He probably wouldn't be home yet, but I figured I could leave a message for him to call me back when he got in.

Rachel answered. "Hello, Max," she said before I could swal-low my mouthful of beer and say anything.

I swallowed and laughed. "How'd you know it was me, Rachel?"

"You were on my mind. You want Daniel I assume."

"Yes, actually. Chief offered to help me with some guests I have coming in next week and I like to take him up on it. Could you have him call me when he gets in."

"He's here now," she said and then there was some rustling on her end and I heard her whisper something and Danny came on the line.

"Hey, Max. Decide you can use me?"

"If you're still game." I told him what little I knew about the women who were coming. "And, except for Sabrina, not one of them has ever touched a fly rod. We'll probably need to spend a couple days just on casting lessons."

"Sounds okay to me. They all about her age?"

"I assume so." Sabrina was thirty. "Sabrina knew one of them in college."

"Heck, women are easy to teach," he said. "Bet I can have them catching fish by the first afternoon." He was probably right. Men were the tough ones. They invariably tried too hard and muscled the rod ruining the cast. Women were indeed different. Whether it's their natural elegance or lack of testosterone, I don't know, but a woman takes to the graceful motion needed almost instantly. "When they arrivin', Max?"

"Monday morning. How about you coming over around seven for breakfast. That way we'll all be here when they arrive."

I could hear Rachel say something in the background and then he said, "Rachel wants to know if I'm comin' home nights."

"Of course. But I'd prefer it if, at least, you could stay through supper each evening." Unlike other fishing lodges, at Whitefork we eat with our guests. It gives us a chance to discuss the day we just had and better plan for the next. Besides, it's usually fun. "Is that possible?"

"Long as Stormy's doin' the cookin'," He laughed, "you couldn't make me leave." He said he'd see me early on Monday morning and, after reminding me that he'd need to borrow everything from rod and reel to waders and wading boots, we hung up.

I still had my hand on the telephone when Stormy clumped up onto the porch with Spotter at her heels. She was sorting the mail, her new half glasses pushed down on her nose. She kicked off her muddy Bean Boots, told Spotter to stay outside and came into the hallway.

"Everything set?" she asked, gesturing at the phone and stuffing a cream-colored envelope into the pocket of her caftan in one motion. She handed me the latest issue of Fly, Rod & Reel and what looked like another bill from my most recent set of x-rays. "Danny gonna help out?"

"He'll be here for breakfast Monday." I drained the beer and opened the magazine to the back. We had a small ad on the "Destinations" page of this issue and I wanted to see how it looked. "I think he's doing it just for your cooking."

She smiled. "Our ad in there this time?"

It was at the bottom of the next to last page and I held the open magazine out to show her.

"Kinda little, ain't it?" She squinted at the magazine page through her glasses. "Considerin' what it cost us." She dumped the rest of the mail in the wastebasket beside the telephone table and then turned and waddled down the hallway. Just as she got to the kitchen's swinging door she stopped and said, "Oh yeah, you got a minute, I got something to show you too."

"Can it wait?" I said, starting for the front door. "I want to look at the dig and then go down to the workshop and see how Rayleen's doing with that hole in the canoe."

She waved me away. "You go ahead. I ain't in any hurry to show you anyways."

"Not more mice," I said but she had pushed through the door into the kitchen and couldn't hear me. Not only had there been an unusual number of mice in the lodge this spring, they were particularly brazen; twice this week I'd awaken to see one sitting on the pillow by my face.

I went out onto the porch. Spotter jumped to his feet and stuck his muddy nose in my crotch. I pushed his nose away and scratched him behind the ears. "You're going to have stop that crotch stuff," I said as we went down the steps and out into the yard. "I don't think the guests we have coming next week will appreciate it."

He barked and then, sniffing ever hole my cane made in the spongy wet grass, followed as I limped down to the excavations.

It was a beautiful spring afternoon and I stopped halfway between the lodge and the dig, leaned on the cane and looked out at the western mountains reflected in lake. There wasn't a breath of air and the only disturbance on the aspic-like surface was from incoming northbound ducks. Why autumn gets top billing in colors department, I'll never know. To me, spring's soft, pastel-tinted budding maples, birch, beech and oaks are far more beautiful than the gaudy golds and reds of fall. It would be like this for another week or so; hundreds of ducks, heads tucked under their wings, floating like feather rafts, waiting for night and the next leg of their journey toward summer.

Although most of my guests prefer to fish the waters of the river, fifteen acre Sweet Lake is really the jewel of the property. Actually not a lake, it is a classic forest pond created and maintained with almost religious fervor by hundreds of generations of beaver. Only twenty-five feet at its deepest point, Sweet lake itself is home to the largest and probably oldest trout on the property as well as loons, osprey, and several species of migrating ducks and geese. Its irregular shoreline hides whitetailed deer, bobcat, pine martin, otter, black bear and a small herd of moose. This time of year, just after the thaw, the lake is perfect for fly fishing. Later in the season, however, as the water warms under the summer sun, the trout seek out the deepest, coolest holes making it better spin cast or bait fisherman's water. Since I allow neither at Whitefork Lodge, summertime Sweet Lake becomes our reflecting pool and the background for quiet, after dinner conversations on the lodge porch.

It wasn't always like this, of course. Several thousand years before Whitefork Lodge was built, and hundreds of years before French trappers wandered the rolling, forested hills . . . in fact, well before northern Vermont's recorded history, Wabnaki Indians summered in the dark spruce, maples and birch on the gentle rise of granite ledge and spaghum moss beside the crystal clear ribbon of fast moving water that would someday be named, the Whitefork River. Sweet Lake wasn't even here yet.

Anthropologists have confirmed that as much as fifteen centuries ago three Wabnaki tribal sects . . . the Wolf, the Salmon and the Squaretail . . . would leave their winter village on the shores of lake Champlain every spring and follow the migrating salmon in the Whitefork River upstream to where the "mountain blocks the rising sun". Today we call this mountain, Morning Mountain and the Wabnaki would build their shelters and council fires in its shadow along the banks of the river and hunt and fish and gather roots and maple sap during the hot months of summer. Four months later, when the nights turned chill and the hardwoods' leaves began to change color, the three Wabnaki sects would burn their summer homes, pack up and return to their permanent village on the lake loaded down with tanned hides, maple syrup, smoked meats and fish, dried fruits, berries and roots, and deerskin bags full of coarsely ground hickory and beechnut flours.

Today, in the springtime when frost heaves the thawing earth, fragments of those pre-history summer days push to the surface. Occasional quartz arrowheads, small pieces of crude pottery, splinters of animal bones and shards of shell from distant shores are found by all of us as we turn over Stormy's vegetable garden or mow and trim the lawn readying the lodge for another season of fly fishing guests.

Is was this kind of treasure that the kids in the dig were looking for.

As I continued down to the excavations, a flock of mallards whistled in overhead and, quacking back and forth, sped out above the lake where they cupped their stubby, pointed wings and dropped with skidding, almost comical splashes onto the glassy surface.

I knew the girls in the hole farthest from the water. Although all four were full-blooded Wabnakis and, for the most part, looked it with their dark eyes, full faces and coal black hair, their names were strictly American melting pot. Tracy Bishop was Red Town High School's all-state field hockey fullback. Her father and mother owned a small twenty-four hour grocery out on Monday Lake that opened as soon as the ice was out. Gretchen and Gretel were Loon Lagering Company foreman, Tom Seeley's twin daughters. And, although I didn't know her parents, Virginia Wingate had babysat my granddaughter on a couple occasions. The long haired, pimply-faced boy with wire-rimmed glasses and a leather thong around his forehead was new. They all watched me approach out of the corners of their eyes. "Finding anything good, Tracy?" I asked as I limped up to the taut string around the perimeter.

Tracy had mud in her short hair. "Hi, Mr. Addams." She smiled and showed me a mouthful of braces. "Kevin found what might have been a fire pit."

I looked at the boy. He was hunched over a three foot in diameter black stain in the otherwise tan wet dirt, carefully scraping at it with a small trowel. "How do you know it's a fire pit?" I asked him.

He scowled at me and pushed his wire-rimmed glasses up on his nose. "That's what the bat . . . our teacher said it probably was."

"You mean, Rachel?"

They all giggled and looked away.

"What's the matter?"

Tracy smiled up at me and blushed slightly. "We call Miss Arneau, bat woman, Mr. Addams."

"You mean because of her cape?" Rachel usually wore a long, dramatic blue black cape instead of a coat.

"Yeah," Kevin said. "And the way she sort of hangs, you know?" He stood and hunched his shoulders in a pretty good imitation of the way Rachel usually stood when she was looking down into the excavation.

The girls giggled again. "We don't say it to her face, of course," Tracy said.

"Here's a piece of it." Kevin picked up a tiny sliver of black between his fingers and held it out to me. "What do you think?"

I took the sliver. It looked like charcoal. "It looks like burned wood to me," I said and handed it back.   ·

He dropped it in a small plastic bag.

I looked back at Tracy. She seemed to be the leader. "What date do you think you're down to now?" I asked.

"Thirteen hundreds." She shrugged. "Who knows."

"How do you find out for sure?"

"Kevin's dad teaches down at the University of Vermont," she said. "They have a carbon dating machine and he gets stuff run through for us."

Kevin was looking out across the lake. "Anybody ever look out there, Mr. Addams?" he said.

"Under the water?"

"Yeah."

"No. I doubt Rachel would like it anyway."

"We know," one of the twins said. "Kevin asked her and she freaked."

"It's too bad," Tracy said, pointing to the charcoal stain at Kevin's feet. "See the way that black mark seems to go out there under the ground toward the water?"

I looked. Now that she mentioned it, there did seem to be an indication there was a lot more of it beyond where they were digging. I nodded. "So?"

Kevin took off his glasses. "So, I'm thinking maybe," he wiped them on the front hem of his sweatshirt, "this might have been one of those big long house council fires we've studied about."

"Yes," the other twin said, "who knows what we might find straight out there under the water. Supposedly it was a burying ground, wasn't it?"

"That's what they say."

They looked at each other and Gretchen said, "So, ask him, Tracy."

"Ask me what?" I said.

"Well," Tracy put her hands in the back pockets of her jeans, "we were wondering if Kevin could dive the lake."

"Dive the lake?" I looked at Kevin.

"Yeah," he said, a big smile lighting up his face. "You know, see what's down there. I got SCUBA certified with my dad in the Caribbean last Spring Break. We dove The Wall in Grand Cayman."

"Beaver Pond's a little different than the ocean," I said. "Lots of sunken trees and other stuff to get hung up on down there."

He shrugged. "I dove Monday Lake all last summer. Sunken

trees there didn't bother me." Monday Lake is the reservoir just
north of town. It had been created by backed up Whitefork River
when the Army Corps of Engineers built The Loon Dam in the
sixties. Almost 400 acres of forest and farmland lay under it.

I sighed. "I thought Rachel said no . . ."

"It's your property, Mr. Addams," Tracy said. "If you said it
was okay Miss Arneau and the tribal council couldn't . . ."

"I don't know." I shook my head. My problem wasn't Rachel
Arneau or her tribal council. It was my insurance. I knew I was
covered for just about every activity above water. Underwater, however, I wasn't so sure about. "Let me think about it," I said. "I'll let
you know tomorrow. Okay?"

They all frowned but nodded. "Okay," they said in unison.

"Good luck." I smiled and hobbled away toward the workshop to see how Rayleen was coming with the patch on our big 19
foot Old Town canoe.

Somehow untouched by the fire we had in the lodge a few
years ago, the one story log, barn-like building we call the workshop sits about fifty yards down the hill from the lodge almost at
the edge of Sweet Lake. Originally a boat house and small stable,
it now serves as a garage, repair center, storage area and, if we make
up the bed in small room on the side, extra guest quarters in a
pinch when the lodge gets full.

The canoe was out in front of the building, bottom up, stretched
between a pair of paint-splattered wooden sawhorses. Behind it,
Rayleen was bent over the electric sander in a cloud of fiberglass
dust. He saw Spotter first, looked up and saw me. He turned off
the sander and pushed his cap back on his forehead. His face was
white around the protective mask covering his nose and mouth.

Like his sister, Rayleen more or less came with Whitefork Lodge
when I bought it. Unlike her, his jobs around the place are less
well defined. In the spring he hangs the window screens, puts in
our dock, cleans and repairs broken equipment and tunes the Jeep.
During fishing season, he drives Stormy in from town at five a.m.
and then goes to work at the Loon Lagering Company. Three days

a week he's on the bottling line with Pete Dromeshauser. The other four, he stays and helps with guests. In the evening, if he doesn't have a church meeting, he joins us for supper and a couple drinks on the porch. Around nine, he drives Stormy home again.

To look at him you'd never know he was Stormy's brother. Although the youngest, he looks the oldest by at least a decade. Where she's plump, pink, and almost bursting with good health, Rayleen is thin, his face gouged with lines. It's as if he was the one, not her, who used to drink a quart of vodka by noon and now squints through the smoke of two packs of unfiltered Camels a day. Although they're both barely five feet tall, the wooden prosthesis that Rayleen wears in place of the leg he lost gives him a stooping limp that makes him seem even shorter. He always wears a red plaid wool shirt and dungaree overalls and I can tell what kind of day he's having by the way he wears the greasy baseball cap that never leaves his head which, no matter how it sits, makes his fine white hair tuft uncontrollably out above his ears and through the caps little air holes like feathers leaking from a cheap pillow.

"How's it coming?" I said, stepping up to the canoe and running my hand over the patch.

He shrugged and pulled the mask down from his face. "I'd say, 'bout time for a new canoe, Max." He slapped the dust from his cap on his trouser leg and returned it to his head. "This baby won't take much more." He patted the canoe bottom. "Mostly patches now anyways."

"Looks okay to me."

"Oh, it'll float all right." He smiled. "Just wouldn't wanta put a foot too hard in a couple spots is all."

"Thanks for cleaning that mess up by the sign."

"No problem. Some folks sure have a stupid way of tellin' other folks they don't like 'em, don't they?"

I shrugged. "You hear we're booked part of next week?"

"Yep." He stooped and scratched Spotter behind the ears. "Passed Stormy going to get the mail. Sabrina and some of her lady friends, right?"

"The friends will want lessons," I said. "So, I'm going to need you to get out two of the Orvis learner rods." Several years ago the Orvis Company down in Manchester donated a dozen of their rods and reels to the fly fishing classes we give in conjunction with the University of Vermont's Center for Continuing Education. "Clean them up and rig some reels with weight forward, floating line."

He looked at my cast. "You gonna be teachin' in that thing?"

"Danny Shortsleeves is coming to help out," I said.

"Danny? Stormy didn't mention that. You sure Rachel's gonna let him?"

I nodded. "Just talked to both of them. He'll be here for breakfast Monday morning. He'll use the days with Sabrina to learn the ropes and then stay on for a few weeks after, at least, until I get this cast off."

He smiled. "Or 'til he and Rachel get all that money." He nodded his head toward the dig. "That gonna be closed up by the time Sabrina comes?"

"No," I said. "One of the women coming with Sabrina is interested in it anyway."

He slowly shook his head. "It's a damn crime, I think. Diggin' around looking for dead people's stuff. A damn crime."

"It's the way we learn, Rayleen."

"Learn." He laughed ruefully. "Ain't nobody's business what them Wabnaki folks done around here years ago. 'Sides, the place where all the good stuff's at is out there." He pointed at the lake.

"That young man over there wants me to give him permission to use SCUBA gear and look."

"You ain't gonna, I hope."

"I doubt it." I watched another string of ducks speed toward the water. "It could be dangerous."

"Ain't that the truth?" He laughed derisively. "'Specially if Rachel was to find out, huh?"

I started back toward the lodge. "Oh yes," I stopped and

turned. "I'm also going to need that slide slow we've got about insects and hatches. I think it's in one of the closets in the lodge."

"It ain't." He thumbed at the workshop. "Seen it up in the attic here just the other day."

"Well, wherever it is, I'll need it."

"Soon's I'm done here," he said pushing the mask back up over his nose, "I'll get it out for you. Need anythin' else?"

I shook my head.

He picked up the sander, turned it on and I stepped back as the cloud of white dust rose around him. Spotter seemed content lying in the shade watching Rayleen so I left them both and limped back up to the lodge alone.

As I entered the hallway Stormy yelled from upstairs, "I'm in the front bedroom, Max. Be down in a second"

I continued on to the kitchen.

Several years ago a fire destroyed the original Whitefork Lodge. None of us was injured, but we lost everything. Fortunately, insurance covered rebuilding. Ruth found the original blueprints in the archives in the cellar at city hall so, with the exception of more electrical outlets, we rebuilt the lodge almost exactly as it had been.

The original Whitefork Lodge was built in 1908 by Daniel Webster's great grandson, a Boston shipping tycoon named, Thornton Randolph Webster. His intention was to create a comfortable, low maintenance retreat for his family and friends and he succeeded. When we rebuilt, with the exception of updating the kitchen, we copied the architect, Wellesly Hinton's plans exactly. Sitting on the highest ground on the point where the Whitefork River joins Sweet Lake, it is a massive rectangle. Two stories of log structure with a porch that runs along the front facing the west over the lake. It has giant shuttered windows, two walk-in field stone fireplaces and wide, rough sawn board floors. Webster spared no expense in it's construction and we didn't either in its reconstruction; The three-foot diameter spruce logs we had brought down from Canada are chinked with river clay just like the original. The fire, of course, spared the foundation and the rip-rap of cut and intricately fitted massive granite boulders still holds everything up. According to old records, two workmen died when the south wall of the foundation buckled and tons of stone blocks caved inward and crushed them. Supposedly, it took two weeks to remove the mangled bodies. Stormy told me that Rachel says she senses the men's spirits under the building.

I took a Camel from Stormy's pack lying on the butcher block food preparation island and was just lighting it when she pushed through the swinging door carrying a pail of vinegar water in one hand and a dripping string mop in the other. Her face was red and a ringlet of rusty hair stuck to her damp forehead.

"I wish I could be more of a help," I said, as she carried everything across the room and disappeared into the pantry by the back door.

"Floor and toilets ain't your job," she said from inside the pantry.

"Still . . ."

"You got other things." She came out of little room and over to the cigarettes. After wiping her hands on her apron, she took one, lit it and then studied me through the curtain of smoke between us.

"What's the matter?" I said, running my hand over my beard. "Pete didn't trim this enough either?"

She sighed, pulled out the cream colored envelope I'd seen her tuck into her pocket earlier and tossed it on the island. It slid to my hand. "That Bolick guy asked Ruth to marry him," she said.

I looked at the envelope. It was addressed to me. In Ruth's handwriting. I looked back up at Stormy. "He what?"

"You heard me, Max Addams. He wants to marry her."

"How do you . . . ? When did she . . . ?"

Stormy slipped a buttock up on the stool across from me. "Called me at home a couple days ago. Told me 'bout it then. Wanted to know how she should tell you."

I picked up the envelope. "And you told her to write me a letter?"

She shook her head. "Told her to tell you face to face." She pointed at the envelope. "She decided to write you 'bout it first."

"How do you know that's what's in here?" The envelope hadn't been opened.

"Just do. Told me she was sendin' it. I been lookin' for it in the mail every day since." She shrugged and looked down at the butcher block. "Didn't want you to just get it without me bein' around."

I slipped my thumb under the flap and tore it open. It was a cream colored card. Her initials, RAP, were embossed in fancy raised script on the front. I opened it.

It was dated yesterday. "Dearest Max," it began. I let my eyes wander over the rest of it, words like "love", "companion", "friend", "commitment" and "perhaps" catching my eye. I looked at Stormy. "I don't believe it," I said.

"Me neither. But it's true."

I snubbed the cigarette in the ashtray. "Dammit."

"Just don't want you to keep thinkin' this thing's your fault. "Cause it ain't."

"Hell it isn't," I said, standing and going to the sink. "Who's fault is it if it isn't mine?" I looked out the window at Stormy's garden. A robin, his head turned to the side, studied the freshly tilled earth. "I'm the one who wouldn't get interested in local politics. I'm the one who couldn't have cared less when she ran for governor. Everyone knows I was glad when she lost."

"Knew you'd act this way."

I turned and looked at her. "I'm right, Stormy. It was always my interests. My problems. Me. Never once did I meet her halfway. Believe me, I've had plenty of time to think about." I tried to smile. "I can't remember ever asking her how her day was." I sighed. "Who can blame her? Along comes this Bolick guy who listens to her. Who acts like he cares about . . ."

"Don't think this wantin' to marry her's an act. He cares."

"Shit. Of course, he cares. I do too. Only she never thought so."

Stormy picked up the card and held it out to me. "Whyn't you read what she says, Max. Maybe it'll . . ."

"I know what it says." I took the card and stuck it in my hip pocket.

"No you don't, Max. Way she sounded on the phone, I don't think she's so sure about any of this . . ."

"She's not sure?" I actually laughed.

"Just read it, Max." Stormy ground out her cigarette.

"Maybe later," I said, going to the back door and opening it. "But it's not going to change anything," I went out, down the steps and over to the garden. The robin eyed me for a second and then flew to the roof of the lodge. I looked up at him. He looked back with one beady black eye and ruffled his feathers. "You don't worry about what happens to last year's girl friend, do you?" I said to him. "You get a new shot at it every spring." He looked at me with the other eye. "Maybe that's the way it was meant to be."

I hobbled around the back of the lodge and through the trees to the river. For the most part, the snowmelt was over and it was running clear. I sat on an fallen birch trunk and listened to the water voices as it bubbled, gurgled and whispered it's way down the rapids, through the chutes, around the boulders and over the hundreds of little waterfalls. As it talked I heard Ruth. And I heard myself on that last night we'd been together. The night that could have once and for all put an end to all this stupidity.

Late last fall I began hearing rumors about Ruth and Bolick. His wife had been killed in a skiing accident seven years earlier leaving him with a three year old child to raise. At first, I let it go as just the kind of bullshit that goes with the territory when you're the not only the first woman mayor in a town the size of Loon, but single, young and very attractive. Also, I found it hard to believe that Ruth could find much in common with a man with a young family. But then, I discovered that Ruth and Doug had attended an out-of-state conference together. I knew it was time to say something.

At first, she denied the whole affair. "I've heard the rumors too, Max," she said when I confronted her. "He's just a friend. I don't see him much, really. Doug and I are on some committees together. He's usually pretty busy down at the University. We've had dinner a couple times is all."

Ruth and I were having an early dinner ourselves by a window in the Loon Hotel's new dining room. It was an unusually balmy Indian Summer night and big red leaves were spiraling down from the two, spotlit, sugar maples just beyond the glass.

Just as our coffee was being poured I hit her with the big one. I told her I knew about the two of them being together at the conference in Manchester, New Hampshire the previous week. "That's a long way to go for dinner," I said.

Even in the candlelight I could see her blush and, after our waiter had poured the coffees and we had declined his list of dessert options, she said, "Doug cares about this town as much as I do. He has ideas that can . . ."

"Did you sleep with him in Manchester?"

"Did I what?" Her green eyes flashed. "The convention was overbooked. We shared a room, if that's what you mean."

"That's not what I mean."

She didn't say anything and looked out the window at the steep east side of Morning Mountain we could see beyond the spotlit maples. From our point-of-view it was just a massive dark shape but I could see the headlights of a car flash occasionally through the thinning trees as it slowly traversed down toward town on the switchback turns of Backside Road.

"Are you in love with him?" I asked finally.

"Oh, Max." She sighed and looked at me. The candle's flame reflected in the tears welling in her eyes. "I don't know how I feel." She looked back out the window.

I didn't know what to say. I lit a cigarette in the candle flame, exhaled and sipped my coffee. I studied her profile.

Ruth and I were introduced by mutual friends just after I bought Whitefork Lodge. I was forty and she had just turned twenty-five. At the time we both had recently been divorced. We dated a couple times and then sort of slipped apart for several years while my fly fishing business grew and she pursued a career in law and politics. About a year after she became Loon's mayor, we rediscovered each other and for the past few years have, more or less, been a couple. I had always assumed we were in it for the long run.

"I need some time, Max," she said, still not looking at me. "We both do."

"What's that supposed to mean?"

"It doesn't mean anything." She took a deep breath. "It just means spend some time apart. Experience new things. Widen our circle of friends."

"As in, get laid by new people like Doug Bolick?"

Her hand lashed across the table like a striking snake and the crack of her palm on my cheek not only knocked the cigarette from my mouth but halted forks and turned heads all the way across the room. My left eye stung and began watering instantly.

Her eyes flashed. "You don't know what you're talking about, Max Addams."

I rubbed my cheek and picked my smoldering cigarette from the tablecloth. I looked around the room. Everyone looked away. I looked out the window this time. A breeze had picked up and the leaves were coming down like giant flakes of rusty snow.

"I'm sorry." She put her hand on mine. "I don't want to hurt you, Max."

I pulled my hand away. "I feel like a fool, Ruth."

"If it's any consolation," she said with a weak smile, "I feel a little like a fool too."

I ground the cigarette out in the ashtray.

She took a breath as if she was going to say something else, then instead, tightened her lips and looked out the window.

I signaled our waiter for the check and when it came, paid it, stood and wove through the tables to the exit. As I got to the door, I glanced back. She hadn't moved and was still looking out the window at the falling leaves.

That was six months ago. It was the last time I saw or talked to her.

A kingfisher swooped through the damp air in front of me and landed, chattering, in a hemlock on the other side of the river. Like the robin, it studied me with one beady eye.

I stooped, picked up a wet stone and threw it at him.

CHAPTER THREE

Except that there were teenagers digging holes in the yard, the rest of the week went by the way every final week goes before the fishing season begins; Rayleen and Stormy arrive at six every day, we have breakfast in the kitchen and then the rest of the daylight hours are spent splitting wood for the fireplaces, tying flies for sale to customers, repairing equipment, trimming weeds, clearing brush, cleaning and cooking and freezing. At 8 p.m. they leave and Spotter and I collapse exhausted in the lodge's reading room. Me, on the leather couch and he, on the floor by the fire. Sometimes, we wake up in the exact positions in the morning.

Although the tension can sometimes become thick as the sap boiling down to syrup in the little sugar houses steaming on the hillsides, nothing more was said about Ruth and the marriage proposal. I, of course, couldn't stop thinking about it and, I guess, carried the pain of the loss around like an extra cast because finally on Sunday, the day before Sabrina and her friends were to arrive, Stormy said something. Spotter are I were on the porch just getting ready to go do our annual inspection of the river and count fish, when she stopped me. "Time someone told you to shape up, Max Addams."

"Shape up?"

"Yeah, shape up. You been mopin' around all week. I'm tired of it. Tired of your snappin' at me and Rayleen. Tired of that long, sorrowful look on your face. Might just be your daughter and some friends comin' up for a few days, but they are customers none the less. Don't think they expect the kinda wake you got goin'. So, get a grip."

"I didn't realize I . . ."

"Well you are."

I sighed and looked down at the porch floor.

"You never read Ruth's note did you?"

I shook my head.

"God, you're stubborn." She stepped up to me and, on tip-toe, quickly kissed me on the beard. Then, just a quickly, she stepped back, straightened her apron and pointed a stubby finger toward the river. "Go out there to that river and make sure we got trout for your daughter. And when you come back, I wanta see a smile on that hairy face of yours. Now git."

Spotter knew as well as I did that you don't argue with Stormy and was off the porch and trotting across the lawn toward the screen of trees between us and the Whitefork River before I had my cane in my hand.

The dig for Wabnaki artifacts was full swing this morning and I waved half-heartedly to Tracy and the twins. They waved back. I could only see Kevin's back but he wouldn't have waved anyway. Yesterday I had turned down his request to dive out in the lake.

Every spring, just before the season begins, Spotter and I walk the seven miles of Whitefork River that run through my property and check to see how our population of trophy-size brook trout fared over the long Vermont winter. As best we can, we also count the landlocked salmon migrating through from Lake Champlain on their way upstream to spawn.

The Whitefork River begins in a series of small beaver ponds about twenty miles across the Vermont border in Canada. It is a gin clear, twisting ribbon that snakes south and west through some of the most beautiful, rolling, forest country in New England. Once it crosses into the state of Vermont it threads together fifty or so mere dots of towns with names like, "Moosenose", "Birch", "Whitetail", "Stoneboat" and "Graniteville". Just north of the town of Loon a dam stops it briefly to become Monday Lake. Once over the dam it curves around town and cuts the steeply walled Gracey Gorge through the Sunrise Mountains. Then it gathers speed again and winds by my fly fishing lodge. Eventually, miles to the south and west, it dumps into Lake Champlain.

Spotter and I began our annual "fish check" on the gravel bar beside the Inlet Pool at the mouth of the Whitefork where it flows into Sweet Lake. Stepping from dry rock to dry rock, Spotter gingerly crossed the river and perched himself heroically on a massive granite boulder. He barked excitedly and began pointing his nose at the pool immediately. I counted thirty big brook trout and the distinct silver flashes of twelve to fifteen salmon holding in the pool. Just upstream, in the rapids, we counted another twenty brookies in pods of three to six behind the bigger rocks.

There weren't always fish like this in my part of the Whitefork River. Before I actually understood the dynamics of the resource I was supposed to be managing, my guests had almost fished us out.

Fortunately, the Vermont Fish and Game Department suggested I adopt a catch and release only policy and it worked. In a little over a year the trout population rebounded. Today, I can offer my guests more than two hundred trout over one pound per hundred yards of water. And some of them are considered to be the largest wild brookies in the east.

I waved Spotter off the rock, indicating that we'd seen enough in this area. He knew the drill and, bounding over boulders and fallen trees, led the way up stream.

Because of the cast on my leg and the precarious footing in some places, it took us most of the rest of the day to do the seven miles. By 4 o'clock we were high above the lodge at the lip of a deep mossy gorge looking down on a vertical drop of roaring whitewater called, Webster Falls.

It had been one of Ruth's favorite places.

I sat on a rock and Spotter sat on his haunches watching me. "The three of us had some nice times up here, didn't we?" I said to him.

He looked at the mossy ground at my feet. I did too and, hard as I tried, couldn't keep from picturing Ruth as she'd been the last

time we'd picnicked on this secluded cliff; wet, naked and writh-
ing playfully beside me.

I looked back at Spotter. "That's what this is all about, isn't it?"

He cocked his head, padded over and pushed his wet nose at
my chest.

I scratched his ears. "It all boils down to sex, doesn't it?" I
looked at the waterfall and slowly shook my head. It was true.
Whether Ruth accepted Bolick's proposal or not wasn't the most
important thing at all. Not right now anyway. Right now what it
really boiled down to was the simple fact that I was jealous she was
having sex with someone else.

*   *   *

There was a Chrysler minivan parked at the lodge when Spotter
and I pushed our way from the river out through the trees and
into the yard. And, although I didn't recognize the car, there was
no mistaking the loud voice of Elisabeth Ross coming from the
front porch. My first instinct was retreat. To fade quickly back into
the budding limbs and wait until she'd gone, but it was too late.
Stormy saw me. "Max," she yelled and waved. "We got ourselves
some visitors." She gave me a pained expression.

The two stocky, waistless women with her on the porch turned
from their positions with their backs to the porch rail and looked.
It was Elisabeth all right. Crisply tailored pink suit, pale blue, pill
box hat perched on her tightly curled bluish white hair. Although
I knew it was impossible at this distance, I was certain I could
smell her nauseating rose perfume from where I stood. The other
woman, dressed in a similar suit of pale, mint green and a dark
green wide brimmed hat, didn't look familiar.

Spotter barked menacingly and, tail down, trotted stiffly up
to the porch steps where he stood, the hair on his neck bristling,
growling faintly.

I limped across the lawn, working up a smile.

"'Lisabeth come out to see the dig," Stormy said as I climbed the steps. "Told her I don't know much about it."

"Hello, Max," Elisabeth said, extending her pale, liver-spotted hand palm down as though she expected me to kiss it. The rose perfume was so thick in the air, my eyes almost watered. I shook her hand and she introduced me to Gertrude Perry the woman in mint. Gertrude didn't offer her hand. She didn't smile either, maybe because of the quarter inch of stiff makeup on her face.

"Actually," Elisabeth said, "we didn't come out to see the dig per se." She looked at Gertrude. "I've heard reports that artifacts of historical significance are being unearthed and thought that, perhaps, as representatives of historical Loon, Gertrude and I should take a look at what's been found."

I went to a rocker, sat and lit a cigarette. Elisabeth wrinkled her nose disdainfully as the smoke curled her way. Loon is one of only a handful of towns in Vermont that hasn't banned smoking in all public places. I'm convinced that we would have long ago been forced to join the smoke-free world if it wasn't for Elisabeth and the rest of her anti-cigarette cronies and their overly zealous campaign against the filthy weed. In fact, John Quinn thinks that cigarette smoking in Loon has risen just because Elisabeth's so vehemently against it. "I'm under the impression that these artifacts, as you refer to them," I said to her, "belong to the Wabnakis. I don't think they fall under your jurisdiction, Elisabeth." I looked out at the dig. The kids were watching us. "Besides, I didn't think that the Loon Historical Society considered Indian history very important."

"Well, we do, Mister Addams," Gertrude said, moving her mouth carefully. "Our children and their childrens' children should be able to see how far our ancestors' hard work has brought us since the area was inhabited by godless savages."

I looked at Stormy. She rolled her eyes.

I laughed. "In other words, you want to make sure they don't unearth a TV set or telephone out there."

Stormy chuckled.

They weren't laughing and Elisabeth's eyes narrowed. "I want to be assured that the Wabnakis and the lifestyle they had and the way they live now is kept in the proper perspective," she said. "These exhibits are used as teaching tools, Max. School age children are very impressionable. As an example, it is well documented that the early red man used hallucinogens. We don't want . . ."

"So, what do you want, Elisabeth?" I wasn't in the mood for this. I stood. "You want my permission to cull through the things those kids are digging up to make sure nothing gets into the Wabnaki exhibit that makes Indians look too good? Or, do you just want to take credit for what they find?"

"I don't think it's necessary to be rude, Max," she said, her nose lifting.

"I don't mean to be rude, Elisabeth," I said, going to the screen door. "I'm sorry. But, I'm not the guy you should be talking to. Ask Rachel Arneau."

"You know as well as we do, that woman's impossible."

"Then, I guess you're just going to have to wait until the exhibit opens to see what we find out here, aren't you?" I shrugged and opened the screen door. "Now, if you'll excuse me, we have work to do." I smiled at Gertrude. "It was nice meeting you, Gertrude." I went inside and walked back to the kitchen where I sat at the island and waited for Stormy.

I was just snubbing out my cigarette when she pushed through the swinging door. "Never thought I'd hear myself say this," she said with a smile. "But, I sure wish Rachel'd been here when them two showed up."

"Sorry to just leave you out there with them like that."

"No problem." She went to the sink and began washing her hands. "Almost had them turned around and leavin' but then you showed up."

"Why don't I like that woman?"

"Question should be," she turned and grabbed a towel for her wet hands, "why are there folks that do?"

*   *   *

As is our custom, Stormy, Rayleen, Spotter and I toasted in the new season on the lodge porch after dinner. The sun had drowned itself in a pool of blood in the lake and now, as the pin-pricks of cold, blue white stars began to blink on in the blackening sky, loons started calling to each other over the cheeping cacophony of spring peepers.

I hung a kerosene lantern on the beam above our heads and, in the warm, yellow glow, we sat in a row in three of the dozen dark green Kennedy-style rockers, our feet up on the porch rail. Snoring softly, Spotter was stretched out on his side beneath our legs. Rayleen and I were sipping Loon Lagers. A big mug of coffee steamed in Stormy's hands.

"Chilly, ain't it?" Rayleen said, pulling the collar of his wool shirt up around his ears.

"It's damp," I said.

"It sure smells nice though," Stormy said, slurping the hot coffee.

It did. The water, wet earth and the smoke from the fire I'd built in the fireplace at dinner all blended into a Whitefork potpourri in the cool night air.

"Too bad them aftershave folks can't come up with a smell like that," Rayleen said. "I'd sure buy some." He pulled is cap down low on his forehead and sipped the beer. A great horned owl hooted up behind the lodge. "And it's too bad Sabrina ain't bringin' that squirt, Elise with her," he said. "Really like that little girl."

Stormy chuckled. "She'd sure get a kick outta The Chief, now wouldn't she, Max?"

I chuckled too. "A real Indian? You bet she would."

"Just occurred to me," Rayleen said. "We ain't had no more trouble since all that trash."

"What?" Storm said. "Whatd'ya call that foul writin' on the Whitefork sign?"

Rayleen sunk a little into his collar. "Forgot about that."

It was something worth trying to forget. The day after Elisabeth and Gertrude were here, I'd gone up to get the mail only to discover that in the night someone had spray painted, "RED NIGGERS" in big black letters on the Whitefork Lodge Sign. Although it had taken all three of us an hour to clean it off, we fortunately were able to get it done just before the kids arrived to work in the dig.

Stormy dropped her feet to the floor and leaned forward in her rocker. "Anythin' we oughta know 'bout these friends of Sabrina's comin' on Monday, Max?"

"I don't know much myself," I said. "I met one of them years ago. She and Sabrina were roommates in college. Asta Singer is her name. Used to take her to dinner with Sabrina and I whenever I'd visit. I guess I felt sorry for her. She was a sad girl then. Her mother had died and her father was too busy resuming dating to care about her or her college life. On top of that, she was really over-weight."

"She the one who works at the museum?"

"Yeah."

"What about this other girl? Pam, whatever her name is?"

"Pam Fiore. She's new to me. We'll have to see when they get here."

"I tell you I run into Richie Norville in town yesterday?" Rayleen said. "Boy's really chompin' at the bit 'bout these girls checkin' in. Come at me from every which way tryin' to get an invite out here while they're around."

"I hope you discouraged him," I said.

"Told him they was all married to professional football play-ers." He laughed. "That shut him up quick."

"He believed you?"

"Sure did. Told 'im them Mets is rough fellas you mess around with their wives."

"Mets? That's a baseball team, Rayleen."

"Whatever." He shrugged. "Don't think Richie knowed the difference either."

"Hope not," Stormy snorted. "Last thing we need around here is a Boy Scout with raging hormones."

The great horned owl hooted again. It had moved to the big maple tree down by the dock. I finished my beer and set it beside my rocker. Spotter snored. Rayleen hummed something I couldn't make out. I put my head back and closed my eyes.

"You gonna give it to him?" I heard Stormy whisper to Rayleen. "Or what?"

"Now?" He whispered back.

"Now."

Rayleen got up and went inside the lodge. In a minute he was back and standing behind my chair. "Max, he said. "I made you somethin'."

I started to turn in the rocker.

"Bring it around here, you old coot," Stormy said. "You want Max to break his neck too?"

Rayleen moved to the porch rail in front of me. In his hands was a pair of strange looking. old fashioned, rubber chest waders. Strange looking because one boot foot was three times the size of the other and attached to different colored leg. "Here," he said with a blush I could see even in the lamp light. "Made this for ya." He dumped the waders in my lap. "Woulda given 'em earlier in the week, but you didn't seem in the mood."

"Thanks, Rayleen." I held them out at arms' length. He had ingeniously cut off one wader leg at mid-thigh and cemented and taped a different, much larger one in its place.

"Taped that there seam inside and out good," he said, running his wrinkled finger along the tape. "Two coats of glue too. Should be water tight as that canoe I patched."

"Try them on, Max," Stormy said.

I toed Spotter out of the way, kicked off my shoe and stepped into the waders. I pulled them up to my chest. My cast leg and foot fit perfectly. "Where'd you get a wader with a foot this big?"

He smiled. "Remember them basketball players we had here fishing year or so ago? One of 'em went 'n left his waders and I hung onto them. Knew we could use them some day. That there's a size twenty."

I pulled the suspenders over my shoulders. "Perfect," I put my hand on his bony shoulder. "Thanks."

"Weren't all my idea," he said. "Stormy had a hand in it, too."

"Had to do somethin'," she said with a laugh. "Don't think our insurance'll cover many more casts."

I sat down again and, with Rayleen's help, took the waders off. I folded them in half and put them beside the rocker. "I'm sorry about all my moping around," I said, putting my good foot up on the porch rail again.

"Still wish you'd read that note," Stormy said.

"I will one of these days."

"Well, just as long as you're done with the mopin', guess I can't complain."

Rayleen looked at me and smiled. "Betcha having a couple pretty young girls around here for a few days ain't gonna hurt, huh, Max?"

I laughed. "I don't think I'm quite that done with it, Rayleen."

"Never know," he said, reaching down between his legs and a scratching Spotter's back. "Never know."

CHAPTER FOUR

On Monday when Stormy and Rayleen rattled down the lodge access road in his old pickup at six-thirty a.m. I was still in bed in my room in the front of the lodge.

They parked directly in front of the porch and I could hear them arguing as they climbed out of the cab and slammed their respective doors. Rayleen's voice faded toward the workshop and Stormy's boots clumped up the lodge steps accompanied by barks of greeting from Spotter. "Get down, you old fool," I heard her say as she opened the front door, "Your feet are muddy. Dammit, Spotter. No. Stay." The door slammed closed and the rubber soles of her Bean Boots squeaked up to my bedroom door. She turned the knob, opened the door and stood there, feet apart, glaring at me. "Max Addams," she bellowed, "it's time to get up. Fishin' season started this mornin', your daughter's comin' and I got a list of things still to be done long as this hallway out here." She slammed the door.

"Make some coffee."

"Intend to," she said, her boot-squeaks fading down the hall toward the kitchen.

I rolled onto my back and stretched. Reflections from the lake danced on the peeled spruce log beans spanning the ceiling above the bed. I was looking forward to seeing Sabrina.

By the time I splashed some water on my face, pulled on my robe and a slipper and limped down the hall to the kitchen, the coffee was done and a full cup was waiting for me under a curl of steam on the butcher block food preparation island. Stormy was at the sink, her back to me as she cracked and stirred a raw egg into the kibbled dog food in Spotter's bowl. He was panting at the back door, his wet nose pushing a dent in the screen. "Hate feedin' him outside," she said, going to the door, bending and placing the bowl out on the stoop. "That dirty bowl's what attracts them 'coons, you know."

I slid onto a stool, leaned on the island and sipped at my coffee. As if herds of mice hadn't been enough, we also had an invasion of hungry, very brazen raccoons already this spring. They had broken into our garbage shed and another night, dug up and eaten the tulip bulbs on the north side of the lodge. Three evenings ago, one of them had even ripped and pushed through the back door screen while Stormy, Rayleen and I were eating in the dining room. It then waddled into the kitchen and carried off half a roasted chicken. "Why don't you just feed him in here?" I said, lighting a cigarette.

"Not this mornin'." She shook her head. "I ain't gonna have them muddy paws of his on this floor. Want this place spotless when Sabrina arrives." She went back to the sink and turned on the water. "When's the Chief get here?"

I looked at the clock above the sink. It was almost seven. "Any minute now, I guess."

"We'll be having red flannel hash 'n poached eggs soon as he does." She went to the refrigerator. "So, unless you're gonna cook, take that coffee and get outta here." She pointed to two plastic sacks of garbage just inside the pantry door. "And take that garbage on your way."

I stuck the cigarette in the corner of my mouth, grabbed the coffee mug and juggled the two garbage bags out the back door, around Spotter and his food, and down the steps to the garbage shed.

"Make sure you close them can lids tight," she yelled from inside.

"Yah, mien commandant," I yelled back.

"And, go get some clothes on."

Rather than go back through the kitchen, I left Spotter eating on the steps and limped around the outside of the building to the front. The lodge, workshop and most of the lake was still in the shadow of Morning Mountain and the air had a little ice in it. In the distance, however, the sun was warming the tops of the budding trees, rimming the mountains with golden light. I was just limping up onto the front porch when Chief Danny Shortsleeves came down the access road in his muddy, yellow VW beetle. Rachel was in the passenger seat. Tappets pinging, he pulled right up behind Rayleen's pickup and turned off the engine. It back-fired twice, tried to re-start itself and then, in a cloud of blue smoke, stopped.

Danny squeezed himself out from behind the wheel. "Mornin', Max," he said across the car when he was standing. "You fish in that outfit?" He smiled at my tattered blue terry cloth robe and one slipper.

"You're real funny, chief." I was tempted to comment on the absurd looking, grizzly bear claw necklace he wore today in addition to the strings of beads around his neck but instead said hello to Rachel as she got out, stood and straightened the hood of the ankle length, midnight blue cape she was wearing.

"Hello, Max." She was a striking woman and, physically, it was easy to see what Danny saw in her. She was the product of a French Canadian father and Wabnaki mother and, except for her eyes, Rachel looked Native American. Tall and straight-backed, her coppery skin was amazingly wrinkle-free considering her age, which I assumed to be within a year or two of Danny's. Her thick, jet black hair was cut straight in heavy bangs just at her eye lids. Nevertheless, of all the things about Rachel you noticed, it was those eyes you remembered. As pale blue as a sled dog's and just as wild-looking, they flashed in the shadow of the cape's hood like they were lit from behind. She gestured toward the lodge. "Stormy inside?"

I nodded. "In the kitchen."

Rachel swept by me and, the long cape flapping out at her sides like wings, up the steps and into the lodge. The kids were

right, she did resemble a bat. I heard her call Stormy's name just
as the screen door slapped shut and Spotter began barking from
the back of the lodge.

I turned to Danny. "What's up with Rachel, Chief?"

"Damned if I know." He rolled his eyes and leaned on the roof
of the car. "She's been actin' real strange lately."

I couldn't suppress a smile. "I've heard she's taking her new
responsibility as Shaman pretty serious."

"Yeah," He slowly shook his head. "I've heard the talk too."
He shrugged. "But, who knows? Myself, I sort of think all this
money we're gonna be getting has kind of gotten to her. It is a lot."

I laughed at the understatement. "It's a lot, all right."

"Me? I think it's gonna be real nice." He patted the roof of the
Volkswagen. "First thing I'm gonna do is get rid of this."

"Is it going to make it back and forth until then?" Red Town is
twenty miles of steep and winding dirt roads northwest of Whitefork
Lodge.

He laughed. "Rachel's taking it into Johnston's this morning
for me to have Dave see if he can figure out what's wrong with it."
Dave Johnston owned Loon's only gasoline station, a Sunoco. He
was also the only one in a fifty mile radius who worked on foreign
cars.

"She's not going to be bringing you every morning, is she?"
Until today, Rachel had been coming out to look at the dig in late
morning in her old black Cadillac.

"Nah. Only today." He looked at his big turquoise-encrusted
watch. "She has to have the Bug at Johnston's in thirty minutes."

"Well, soon as she leaves why don't you see Rayleen." I pointed
toward the workshop. "He's down there. He'll show you the rods,
reels and waders. You can pick out what you want."

"Look what I dug out of mothballs." He leaned in through the
VW's window to the back seat and pulled out a khaki fishing vest
so faded it looked white. An old fashioned string net hung from a
D-ring on the back. "Found this baby with some of my wife's
things I thought we'd thrown out." He patted one of the bulging

pockets. "Most of my old flies, too." He waved the net. "Even got my own net."

I smiled. "We don't use that kind of net anymore, Chief."

He frowned.

"Not good for the fish," I said. "Now that everything's catch and release, we use soft nylon nets. Rayleen'll find one for you."

"Catch and release, huh?" He laid the vest on the roof of the car. "You don't kill anything?"

I shook my head. "Only if it's an accident."

"Damn," he said. "I was lookin' forward to some trout fillets dipped in milk, breaded and fried in bacon grease."

"You'll have to buy them at the store if you're working here, Chief."

He pulled a cigar from his pocket and stuck it in his mouth. He didn't light it. He looked up at the lodge. "At least it still looks the same around here," he said. "I haven't been out since you rebuilt. Just like the old place pretty much, isn't it?"

"We tried." I drank the last of the coffee and dropped my cigarette butt in the empty coffee mug.

He looked at the cabin we had built down by the water. "That's new though, huh?"

"We had quite a few logs left over," I said. "Guests seem to like it."

He nodded. "Looks real cozy."

Adding the cabin had been Stormy's idea. Perched on a granite outcropping with a spectacular view of the river and the lake, the cabin is constructed of the same big spruce logs as the lodge. It has a bedroom, bath, big stone fireplace and a large deck on the river side that you access through sliding glass doors. We even tucked a small, hotel-style refrigerator inside the cabinet in the corner by the door. It'll hold a case of beer or couple bags of ice. Although we charge almost twice as much for a cabin stay as we do for a room in the lodge, fisherman who want a feeling of privacy and the illusion of rustic seclusion seem more than happy to pay it. Sabrina had requested we make it ready for one of the girls in her party. Whoever the lucky young woman would be, it was easy to guarantee she was going to enjoy the fire crackling at the foot end of the king size bed and the big Jacuzzi bathtub with the view of the lake.

"Sure be nice if the weather stayed like this all week," Danny said. "And look there." He pointed at the lake. "Somethin's hatching. We even have fish rising this morning."

I nodded. Perfect bulls-eye rings were suddenly appearing all across the glassy surface of the water. "I thought I'd do a little fishing from the dock after breakfast," I said. "Join me if you want."

"I will," he said, still looking at the lake. "That's little stoneflies I bet."

I squinted back at the rise forms on the lake. He was probably right. Stoneflies were the first significant insect hatch of the season at Whitefork Lodge.

"Might be able to teach your guests casting and catching at the same time," he said. What he meant was we might not even have to take the women to the river to catch trout. They'd be learning to cast on the dock without flies on their lines and once they mastered it, all Danny and I would have to do is tie on imitation stonefly nymphs and they'd be fishing.

"That would make it pretty easy," I said.

"That it would." He rolled the unlit cigar in his mouth. "Well, guess I better go see Rayleen." He threw the vest over his shoulder. "When's breakfast?"

"You'll hear the bell."

He nodded and, as I watched him lumber down across the lawn, a small noise from the porch made me turn. It was Stormy carefully letting herself out the front door. She eased the screen door shut and then tip-toed down the steps to where I stood. "Get that witch outta my kitchen, Max," she whispered. "She's wavin' a bunch of smokin' grass around in there and chantin' like lunatic."

"Why?"

"Says she's cleansin' the kitchen's aura, or some crap."

"Humor her. She'll be gone in a minute."

"I ain't got time for this nonsense." She jammed a cigarette in her mouth and lit it. "Told her I do my own cleanin' but she says that ain't what she's talkin' about. Doesn't want the Chief's food prepared in negative space. Whatever that means." She shook her head in disgust and sat on the steps. "Just lit up some handful of dried grass, blew out the flames and started spreading weird-smellin' smoke an' ashes all over my counters. Go get her outta there, Max."

"All right." I sighed. "I'll try." As I started up the steps, Rachel burst out the door, swept out onto the porch, between Stormy and me and down to the VW, where she opened the door and looked back at us.

"There," she said. "You're fixed." She gathered her cape around her, she climbed in and started the engine. "Remember, Stormy, Danny's lactose intolerant."

When she'd backed up. turned around and the noisy little car's engine had faded away up the access road toward route 16, Stormy slowly stood. "I want you to tell the Chief," she said, as we entered the lodge, "to tell her to stay outta this buildin' unless she's invited." I stopped at the door to my room and she continued on down the hallway toward the kitchen, cigarette smoke trailing behind her just like it had from Danny's VW. "You tell him that if she comes in here again," she shot a frown my way as she entered the kitchen, "that woman's gonna need more'n black magic to protect her." Then she pushed through the door and was gone. "And light the fire in the dining room." I heard her say.

Like the original Whitefork Lodge, the first floor of this new one is cut into four basic living areas. The hallway runs straight back down the middle from the front door, the full depth of the building. At the back on the left, where Stormy had just stood, a swinging door with a round window at eye level, opens into the kitchen, pantry and laundry room. On the right a doorway leads to the library like reading room and a small storage room. Another door, just forward of that on the same wall, opens onto the stairs to the cellar. The stairs to the second floor are in front of that. My new apartment and its bathroom are on the first floor and look out over the porch and lake on the left front of the lodge. The dining room does the same on the right.

I went into the dining room.

Of all the rooms in the lodge, the dining room gets the most use. Not only are all meals served there but, it's the place everyone congregates before going out to fish and after coming back. Part of it's popularity, of course, is the fact that the bar is located in there. But I like to think it's more than that. Not only is it the largest room, it's really the heart . . . and the personality of Whitefork Lodge. On top of the polished, random-widths of yellow pine floor planking, two, thick, nine by twelve oriental rugs help define the eating and sitting areas of the room. Rayleen built the long plank dining table from an old barn door. Sealed with an inch of clear resin it sits along the four front windows under two large electrified chimney lamps taken from a country store up in Graniteville. I have them on rheostats and they can be turned down to simulate the warm glow of kerosene during dinners. The table, which will sit twelve in a pinch, today had only eight captain's chairs around it—three on each side and Stormy's and mine with the higher backs at the ends.

In the back half of the room there's a small leather couch, coffee table and two stuffed chairs facing the massive stone fireplace. "You could rig a rod in that thing," my friend John Purcell said of the fireplace the first time he saw it. To my knowledge no one's tried but the carefully fitted, river-polished stones literally dominate the entire back wall. Even the three by five Peter Corbin oil I have above the mantel is all but lost in the mass of granite shapes and colors.

This morning Stormy had put an earthenware crock filled with bright yellow daffodils from the yard on the dining room table and I noticed new candles with untouched wicks standing from every candlestick. The placemats we seldom used—the ones with Whitefork Lodge and the jumping brook trout embroidered on them—were stacked and ready on the sideboard beside my Dale Weiler sculpture of a river otter chasing a small trout through a tangle of tree roots. The glassware in the hutch was spotless and as I passed the big wooden cupboard on the way to the fireplace to build the fire for breakfast, I could smell the silver polish. The usual pile of hunting and fishing magazines on the coffee table by the hearth was gone. In their place was a large picture book of Vermont, a recent issue of COSMOPOLITAN and Orvis' new fly-fishing Catalog for Women.

Someone had already prepared the fireplace and, over wads of newspaper, they'd arranged a neat pile of birch kindling and three split apple logs. All I had to do this morning was make sure the flue was open and touch the thing with a match.

I watched the flames lick up through the kindling and when I was sure it was going, set the screen in front and, carrying the coffee mug, went to my room to dress. I also needed to rinse the cigarette butt out of the mug. If there was one thing Stormy hated it was cigarettes anywhere but in ashtrays.

* * *

I'm positive that, for many of our regular guests, returning to Whitefork Lodge every season is as much about eating Stormy's food as it is catching trout. She has had so many requests for this or that recipe that she finally fired up the lodge computer and wrote them out, adding a few kernels of "Stormy-isms" to the narrative. Skip Willit's daughter, Kate added some pen and ink illustrations and we found a small publisher down in Bennington who printed and bound a few hundred copies. It's called, "Stormy's Whitefork Lodge Cookbook" and I now offer it for sale in the "Shelf Shop" in the reading room where I have available other things guests might need or want like line, leader, tippet, the flies I tie, strike indicators, embroidered Whitefork Lodge patches, our Whitefork Lodge caps and tee shirts and, of course, the green Whitefork Lodge coffee mugs.

Red flannel hash is just one of the masterpieces Stormy creates in the kitchen. It starts several days before as a classic, hearty New England boiled dinner of corned beef, salt pork, carrots, onions, cabbage, turnips, potatoes and beets. She always makes twice as much as we'll eat and refrigerates the rest. It's these leftovers that are chopped, combined and fried in salt pork fat to make the hash. The beets give it its color and name and it's served crispy brown on the outside with perfect poached eggs sprinkled with fresh ground pepper and snips of chive scattered on top.

When his plate was set in front of him, Danny's big flat face beamed. "My God, Stormy." He closed his eyes and inhaled the rising aromas dramatically. "If this tastes even a fraction as good it smells, I swear I'm your slave forever."

"Pass me some a that there raisin toast, Max," Rayleen said, gesturing with a fork dripping egg yolk at the stack of toasted homemade bread. "And that butter, Chief, if you don't mind."

Once everyone had what they wanted, we ate in silence. The fire snapped on the other side of the room and occasionally Spotter whined from the window behind my back where he stood on his hind legs, front paws on the sill, fogging the glass with his wet nose and dripping tongue.

We were just picking the last crumbs of warm cinnamon maple coffee cake from our plates when the phone rang. Stormy pushed her chair away and went out into the hallway to get it. I could hear her hello. "Whitefork Lodge. Stormy speakin'." There was a pause and then she said, "Sabrina baby. Hello. Where are you?" Another pause. "Yes. Okay. Sure. See you then." She hung up and came back into the room. "That was Sabrina on her car phone. They're down in White River Junction. Should be here in a couple hours or so." She began clearing the dishes.

"What can I do to help?" Danny said, pushing his chair back from the table.

"You could consider takin' that bearclaw necklace off, for starters," Stormy said with a laugh, heading for the kitchen. "Max, you come with me. You can dry."

Danny fingered the necklace and looked at me. "What's the matter with it, Max? Is it too much?"

"Yeah, Chief." I nodded. "It's a bit much."

*   *   *

In a pair of chest waders he'd gotten from Rayleen and his faded old vest, Danny was already casting in the lake in the sunshine when I joined him after dish duty. He was waist deep in the water to the left of the dock. Cigar smoke clung to his big head like a cloud on a mountain. Spotter was at the end of the dock, tail out straight behind him, pointing at the water. "Caught three nice ones already, Max," he said, the line whistling by his head. "You've got some good lookin' brookies in this lake." He shot the line and thirty yards out I saw the fly plop into the water.

"What are you using?" I sat on one of the overturned canoes and began rigging my rod.

"Weighted stonefly nymph." He began stripping the line back toward himself in short jerks to imitate a swimming insect. "I been letting it sink about two feet and then strip it back. Have had a hit on just about every other cast . . . whoa . . ." His line pulled taught and the rod bent. "See. Another one."

As the trout on his line dove and Danny's reel buzzed, I strung my line through my rod's guides. By the time he'd brought the brook trout to hand and released him, I had tied a small, marabou muddler onto my tippet and limped out to the end of the dock beside Spotter. I began false casting, shaking out my winter-kinked line.

He rinsed his hands in the lake and watched my cast. "What'd you tied on, Max?"

"Muddler," I said, shooting my line out over the water to a fading rise form about twenty yards out. "I want to see if I can get them to strike at something on the surface." As far as I'm concerned, there are really only four flies needed for the trout and salmon at Whitefork Lodge; the olive wooly bugger, the bead head prince, the tan elk hair caddis and the muddler. The muddler's the most versatile. Depending upon the way you fish it, the muddler can be used to imitate anything from an adult caddis fly or grasshopper to a wounded minnow. I work a little color into some of the muddlers I tie and the one I had on now sported a yellow marabou feathered tail. It landed just to the right of the rise form's ripples and I quickly gathered in the slack in the line. Then I twitched the fly, counted to ten and scooted it toward me six inches or so. Another twitch and I waited. Spotter barked at it.

"What the hell's Spotter doin'?" Danny said. "Been posed like that ever since I waded in here."

"He's pointing out where the fish are," I said, not taking my eyes off the muddler.

"Pointing? No shit?"

"No shit. Wait until you see him in the river. He can find trout that I can't see from mid-stream wearing Polarized sunglasses."

"No shit?"

"No shit."

There are coon and fox hounds, rat terriers and bird dogs, but, as far as I know, until Spotter, there's never been a fish dog. Just how much of his ability to spot trout is memory, I'm not sure, but he's infallible.

In the winter trout crowd themselves caudal fin to caudal fin in the deepest spring holes where the water temperature is dependably the highest. As soon as the snow melts and the river begins getting sunshine, they tend to return to the same holding areas they use year after year. The brookies scatter through the riffles and into the eddies and pocket water behind boulders. Some move into the lake and return to their favorite spots under fallen logs or rock formations on the bottom. The few brown trout we have in the Whitefork hunker beneath the mossy overhangs along the banks and at the bottom of some of the deeper plunge pools. Since I insist on catch and release, once Spotter knows where the trout are, they're always there. Spotter's so good at pointing them out that sometimes it's embarrassing. More than once I've positioned a customer in the Whitefork only to look over at the bank and see Spotter sitting on his haunches watching us. I am positive that, if he doesn't like the place I've picked, he slowly shakes his head "No" and then points with his nose to the spot in the river where he knows the fish really are.

Spotter whined. He looked from my muddler out on the water to me and back again. I gave the fly another twitch and, just as I was about to scoot it toward me another six inches, the water around it bulged and something large sucked it under. I lifted my rod tip and the line tightened and thrummed, my reel buzzed and the fish, whatever it was, headed straight for the far side of the lake.

"Bet that one's a salmon," Danny yelled. "Look at him go."

I did and I let him run for a few seconds then palmed the reel, putting tension on him. He jumped. Like a piece of twisting stainless steel, he cart-wheeled backwards in a shower of water. It was a salmon. Not as big as they can get, but strong. I quickly reeled in the line slack and, feeling the tension once more, he jumped again, this time tail-walking and shaking his head like bass or sailfish. When he slapped back down in the water I could hear the "whack" and a large flock of mallards rafting not far away thundered into the air with quacks of alarm. Jabbering and scolding, they circled the lake, most of them not quite sure what had alarmed them. The fish was tiring now and, cranking the reel hard, I gained more than half my line back. He was getting close to the dock and I could see the sun flash off of his silver sides as, just beneath the surface, he twisted against the line. Then he jumped, clearing the water this time by almost two feet. Another cartwheel, a "whack" and my line went slack. He'd broken off.

"Yessir," Danny said, as I reeled in the loose line, "that was a salmon all right." His cigar pumping smoke like a steam ship, he waded over to the edge of the dock nearest my walking cast and leaned his forearms on the planks. "Once they start that cart-wheelin' stuff, might as well just let 'em go. Especially fishin' barbless hooks like you do."

I reeled in the remainder of the line. I held it out for Danny to see. The muddler was gone. So was most of my tippet. Danny laughed. "Sex urge is a powerful thing, Max. I'd say that old boy had other things on his agenda this mornin'. He wasn't about to waste time with you."

By the time I'd changed to a stronger tippet and tied on a new muddler, Danny was back in his spot and had another brookie on. "Funny," he said, sliding the hook from the fish's mouth and watching it swim away, "you'd think it would be just the opposite."

"Opposite?"

"You'd think it would be the salmon taking my nymph and the brookies who'd rise to your muddler. Go figure, huh?"

I nodded. None of it made any difference really. Even the fact that I was forced to stand on the dock, it was great to finally be back out casting for fish. It had been a long, cold winter and, for me, the salmon's intense, wild energy had run right up my line into me like an electrical charge. I felt restored.

I began casting again. This time at a place Spotter was pointing to nearer the shore where a clump of young birch cast their skinny, cross-hatch of shadows out on the water.

I placed the new muddler as close to the water's edge as I could and then, stripping it fast back toward me, I tried to make it look like something which had fallen from the trees and was now swimming for its life.

It worked and instantly a large dark shape slid out from under the shade of the bank and, making a "V" wake like the shark in "Jaws", bore down on my fast moving fly. The fish chomped the fly and turned in one movement, hooking itself. My rod bend hard and, as I let him have a little line, I could see his dark, spotted back in the clear water, the yellow feather caught in the corner of his mouth. It was a very large brook trout and he had no intention of getting anywhere near me.

"Watch them roots there, Max," It was Rayleen. I hadn't noticed him watching. He stepped into the clump of birch and hung precariously on a slender trunk, squinting down into the water at the struggling fish. "He's gonna wrap ya and break off."

I kept tension on the fish, reeling slowly, trying to move him from the root-tangled water near the bank. "Feels like he's got legs," I said. It felt like he had feet planted belligerently on the bottom.

I got an inch of line back. Then two. Then, all of a sudden, I was cranking hard as the big trout sped directly toward me.

"He's goin' under the dock," Rayleen yelled. "Look out. Chief. He's comin' your way."

It was too late. I couldn't reel in as fast as the fish swam and he shot under the dock, out the other side, around Danny's legs and then turned right and headed for deep water. My line pulled tight under the dock and around the backs of Danny's waders. He danced clumsily backwards pulling the line tighter. Just as I thought my almost "U" shaped rod might break, Danny tripped and fell ass first into the water, the line broke and the big brook trout was gone. This time, not only did I lose my fly and tippet, but about twenty feet of expensive, weight forward, fly line as well.

Spotter was barking and Rayleen was laughing so hard he almost lost his grip on the birch sapling and fell in himself. Danny had gone completely under and, for a second, all I could see was a cigar floating between two braids. Then he came sputtering to the surface, water pouring from the tops of his waders and the pockets of his vest. "Goddam," he bellowed. "Goddam, that water's cold."

I was laughing now. "Good thing Sabrina and her friends aren't here yet," I said, holding the broken line. "Some guides we look like."

Danny snatched his cigar from the water, jammed it in his mouth and slowly slogged for shore. Rayleen helped him out and up on the grass. "Rachel told me this was gonna happen," Danny said, sitting on a canoe. "Told me to stay outta the lake."

After Rayleen and I helped Danny remove the waders, he gave all of his clothes to Stormy who said she could dry some of them in the drier. "They'll be out in a half hour, Chief," she told him. "Question is, what have we got around here for you to wear in the meantime? Maybe you can find him somethin', Max."

I tried. But the only thing of mine that fit the big Indian was the quilt from the bed. So, after taking a shower in my bathroom to warm up and rebraiding his hair, Danny wrapped the big blanket around his shoulders and went out to smoke a fresh cigar in the warming sun on the porch and wait for his clothes to dry.

And it was this specter that greeted Sabrina and her friends when they arrived ten or fifteen minutes later.

I was inside, putting a couple more apple logs on the fire in the dining room when I heard a car pull up in front. I went to the window and peered out.

There, standing on the top step was Danny, wrapped in the quilt, his smoldering cigar jutting from his big face. His right hand was raised in greeting. In front of him sat a new, forest green Jeep Cherokee with New York plates. Sabrina was at the wheel. Her two female passengers, their eyes wide with disbelief, stared and pointed from behind the security of the closed side window.

CHAPTER FIVE

Sabrina and her friends were crammed in the front seat of the station wagon. Suitcases and garment bags took up the rest of the interior of the big car and there were more tied to the roof rack.

"How many days they stayin'?" Stormy said with a chuckle, as she, Rayleen and I came out of the front door.

Sabrina jumped out from behind the wheel and, with her long auburn hair bouncing, ran around the front of the car and up the steps. "Daddy," she said as we hugged. "How's the leg? You okay?"

I held her at arms' length. Except for my blue eyes, she was like looking at my wife when we first married. "It's my ankle, not my leg." I laughed. "And, of course, I'm okay."

After hugging Stormy, kissing the cap off of a blushing Rayleen and giving Spotter a good rump scratching, Sabrina looked at Danny. "Chief Shortsleeves? What are you doing here?" She fingered the quilt. "And what's with this cigar store Indian thing?"

"Gonna help teach your friends casting for one thing." Danny smiled and took her hand. "Gonna be helpin' your father this summer for another. Didn't think you'd remember me after all these years."

"Of course, I remember. I remember your wife too."

"She passed on," he said.

"Oh," Sabrina squeezed his big hand, "I'm sorry."

"That's all right." He smiled. "It was a long time ago. Ten years."

"It's been that long since I've seen you?"

"At least."

"We're dryin' Danny's clothes," Stormy said with a smirk. "Fell in the lake, is what he did."

"Your father tripped me," Danny said.

Sabrina looked at me. "Tripped . . . ?"

"I'll tell you about it later," I said. "Let's help you get unloaded."

"And tell them friends of your's it's okay to get outta that car," Stormy said, peering at the car, "Though he might look it, Chief here ain't gonna scalp nobody."

Sabrina looked down at the Jeep. "Asta. Pam," she said. "Hey you guys. Get out of that car and meet some of my most favorite people in the whole world."

As the car doors opened, Sabrina put her arm around my waist. "Sorry again about you and Ruth, Daddy," she whispered.

"Hello, Mister Addams," the slim, very pretty brunette in the tight jeans and snug red sweater said, as she came up the steps. "I'm Asta Singer." She thrust out her hand and I took it. "Remember me?"

"Yes, of course, I remember you." I did my best not to look astonished but, Asta had changed since those days at Wellesley. Not only had all the pounds been shed to reveal a great little figure, the self conscious, frightened little girl expression I remembered always being in her eyes had been replaced by a stare that was wary and challenging. "How are you Asta?" Her grip was like a man's.

Before Asta could answer, Sabrina put her hand on Asta's arm and introduced her to the others. "This is my friend, Asta Singer, everybody. Asta and I have known each other since college. Now she's a curator at the Museum of Natural History in New York City."

Asta's smile faded. "Assistant curator." She dropped my hand. "For now."

Sabrina turned to the leggy blond in the green JETS sweatshirt and loose-fitting green satin running shorts still standing on the steps. "And this is Asta's friend, Pam Fiore. Pam works with Asta at the museum as a . . . as a . . . what, Pam?"

Pam tossed the blond hair from her face, came up the last porch step and smiled. "I'm a just a tourist guide, really." She had traces of a southern accent.

"Yes, a guide," Sabrina said. "But from what I heard coming up here, not for long." She looked at us. "Pam's a dancer. Has a part in the chorus line of a new musical coming out this Fall."

"Only second line, but it's a start." Pam smiled and extended her hand to me. "Nice to meet you Mister Addams." She smelled of cinnamon and her eyes were as green as the new grass out on the lawn behind her head.

I shook her hand, "Welcome to Whitefork Lodge, Pam."

Sabrina then introduced Danny, Stormy and Rayleen and I stepped aside as they all said hello and the girls stepped up and reaching in, around and over each other, laughed at the sudden awkwardness of it all and shook hands.

"This place is as beautiful as Sabrina has told us, Mister Addams," Asta said, looking up at the lodge. "I think I'm going to love it here."

"I think you're old enough to call me, Max, Asta."

"Oh yes. And this is Spotter," Sabrina said, stooping and hugging the dog to her breast. "The world's only fish dog."

Asta frowned and took a step away as though she thought she might have to hug the dog next. "I'm not a dog person," she said when she saw I'd noticed her distaste.

"Well, I am." Pam squatted, pulled Spotter between her bare thighs and rubbed his ears. "Aren't I, you big, old puppy?" She looked up at us. "My Papa raised blue tick's when I was a little girl."

"Where was that, young lady?" Stormy said. "You got yourself a tiny bit of accent I can't place."

"North Carolina," Pam said. "Little town in the mountains about fifty miles west of Asheville. Fullersburg?"

Stormy shook her head.

Pam smiled. "Nobody's heard of it." She gave Spotter one last scratch and gracefully stood.

"Nobody ever hearda Loon, Vermont, neither," Rayleen said, "'til Max got up here."

We all laughed.

"So," Stormy said, going down the steps to the big Jeep, "which one of you gets the cabin?"

Sabrina nudged me. "We played "flip-the-coin" in the car coming up, Daddy." She followed Stormy to the car and opened the tailgate. "Pam won the cabin." Flip-the-coin was a long car trip game we played when Sabrina was a little girl. You flipped for anything and everything . . . road signs, other cars, cows . . . and the person with the most stuff by the time we got where we were going was the winner.

"That's where Pam's staying?" Asta pointed at the little log building out by the water. "Way over there all by herself?"

"If you'd rather stay in the lodge, honey," Stormy said to Pam, "just say so. I got plenty of empty rooms upstairs. Rayleen! Get down here and help."

"No, it's perfect." Pam pushed by Asta and started down the steps. "It looks just like the pictures in the brochure."

Rayleen hobbled down to the Jeep.

"Your clothes are dry enough by now, Chief." Stormy began yanking suitcases out to the ground and pushing them with her foot to Rayleen. "Go get dressed and then get right back out here. We ain't luggin' this pile without you."

Pam leaned into the back seat and the backs of the loose shorts hiked up. "Don't change on my account, Mister Shortsleeves," I heard her say with a laugh. "Big men wrapped in blankets are just what I'd like on this vacation."

Stormy laughed back. "Don't wanta mess with that big man, honey. He's spoken for." She winked at Danny and lifted a large embroidered suitcase to the ground. "Marryin' his high school sweetheart in a coupla weeks, ain't you, Chief?"

Danny's coppery skin seemed to redden slightly as he smiled and nodded. "Yep. Sure am. 'Bout time, too."

"Really, Chief Shortsleeves?" Sabrina said. "When?"

"May 12th."

"You knew her in high school?"

He nodded. "We kinda got back together after Winnie . . . my wife was gone."

"Com'on," Stormy said. "Let's stop yammerin' and get these girls moved in."

Asta and Pam had a lot of questions about the lodge and the logs and Daniel Webster's great grandson and, as a result, it took the better part of a half an hour just to get all of their luggage out of and off the Cherokee and up onto the porch. My leg made it impossible for me to be of much use beyond unloading so, while Danny, Rayleen and Stormy finally showed everyone to their respective lodging, Spotter and I went into the dining room to finish rebuilding the fire I'd started when they arrived and make a pot of coffee in the Bunn we have set up on the sideboard. I could hear the thumps and clumps of feet and dropping luggage in the rooms above my head.

I'd just finished measuring out twelve cups of something called, "Caribe Hazelnut" into the filter when Sabrina came into the room. "Oh, it's so great to be here, Daddy." She went to the fireplace and stood looking into the flames.

I looked at her over my shoulder. "You unpacked already?"

She shook her head. "I'll do it later." She smiled. "And I've heard Stormy's spiel about the sensitivity of septic system a million times." She sniffed at the air. "I smell hazelnut coffee. When did you start drinking that junk up here?"

"Stormy made me get it for you and your friends," I said. "Pretend you love it." I pushed the START button on the machine and joined her. When she was a baby she looked like me. Now, with her clear white skin, straight nose and lush, auburn hair Sabrina was an unnervingly beautiful duplicate of her mother at the same age. She even unconsciously pulled on the strands of hair around her right ear like Marge always did.

"I hope I didn't say anything wrong to Chief Shortsleeves." She turned and looked at me. "I had no idea his wife died. What happened?"

"They only assume she died," I said. "She disappeared about ten years ago."

"Disappeared?"

I nodded and lit a cigarette. "She was an alcoholic. Really pretty bad, I hear. Stormy knows the whole story but, basically, one day Ginny just packed an old leather suitcase, left and never came back. Most of it happened before I moved here but I guess she was always getting drunk and wandering off somewhere and Danny was always going and getting her and bringing her back. This time Danny couldn't find her. And neither could the sheriff's department or the state police."

"That's so sad, daddy."

"Yeah. I think it's taken Danny a long to time to get over it."

She smiled. "Well, at least he's happy now. What's this woman he's marrying like?"

"Not a favorite around here, I'm afraid. Stormy thinks the woman's crazy." I shrugged. "And I'm not exactly nuts about her either."

"Oh well, as long as they like each other."

"I think they like each other fine," I said. "In fact, they're going to be one of the richest couples in northern Vermont in another month or so."

Her eyebrows went up.

"Danny's wife's money. Freeing him to marry isn't the only benefit of his ten year wait. It also's freeing a ton of money his wife inherited."

"Really?"

I shrugged. "Again, you'll probably have to ask Stormy but, the rumors I've heard say the stocks, bonds and cash her father left her are now worth ten million or so."

"Ten million dollars? Chief Shortsleeves? What on earth would he ever do with ten million dollars around here?"

I smiled. "I think it's Rachel who has the plans for the money."

"Rachel? The high school sweetheart?"

I nodded. "It's pretty well known that she wants to the

Wabnakis to get in on the gambling action that all the other Indian tribes in the country are cashing in on. She's already petitioned the State Gaming Commission. She wants to build a hundred acre casino and entertainment complex on Robinson Mountain."

"Up by the ski area?"

I nodded. "The ski area would be part of it."

"Say goodbye to quiet Loon, Vermont."

"Yeah."

"What are you going to do, Daddy?"

I shrugged. "Hope the Gaming Commission keeps turning her down, I guess."

"That kind of money can be pretty convincing."

"Tell me about it."

She ran her fingers over the River Otter sculpture. "This is new, isn't it?"

I shook my head. "I think Stormy put it away last time you were here with Elise." My grand daughter is around 18 months old and when she's visiting we usually move anything and everything that she could hurt herself with or break to the security of my bedroom.

"You'd have to lock it up if she were here now." Sabrina laughed. "The little demon has learned how to open doors. She's a real escape artist. Even climbs out of her crib in the middle of the night. I woke up at three the other morning and there she was at my side of the bed, thumb in her mouth, just staring at me."

I laughed. "I can just picture it."

"It's not very funny when you have to get up as early as we do."

"Well, you're here now," I said. "You can sleep all day if you want."

"I just wish I could make David like it as much up here as I do," she said, flopping down into a chair.

I sat on the small couch. Her husband, David seldom visited the lodge and when he did, he usually spent most of his time in a rocker on the porch with his briefcase open in his lap and his cellular phone flipped open at his ear, buying and selling whatever it was that he bought and sold on Wall Street. "How is my only son-in-law?" I said, more out of courtesy than real interest.

"I don't know, Daddy." She shrugged. "We both work so hard. It's like, after picking Elise up from daycare, we eat, put her to bed and that's it." She sighed. "I don't think we've had a real conversation, much less anything else, for months."

"What about weekends?"

"David has joined a club. He plays tennis with the guys most weekends." She shrugged again. "Last Saturday he didn't even come home. They were in a tournament down in Princeton, New Jersey." She smiled weakly and put her sneakered feet up on the coffee table.

"What do you do when he's gone?"

"Elise loves the Central Park Zoo." She smiled wanly. "But I can't tell you how tired I am of that place."

"Sounds like you needed to get away."

"I'm not the only one."

I raised an eyebrow.

She looked over her shoulder toward the door and lowered her voice. "Asta just broke off her engagement a couple weeks ago. She found out her fiancé has been . . . you know . . . with other women." She rolled her eyes. "I think the invitations were already in the mail."

"Poor kid."

"Yeah." She nodded. "That's one of the reasons I agreed when she pushed about getting out of the city and coming up here."

"It was her idea to come up here?"

"Mostly." She shrugged. "We only casually talked about it over lunch one day . . . how it might be nice to get out of the city and away from . . . well, you know who. Anyway, she sort of said yes but, then she moved out of the boyfriend's apartment and in with Pam and, I guess, saw the article in the TIMES about your dig. After that, she started calling me at work every day. There was no changing her mind." She smiled. "Fortunately mother was coming for a visit anyway."

I sighed.

"That sigh," she said, reaching across the coffee table and patting my knee. "is the other reason I agreed to bring her." She smiled. "I kind of figured you and Asta might find a lot in common."

I frowned. "You did, did you?"

"Yes, I did.' She sat up straight and pushed her hair over her shoulder. "And I still do."

"Like what?" I laughed. "A support group?"

"Don't make fun, Daddy."

"What then?" I was still smiling. "Is my little daughter trying to fix me up?"

She frowned. "No, I'm not trying to fix you up. I'm only trying to get you to lighten up. Upstairs Stormy told me how you've been, Daddy. Ruth is a wonderful woman but, it's not the end of the world if she's gone. There *are* other people out there, you know."

I sat forward and took her hand. "Listen, sweetheart. I know you've been worried about me." I shook my head. "But, don't be. I'm fine. Things couldn't be better. My daughter's here, fly fishing season just began," I tapped the cast, "and the doctor told me last week that finally this thing is healing. What more could I want?"

She sighed this time. "Why don't I believe you?"

"Why don't we change the subject?" I lit a cigarette. "Tell me about this other girl. What's her story? How does she fit in this little soap opera you've got going here?"

"I don't really know what Pam's story is, Daddy," she said. "I never met her before she climbed into the car to come up here. I do know she and Asta have been friends for a couple years. Like I said, Asta's been living in Pam's apartment since the boyfriend thing. I actually thought it was just going to be Asta and me up here but . . . well, we didn't have much choice. I guess Asta couldn't just up and go without Pam . . . all she's done for her, I mean . . . Asta wanted her to come . . . practically begged me . . .so, well I . . ."

"She's a dancer?"

"Pam? I guess. She's certainly got the body for it." She smiled.

"As if you haven't noticed." Her smiled faded to a frown. "What she does do, is flirt."

I smiled. "That I noticed."

"You mean that thing with Chief Shortsleeves? That's nothing, Daddy. You should have seen her coming up here. I've never been so embarrassed. Pam hit on everyone. Gas station attendants. Toll takers. Truck drivers we passed." She smiled ruefully. "Even the voice in a McDonald's Drive-Through."

"I'm sure she's just having fun."

She smiled at me. "Well, you just better watch out, Daddy." She reached over and patted my forearm. "The cabin wasn't the only thing Pam won at flip-the-coin."

"Com'on . . ."

"Seriously, Daddy." She laughed. "I had a copy of the Whitefork Lodge brochure in the car coming up and Pam saw your picture. She insisted on flipping for you and you should have heard her when she won."

I laughed. "I wonder how Pam feels about it now that she's met the old, weather-beaten guy in person."

CHAPTER SIX

The coffee gurgled, sputtered and hissed to a finish.

I poured each of us a cup and Sabrina and I walked out onto the porch into the sunshine and stood looking at the fish rising on the lake and talked about her job as an advertising agency media buyer, Elise's daycare, the cost of living in New York City and her mother's new husband, whom neither of us liked.

Finally, however, the feeding trout dimpling the water were too much for her to resist. She gestured to my rod and vest hanging on the pegs by the door. "Would you mind if I borrowed your rod and a couple flies and went down on the dock and fished for a few minutes, Daddy? Just until everyone's done unpacking?" She drained her coffee and set it on the rail.

"I haven't written you a license yet."

"Com'on, Daddy. You can do that later. Who's going to know?" She dug a box of dry flies out of the vest. "You want to come and watch?"

"I can see from here."

She grabbed my rod and almost ran down across the lawn to the dock. Spotter, his pink tongue flapping in the corner of his grin, galloped ahead of her and took a position out on the end.

It took her only half a minute to tie on a fly and, in another half minute, the sunlight was reflecting from her line as she gracefully began false casting, building a long loop behind her. Spotter barked and pointed and a trout rose forty feet straight out. Sabrina turned toward it, shot the line and it unrolled smoothly out over the water, straightened and settled on the surface. Although I couldn't see her fly from this distance, Sabrina's accuracy with a fly rod rivaled mine and I knew it had dropped perfectly in the bulls-eye of widening ripples. Her rod was parallel to the water and she and the dog appeared to freeze as they concentrated on the floating fly.

I hooked a couple fingers through the handles on our coffee mugs and just as I was turning for the door there was a splash and I turned back to see Sabrina quickly raise her rod. It curved and vibrated and I could hear the high pitched buzz of the reel. Spotter barked and the fish on her line headed for deeper water. "Wow! First cast, Daddy," she yelled. "First cast."

I waited and watched her gently play the fish. After she had reeled the trout in, stooped and scooped it from the water, she held it up for me to see. It was a thick bodied, fourteen incher. Spotter, his tail almost wagging him off the dock, strained to lick at it.

I smiled and waved. "Not bad," I yelled. "What do you have on?"

"A muddler," she yelled back, "of course."

*   *   *

Rayleen and Stormy were both in the kitchen.

He was sitting on a stool at the food preparation island scratching at something under his cap. She was at the sink, wrestling stuffing into the big turkey we were having for dinner. A cigarette smoldered in a full ashtray beside the little clay pot of parsley on the windowsill.

I put the coffee cups in the dishwasher and slid onto a stool across from Rayleen.

"Ain't seen this many good lookin' women in one place," Rayleen whispered, "since that hospital ship they stuck me on after my leg was shot off. God, was them nurses somethin'."

Stormy turned her head. "What're you whisperin' about, you old coot?"

"He was just commenting on our attractive guests," I said, shifting on the stool to take the weight off my leg. For some reason it had begun aching. "And I agree."

"They are a cute little bunch, ain't they?" She didn't turn.

"Don't know what's eatin' that Asta though," Rayleen said, scratching again under his cap.

"Asta?" I said. He had help carry her several bags upstairs.

He nodded. "She sure has a nasty streak."

Stormy turned. "You watch your mouth, you old fool." She shook a handful of stuffing at him. "Them girls are Sabrina's friends."

He blushed and shrugged. "Well, it's true." He looked at me. "Shoulda seen it, Max. I just said to her about how she really missed out by not gettin' the cabin and how lucky that there Pam is and, next thing I know, she's damn near bitin' my head off. Snarled at me, she did. Said somethin' 'bout Pam pushin' her luck or like that and snatched a bag right outta my hand so hard almost clean pulled my arm off."

Although she didn't say so, I didn't think Sabrina wanted the Asta-Pam soap opera going any further than me so I just said, "I think maybe she's just tired from the trip. Sabrina told me Pam and Asta are very good friends."

"Couldn't tell by what I seen." He dug harder at whatever was in his scalp. "That little girl had fire in her eyes . . ."

Danny pushed through the swinging door. "My God," he said with a big smile. "Sure hope Rachel doesn't find out about this."

"Find out about what, Chief?" I pushed a stool his way.

He straddled it and sat. "These beautiful young women. No offense, Max, but your daughter's got a couple sexy little friends, by God. And that Pam . . ."

I laughed. "We were just talking about it."

"And now you're gonna stop talkin' 'bout it," Stormy said, pointing at the three of us. "These little ladies come up here to relax and learn to fish. They don't need three men . . ." she glared at Danny and Rayleen, " . . . two old enough to be their granddaddies . . . all who should know better . . . droolin' over 'em." She leaned on the island and looked each one of us in the eyes. "I hear any more of this sexist talk," she pulled down a ladle from the rack of hanging pots and pans above us and shook it in our faces, "I'm gonna brain each one of you. Understand?"

*   *   *

Saturday is dump day in Loon and I supervised while Danny helped Rayleen wrestle the three big, green plastic lodge garbage cans into the bed of his pickup. Going along to the dump is one of the highlights of Spotter's week and he was already in the truck cab whining impatiently and pacing the seat. I swear, if he could drive, he'd have the engine idling and his paws on the steering wheel. He is fun to watch at the dump. He becomes almost puppy-ish as he weaves excitedly among what must be a paradise of rich aromas, fresh bear and raccoon tracks and flocks of chaseable crows.

After Rayleen and Spotter rattled up the access road, Danny and I each got a cup of coffee, pulled two rockers up to the porch rail, put three feet up and waited for our new customers to make the next move. Sabrina was no longer fishing on the dock, but I had told her earlier that, once she and her friends were settled, Danny and I would be available to meet with them to block out a day-by-day instruction/fishing schedule comfortable for everyone.

Danny looked liked he was dozing in the sun when Sabrina came down the front stairs and out onto the porch. Asta was right behind her.

Danny jumped to his feet.

"There's fresh coffee inside," I said.

"We're fine, Daddy," Sabrina said, sliding into a rocker. "And sit down, Chief Shortsleeves. You don't have to do that for us up here."

"Yeah," Asta said, going out to the top step. "Just pretend we're men."

Although it was a typically chilly April day, the warm sunshine felt good and for a few minutes the four of us watched the ducks arrive and leave out on the lake. It was already beginning to be obvious to whom all the luggage belonged. Sabrina was wearing the jeans and sweater she'd arrived in but Asta had changed to fitted khaki trousers, suede desert boots and a belted khaki shirt with more pockets than my fishing vest. Hanging from a gold chain round her neck was what looked like an oval of smooth ivory inset with an emerald cut topaz that matched her big eyes. She looked like she was going on safari. "Is that the dig?" she asked, pointing out at the holes in the yard.

I nodded. "That's it."

She took Sabrina's arm and pulled her to her feet. "Com'on, 'Brina. Let's go look at it. You mind, Max?"

"Not at all."

As we watched them walk across the lawn, Danny said, "Wonder where Rachel's students are. I thought you had them kids digging out there from dawn to dusk."

"They are a bit late today." I looked at my watch. "But then, they are kids. And it is Saturday morning."

We watched Sabrina and Asta at the holes. When Asta climbed down into the one closest to the lake, Danny got to his feet. "What's she doin', Max. She shouldn't be down in there."

"Relax, Chief." I put my hand on his arm.

He sat reluctantly. "What if she disturbs somethin'?"

"Of all the people who've been in those holes since they were dug," I said, "I think Asta is probably the most qualified."

"Maybe, but . . ."

"I think you'd better get used it. Those holes are one of the reasons she's here."

He sighed and looked over at the cabin. "Wonder where the blond girl is?"

"Pam?"

He nodded. "I've got me the distinct feeling we're gonna to be doin' a lot of this the next couple days, Max."

"Waiting?"

He nodded again and drained his coffee.

I laughed. "You're getting a good taste of what this business is all about. You do what the customer wants, when they want and, usually, how they want. All you can do is make suggestions." I smiled. "And wait."

"Here she comes."

I looked. Pam stood in a shaft of sunlight on the cabin's little covered porch and appeared to take a deep breath. Her golden hair was twisted loosely on top of her head. She had changed to khaki also but, instead of slacks and a safari jacket, she wore a loose flannel shirt over a tee shirt and pocketed shorts. As she walked up the lawn toward the lodge the long dancer's muscles rippled under the tan skin on her thighs. She stopped at the bottom step. "What's going on?" she said, nodding toward Asta and Sabrina out in the yard.

"Asta's checking out our dig," I said. I could see that Pam's thighs and upper arms were covered with goose bumps and, although I quickly looked away, couldn't help but notice that she wasn't wearing a bra under the tee shirt.

She looked at Danny. "That nozzle on the bathtub we were trying to figure out earlier is for Jacuzzi jets."

"That's what it is." Danny looked at me and smiled sheepishly. "I couldn't tell her much about the cabin, Max. Sorry."

"You get everything else figured out?" I asked Pam.

"I can't seem to get the shower to work." She smiled. "Too bad. What a view there is from that tub."

"I'll have Rayleen look at it when he gets back," I said. "He'll have it fixed before dinner. Okay?"

"No hurry." She looked back out at the dig. Asta and Sabrina were now coming back toward the lodge. Asta was dusting her hands on her trousers. "What do the think they'll find?" Pam said. "The people who are digging, I mean."

"My people used to camp right here thousands of years ago," Danny said.

Pam looked out at the lake. "They certainly had a nice swimming pool."

"Lake wasn't here back then," he said.

"Wow. It's really cool," Asta said, as she and Sabrina came back up onto the porch. "They've dug down about five feet. Small quadrants. It looks real professional. You should see it, Pam."

"Maybe later." Pam sat up on the rail in front of me, crossed her legs and looked at Sabrina. "What you should see is the furniture in my cabin."

Sabrina slid up beside her. "You mean the armories and big beds?"

"You have them too?" Pam said, obviously a little disappointed. "Do you have a refrigerator too?"

"Only the cabin has its own refridge," Sabrina said. "But every room up here has the antiques."

"Where did find you the stuff, Max?" Asta said. "It's incredible."

"We picked them up at an auction," Ruth had found the large, ornately carved, fruitwood beds and matching armoires that we had in the main lodge bedrooms at an estate sale down in St. Johnsbury. She had once dated the auctioneer and we got them for next to nothing.

"I can't believe your beds are as big as the bed in the cabin," Pam said, holding her hand out in front of her. "The mattress is this high." She smiled coquettishly at Danny and me. "Which one of you is going to come down there tonight and help me get up in it?"

I saw Asta's hands ball into fists. "I'm getting some coffee," she said and pushed by us and into the lodge.

"Get me a cup?" Pam yelled after her. "Black?"

Asta returned sipping on one coffee. She glared at Pam over the rim. Pam looked like she was going to say something but instead helped Sabrina arrange five rockers on the sunny end of the porch. Once we were all seated we worked out a rough schedule for their stay.

Asta indicated that, not only was she interested in watching the dig in progress, she hoped to do some shopping while she was here. Despite Danny's description of the cold water this early in the season, Pam said she might like to try and swim each day as well as have time to rehearse her dance routines on the cabin deck. Sabrina let me know she intended to take the girls on a couple sightseeing tours. "I want to show them the town, the dam and Monday Lake," she said. "Also, Daddy. I hope you're going to take us all for a drink at The Starlight." She knew that I didn't like to waste time drinking with guests when there were trout to catch and narrowed her eyes as if expecting me to disagree.

I didn't. "Then, it sounds like mornings are going to be our best bet as far as fly fishing," I said and looked at each of them. No one disagreed, so I continued looking now at Pam and Asta, "I also know that there's a good chance one or both of you aren't going to like it." I smiled. "If it gets that way for you, don't worry about it. I certainly won't be offended." I nudged Danny. "And neither will Chief."

He nodded and blew a stream of cigar smoke into the air. "There's plenty to do up here besides fly fishing."

"Until then," I said. "Let's tentatively set aside from just after breakfast until noon each day as official time for instruction and eventually, real fishing. Anyone who wants to spend more time can. Danny and I will always be available. Those who don't want to, don't have to. Okay?"

"Why not start them today?" Sabrina asked.

"Yes," Asta said, fingering her necklace. "Can't we start fishing today?"

I smiled. "If everyone wants to."

They wanted to.

"Alright," I said, standing. "Let's all meet down at the workshop over there in, say," I looked at my watch, "fifteen minutes and Chief and I will get you outfitted with rods and reels."

*   *   *

Sabrina had brought her own equipment and, after getting it from her room, pulled on her waders and vest and, carrying her rod, walked down to the mouth of the river to fish. Not only didn't she need lessons, she said she didn't want to be in the way as Danny and I worked with Asta and Pam. As it turned out, our first casting lessons were delayed an hour anyway because, just as Danny and I had Asta and Pam lined up on the dock with their rods and were showing them the correct grip, Stormy rang the bell for lunch.

We leaned the rods against the canoe rack and, with the girls hurrying ahead up to the lodge, Danny and I followed.

"God," he said, looking wistfully after the girls. "I don't care what Stormy says about being sexist, Max. You ever seen anything so pretty?"

It was a sexist observation but, I had to admit he was right. There is something about the way a woman moves when she walks. Especially if she knows you're watching. They both knew and, as they went up the stairs in front of us, they looked back over their shoulders and smiled.

Lunch was another Stormy Spectacular and the girls ooed and ahhed as they moved along the buffet on the sideboard taking thin slices of maple-cured ham, big spoonfuls of cheddar cheesy escalloped potatoes laced with green onions, thick warm chunks of yeasty, freshly made honey oatmeal bread and dark green spinach salad with sweet bacon-sesame seed dressing.

We were all seated and eating when Sabrina came up onto the porch, stripped off her waders, leaned her rod against the logs and came into the dining room. Her cheeks were red and she'd tied her beautiful hair back into a ponytail with a piece of clear nylon leader. "I could smell that turkey you're cooking for dinner all the way down at the river," she said to Stormy, grabbing a plate and starting on the buffet. "Daddy, the trout in the river are beautiful this year. Just beautiful. And the salmon. Wow." She turned and came to the table with the plate loaded. "They really jump, don't they? I had a small one on and he literally did backflips completely out of the water."

"You have salmon up here?" Asta said.

"Landlocked salmon," Danny said, chewing a mouthful of ham.

"What's a landlocked salmon?"

"Used to be an ocean-going fish like every other salmon," Stormy said. "Until the glaciers moved through here millions of years ago. Ice cut 'em off. And they adapted."

"The salmon we have here are only around in the spring and fall," I said.

"If they're not here all the time," Pam said, "where do they come from?"

"Lake Champlain mostly," Stormy said. "Though a few come from some of them smaller lakes between here and there."

Asta looked puzzled. "But why?"

"Why do they come up the river?" I said.

"Yes." She nodded. "I mean, are they hungry, or what."

"I guess you could call it a hunger." I smiled. "They swim up here to spawn."

"Spawning?" Pam smiled and looked at me from under a wave of hair. "I thought I felt something romantic in the air up here."

Asta glared at her. "You would."

CHAPTER SEVEN

By one-thirty Danny and I were back out on the dock teaching Pam and Asta to cast. Sabrina was on the lodge telephone trying to convince my ex-wife that modern parents didn't force children to eat anything they don't want. "Elise will eat carrots, Mom, when her body tells her it needs what's in carrots," I heard her say as I limped out the door after the others.

As usual, Spotter didn't understand that we were only learning and not fishing and immediately took a determined point at a spot on the bank fifty feet away under the cluster of small birch along the shore. And, of course, I had to explain to Asta and Pam what he was doing and why. But once Danny and I got the two of them casting, they took to the graceful ten o'clock to two o'clock motion in a matter of minutes and lines whistled back and forth over the dock in beautiful, tight loops.

"Wait a bit longer for the line to unroll out behind you, before you cast forward." Danny said to Asta, "That's it. Great."

"Remember," I said to her as she shot twenty feet of line out over the water, "Wherever you point your rod tip, that's where the line's going to go."

"It doesn't do that for me," Pam whined. "Help me Max. The line always goes over there no matter where I point the rod."

She was having a common problem and I stepped up behind her, put my arms around her and, like a golf instructor teaching someone to putt, put my hand over hers on the grip. I could smell the cinnamon again. "You're twisting the rod on your forward cast, Pam," I said, now helping with the casting movement. "Keep your thumb on top of the grip. Put it in this position." As I moved her thumb under mine, I felt her buttocks press firmly back against the front of my trousers.

She turned her head. Her lips were on my beard and I felt her buttocks move again. "I like this position," she whispered.

I dropped her hand and stepped quickly away. I think I was blushing. I looked at Danny and Asta. It didn't appear that they'd seen anything. I looked back at Pam. Her line was still whistling overhead and her eyes were still on mine. "Cast it," I said. "Now."

She cast forward, released the line and it shot straight out across the water. A perfect cast.

"That was good, Pam," I said. "That's the way to do it."

"Thank you."

"Try it again."

She smiled at me from under a lock of golden hair and, for a second, I was afraid she was going to say something else but, instead, she looked out at the water and began stripping in the line to cast again.

"You know what, Max," Danny said, as he stood back and watched them cast. "I think we could all do some fishing. What do you think?"

"They're ready," Sabrina said. Now in her waders and vest, she was sitting on the patched bottom of the Old Town. I wondered how long she'd been sitting there and if she'd seen Pam's flagrantly suggestive body language.

"Sure, let's try it," I said to Danny. "There's no better teacher than the real thing."

There was nothing rising on the water so it was Sabrina's suggestion that we add sinking tips to our lines, tie on small weighted olive woolly buggers and fish deep from the canoes out on the lake. "Danny told me he was catching brookies on weighted flies this morning," she said.

I asked how she suggested we do it with five people and only two canoes. It is hard enough for two people to fish with a fly rod from a canoe when both know what they were doing. As proficient as Asta and Pam had become, they were still neophytes and having them wildly slinging weighted flies around my head was not my idea of fun.

"Since my waders are already on," Sabrina said, "why don't Spotter and I fish from here as far as I can wade out. You guys split up and use the canoes. Later, I can trade with someone."

It sounded good.

"It's all right with me," Danny said, striding up to the canoes and turning over the small red one. "Who wants to ride in my yacht?"

"Me." Asta's hand shot up. "Me. How many chances do you get to ride in a canoe with a real Indian?"

"Native American," Pam said.

Danny smiled broadly, his gold teeth glinting in the sunlight. "Wab-na-ki," he enunciated, dragging the smaller canoe to the water and pushing half of it in.

"Why can't we use that bigger canoe?" Asta said, placing their rods in the stern.

"Max needs room to stretch his leg," Danny said, setting his vest beside the rods. "Besides," He pointed at the big Old Town and laughed, "look at the patches that thing. It'll probably sink before it's ten yards out."

"You sure about this?" I said to Sabrina. "I can stay here with Spotter and fish from the dock. Or even the water. Rayleen made a special pair of waders just for my cast that I'd like to try anyway. You can go in the canoe with Pam."

She laughed. "You're the guide, Daddy. With nothing rising, I would only be guessing where to take her out there."

"I guess it's you and me, Max," Pam said softly from right behind me.

Sabrina went to the workshop and got two flotation cushions for each canoe and then while Danny was getting Asta positioned in the bow of his, Pam and Sabrina flipped the big Old Town and carried it out onto the dock where they set in the water. She then held the gunwale while Pam slipped off her sandals and gingerly stepped into the bow. I climbed awkwardly in and sat in the stern.

I wedged my vest between my good foot and my cast. Rods were next and then the paddles. "I'm afraid I don't know how to use this, Max." Pam held the paddle above her head and looked at me over her shoulder.

"Put it in the bottom of the canoe," I said. "I'll paddle."

She turned in her seat and faced me. "Then I can ride like this. Okay?" She stretched her tan legs out in front of her and leaned back on her elbows like we were going for a ride on some pond in Central Park.

I grit my teeth.

Sabrina was still holding the gunwale near my arm. She leaned and put her face near my ear. "I can see your jaw muscles working, Daddy," she whispered. "Relax. I doubt she'll jump you in this thing." And then with a laugh she pushed us off.

Danny and Asta, both paddling like they'd been doing it together for years, were already fifty yards out. I put on my sun glasses, dug with my paddle and Pam and I surged out into the widening "V" of their wake. It looked like they were headed to the far shore where the deep, green water on this side of the beaver dam is a trout soup this time of year.

Pam didn't take her eyes off of me and occasionally trailed one hand or the other in the clear, cold water as I pointed us away from Danny and Asta and to the right, toward the north shore where I knew sunken logs and submerged trees usually hid some big brookies and an occasional brown.

After about two hundred yards of staring at me, she said, "I think I should apologize, Max."

I paddled and didn't say anything. I looked beyond her.

"Yes." She sat up. "From the look on your face I know I should apologize."

I kept paddling.

"I was out of line on the dock. I made you uncomfortable. I'm sorry."

I smiled. "Apology accepted."

"It's my biggest problem," she said, pulling her knees up to her chest and wrapping her arms around her legs. "I've always been a flirt. My momma was. My sister is. My Daddy's in his late eighties and he's incorrigible. Nurses at the home he's in won't sponge bathe him anymore, he's so mischievous."

I shrugged. "No harm done."

She peered into the deep water. "It's just that, well, I see someone who I think is attractive, I want to let them know. You know?"

I nodded and slowed the canoe. We were approaching the place I wanted to anchor. The ghostly shapes of tree trunks and tangles of limbs slid beneath us.

"Sometimes, I guess, I pick the wrong times," she said.

"Don't worry about it," I said. "We're here." I dropped the small anchor over the side and I watched it vanish into the darkness near the bottom.

She was still looking at me. "Just so long as you're not mad at me, Max." The anchor line pulled taut, the canoe jerked and then turned lazily, the sun following her golden hair like a spotlight.

"I'm not mad." I laughed. "Hell, I should be flattered."

She sighed and looked back into the water. I sensed there was more she wanted to say. When she didn't, I took a box of flies from my vest, opened it and showed the contents to her. "These are called streamers," I said, plucking a small, weighted, olive wooly bugger from the bunch and tying it to the tippet on the end of the line on her rod. "And this thing I'm tying on your line is a wooly bugger."

"Looks kind of like part of one of my daddy's pipe cleaners. One of the dirty ones, of course."

I smiled and pulled the knot tight. Her description wasn't too far off. Not a lot more than chenille yarn and a hackle feather wrapped around a hook, the wooly bugger is a deceptively simple fly. I tie a variety of colors and sizes; everything from little number 14 yellows with short orange tails to big black number 2's. Depending upon its color, the size you pick and how you fish it, it can look like a stonefly or mayfly nymph, a crayfish and, I suppose, if a trout is gullible or hungry enough, even a minnow. Today, however, we were hoping it looked like a big, juicy dragonfly nymph swimming desperately for the surface. "It'll look a lot different wet and under the water," I said, handing her the rod.

She took it and my hand too. "Max. For God's sake." She wasn't letting go. "You act like I'm just another fly fisherman."

"You are." I pulled my hand free and took off my sun glasses. "And you're here with my daughter and will be for the rest of the week." I smiled. "There's a time and a place for everything." I pointed to her rod. "And now it's time to do what we came out here for."

She frowned at the rod. "I don't know whether I'm going to be able to handle this."

"It's no different than when we were on the dock."

"I know," she said, turning in her seat and looking into the water. "That's the problem."

To me, the best part of fly fishing has always been using the dry fly. Whether it's fishing the Whitefork River or Sweet Lake, I try to fish the surface whenever I can. Fishing anything deep reminds of fishing with my uncle as kid when we'd dangle worms from bobbers. I hated it. Even when all indications are that I can't or shouldn't, I still want to fish a dry fly. So, when I'm guiding a guest using a subsurface fly like I was with Pam today, I simply let them do it.

"Aren't you going to fish too?" Pam said, turning slightly in her seat and beginning to false cast line out over the water.

I shook my head. "I'll watch you for a while." I pointed to a spot on the water halfway between us and the shore. "Can you put your fly right about there?"

She turned farther sideways, the rhythm of her cast never missing a beat. "I think I can."

"Try." With my Polarized glasses I could see the faint shape of a giant tree trunk on it's side about fifteen feet under. I'd also seen what looked like sunlight glinting off the sides of trout as they swam just beneath it. "I think you might get some action there."

"Action, huh?" She gave me a look from the corner of her eye and then shot the line. Just above its own reflection, it unrolled out over the still water, straightened and, wooly bugger first, settled on the surface. As she'd been taught on the dock, Pam began to strip it back.

"No," I said. "Don't strip it in this time. Let the fly sink. Wait."

She stopped stripping. "How long?"

"Thirty seconds."

We watched as the wooly bugger sank. She dusted something from her thigh and the canoe rocked slightly. A big yellow and black bumble bee droned out over the water, circled us and then droned back into the shade of the trees on the shore. A small turtle's dark head popped up in the water just off the bow. It blinked its wet eyes at Pam and then slid back where it came from. Ducks quacked overhead and I heard Danny laugh on the other side of the lake.

"Now?" she asked.

"No. Wait a few seconds more. You want it down where the fish are."

"But, it's going to get caught in all that stuff down there."

"Okay," I said. "Start stripping it back."

She began to yank the line toward her.

"No. Not like that. Slower. Short little jerks. Only a couple inches at a time." I smiled. "Try to make the fly look alive. Like it's swimming toward the surface."

"Like this?"

"Perfect . . ." I'd no more than said it when I saw a flash of bronze under the water and her line was yanked tight in her hand. Her rod tip bowed. "You've got one," I yelled.

"But, but what do I do?" The fish was tugging hard on her line and I could see it twisting just below the surface ten yards out.

"Keep holding the line with that hand and reel in the slack that's lying in the canoe with the other."

"Like this?"

"Yes."

She reeled the loose line onto the reel.

"Now, let go of the taut line."

She did and the reel buzzed loudly as the trout, feeling the reduced tension, dove for the bottom. "Lift your rod tip," I said. "And press your left palm on the edge of the reel. No. Like a brake. There. Yes, like that. Now keep the rod tip up and start reeling him in."

She began reeling. Her face was flushed. She was smiling. "Wow. He's so strong." The long muscles in her tan forearms stood out.

"Don't reel too hard," I said. "You don't want him to break off."

"Oh, look. I see him." She pointed and the reel buzzed as the fish took line. "Oops." She quickly resumed palming the reel and then began cranking again. "It takes two hands, doesn't it?"

I smiled. "You're doing fine." I unhooked the net from my vest and laid it across my thighs.

"You're going to have to help me take him off the hook, Max," she said. "I've never touched a live fish before."

"Try to maneuver him toward my end of the canoe," I said.

Her reel buzzed loudly again as the trout pulled toward the shore. "He won't come," she yelled.

"Just keep tension on him," I said. "Feel him. When he pauses, reel him toward you." I watched her play the fish. Her dance training as obvious. I doubt she realized it but it was sort of a seated ballet. Even in the confines of the canoe, the tug-of-war with the trout was translated into graceful moves and poses. The rod had become a wand in her long fingers and when she raised her arms to lift it, it's curve became her curve, down her arms to her shoulders and then repeating itself in reverse along her spine to her buttocks. Her breasts, rib cage and stomach pushed out tight against the tee shirt. Her toes pointed. Her calves flexed. Sweet Lake had become "Swan Lake".

"You're making me nervous, Max," she said. "Staring at me like that." A thick coil of golden hair had come undone and now looped, spring-like, at her flushed cheek. A small piece of pink tongue stuck out from the corner of her mouth. "You could help, you know."

"You're doing fine." The trout, a thick bodied, two to three pound brookie, was tired and now finned slowly only a few feet from her end of the canoe. I could see the wooly bugger in the corner of its mouth. I slid the head of the net into the water. "Work him over here."

She did and, after a short burst of twisting and flailing, he slid into my net. I lifted him from the water. "Nice job, Pam," I said, slipping the barbless hook from his jaw. "Nice job."

She pushed the lock of hair away from her eyes and beamed. "He's beautiful isn't he?"

"Here," I held the net out to her, "you put him back." The trout's golden eye rolled and his gills pulsed.

She frowned. "But I want the others to see him."

"We don't keep fish up here," I said. "They all go back to be caught again."

"Really?"

"Really. I thought you knew. Sabrina said you were reading our brochure on the way up here."

She smiled. "I only looked at the pictures." She held her hands tentatively over the fish. "What do I do?"

"Just gently pick him out of the net with both hands."

She gingerly lifted the fish from the net. "Oh, he feels like a muscle."

"Now hold him in the water. But, don't let go."

She held the fish over the side. "Now what?"

"Move him back and forth," I said.

"Why?" She began moving the trout back and forth just below the surface.

"You're giving him artificial respiration," I said. "Without doing that, if you let him go now, he'd probably die."

"How long do I do this?"

"When you feel him begin to struggle, he's okay. Then just release him and let him swim away."

"Now?"

"If he's struggling."

"He's twisting." She lifted her hands from the water and we watched the trout dissolve back into the lake. "Bye, trout," she said and looked at me. "That was fun, Max. Can we do it again?"

I laughed. "You can do it until Friday."

She picked up the rod and began untangling the line. "Did your mayor girl friend like to fly fish?"

I sighed. "How do you know about her?"

"Sabrina told us coming up," she said. "Wasn't she supposed to?" The curl fell in her face again.

"I guess everyone else knows," I said. "Why not you?"

"I've never had anything like that happen to me." She glanced at me around the curl. "I guess I've always been the other woman." She had her line untangled and was beginning to false cast again. "Should I put the fly in the same spot as before?"

"Sure." I squinted at the water. "But maybe a little more to the right this time."

Her eyebrow arched under the curl of hair. "What's a little more?"

I pointed. "Like six feet."

Again her presentation was almost flawless and the wooly bugger landed and began to sink exactly six feet from where it had the first time. "Now I wait?" she asked.

"Not as long this time," I said. "It's shallower there."

"Say when."

We waited.

"Do you know this guy who wants to marry her?"

"Nope."

"I'd think a place a small as this, you'd know everybody."

"I don't know him."

"Do you think she's going to marry him?"

"I suppose." I pointed at the water. "Start stripping now. You don't want it to catch on the bottom."

She jerked on the line and it pulled tight in her hand. "Oh, oh," she said and jerked again. The line pulled tighter, her rod bent and the canoe pulled toward it. "I think it went too far down, Max. I'm stuck."

"Lower your rod and point the tip at the place where the line enters the water. Then pull."

She did as I instructed and the canoe moved again. "Darn, she said. "I think it's really stuck."

"Here, let me help," I said and, folding my cast under me, carefully knee-walked to the center of the canoe where I could reach her rod. "Hand me the rod."

"No, Max." She frowned. "I got it stuck. I'll get it unstuck."

I sat back on my heels and watched her struggle with the bending rod. "Be careful you don't snap the rod," I said. "I'd rather we lost the fly."

"Don't worry," she said, really pulling now. "See. It's moving."

She was right. The line was slowly coming toward her. "I think you're hauling a piece of the bottom up with it," I said.

"Whatever." A big piece of her tongue was in the corner of her mouth now. "It's sure heavy."

"Probably a branch." I peered into the water. "If you can get it close enough, I'll grab it."

"I see it, Max." She was filling the canoe with loose line as she pulled it in. "It looks like a ball."

I tipped my sun glasses. I could see it also. "It certainly isn't a branch," I said. It looked like large clump of lake bottom.

"Here." She shoved the rod in my hand. "Keep pulling." The canoe tipped a bit as she leaned slightly over the side, thrust her hands down into the water and reached for the thing caught on her line. "I've almost . . . there . . . I've got it . . ." She lifted whatever it was to the surface and her eyes went wide. She screamed, dropped it back into the water and sat hard in her seat. The canoe rocked violently. "Oh, my God, Max! It . . . it's . . ." She put a hand to her mouth. Her face was white, " . . . it's a . . . it's a skull."

I looked into the water. Although it was now cloudy with

bottom silt, I could see the wooly bugger hooked firmly in the left eye socket of a muddy, human skull.

I reached into the water and grabbed for it. Just my luck, my finger hooked through the soft mud in the other eye socket and, fighting a sudden wave of nausea, I quickly lifted the skull into the canoe and dropped it on the floor, where it rolled back and forth, drooling mud on the vest between my feet.

"My God, Max," she said, pushing herself as far into the bow as she could. "Who's is it?"

"Your guess is as good as mine." I toed the tannin-stained cranium with my boot. The lower jaw was missing and only one black molar peaked through the thick scum and mud in the back half of the upper jaw. A stonefly pupae slithered from the nose hole. I looked into the water. "I wonder if the rest of it's down there."

"Throw it back, Max. Please."

I looked across the water to the lodge. The high schoolers had arrived while we'd been fishing. Their cars were parked in the turn around and I could see what looked like Kevin, Tracy and the twins up to their waists in the holes.

"Please, Max. Please get rid of it."

I shook my head. "I don't think we should. Not yet anyway." I gingerly lifted it from the floor of the canoe and began picking the mud from it. "I'll be interested in what Chief thinks about it. Asta too, for that matter."

"Asta?" Pam laughed, a little deliriously, I thought. "I'll tell you what Asta will think about it, Max. She'll be really pissed. She'll think that now I'm trying to take her job too."

I frowned. "Too?"

"Yes, too. I'm positive she thinks I'm one of the ones who was screwing her fiancé."

CHAPTER EIGHT

"I can't believe it, Daddy," Sabrina said. "You just hooked it with a fly?"

I nodded and smiled at Pam. Really afraid of what Asta might think, Pam had made me promise I'd take credit for hooking the skull. "I thought I'd caught a branch or something," I said.

Pam, Sabrina and I stood in a half circle watching Kevin, Tracy and the Twins squatting at the water's edge with the skull. I had called them over to see it as soon as we'd tied the canoe to the dock.

"It certainly looks old enough," Tracy said, carefully turning the skull in the water as she cleaned the mud from it.

Kevin looked wistfully out at the lake. "There are probably hundreds more out there."

"Boy, this is sure better than a bunch of broken bowls," Gretel said, reaching in a picking at the dark mud packed around the molar and in the other tooth sockets. "Are you going to let us have it, Mister Addams?"

"Yeah," Kevin said, taking the skull from Tracy, "My dad won't believe this dude."

"Dude?" Tracy snatched it back. "How do you know it isn't a woman?"

He roughly turned it in her hands. "This's why," he said, sticking his finger in the jagged two inch wide hole in the top back of the skull. "Look at that hole. This dude was killed in battle probably. And women Wabnakis didn't fight in battles, stupid."

"He wasn't very big," Gretchen said, taking the skull from

Kevin and holding it beside her head like she was posing for a picture in a mall photo booth. "Look. My head's lots bigger than his."

"That's 'cause you're so stuck up," Gretel said, taking the skull from her sister. "Nobody's head's as big as yours." She turned it in her hands. "I wonder where all his teeth are."

"Out there under the water," Kevin said. "Where the rest of him is." He looked at me. "Where exactly did you find him. Max?"

"About twenty yards out from that thick bunch of spruce there." I pointed.

He looked. "Like about where those mallards are landing?"

"Exactly." Half a dozen ducks were just skidding onto the water where Pam and I had been fishing.

"What's all the commotion down here?" It was Stormy, a contrail of cigarette smoke streaming behind her, coming down through the yard. "Somebody else fall in?"

"Daddy and Pam found a skull in the lake," Sabrina said.

Stormy pushed through the half circle. "Skull? What kinda skull?"

"A person's skull." Gretel handed it to Stormy. "He was killed in a battle. See," she pointed, "there's a hole in his head where he was bashed by a tomahawk."

"We don't know any of that," Tracy snapped.

Gretel blushed. "Kevin said . . ."

Tracy rolled her eyes.

Stormy turned the skull in her hands then looked from Pam to me and back again. "What do you mean, you found it?"

"I caught it," I said.

Pam smiled and nodded. "It almost broke his rod."

"Can I talk to you, Max?" Stormy nodded away from the group. "In private?" She handed the skull back to Gretel and walked up into the yard.

I followed.

"Rachel's gonna freak," she said, when I was at her side. "That woman's gonna blow a gasket when she sees that thing. She's been out here every day just makin' sure nothin' like this happened and now you go and do just what she's been tryin' to avoid."

"Dammit, Stormy. Relax." I lit a cigarette and looked back at the group by the water. They were all watching us. "We weren't looking for anything. We were fishing. And that lake may be sacred ground, but I own it."

"Maybe you do," She took a final drag on her cigarette, stooped and snubbed it in the grass, then stuffed the butt in her apron pocket, "but I think you oughta take that thing right back out there where you got it and put it back."

I shook my head. "I'd like Asta to look at it. I mean, now that we've got it. Also, I think Chief ought to have a say in what we do with it, don't you?"

She shaded her eyes with her hand and squinted at the lake. "That him out there by the beaver dam?"

I nodded. "He's fishing with Asta."

"You don't mind, I'll go ring the bell for them. Ask me we should decide this thing 'fore Rachel comes back to pick him up tonight."

I nodded and walked back down to the group at the water.

Kevin was holding the skull now. "We want to take this into town, Max. Show it to my dad before Miss Arneau sees it and makes us put it back."

"Yes," Tracy said. "He'll carbon date it and . . ."

The bell began ringing.

"What's that for?" Sabrina frowned and looked at her watch. "It's bit early for supper, isn't it?"

"Stormy's calling the Chief in," I said, looking at Tracy and Kevin. "We're not doing anything with this guy," I took the skull, "until he and Asta take a look at it."

*   *   *

Stormy paced the length of the porch chain smoking as Danny and Asta took their time coming back across the lake. I couldn't blame them. They didn't know why we called them in and fish were now rising everywhere. I could see both of their rods flash in the sunlight as they stopped their paddling often to cast and catch trout.

Kevin, Tracy and the twins were waiting too and sat, talking softly, out in the grass halfway between their cars and the dig.

The skull was on the porch rail. "Kind of makes it look like Halloween up here," Pam said, coming up onto the porch. She'd gone to the cabin and changed from the skimpy shorts and tee shirt to a loose pair of thick, brown corduroy trousers and a thick, thigh-length navy blue sweater. Unfortunately, they made her look no less attractive.

"Too bad all that dirt won't come off the mouth," Sabrina said from her seat in the rocker beside mine. "It's kind of gross." The kids had done their best to clean the skull but whatever the black scum was on the single molar and upper jaw wouldn't wash off with water. Kevin wanted to pick at it with his pocket knife but, since there was a good chance it was going right back in the lake where it came from, I suggested he wait until Danny and Asta saw it.

Just as Danny and Asta got to the dock, Rayleen pulled in with our empty garbage cans bouncing around in the old International's bed. Spotter, his nose suddenly in the air, leapt from his perch in the truck bed to the ground and made a bee-line for the skull. Rayleen stopped in front of the porch, climbed from the cab and saw the skull. He pushed his cap back on his head. "Lordy, what've you got there, Max?"

"Trouble," Stormy grumbled, still pacing.

"We think it's a Wabnaki warrior," Sabrina said.

Rayleen limped up onto the porch and went to the skull. Spotter was cautiously sniffing at it the way he did everything he didn't recognize; as though it might lash out and bite him at any second. Rayleen pushed the dog out of the way. "Can I touch it?" he asked.

I shrugged.

He picked up the skull and turned it in his hands. "Little

people, wasn't they?" He looked at me. "Where's the other part of his mouth?"

I pointed at the lake.

"Who found it?"

"Max did," Pam said.

"What's this goop where his teeth's supposed to be?"

"We don't know," I said. "Maybe Asta will be able to tell us that."

"Hey, Rayleen," It was Danny. "Whatcha got there?" Carrying their rods, Danny and Asta came up onto the porch.

"Max pulled a skull from the lake," Stormy said.

"Really? No kidding?" Asta leaned her rod against the wall and went to Rayleen. "Wow. Let me see that." She took the skull from his hands, turned it in the sunlight and expertly traced the cranium cracks with her finger. "Wow."

Danny sat on the porch rail and looked at me. "Out in the lake, huh?"

I nodded.

He held his big hand out to Asta. "Let me see that thing, honey." She gave it to him and he held it out at arm's length. He looked like he was auditioning Hamlet. "Not very big folks in those days, were they?"

"What I thought too," Rayleen said.

"It must be one of the ancient ones, huh Danny?" Asta said almost reverently. It was obvious that, besides fishing, Danny had been regaling her with his famous stories out on the lake.

He looked at me. "What're you gonna do with it, Max?"

"That's why I rung the bell for you," Stormy said. "Figured you'd tell us."

He sighed and handed the skull back to Asta. "Hell, I'd like to keep it for the exhibit." He pulled a half smoked cigar from his vest and stuck it in his mouth. "But I don't know about Rachel." He struck a match on the rail and stuck it to the end of the cigar and a cloud of smoke formed around his head. "This is exactly what she's been afraid might happen out here. She takes that N.A.G.R.A. law pretty seriously."

Sabrina frowned. "What law?

"The Native American Grave Repatriation Act," Asta said. "It protects American Indian burial sites as sacred. The people in New York I work for are challenging it in court right now. It says ancient physical remains cannot be tested, should be left alone and reburied when and where they're found. It's a pain."

"That's what I been tellin' everybody all along," Rayleen said. "Ain't right diggin' up dead folks."

"No, it's probably not right, Rayleen," Danny said. "But, hell, that exhibit we got at the historical society could sure use something liked this. Having a human head on display'd be a real drawing card the day we open, you ask me." He looked at Asta who was now sitting on the arm of Sabrina's rocker hugging the skull to her breast. "The whiteman's exhibit has three skeletons in it," he said. "Personally, I don't see why the Wabnakis gotta be so prissy different."

"It's not like we went looking for it," Pam said.

"It's your call, Chief," I said.

Stormy nodded. "You're the one's gotta deal with Rachel."

"I'll deal with her," he said. "What's done is done."

"I don't see what the big deal is," Sabrina said. "If somebody gets offended then all we've got to do is put it back in lake, right?"

"Put it back?" Asta wrapped her arms around the skull. "This could be hundreds of years old. It should be studied." She ran her fingers over the brow this time. "Look at how high this forehead is and how wide these eye sockets are. Even the color of the bone." She turned it over. "And this tooth. I can't begin to tell you how much can be learned just from . . ." Her eyes widened. "Hey, look." She held the skull out to Sabrina. "See, there's a cavity in it."

Sabrina squinted at the tooth and the rest of us circled around Asta taking turns looking at the tooth. It was a cavity all right. A big one. It was packed with the black stuff.

"Once that goop is washed out," Asta said, "they can tell just from the type of decay what kind of diet this man had." She looked at me. "I happen to know that the museum pays good money for things like this, Max. I could call my boss. Just to see what she might bid on . . ."

I shook my head. "I think right now we'll wait until the Chief tells Rachel and then we'll see what the Wabnakis want us to do with it." I looked at Danny. "If you want, we'll wrap it in a plastic bag so you can take it with you."

"Nah." He shook his head. "Just leave it like it is. We'll just be showin' it to Rachel when she comes to get me tonight anyway. You can wrap it then, if she wants."

While we were talking, Kevin had come across the lawn and now stood at the bottom of the steps. "Mister Addams? Can I talk to you for a second?"

"Sure. Shoot."

"No." He blushed. "In private."

Kevin and I walked out into the yard a few paces. "What's up?" I said. I hadn't noticed before in all the commotion, but he had quite an abrasion and knot on his left cheekbone.

"We were just talking," he said, gesturing to Tracy and the twins who were now up at their cars. "There must be tons more bones and stuff out there in the lake where you found the skull. And well, we were thinking . . ."

I knew where he was going and I shook my head. "I don't think so, Kevin. I told you before, it's too dangerous to be diving out there."

"Yeah, but, since you already have the skull, what's the harm in getting the rest of it?"

I shook my head. "I just heard that we might be breaking a law as it is. I don't want to push our luck. Okay?"

He nodded slowly. "Are you going to, at least, let me show the skull to my dad? Let us get it carbon dated?"

"I'm not sure. I think we've decided it's going to stay right here at the lodge until The Bat sees it."

He frowned. "Then we can kiss it goodbye . . ."

"We don't know that yet. Chief Shortsleeves seems to feel pretty

T

strongly that it would be quite a drawing card at the museum." I
pointed to his cheekbone. "What happened there?"

He shrugged. "Nothin'."

"That's a pretty big goose egg to be nothin'."

"You wouldn't understand, Mister Addams. It's an Indian thing."

"Try me."

He sighed. "Bunch of Loon High School guys chased us out
here this morning." He touched his cheekbone. "I got mad, but
there were four of them. That's why we were late today."

"Com'on Kevin," Gretel waved from the cars, "I gotta get
home."

"Yeah, Kevin," Tracy yelled. "We told your dad you'd be home
an hour ago."

"Okay, Okay," he yelled and then turned back to me. His face
was full of hope again. "I gotta go, Mister Addams but if The Bat
says she wants to keep it, maybe she'll want the rest of it."

"Who knows," I said.

"I sure would," he said. "I mean, if I was the dead guy and
that was my skull. I'd want my all of me together, no matter where
I was."

"Unfortunately," I said, "that's probably The Bat's feeling too."

*   *   *

Sabrina and I were alone in the reading room. I was sitting on the
stool in front of my fly tying table and she stood behind me, mas-
saging my neck. Favoring the cast on my leg, the way I had to
when I tried to walk without the cane, cramped the muscles at the
top of my spine. By dinnertime, I usually could barely turn my
head.

Stormy was in the kitchen getting dinner ready and Danny
had taken Pam down to the dock to try for more trout. Asta and
Rayleen were out in the workshop looking for something non-
caustic in which to soak the skull. No matter what Rachel decided, Asta felt the scum around the teeth should be removed.

"There's one other thing I'd like to do while I'm here, Daddy," Sabrina said. "If you don't mind."

"What do you want to do?"

"I'd like to call Ruth. That be okay?"

I nodded. "Sure."

"Maybe I can go to town and see her."

I nodded again.

"Stop moving your head, Daddy." Her thumbs pushed into the flesh above my shoulders, the pressure just at my threshold for pain. "It feels like you've got rocks in there." Her thumbs dug harder.

"That's my body tensing up." I laughed. "It knows if it doesn't, you'll dig two thumb-size holes in me."

"Don't be such a baby. Relax."

I exhaled and tried to relax.

"I want to hear it from Ruth," she said.

"That she's getting married?"

"Yeah. Stormy doesn't seem to think it's going to happen. Ruth hasn't said yes yet."

I sighed and she didn't say anything more. The fingers dug.

Finally she said, "Pam says you're a great teacher."

"Good."

"Thanks for being so nice to her. I saw what she did on the dock. Did I tell you she was a flirt or what?"

"I guess things like that go with the territory," I said. "I don't like it but . . . Ouch." I winced as she pushed beyond the threshold.

"You didn't hook the skull, did you?"

I shook my head. "How'd you know?"

"Even I know you don't fish sinking flies."

I smiled.

"Why the ruse?"

"Pam doesn't want Asta to think she's trying to take her job or something like that."

"What?" She spun me around on the stool so I was facing her.

I told her what Pam felt Asta thought about the boyfriend.

"That's Asta." Sabrina chuckled. "She thinks everybody's the one. Will probably think I was sleeping with him next."

"What I can't figure is," I said, "if that's what she thinks, why did she want Pam along on this trip?"

She shrugged. "Maybe she thought she could confront her on neutral ground. They are friends, you know."

"They don't act it. Or, at least, Asta doesn't."

"Like I said, that's Asta."

I shook my head. "Oh, brother."

"It'll iron itself out, Daddy. Don't worry about it. Now that you've found the skull, Asta's in heaven anyway." Sabrina turned me back around. "She's probably forgotten all about everything else."

"She's going to be pretty unhappy if we have to put it back."

"Oh, don't worry about Asta." She dug her thumbs into me again. "She'll find a way to get some mileage out of it no matter what happens to it." She turned me around on the stool again, leaned and looked me in the eyes. "Meanwhile, Daddy, that skull should make you realize that life's too short to go around moping." She ran the tips of her fingers over my beard. "I don't like seeing you look so sad. It makes you look old. You're a handsome guy. Smile a little."

"I have been smiling."

"You're getting better." She spun me back around and her fingers dug into my shoulders again. "But I think you need to have more fun."

"Fun?"

Stormy's dinner bell began to ring. Sabrina gave my shoulders one last dig and patted my back. "Yes, fun. Go with the flow, Daddy." She went to the door and turned. "People come up here to Whitefork Lodge to fish, yes. And it's your job to make sure they catch them. But remember," She smiled, "they also just want to have fun. I think that's your job too." She gave my shoulders a final squeeze and disappeared into the hallway.

*   *   *

It was like Thanksgiving.

Twenty golden pounds of moist, range-fed turkey, four pounds of apple/mushroom stuffing, two heaping bowls of homemade cranberry relish, steaming brussel sprouts swimming in butter sauce, mashed potatoes in more butter, sticky-hot maple-candied yams, a basket of hot rolls and a milk pitcher full of Stormy's decadently rich, dark gravy. All washed down with a couple half gallons of crisp, cold California Chardonnay.

And like Thanksgiving, we all ate too much too fast and by the time it was over, were too stuffed and uncomfortable to move without pain, much less go back out on the lake and fish. Instead, we sat on the porch—Rayleen, Chief, Asta, Pam, Sabrina and I—almost comatose, in a long line in the rockers and sipped coffee and watched the sun set over the lake.

"I'm going to have to start exercising tomorrow," Pam had said, rubbing a hand on the back of a thigh. "I'll bet I put on ten pounds just today."

"It couldn't happen to a more deserving person," Asta mumbled.

Pam sighed. "Oh, Asta . . ."

Asta frowned but didn't say anything.

"Strange how quiet it is," Rayleen said, going to the porch rail and looking out over the still lake. "Them peepers should be chirpin' full tilt by now."

"Thought somethin' was unusual," Danny said, looking also. "And where's all the ducks?"

They were right. There was no breeze either. It was like looking at a mural on the wall in the dentist's office.

"I told you we should have put that skull back, Max," Pam said.

Asta laughed derisively.

"I'm serious," Pam said. "Maybe it's like what happened when they began removing things from Tutakaman's tomb. A curse. First the animals and birds died. Then the diggers. Then, even the man who led the dig, Sir Edmund Grange, died mysteriously too."

"You can see why she's such a good guide," Asta sneered. "Even she believes the crap they make her tell the tourists."

"It's true." Pam stamped her foot. "Every one of them died."

"Yeah, they died all right." Asta rolled her eyes. "But it wasn't a curse. They died of complications from a respiratory infection caused by mold spores in the air in the tomb."

"Oh yeah?" Pam folded her arms across her chest. "Then why did they call it, The Curse of King Tut?"

"They didn't know it was mold spores then." Asta looked at the rest of us. "They didn't even know from mold spores in those days. We've only discovered that part in the last ten years. Back then they called it a curse to keep the grave robbers away."

Pam blushed and looked at her feet.

"Com'on, you guys," Sabrina said, putting her hand on Asta's. "We're supposed to be here having fun. Let's not let some stupid skull ruin everything."

"Hear. Hear," Danny said.

"Well, I recommend keeping things tomorrow morning like they were this afternoon," Asta said. "Chief Shortsleeves and me in one canoe. Max and Pam in the other." She looked at me and smiled. "Is that all right, Max?"

I laughed. "If we can move tomorrow."

"Do we have to go out on the lake?" Pam made a face. "I think it's kind of spooky out there."

"Hey, maybe we could all fish together down at the inlet pool," Sabrina said. "There aren't that many trees there to get hung up on and it was great when I was there today. And maybe we can take a lunch and picnic up under those pines on the point. Do you think Stormy would mind?"

"Would Stormy mind what?" Stormy pushed through the screen door. She was rubbing her hands together. I smelled hand lotion.

"Making us a picnic tomorrow," Pam said.

"No problem," Stormy said, going to the porch rail and putting one cheek up on the rough wood. "Rayleen can bring it down to you at lunchtime."

"Ain't gonna be me," he said, looking from Stormy to me. "I told ya both I was gonna be gone tomorrow. Whole week almost. It's the tent raisin' and the Church's spring vacation week baptisms, remember?"

"Already?" Danny said. "Little early for outdoors ain't it?"

"Got us a new tent," Rayleen said. "Portable heaters too. Kerosene. Good enough for this weather."

"You go to church in a tent?" Asta said. "Like a revival thing?"

"Dunno whatcha call it," he said. "But, yep, it's in a tent."

"What denomination is it?"

He scratched his head. "Well, we call it Lord's Workers, if that's what you mean."

"No, I meant like, Methodist, Catholic, Presbyterian. Like that."

He shrugged. "Don't think we're any of them." He looked at me for help.

"I think you'd call Rayleen, a Born Again Christian," I said.

"God botherers, I call 'em," Stormy snorted.

Ever since a near death experience during the war, Rayleen's has always flirted with one religion or another. And he isn't alone.

In the ten plus years I've lived up here I've watched our part of northern Vermont become a hot bed of fundamentalist Christian teaching. Stormy says that it started in the sixties with the hippies and their refusal to go to Viet Nam. "Them long hairs run to Canada," she said. "After a while, they got homesick and sneaked back down across the border into Vermont. Old timers up here didn't hassle them, so they set up them communes and stayed. Now most of 'em are in their forties and fifties. Got families and homes up here and, to them, these new folks like Rayleen's bunch and their crazy religions are entitled to the same tolerance they got."

Word spread and every loosely organized group from Louisiana to L.A. claiming a direct line to the Almighty, gave northern

Vermont a try. Some of them, like Rayleen's Lord's Workers' church, are solvent enough to lease space in one the many old, empty, brick, factory buildings in town and move outside when the weather warms. Others, like the bible thumping *Witnesses for the Cross*, and *Voice of the Mountains*, pitch big tents in local farmers' hay fields only in the summer. When the weather turns cold, they move south.

Although their arrogance wears a little thin, I don't mind them. And as long as they don't come knocking on the lodge door preaching creationism to me or my guests, they don't really bother me. They run their own school and, at least for now, seem disinterested in active involvement in local politics. Rayleen is good about it around Stormy and me and, as far as I know, has never tried to force feed his beliefs onto anyone else either. In fact, I'm still not sure how he hangs in there with them in the first place. The Lord's Workers church is against just about everything he cares about. Stormy thinks they tolerate his tendencies toward alcohol, bars and swearing because they use him as an example. "Either that," she says with a laugh, "or like I been suspectin' all along, they're just plain stupid."

"Think I better be goin'," Rayleen said, looking at Stormy. "You 'bout ready to go?"

She shook her head. "Think I'll stay here tonight. Save you the extra drivin' in the mornin'."

He nodded, went down the steps and out to his pickup. "I'll try'n be back 'fore you girls leave on Friday."

"See that you do," Stormy said.

The girls and Danny said goodbye. I waved.

Sabrina turned back to Stormy. "I'll help you with the picnic, Stormy," she said. "Just ring the bell tomorrow when lunch is ready and I'll come up to the lodge and help carry it down."

"We all can help," Asta said. "And we want you to picnic with us, Stormy."

"How anyone can talk picnic right now," Danny said, patting his mountainous belly, "I don't know . . ." He was drowned out by the sound of his yellow VW sputtering, clacking, clanking and backfiring down the access road.

As the headlights illuminated the porch, I laughed. "Doesn't sound like Dave Johnston was able to fix much, does it?"

Rachel honked. I could see her face lit by the faint green glow of light from the dash. It seemed to float, disembodied in the little car's dark interior.

Well," Danny stood, "here goes." He scratched Spotter's ears as he walked by and went down the porch steps where he stopped and turned. "If I'm not back in two minutes," he laughed, "call the sheriff."

We watched Danny walk to the driver's side window of the VW. Rachel rolled it down and he put his big hands on the roof. I couldn't hear what he was saying but, about thirty seconds into it, Rachel screamed something in Wabnaki and leapt from the car almost knocking him over. "Inushuk! Inushuk," she yelled as she stomped toward us. "La coot oray, inushuk. Goddammit!"

"Oh, Jesus," Stormy said, backing into the lodge and quickly pulling the screen door shut in front of her. "Here it comes."

CHAPTER NINE

My cast was cumbersome but I could move if I wanted to and I intercepted Rachel on the porch steps. "Calm down, Rachel," I said, holding up my hand. "You're not coming up here until you calm down. I have guests."

She stopped on the bottom step. She was breathing hard. Her wild blue eyes flashed, but she lowered her voice. "I knew this would happen. Damn those kids. I told them to leave bones alone . . . I'll flunk all of them . . . I'll . . ."

"I found the skull, Rachel," I said. "Not your students. I found it . . ."

"You?! What were you doing in our dig . . . ?"

"It didn't come from the dig. It came from the lake." I pointed toward the dark northern shoreline. "Way over there."

She turned and looked. When she turned back, her face appeared drained of color. "How . . . ? How did you . . . ?"

"He caught it fishing," Pam said. "We didn't even know what it was at first and . . ."

I gestured to Pam to silence her. "A fly hooked it," I said to Rachel. "It was an accident."

Rachel sighed. Her color wasn't coming back, but she seemed calmer. "I thought . . ."

"We know what you thought. And I know how you feel. We haven't damaged it." I gestured toward the lodge. "It's right inside."

"We been waitin' for you, dear," Danny said, coming up beside her. He put a big hand on her shoulder. "Wanted to let you decide what to do with it."

She didn't look at him and instead tried to see by me into the lodge. "May I see it, please?"

"I'll get it," Asta said, going quickly inside.

"Maybe we should all go in," I said. "The light's better there."

The skull was up on the mantel in the dining room so we filed in there. Danny and Rachel sat at the table. The rest of us stood. Asta took the skull from the mantel and brought it to the table. "Here it is." She set it carefully in front of Rachel.

Rachel's eyes widened and she sat back in the chair. "Ohhh .." She actually looked like she might faint.

"What's the matter, dear?" Danny said.

"I . . . I . . ." Rachel tentatively reached out and touched the skull's forehead. "I . . . I . . . it's just that I don't think I've ever been this close to . . . to our ancestors."

Asta pulled up a chair and sat across the corner from Rachel. "It is pretty impressive." She turned it on the table top. "My guess is it's a thousand years old, at least."

Rachel frowned and pulled the skull from Asta's hands. "And who are you?"

Danny introduced Asta, Pam and Sabrina. "Asta works at the Museum of Natural History in New York City. She knows about stuff like this."

Rachel's eyes narrowed and she put her other hand on the skull. "And you'd like to have it, I assume."

"Yes," Asta said, with a shrug. "To study, of course."

"Of course." Rachel lifted the skull, turned it upside down and studied the upper jaw and molar. I heard her stop breathing for a second and her hands shook slightly. She quickly put the skull back down on the table and, gripping it as though it might fly away, looked at Danny. "Out in the car's my prayer shawl," she said. "Get it."

Danny looked at me, rolled his eyes and stood.

When he was gone, Rachel said, "This must be returned to the lake." She was now gripping the skull so hard the knuckles on her hands were turning white.

Excuse me, but," Asta reached for the skull, "if you squeeze it like that, you could damage it."

Rachel swept Asta's hand away. "I know what I'm doing, thank you."

Danny came in with the prayer shawl. It looked like the old Navaho print afghan Stormy sometimes threw over her shoulders when the lodge was chilly.

Rachel snatched it from his hands, unfolded it and after setting the skull in the middle, quickly wrapped it up. She stood, pulled the hood of her cape over her head and went to the front door. "I'm going out onto your dock, Max. I'd like not to be disturbed."

"My God," Asta said. "You're just going to toss it off the dock?"

Rachel didn't answer, opened the door and was gone.

Danny sat in her seat at the table and put a hand on Asta's. "Don't worry, honey," he said. "She ain't throwin' it anywhere. She's just gonna pray over it."

"But, she said it had to go back."

"If it does," he said, "she'll have a Deganaweda to do it."

Sabrina frowned. "A what?"

"Sorry." Danny smiled. "A burial ceremony. Most of the tribe will have to be present." He looked at Stormy. "You've been to one, haven't you Stormy?"

"Last year." She nodded. "When Mildred Little Bear passed on." She looked at Sabrina. "Lots of moanin' and groanin' mostly. Whole damn tribe was there it seemed."

"Not all of 'em," Danny said, with a smile. "Someone from each family though." He looked back at Asta. "We believe we are all the same blood so everybody's related, you know? We all morn, no matter who dies."

"Wow," Pam said. "You mean, you're going to have a big Wabnaki funeral ceremony right here?"

"But," Asta was looking out the window, "but, why?"

"Question is, when?" I asked. The Saturday immediately following Sabrina, Pam and Asta, we had a big group from the Boston chapter of Trout Unlimited booked in for a week of serious fishing. I hadn't said anything to anyone but, I wanted the dig, and now the skull thing, over and done with by then.

"Hafta ask Rachel about when, Max," he said. "She's the Shaman."

Sabrina joined Asta at the window. "What's she doing out there, anyway?" She pressed her face to the glass.

I joined them and we both peered out into the darkness toward the dock. Rachel was just a black shape silhouetted against the abyssinian darkness of the lake. I squinted. She held the shawl-wrapped skull high above her head. She was swaying back and forth. "Stormy," Sabrina said. "You should see this. If she's not careful, she's going to fall in."

Stormy, Pam clustered at the other window. Danny stayed seated and lit a cigar.

"Looks like somethin' from that ROOTS movie," Stormy mumbled.

"She's askin' permission from the four corners," Danny said, his cigar smoke now clouding the end of the table. "Settin' things up for the Deganaweda with the wind, lightnin', rain and sun."

"Well, she musta got it 'cause she's coming back," Stormy said, stepping quickly from the window. "I'm goin' to the kitchen. You come get me, Max, when all this is over." Her Bean Boots squeaked down the hall.

"Stormy don't like Rachel much," Danny said. "does she?"

I smiled. "I don't think it's that, Chief, as much as it's the fact that she's probably the only one of us who actually believes the mumbo jumbo stuff."

He frowned. "You don't think I believe?"

I shrugged. "I sort of thought you were . . ."

He shook his head. "I grew up with Shamans, Max. I seen 'em do lots of stuff nobody can explain. Hell, even before the tribe made her Shaman, I seen Rachel cure arthritis and turn breach babies in the womb. Years ago, she made the lumps in wife's breasts go away."

"Were your wife and Rachel friends?" Sabrina asked.

T

"After the lump thing, they sure were. Did damn near everything together. Like sisters, almost."

"Wasn't she jealous?" Asta turned and leaned her back against the window. "I mean, didn't your wife know that you and Rachel had been high school sweethearts?

"'Course she knew. But why would she be jealous? We were man and wife." He shrugged. "Rachel and I didn't start up again until after my wife was gone."

The front door opened and Rachel swept in. She carried the blanket-wrapped skull directly to me. "I want this to be your responsibility, Max," she said, handing it to me. "I'm going to arrange a Deganaweda for Wednesday night after the moon rises. It will only last an hour. Then this will be finished."

I set the bundle on the table. "What do you want me to do with it?"

"Keep it wrapped," she said. "It's pure now." She looked at Asta. "I don't want anyone touching it."

"Why don't you just take it with you?" Asta said, bitterly. "Then you'll be sure nobody touches it."

"This is where the spirits of our ancestors are," Rachel said simply. She looked back at me. "Put it somewhere safe. I'll be back on Wednesday morning to prepare it for burial." She looked at Danny and pointed to his cigar. "Now, put that obnoxious thing out and let's go home." She dramatically turned and, without saying goodbye, swooped back out the door. Danny gave me a nod, indicating he wanted me to follow him into the hallway.

I did. "I hate to do this to you, Max," he said. His voice was low. "But I think I ought to stay in Red Town tomorrow morning. Rachel's gonna need help getting this Deganaweda set up. Lot of folks to contact and only a couple days to do it."

I shrugged. "Do whatever you feel is necessary. Sabrina can help me in the morning."

"You sure?"

I opened the door for him. "I'm sure."

After Danny and Rachel rattled up the access road in the little

VW, I took the skull to the kitchen and put it in the refrigerator in
the space vacated by the turkey. Stormy was hanging our big aluminum pots on the iron rack above the island and I told her what
had transpired in the dining room after Rachel returned from
the dock.

She wasn't very happy about any of it. "Criminy, Max," she
said. "I don't want some dead guy's head in my 'fridge. Why can't
you just put it in your room?"

I reminded her of our rodent problems. "The refrigerator's the
only place mice can't get into."

She sighed and sat on a stool. "A funeral Wednesday night, huh?"

I nodded and took one of the unfiltered Camels from the pack
at her elbow and lit it. "You've got to admit," I said, coughing at
the harsh smoke. "Rachel wasn't nearly as bad about this thing as
we thought she'd be."

"Don't care, Max. Don't like that woman one bit." She pulled
a cigarette from the pack, looked at it and put it back. "And, what
about that poor little Asta? She was so excited 'bout havin' the
skull to study. Now she can't even look at it."

"As far as I'm concerned," I said. "She can study it all she
wants in next couple days."

"You can't do that, Max. Rachel's got a spell on it. She'll know.
And then . . ."

"How's she going to know?"

"She'll know, Max. I'm tellin' you, she'll know." Stormy looked
at the refrigerator. "Thing's prob'bly wrapped special to boot. She'll
know we unwrapped it. That woman'll take one look at that blanket and, I know, all hell's gonna break loose."

"We'll see," I said.

"And you don't wanta put Chief on the spot."

"He's not coming back until this is over. Said he wants to help
Rachel with the Deganaweda arrangements.

Spotter barked outside the back door.

She stood and went to the door. "Think I'll go upstairs and fix
my room." She opened the door and Spotter came in, sniffed at his

food bowl and then licked the floor around it. "I'll take that little one at the top of the stairs, you don't mind."

"Fine with me."

She stepped out onto the back stoop and took a deep breath. "Smells like we're gonna get a little rain by mornin'."

"Maybe The Lord's Workers will call off the tent raising."

"Fat chance of that," She came back inside and closed the door. "They got collection plates to fill."

Well," I stood and snubbed out the harsh little cigarette, "as long as it doesn't rain Wednesday night," I said. "I want this skull thing done with before Sabrina leaves."

*   *   *

Stormy went to make the bed in the small room at the top of the stairs and, opening a Loon Lager, I wandered back out through the lodge. Spotter clicked along behind me. No one was in the dining room but a bottle of gin was on the sideboard. I could hear conversation from the porch.

Pam, Sabrina and Asta were in the rockers with their feet up on the rail. The only light was from the dining room windows behind them. They'd all slipped on odd jackets of mine from the pegs just inside the door. It was getting chilly. I could smell the gin and cigar smoke. I slipped on a sweatshirt and Asta turned as I stepped out the door. "Where is it?"

"I put it in the refrigerator."

"I made us some killer martinis, Daddy," Sabrina said and lifted the stainless shaker from the porch floor. "There's enough in this shaker for one more. Want it?"

I gestured with my beer bottle, shook my head and sat on the top step beside Spotter who was now sitting as he does sometimes, just watching and sniffing the dark. The peeper chorus had resumed and several bull frogs had joined in, their groaning croaks ricocheting around the lake.

"The frogs are back," I said, sipping on the beer.

"Some curse," Asta mumbled.

"Yeah but, the stars are gone, now," Pam said, sipping carefully from her big martini glass.

"Clouds. Stormy thinks we'll have rain by morning." I could see the glow of a cigar ash from Asta's rocker. "I see the Chief taught you more than how to catch fish today," I said to her.

Asta laughed. "Actually I've been trying to teach him." A cloud of smoke drifted out over the yard. "That Macanudo wrapper on those old things he smokes is so bitter. I told him I was going to send him a box of these Don Perones as soon as I get back to the city."

"You call New York tonight?" I asked Sabrina.

"Oh, damn." She sat forward and set her glass on the floor. "I forgot in all the commotion." She stood and went to the screen door. "Knowing mother, she probably thinks we were all killed up here."

"Someone was," Asta said. "About a thousand years ago."

Sabrina went inside to the phone. I looked back at Asta. "You really think the skull's that old?"

"At least." The cigar tip glowed orange.

"How can you tell? I thought you need carbon dating for . . ."

"That's for exact age, Max. I'm just comparing it to some of the pieces of that age we have at the museum. The skull you put in the refrigerator has a lot of the same characteristics."

"Like?"

"Size, for one thing. Of all the bone structures in the human body, the cranium has shown the most growth in the past several thousand years. Our lake man's skull is no where near as large as modern man's."

"Maybe he's a child," Pam offered.

"Not with that molar," Asta snapped.

Pam sighed, dug the little olive from her drink, put it in her mouth and chewed thoughtfully. Asta resumed sucking on the little cigar. Something splashed out on the dark lake. Spotter got up from the step, walked out into the yard and I heard him exhale as he flopped in the grass. "Do we have to obey her, Max?" Asta finally said.

"Rachel?"

"Yes. This thing about not touching the skull. She can't be serious."

"She's serious," I said. "But I don't think it's going to hurt anything if you want to continue studying it."

"Really?"

"Really. As long you don't take it apart or damage it in some way, I really can't see what difference it could possibly make."

"I want, at least, to get some good photographs of it before it goes back into the lake."

"It doesn't sound like that could hurt it."

"Of course, I wish it were cleaner," she said. "Around the upper jaw, you know?"

"Why don't we just soak it overnight in some vinegar and water?" Pam said. "That might loosen up the goop on the tooth."

Asta sat forward in the light from the window. "Could we, Max?"

"Hell, I don't know why not." I sighed and looked out a Spotter in the grass. He had rolled into a line of window light and was now on his back. His forepaws twitched. "Stormy uses vinegar and water on just about everything around here and it hasn't hurt anything yet."

Sabrina came back out on the porch and flopped into her rocker. "Good God," she said, picking up her martini and drinking most of it. "I've only been away a day and already the wheels are coming off down there."

"Elise all right?" I asked.

"Oh, she's fine. It's David. He's out of underwear. He's out of socks. Mother's cooking is upsetting his stomach. She thinks he should take them to the Empire State Building tomorrow. He wants to play tennis." She drained the glass. "All the time I was talking to David, Elise was in the background screaming, 'Mama, be home'." She looked at Asta. "Be glad you're not getting married. It's a pain."

"I *am* glad I'm not getting married." Asta tossed her cigar out into the yard, stood and looked down at Pam. "I just don't like what caused it." She looked at me. "Can I go into the kitchen and try the soaking thing, Max?"

"Need help?"

She shook her head. "Just tell me where the stuff is."

"Vinegar's in the cupboard. And the big bowls Stormy uses for making bread are in the pantry."

"What's going on?" Sabrina said, looking at me. "You're not going mess around with the skull after what that woman said," she looked at Asta, "are you?"

"I'm letting Asta take some pictures of it, if that's what you mean. And I'm letting her soak it overnight in vinegar and water so it's a little cleaner."

"But, Daddy. Rachel said . . ."

"I know what she said. But this is my lodge. And that skull was found on my property. We're not going to hurt it. Asta's only going to take some pictures of it."

"Com'on, Sabrina," Asta said. "I need this. It's really important right now. Even if I only take pictures and write a report. Associate curators don't usually get chances like this."

"I hope you guys know what you're doing," Sabrina said.

"I do," Asta said and the screen door slapped behind her as she went into the lodge.

After we heard Asta enter the kitchen, Pam said, "Asta thinks the museum's going to let her go."

"They're going to fire her?" Sabrina picked up Asta's martini glass. It was half full. "Why?" She took a sip.

"Asta's not the only one. They're cutting back on the number of Associate Curators at the museum. There are fifteen of them, including Asta. I heard the new director wants that number down to three by June."

"But, why Asta?" Sabrina drained Asta's glass. "I thought she was one of the fair haired . . ."

"Not with this new woman," Pam said. "Besides, Associates are supposed to be constantly presenting the museum with potential material and ideas. Asta hasn't contributed anything for nearly a year."

"She's had problems, for God's sake."

"I don't think the museum cares about her personal life, Sabrina."

"Poor Asta." Sabrina drained Asta's glass and looked at me. "I guess you're right, Daddy. What she needs is more important than what Rachel wants."

"I didn't know about her job problems," I said. "But if she gets good enough pictures of the skull, maybe she'll get some sort of credit or something for it."

Pam smiled. "I'm sure that's exactly what she has in mind."

*   *   *

About thirty minutes later, Stormy called down from an upstairs window and said she was going to bed and would see us all in the morning. A few minutes after that, Asta came to the screen door and said she was doing the same. "The skull's soaking and I put it back in the refrigerator, Max," she said. "It's in a big bowl. The shawl thing is folded on a stool, okay?"

Sabrina was the next to go and, gathering up the martini glasses and the shaker, kissed me on the forehead and went inside. I was tired too, but Pam didn't seem to be going anywhere.

The warm yellow light from the dining room window back lit her golden hair and made even the old red plaid jacket of mine she had on look good. Her face was dark. "I kind of wish now that I could tell Asta I was the one who found the skull," she said.

"If you think it will help, go ahead."

She shook her head and the light skimmed her cheek and caught for a second on her lips. "No. It's too late."

I lit a cigarette and didn't say anything and listened to the frogs. The peepers had all retreated into the mud and were quiet now. An owl hooted up behind the lodge.

"Was that an owl?"

I nodded. "A great horned owl." Another answered from across the lake.

"Sabrina said you used to work in New York City."

"Yeah. Advertising."

"How did you end up here?"

"Got fired." I smiled at her. "And divorced. No reason to stay in the city anymore."

"I'm sorry."

"Don't be." I laughed. "It was the best thing that ever happened to me."

"But, how did you know how to run a lodge?"

"I didn't." I laughed. "Stormy came with the place. She was only supposed to stay a month until I got my feet on the ground but, as you can see, she never left." I smiled. "Thank goodness."

"She sure can cook."

I nodded. Stormy did a lot more than cook and clean. She kept the lodge books, did our income tax returns and generally kept me from over-extending, over-promising and over-booking. I knew that if it wasn't for Stormy, Whitefork Lodge would have gone under years ago.

The owl hooted again up behind the lodge and was immediately answered from across the lake.

"It sounds like they're talking," Pam said.

"They are." I nodded. "It's mating season."

She pulled up her collar. "Are you dating anyone, Max? I mean, now that . . ."

I shook my head.

"Why not?"

I shrugged. "Too busy, I guess." I lifted my cast-covered leg. "This thing hasn't helped much either."

"How did you do it?"

"Slipped on some ice." I pointed toward the cabin. "Right over there, as a matter of fact."

"You stay up here all winter?"

"Not usually. In January I go south with a friend to fish."

"Female friend?"

"Male. This year, because of the leg, I couldn't."

The owls hooted again. Now they were both out near the lake. "Don't you get lonely, Max?"

I shrugged.

Her rocker stopped moving. "I wish I'd known you were up here all by yourself." She stood and went to the porch rail. She leaned on it and looked up at the sky. I could smell the cinnamon again. "It can get pretty lonely in The City too."

"For you?" I laughed. "That's hard to believe."

"Well, believe it." She turned and faced me. "If I was asked out by every guy who made a pass at me I'd be booked twelve hours a day seven days a week. But nobody does. I had only one date last year. One. And he was a fat banker old enough to be my father. He was a pig. He took me to dinner on the east side and kept putting his hand between my legs under the table. I left before the appetizers. "

"I'm damn near old enough to be your father, Pam."

She laughed this time. "You don't try to feel me up under the table. In fact, you don't try anything."

I snubbed my cigarette on the floor and put the butt in my shirt pocket. "I thought I explained all that out on the lake today."

"I know. I know." She walked around behind my rocker and stopped. "The Max Addams' Code Of Northwoods Ethics." She chuckled and I felt her hands on my shoulders. "Everyone has a good time but him." I felt her fingers brush the top of my head and then she went down the steps into the yard, bent gracefully and scratch Spotter's belly. He groaned. She smiled up at me once more and then she straightened, tossed her hair back and faded into the darkness toward the cabin.

As I watched the lights in the cabin come on, I reached up and touched my head where she'd touched me and when I held my fingers to my nose I could smell cinnamon again.

I smoked another cigarette and watched Pam's occasional shadow on the cabin curtains until she turned out the lights. Then I rearranged the rockers and called to Spotter. He got slowly to his feet and followed me inside, down the hallway to the kitchen where I took my vitamins. I opened the refrigerator and peered into the big bowl now sitting in the center of the top shelf. The skull stared indifferently back at me from just beneath the surface of the amber vinegar and water solution. Some flecks of black floated in the bubbles around the edges. I poked my finger into the liquid and pushed at the skull. Bubbles containing more black flecks rose. The solution was working. It was methodically eating the build up away.

"I think I've got the same thing happening," I said to the skull. "Only with me it isn't vinegar. It's cinnamon."

CHAPTER TEN

Loud pounding on the lodge front door awoke me the next morning at six a.m. Spotter barked from his spot on the foot end of my bed as I rolled over and peered out my window. It was Loon County Sheriff, Simon Perkins. Richie Norville was standing right behind him with his hat in his hands. Both were in yellow rain slickers. Their tan squad car with the green Loon insignia on the doors idled out in front of the porch, its wipers flip-flopping big streaks across the wet windshield.

I groaned, put my feet over the side of the bed and sat up.

Perkins pounded again. Spotter jumped off the bed and whined at the closed bedroom door.

"I'm coming," I said through the partially open window. "Don't wake up the entire lodge, huh?" I went to the bathroom, pulled my robe over my nakedness and looked in the mirror. I'd stayed up too late last night.

Sheriff Perkins knocked again and, as I limped to the door to my room, I heard Stormy open the front door. "You wake up our guests, sheriff," she said. "and you ain't gettin' my vote this November."

I stepped into the hallway and stood behind Stormy. She was in a robe too. It was red faded to pink. An unlit Camel was stuck behind her ear. Her braid was wrapped around her head and encased in a thin scarf.

"Morning, Stormy. Max." Perkins tipped the wet brim of his smokey hat.

"Hi, Max," Richie said, trying to peer around all of us into the lodge. "Stormy."

I frowned. "What's going on, Simon ?"

"Heard last night that you found yourselves a human skull out here," Perkins said.

I nodded. "Out in the lake."

"How'd you hear 'bout that?" Stormy said.

"Those kids from your dig out here were telling everyone who'd listen last night that you found a skull with a hole in it."

Stormy frowned. "What were them kids doin' in Loon instead of Red Town?"

"Don't know," he said. "But one of them even went so far as to say that this guy was hit over the head with a tomahawk."

I laughed. "Nobody knows any of that."

He didn't laugh. "That's why we're here, Max."

I frowned.

"Do you think I could see it?" he said.

I shrugged.

"Whyn't you turn off that squad car, Richie," Stormy said and then looked at Perkins. "And both of you come inside out of the wet. I'll make us all some coffee."

"That would be real nice, Stormy." Perkins tipped the hat brim again. "Thank you."

While Richie ran out to the squad car, Perkins took off his slicker and hat and hung them on the pegs by the door. Then Stormy and I led him into the dining room where she went to the Bunn and began making the coffee. Perkins sat the end of the table in my chair and I quickly got a fire going. You could see where Richie got the inspiration for his brush cut hair. The only way the white stubble on Sheriff Simon Perkins' head could have been shorter was if he shaved it. He was about my height, maybe an inch taller and looked to be in much better shape. His shoulders were Marine-square and his belly was as flat as a fourteen year old's. He had a nose that had been broken more than once, faded blue eyes and a wide thin mouth I'd never seen smile except in the re-election posters now all over Loon. A pale scar divided his left eyebrow. He had been a State Police Lieutenant in Vermont's larg-

T

est city, Burlington when, a little over a year ago, he'd been asked by Ruth to replace Loon's current sheriff who had resigned for health reasons. It was only supposed to be a temporary assignment but Perkins liked the job and, after settling the divorce he was in the middle of, he moved into an apartment overlooking the river. Rumor was, he took a massive cut in pay but, I guess, life in Loon had other advantages when compared to Vermont's largest city. Now he wanted the job for real and indications were he was going all out to get it. I wasn't so sure he was going to get my vote in November, however. Not only was the man humorless but, as a leader, seemed . . . to me at least . . . a bit too political. More than once in his short tenure as acting sheriff, he'd been called upon to take a stand and didn't. Our current situation aside, Ruth needed as many people in government as she could get that she could trust to stand by her when push came to shove about Loon's drug problems, ever present poverty, growing traffic or recent racial tension.

Richie came in and, after hanging his slicker and hat beside the sheriff's, sat at the table across the corner from Perkins. "This rain really sucks," he said, wiping the wet from his face with his sleeve.

Perkins frowned at him. "You lock the squad car?"

"Ah, er," Richie blushed. "no sir. I forgot . . ."

"Go lock it."

"But . . ." Richie frowned.

Perkins sighed. "Son," he said, "you're supposed to be learning this job and being a good law enforcement officer is knowing how to follow procedures. Whether it's remembering to read the Miranda, cleaning your weapon or locking up the squad car, those are procedures you follow. Understand?"

Richie nodded and stood.

"Now, go lock the car."

I followed Richie to the hall and, as he went out the front door and ran to the squad car, I went into my room and pulled on some jeans and the thick, green cable-knit sweater Ruth had given me for my birthday. I put a moose hide moccasin on my good foot, hobbled down to the kitchen and after removing the big bowl from the refrigerator, lifted out the skull, rinsed it in the sink and dried it off. It looked a hundred percent cleaner. Then I wrapped it in Rachel's prayer shawl and carried to the dining room.

Richie was back, the coffee was done and Stormy was pouring four mugs on the sideboard. "Sheriff?" Stormy held out a mug. "You or Richie want cream or sugar?"

They both wanted it black and once we all had our mugs, I set the ball of blanket in front of Perkins and Richie, and Stormy and I sat at the table with them. "What's your interest in the skull, Simon?" I said, helping him unwrap it. The smell of the vinegar was still strong.

"What's that smell?" Richie said.

I told them about soaking it in vinegar.

"See this." Perkins hefted the skull in his hands and studied it. "Something made this hole in the skull here." He stuck his finger in the jagged hole in the back of the cranium. "And if the hole happened before death, that makes it murder."

"Murder?" Stormy laughed. "That thing's a thousand years old, if it's a day. What'd'ya mean murder?"

Perkins gently turned the skull in the light. "First of all," he said, "you don't know how old it is."

"Sure looks old." Stormy lit the cigarette from behind her ear. "Look at the yellow color of that bone."

"That could be stain, Stormy," he said. "Tannin in the lake water could do something like that in a matter of months."

I drained my coffee cup and got up for a refill. "So, what are you saying, Simon ?"

"Like I told Richie here," he said. "There's procedures we follow. And when it comes to suspected homicide, I gotta investigate."

I came back to the table. "Even when it's centuries old?"

"Until we know it's centuries old, Max, I gotta deal with it like it happened yesterday or last year or ten years ago. That's the procedure."

"Then this is an official visit?"

He shook his head and looked at Richie. "Official visit we'd need what, Richie?"

"A warrant, sir."

"That's right." He nodded. "And how would we get that."

"We . . ." Richie blushed slightly, " . . .we'd have to go to Judge Emery with an affidavit that proves probable cause."

"And what is probable cause, Richie?"

"It's . . . ah," Richie scratched his head and shut his eyes, "a reasonable ground for belief," he was quoting from memory, "but without evidence justifying a conviction, but more than bare suspicion." He opened his eyes and smiled.

"Right. Probable cause concerns circumstance in which a person of experience believes a crime has been committed." Perkins put his hand on the skull and looked at me. "In this case, Max, murder."

I sighed. "Com'on, Simon . I've got a guest sleeping upstairs right now who just happens to work at the Museum of Natural History in New York City. She says this thing is, at least, several hundred years old."

"Based upon what?"

"Her knowledge of similar skulls, for one thing."

He sighed this time and tapped the skull with his index finger. "I've seen quite a few skulls in my time too. And hundreds of head wounds, Max." He put his finger in the cranium hole again. "And, you see, I could easily say this is a bullet hole." He held his finger in the hole at an angle. "That the angle of trajectory was down, about like this." He turned the skull over. "Which would explain the missing lower jaw. It was probably shattered and the fragments dispersed during decomposition."

"Too bad there aren't any teeth," Richie said, running his finger along the empty tooth sockets. "Could tell how old it is in about two seconds if it had fillings."

I suddenly noticed the molar was missing and looked at Stormy. I could see in her eyes that she'd seen it was gone too. She gave me an almost imperceptible "no" shake of her head. I looked back at Perkins. "So, what are you saying, Simon ?"

He set the skull upright and began to rewrap it. "I'm saying that you have two choices, Max. You can cooperate by letting me take this thing now. I quickly ship it down to the state police forensic lab in Montpelier and in a week we not only know when he died, but have a pretty good idea of how."

"What's the other choice?"

"I go get my warrant and come back out here and take it."

I pulled the wrapped skull to my side of the table. "It's not mine to give, Simon . The Wabnakis have already claimed it. Rachel Arneau was here last night. They're going to re-bury it in the lake."

Richie raised an eyebrow. "The Wabnakis are going to put it back? Can they do that?"

"Got themselves a law says they can," Stormy said.

Perkins was turned and looking out the window. The rain was coming down harder. I wondered how Rayleen and The Lord's Workers were doing out at Monday Lake. When Perkins looked back he said, "I've read about N.A.G.R.A., Max. But Federal law says you can't re-bury the corpus delicti in until a murder investigation is finished. No matter who's relative it is. And by this afternoon, I guarantee this will be an official murder investigation."

"Then go talk to Rachel and the Wabnakis," I said.

"Max." He slowly shook his head. "I'm trying to do this thing so the least amount of people are . . . you know, upset. You, of all people, should understand the delicacies of campaigning for office. I need those votes out there in Red Town just like I need yours here at Whitefork."

I handed the skull to Stormy. "Put this back in the kitchen, Stormy, will you?" I looked at Perkins. "Danny Shortsleeves is a friend of mine and I'm not going to jeopardize that by letting you turn all of this into some kind of political maneuver. If you think there's been a murder committed, then go get your warrant. Until then, the skull stays here, just like I told Rachel it would."

"You're making a mistake, Max."

"I don't think so."

Perkins stood. His cop belt squeaked. He walked around the table to the door. Richie jumped up and I stood. "I'm not going to Red Town, Max. You've got what I want right here." He looked at his watch. "I'm going back to town, Max. Judge Emery should be in chambers in a couple hours or so." He walked into the hallway and took his slicker from the peg. "I'll get my warrant and be back." He slipped it on.

Richie did the same and I went with them to the door. "And just remember," Perkins said, screwing his hat onto his head, "if I find that skull's only been in the lake a short while, then everybody who was here at the time is going to be murder suspects."

"Bet we have to drain the lake too," Richie said. "If divers can't find the rest of it." A toilet flushed on the second floor and Richie craned his neck to see up the stairs. "How are the fly fishing babes, Max?"

"They're fine, Richie."

He held the door open for Perkins. "You tell them, if they get bored out here, just give me a call." Perkins went out onto the porch and Richie lowered his voice. "All they gotta do is call 911 and ask for Richie." He smiled and the door closed behind him.

When the squad car was gone I went into the kitchen where I found Stormy up to her forearm in the liquid in the big bowl.

"What are you doing?"

"Lookin' for that damn molar," she said. "You put that skull in this mess?"

"I told Asta she could soak it a bit. She wanted to get it cleaner so she can photograph it."

"See what happens when you let someone touch it, Max." She lifted something from the brine, held it between her fingers and squinted at it. "Hand me my readin' glasses." She nodded her head at the butcherblock island.

I handed them to her. She put them on, studied whatever it was between her fingers, made a face and tossed it into the sink. "Told you to leave it be like Rachel said." She stuck her hand into the bowl again. "But no. You gotta go and do it one worse. You gotta let one of our guests soak it over night. And now it's fallin' apart."

"It's not falling apart," I said. "One tooth just fell out."

"One tooth? That was his only tooth."

"Just give it to me and I'll glue it back in. Nobody'll know."

"I don't think it's in here," she said, gesturing to the pot rack above the island. "Give me that spaghetti strainer."

I gave it to her.

"No." She pushed it back at me. "You hold it while I pour this mess through."

I held the strainer over the sink and she carefully poured the liquid through it.

The tooth wasn't in the bowl.

Stormy sat hard on a stool, took the cigarette from her pack and lit it. "Dammit, Max." She blew a stream of smoke at me. "Why do you always gotta go off and do just the opposite of what folks want you to do?"

"We'll find the tooth," I said. "Don't worry about it. Asta probably has it. It must have fallen out last night."

"You better hope."

"Why didn't you want to tell Simon it was missing?"

"Ain't none of his business. 'Sides, I don't want Rachel knowin' we mighta done somethin' to hurt that damn skull."

"She'll never know the difference."

"I'm tellin' you, Max. I'm thinkin' she knows already and she's playin' with us." She went to the sink and began washing her hands. "Now go find somethin' to do. Tooth or no tooth, I gotta start breakfast."

*   *   *

As I walked down the hall I could hear the showers running in both bathrooms upstairs. I checked the fire in the dining room, put two more logs on the coals and then crossed the hall and went into my room. As I shut the door, I noticed an unfamiliar pale green, flannel robe lying on my bed at the same time I heard the shower water running in my bathroom.

I crossed the room. "Sabrina?" I said. There was no answer.

The bathroom door was ajar and I looked in. A towel from the cabin was draped over the sink. The aroma of cinnamon was strong in the steamy air. There, framed behind the wet, pebbled glass of my shower door was Pam Fiore. Her eyes were closed and her head was bowed in the shower spray as she rinsed suds from her long blond hair. I should have immediately turned and left but I didn't. I stood there, like a school boy's first peek in the girl's locker room, and stared. Except for the women in SPORT'S ILLUSTRATED's Bathing Suit Edition, I'd never seen anyone like her. Her body, albeit slightly distorted behind the glass, was classic. There were no bathing suit lines. Just curve after curve of caramel colored skin. Her dripping breasts moved slightly as she pushed the hair from her face and turned, saw me and smiled. "Hi Max." She didn't cover up or seem startled. "I hope you don't mind. My shower in the cabin still doesn't work and all the ones upstairs were being used." She raised one leg and ran her hand down the shin to the ankle. "Sabrina told me I could use yours."

"I—I—I'm sorry." I couldn't look away. "With so many things going on yesterday, I forgot to tell Rayleen to . . ."

"That's all right."

"I'll take care of it myself right after breakfast."

"Really. I don't mind, if you don't." She turned off the water and opened the door. "Would you get me my robe?" She reached for the towel on the sink. Even wet, her pubic hair was so pale it appeared non existent. "I left it on your bed, I think."

I backed quickly away into the bedroom. She was out of the shower stall now and I heard the glass door slide closed as I felt behind me on the bed for her robe.

She came out of the bathroom toweling her hair as my fingers closed on the green flannel fabric. Her breasts danced stiffly as her arms moved. Her nipples were the color and size of pink pencil erasers.

She wrapped the towel, turban-style, around her head and I held the robe out at arm's length. I could feel the heat from her water-warmed skin as she took and slipped it on.

She wrapped the soft robe around her nakedness and tied the belt. Two dark wet spots appeared as the pale green fabric soaked up the water on her breasts. "Are you all right, Max?"

I cleared my throat. "Stunned, I think. A little stunned. It's been a while since I . . ."

She smiled. "Since you've had a nude woman in your room?"

I laughed. "That too."

CHAPTER ELEVEN

Sabrina was seven when her mother and I divorced. It was not very amiable and, as a result, the court only granted me one long week-end a month and two weeks in the summer to be with my daughter for the first several years.

Most of our time together was spent at the lodge and I did my best to make it meaningful. I took her hiking and canoeing. I showed her how to build small, smokeless campfires in the woods, taught her the tracks, calls and even the scat of the animals and birds. We camped out and slept under the stars. In the winter we skated on Sweet Lake, made snow caves and melted snow water to make hot chocolate. She learned to fly fish and to appreciate the surroundings in which one did it. By the time she was eleven, she was tying some of her own flies on her own little vise beside mine in the lodge reading room. Although some people criticized me for treating her more like a son than a daughter, Sabrina loved it all and, I think, benefited from the experience. Besides, through her mother, who at that time still lived in Manhattan, she was able to attend museums, go shopping and see all the Broadway shows she needed. I never thought about taking her to baseball games or fancy restaurants or buying her pretty dresses. I loved the mountains and woods and the wild water and it only seemed natural that I teach her to do the same.

For Stormy, little Sabrina's visits were, I believe, initially a form of therapy. Years earlier, she had lost her own child in the second trimester and, in the process, the ability to every have another. For every memory I created for Sabrina in the outdoors, Stormy matched it with something special from the kitchen. And then some.

In fact, it's the memories of sharing Stormy's kitchen creativity that surface first whenever Sabrina and I reminisce about those early days of the divorce. She can recall the time we watched a Whitetail fawn be born, but not as distinctly as she remembers helping Stormy to make jams in the summer, crush apples in the fall for cider, boil sap for maple syrup, hang meats in the smoker, stuff sausage casing or pick ripe tomatoes in the garden. Her memory of the food we cooked over campfires in the woods is almost blotted out by food from Stormy's oven; the special roasts, foot high pies, fresh baked breads, muffins, and, of course, the breakfast pancakes Stormy always made when Sabrina visited. They laughingly dubbed them, "platecakes" because they're so large in diameter that each one overflows the largest dinner plate.

This morning, however, the platecakes Stormy especially made for Sabrina and her friends didn't get he kind of reception they deserved. We were all at the table but everyone was too interested in what Sheriff Perkins had said to eat anything.

"He actually said he was going to get a warrant and take the skull?" Asta said. "That he was going to get it dated?"

I shrugged. This morning, she wore a bright red silk blouse under a blue dungaree outfit with knee high leather boots. Her necklace—the bone amulet with the topaz—hung against the skin in her open collar.

"That's what he said, honey," Stormy said.

"Can he do that?" she said.

I nodded.

"When?"

"He made it sound liked he'd be back today," I said.

"Well," she said defiantly, "we, we can't let him. It belongs to the Wabnakis. They have to rebury it."

"I thought you were against the Wabnakis putting it back in the lake," Sabrina said. She was wearing a long, ankle length, green skirt, Doc Martin's and a darker green sweater.

"Yeah," Pam said. "Now because of the sheriff, the skull will be officially tested just like you want." Obviously ready to practice her dance routine, she was in black leotards, sneakers and the bulky sweater she'd worn last night. Her blond hair had been loosely braided into two pigtails and bound with rubber bands. I found it hard to look at her, however, without seeing her as she looked in the shower. "I thought you felt that . . ."

"The police could . . ." Asta appeared flustered, " . . . they might hurt it. There's a special way to handle things that might be that old. You don't just . . ."

"We ain't handlin' it so good ourselves," Stormy said. "Already the tooth's missin'."

Asta frowned. "What?"

"The tooth is missing," I said. "I assume you have it."

She shook her head, pushed back her chair and stood. "Are you sure?"

"It ain't there," Stormy said. "No teeth at all, now."

Asta started for the kitchen at a trot. "Maybe it fell out in the vinegar solution." She disappeared into the hallway.

"Checked that too," Stormy yelled after her.

"What did the sheriff think about the tooth being missing?" Pam asked.

"He don't know about the tooth. We didn't tell him."

Asta came back into the room carrying the skull. "It is gone." She sat back in her chair and set the skull on her plate.

"Please, Asta," Pam said, wrinkling her nose. "There's food here."

Asta frowned but got up and carried it over to the coffee table.

"I told you that if you cleaned it too much it might fall apart," Pam said.

"Dammit, it didn't fall apart," Asta said.

"Well, that molar's gone, honey." Stormy said to Asta. "And we was hopin' you had it."

"Well, obviously I don't have it, dammit," she said. "And I assume it was there when I put the whole thing in the refrigerator."

"Maybe Rachel dropped it out on the dock," Sabrina said. "And what about the prayer shawl? Did you guys check that?"

"It isn't in the shawl," I said.

"How about on the floor in the kitchen?" Pam asked. "Or under a counter."

"Looked there myself, honey," Stormy said. "Nothin'."

"Look," Asta had been working herself up to being angry and now she was. "It'll turn up, all right? It was my responsibility. Max trusted me. And I'll find it." She put the skull on the coffee table. "Now would everyone just stop worrying about it and eat?"

"Well," Stormy said, "you don't hafta get all riled up about it."

Asta sighed. "I'm sorry." She came back to the table and sat hard in her chair. "It's just that it now sounds like I get screwed no matter how this thing works out. As of this afternoon, the skull will be gone. I can't study it in that length of time. Not well enough to impress my boss at the museum anyway."

"Why don't you take the pictures as soon as we eat?" Sabrina said.

"That's a great idea." Pam smiled at Asta. "It's not even nine o'clock."

Asta nodded her head thoughtfully and then frowned. "I just hope my little snap shot thing will be able to . . ."

"My second husband was a professional photographer," Stormy said. "After he passed on, I had Rayleen put some of his picture equipment out in the workshop. Pretty sure there's a camera or two in one of those boxes. Some flood lights, too." She patted Asta's arm. "Why don'tcha go take a look. You're welcome to use what you want."

"Are you sure, Stormy?" Sabrina looked concerned. "I mean, after all . . ."

"Hell. What good are they to me? Somebody might just as well get some use outta them."

"Hey," I said. "Let's not forget about the tooth."

Asta stood up. "I told you, Max, I'll find it and I will."

"Maybe Rachel just took it," Pam said it so quietly I almost didn't hear her. "Anybody think of that?"

"Sure," Stormy said. "It crossed my mind. Wouldn't put nothin' past that woman."

Pam pulled on a pigtail. "We wouldn't have noticed it was gone."

"But, why would she take it?" Sabrina said. "What would she want with a tooth? Besides, I thought she left the skull here because it couldn't leave the sacred area or something like that."

I nodded. Sabrina was right. "Look," I said. "The best bet is out on the dock. Or in the water near the dock. We can all go look after breakfast."

"I told you, I'll find it," Asta said, her smile not exactly disguising the fact that she was irritated again. "If I need your help, I'll ask."

I sighed, forked a platecake and dropped it on my plate. It bounced like cold rubber.

"I'll make some more," Stormy said, taking the platter.

I shook my head. "Not for me," I said.

"Me either," Pam said. "I shouldn't eat so much before I exercise, anyway."

Sabrina put her arm around Stormy. "Maybe, we can have platecakes tomorrow."

Stormy shrugged. "Easy enough to make." She gestured to the bowl of sausage. "Anybody gonna eat those things?"

"Maybe he hasn't had breakfast," Sabrina said, pointing out the window.

We all turned and looked out the windows into the rainy front yard. Kevin, in a dark green slicker and baseball cap, was just climbing out of his big, jacked-up Bronco.

"What? Who?" Asta got up and went to the window. She wiped a circle in the fog on the glass and peered out. "What's that blue, rolled up thing he's carrying?"

Stormy joined her. "It's a big tarp," she said. "He's prob'bly gonna cover them holes is what he's gonna do." She looked back at me. "Somebody oughta go help that boy, Max."

"I'll go," Sabrina said, standing and heading for the hallway and the coats.

"Wait up, Sabrina. I'm coming too." Asta pulled her necklace over her head and handed it to Stormy. "Hold this for me, Stormy? One thing misplaced this morning is enough."

"Tell Kevin, I'll have a couple hot platecakes waitin' for him in here when you're done," Stormy said as they went out the door. "Looks like he could use a little more meat on them bones of his."

The door slammed and we watched Sabrina and Asta run down the porch steps into the yard and dodge the puddles to the dig where Kevin was just beginning to unroll the tarp.

Stormy turned from the window and handed me the necklace. "You better hang into this, Max. Knowing me, it could get cooked into a platecake." She grabbed the platecakes' platter and headed for the kitchen.

Only Pam and I were left at the table. I let the necklace dangle from my fingers. "I wonder if Danny's seen this. It looks like it might be American Indian."

Pam smiled. "I hate to disappoint you, Max, but Asta's fiancé had a guy in Greenwich Village make that for her birthday. I think he was Jewish."

I turned it over in my hand. "What kind of bone is it? Do you know?"

"Asta said it's a piece of a 1200 year old human thigh bone from a dig the museum did in Montana. The Topaz is her birthstone."

I laid it on the table between us. "I've got a feeling this is sort of the kind of thing Rachel and the others are so worried about." I pushed it toward her with my finger. "Pieces of their ancestors becoming knick-knacks and jewelry."

"It is sort of gross," Pam said, "when you put it like that." She pushed the necklace back to me.

I picked it up and dropped it in my shirt pocket.

The front door burst open and, shaking rain water from their clothes, Sabrina, Asta and Kevin pushed into the hallway. Kevin's green baseball cap had "U.V.M." embroidered in gold on the crown. He was talking excitedly, " . . . at about thirty feet, just above the biggest piece of brain coral I've ever seen, I turned around and there the dude was." Sabrina and Asta hung up their coats. "I'd never seen a sea turtle like him. His shell had to be five feet across and he was just looking at me like . . ." Kevin saw Pam and I watching. "Oh, hi, Mister Addams. Good morning, mam." He blushed slightly.

"How are you, Kevin?" I said.

Sabrina stomped her feet. "It's raw out there, Daddy. Feels almost like it could snow."

"It could." I shrugged. "It's April in Vermont."

"I'm not going on any picnic today," Asta said, rubbing her upper arms and crossing the room to the fireplace. "Did you know that Kevin SCUBA dives? That he has his own equipment?" Her hair was wet.

Sabrina and Kevin joined her at the fireplace, where she and Asta linked arms behind him as they all stood with their backs to the flames. "He was telling us about diving a place on Grand Cayman Island called, the Wall," Sabrina said.

Kevin beamed.

"Kevin and I have talked about it," I said and looked at Kevin. "Speaking of talking, Kevin. I thought I asked you to keep this thing quiet in town."

"What town?"

"Loon."

"I didn't say anything to anyone in Loon," he said. "In fact I haven't been in Loon in a week."

"Sheriff Perkins was here this morning," I said. "He said, it's all over town. That you guys were telling everyone."

"It wasn't us." He looked at the others. "Honest." He looked back at me, his eyes wide. "Honest, Mister Addams. The girls either. None of us were in Loon. We went straight to Red Town. Honest."

I sighed. "I believe you, Kevin." I actually did.

Asta looked at Kevin. "Well, however he found out, the sheriff's going to come with a warrant and take the skull away."

"What? Where?"

"We don't know where," she said. "Some cop place probably. But you better tell Rachel that the police are going to be messing with her ancestor's head and it'll be quite a while before she gets to rebury it. If ever."

"Asta!" Sabrina shook her head. "You don't know that."

Asta made a face, turned and faced the fire.

Pam stood and gathered several of the dirty plates. "I don't see what everybody's so upset about." She stacked them on top of her own. "The skull might not be old at all." She looked at me. "It might not even be Wabnaki." She carried the dishes to the doorway and stopped. "It might be just like the sheriff said. It might be somebody else entirely."

Stormy came into the room with a steaming platter of platecakes. "Honey," she said, setting them on the table. "that there skull might be the missing link for all we know, but if I know Rachel, sheriff or no sheriff, she ain't gonna let nobody find out. Not without a fight, anyways."

As Pam disappeared into the hallway, Stormy motioned to Kevin. "Here you go, Kevin. Eat 'em while they're hot." She looked at me. "Get the boy a plate, somebody. And some silverware."

Kevin sat at the table.

Sabrina got a plate and silverware from the drawer in the sideboard. "Hey. I've got an idea." She came across the room. "Since it's obvious we aren't going to have our picnic, why don't we all go to the Starlight for lunch?" She placed the plate in front of Kevin and arranged the fork, knife and spoon around it. Then she removed his cap and hung it on the back of the chair. She looked at me. "I'm going into town to see Ruth this morning."

"Ruth? When did you talk to her?"

"This morning. I told you I was going to."

"She was in her office on Sunday morning?"

"She said she goes up to Red Town and reads to the pre-schoolers on Sunday, Monday and Tuesday afternoons, so she was trying to get a little ahead on her paperwork."

"When did she start this?"

She shrugged.

"Com'on Sabrina, when did she start reading to kids?"

She looked at the floor.

"It has to do with Bolick, doesn't it?"

"I guess. She said he was involved in some program the University's got for Native Americans." She frowned. "Why?"

"Nothing." I sighed. "I guess I just never knew she liked kids."

"Well, she does now."

"And I guess it's none of my business, is it?"

"Not if you don't want it to be." She let out her long sigh. "Anyway, I mostly called just to say hello but she suggested that if I had time, I should come to her office." She gestured to the fogged windows. "All this rain I figured I had the time."

I watched Kevin fork almost half a platecake into his mouth.

She sat beside me. "Are you sure it's okay, Daddy?"

"Why not." I shrugged. "You've known her almost as long as I have."

"Okay . . . so we'll do the lunch at the Starlight then?" She smiled. "I can't wait for these guys to see the place."

I nodded.

Pam came back into the room. "What place?" She sat back in the chair beside mine.

Sabrina told her about lunch at The Starlight. "You won't believe the burgers they have there."

"It sounds different," Pam said.

I looked at Stormy. "You mind?"

"Starlight could be pretty crowded," she said. "Lots of boys ain't gonna be workin' 'cause of this rain."

"All the better." Sabrina laughed. "I could take a room full of handsome lumberjacks about right now." She turned and smiled at Asta. "Right?"

Asta scowled at Pam. "I'm not the one you should be asking."

Pam looked at me and quickly looked away.

"What time do you want to meet?" I asked Sabrina.

She looked at her watch. "I could meet you all there at, say, twelve-thirty?"

I looked at Stormy and she shook her head. "Not me," she

said. "You folks go ahead. I like Skip and Lo Ming but, that food of theirs gives me gas."

"Too bad Rayleen's not around," Sabrina said. "He could join us too. I feel kind sorry for him. Out there in all this weather."

"Once the tent's up," I said. "he should be fine."

"Them God Botherers are all wet anyway," Stormy said. "Little more ain't gonna hurt nothin'."

*   *   *

Kevin ate four platecakes. He also ate the cold sausage in the bowl, three oranges, drank two big glasses of milk and cleaned every drop of syrup from his plate with his spoon. The way he looked around the table when he was finished, I think he would have eaten more if we'd offered it. "Thank you, Stormy," he said, pulling on his cap and standing. "I'll have to tell my dad about those things. He thinks he's a pretty good pancake chef but, compared to these, his are pretty lame."

Stormy smiled, put her arm around him and, she and Asta walked him to the door. "Nothin' to it," she said. "Just tell him to pour 'em big on the griddle. Real big."

Asta continued with him outside and, as he went to his Bronco, she stood in the shelter of the porch roof. They appeared to talk a while and although I couldn't make out what they were saying, the way he stood there at the car door ignoring the rain, he seemed very interested in the conversation.

Stormy was watching them also. She chuckled. "That young man ain't gonna forget this mornin'."

"Neither will Asta." Sabrina laughed. "She's finally found someone who speaks her language."

Pam stood. "I'm going to go to the cabin rehearse my routines." She smiled at me. "Any chance you can get that shower fixed, Max? I'm going to need another one when I'm done."

I shrugged. "I can try."

"Just come down anytime." She began gathering up Kevin's dishes.

"Leave the rest of them dishes, honey," Stormy said. "That's my job. You done enough already. You go do what you're gonna do."

Pam took the dishes to the kitchen anyway and then went out the front door as Asta entered and went straight to the fireplace. "Brrr. Sabrina's right. It should be snowing."

"What's on your agenda for the rest of the morning?" I asked her.

"I'm going to find the tooth," she said. "And then I'm going try to take some pictures."

Sabrina looked at her watch. "I think I'd better be going, Daddy. Ruth'll be expecting me."

I nodded.

"Anything you want me to tell her?"

"Nope."

She stood there in the door, I think hoping I'd say something more. When I didn't, she gave me a look of exasperation, turned and I listened to her feet run up the stairs.

"Oh, yes, Stormy," Asta said. "My necklace . . . ?"

"I give it to Max."

I pulled it from my pocket and tossed it the three feet to Asta. It was a stupid thing to do. She wasn't expecting me to throw it and it bounced from her hand and clattered on the floor. "I'm sorry," I said, reaching for it.

She beat me to it. "I never could catch anything." She studied it. "No harm done, Max." She put it over her head. "I don't know why I should care anyway. Considering who gave it to me."

*   *   *

About fifteen minutes later, Sabrina left for town without saying goodbye. Stormy had gone to the kitchen to clean up breakfast and start supper. Asta had slipped on a jacket and old hat of mine and went out to the dock to look for the tooth.

I decided to take the opportunity to finally shower and dress.

I went to my room and undressed in the bathroom. As I turned on the shower water, I noticed a plastic bottle of shampoo on the ledge. It was still open and I sniffed it. Cinnamon. I screwed on the cap and set it on the sink. I stepped into the spray and closed the glass door. The bar of soap was still wet.

I sighed. Pam was right. It had been a long time. I hadn't had a date since that last dinner with Ruth. I hadn't cared at first. Then I'd broken my ankle and the days had just stretched into weeks and then become months and, I sort of lost interest. I tied flies, read my backlog of videos, books, magazines and even went to a couple of real movies alone in Loon. Every now and then, I ate dinner or just had a few beers at The Starlight and, other than Skip and Lo Ming Willits' doe-eyed daughter, Kate who bartended some nights and I think has a crush on me, I don't think I even noticed whether there were other women in the room.

What was I waiting for? Ruth to change her mind? I almost laughed out loud in the spray. No chance of that. And the skull? Hell, it wasn't my problem. Asta would find the tooth and get her photographs and Rachel or Perkins would take it from there. It was out of my hands.

So, what's your problem, Addams? I thought, as I soaped up. Sure Pam's a flirt. So what? Nobody's going to think any less of you if you decide to flirt a little back.

"Go with it, Daddy," Sabrina had said. "Have some fun."

I turned slowly in the spray and rinsed off. All right, dammit, I thought. I will. I'm tired of being alone. If the opportunity presents itself, I'll go with it. I'll have some fun.

CHAPTER TWELVE

After I dressed, I went into the hallway where I put a Whitefork Lodge cap on my head and slipped on my khaki barn coat with the green blanket lining. Then, with Spotter waddling dutifully at my heels, I limped down through the dismal gray wet to the workshop to see what Rayleen had in the way of plumbing tools that might fix the cabin shower. I could hear the quacks of ducks out on the lake but couldn't see them, much less the water in the thick, wet, gauzy air. Even the workshop was a diffused ghost shape as I approached. I could hear the throbbing beat of music coming from the cabin. The lights were on in the two front windows and their yellow glow blurred in the gloom as though under water.

As I neared the workshop, I heard tapping coming from inside. Nose to the ground, Spotter continued on around the far side of the workshop and I went in.

At the workbench against the far wall, Asta, with her back toward me, stood in a puddle of light from one of the shaded bulbs that hung at intervals above the sixteen foot work surface. I could see a small hammer in her hand as she gently tapped at something in front of her.

"Need some help?" I said as I crossed the room.

"What ...?" She dropped the hammer and spun around. "Oh, Max. You startled me." She put her hands in her pockets.

I joined her. Her necklace lay beside the dropped hammer. I gestured to them. "What's the matter?"

"Nothing." She snatched up the necklace and quickly put it around her neck. "The Topaz was a little loose is all." She tucked the oval of bone into her collar and smiled. "Probably got knocked when I dropped it."

"Here," I reached for it, "let me look."

She backed away. "No. It's fine, Max. I fixed it."

I shrugged and went to the far end of the workbench where I pulled Rayleen's red steel toolbox off the shelf. "I take it you haven't found the molar."

"I looked a little but then I noticed the stone in the necklace was loose. I wanted to fix it first."

I opened the toolbox and stared at the tiers of trays that rose with the lid. It smelled like oil. Every compartment was full; at least a dozen different screwdrivers, all kinds of pliers, a claw and a ballpeen hammer, a socket wrench set, a small soldering iron, solder, flux, wire cutters, a coil of wire, plastic electrical tape, masking tape and, of course, my tool of choice, a big roll of duct tape. I looked back over at Asta. She was watching me. "You want something?" I said.

She shook her head. "I was just wondering, since you're here, if you would find that box of photo stuff Stormy was talking about?"

"Sure." I closed the toolbox and walked to the center of the room. A rope with a loop on the end hung from a trap door in the ceiling. I pulled the rope and, creaking and groaning, the door swung down revealing stairs mounted on the other side. "If it's anywhere, it's up here." I folded down the ladder-like steps and started up.

"You want me to go up there, Max?" she said. "I mean, your leg and all . . ."

I shook my head. "I just hope the box is marked." I pointed to the wall behind the workbench. "Flip that switch on the left over there, huh?"

She clicked the switch and the bare bulb hanging from the ceiling in the small attic turned on. Something . . . more mice probably . . . scurried away into the darkness under the eves.

It had been a long time since I'd been up here. Besides the normal accumulation of broken fly rods, tires, chairs, broken lamps, picture frames and cardboard wardrobes you'd expect us to have after almost a dozen years, all of Sabrina's toys were here too. There was the doll house Rayleen had made for her from willow saplings to look like the lodge. Several dolls' heads stared blankly at me from a cardboard carton. In a cluster, cocooned in cobwebs under the eves, was Sabrina's tricycle, her red wagon and the seat to the swing that we used to have hanging from the beech tree where the cabin now stands. Stormy's husband's things were wedged in neatly beside them; his camera tripod, three clamp-on floodlights and a stack of beer case-size boxes, all magic-markered in black in Stormy's big block letters. I grabbed the floodlights and, pushing the box marked, CAMRAS & LENZS ahead of me with my cast, worked my way back to the stairs. "Asta?" I yelled down through the hole. "Now you can help me."

The box contained four cameras and several lenses wrapped carefully in pages of a year old Loon Sentinel. Asta chose the small automatic Nikon. "I only have 35 millimeter film, Max," she said and pointed at the Hasslebladtt she'd unwrapped first. "I don't even know what size film that thing takes." She fingered the lenses which we'd laid out in a row. "Question is, which one of these should I use."

"I think the little one is for regular shots," I said. "Those big ones are telephoto."

After helping her assemble the camera and make sure its battery still worked, I left her there fiddling with focus and f-stops and shutter speeds and carried the toolbox across the yard to the cabin. The lights were still on and sweet-smelling woodsmoke was now curling from the chimney. As I limped up on to the stoop to the door, I noticed the music I'd heard earlier was gone.

I knocked.

"Is that you, Max?" Pam said from somewhere inside.

"No. It's the plumber." I laughed. "I hope."

"I hope so too," she said. "Come in."

Pam was lying on her back on the floor in front of the fireplace in a pair of dark blue, nylon running shorts and a white sports bra.

She was slowly lifting one tan, polished knee, then the other, to her chin. Her toenails were bright red. "Close the door, Max. There's a draft down here." Firelight flickered in the sheen of perspiration on her skin. The aroma of cinnamon was strong.

I closed the door. The big bed was still unmade. Like mine in the lodge, only one side had been used.

"Don't pay any attention to me," she said, straightening her legs and pointing her toes at the ceiling. "I'm just doing my cool down." Curls of damp hair stuck to her flushed cheeks.

A log on the fire snapped.

She smiled. "You look official."

I smiled back, stepped around her and went into the bathroom. The robe she'd worn in my room was in a pile on the floor. The shelf above the sink was edge to edge bottles and open jars. A hairbrush lay on the toilet seat lid.

I set the toolbox on the edge of the big tub. "What happens when you turn on the shower," I said, opening the box.

"Nothing."

"I mean, does it make any noise?"

"It gurgles a little."

I leaned in and twisted the hot water on. Water rushed from the tub faucet and I moved the lever above it from "TUB" to "SHOWER". Before I could get out of the way. water thundered down out of the showerhead drenching me from the shoulders up. "Jesus!" I said, jumping back.

"What's the matter, Max?"

"I guess nothing's the matter." I stood, took off my cap and shook it over the tub. "The shower seems to be working fine."

"Really?" She came into the bathroom, went around me to the tub and put her hand in the spray. "How did you do it?" She looked at me over her shoulder.

I pointed to the lever. "I flipped that thing up to where it says, 'SHOWER'."

She looked at the lever, then leaned in and flipped it down. The water stopped coming out of the showerhead and began pouring from the tub faucet. She flipped the lever back. As the water resumed spraying from the showerhead, she turned and looked at me. "You must think I'm really dumb."

I shrugged. "Danny was supposed to show you . . ."

She put her fingers on my beard. "You're all wet, Max."

I smiled. "I hadn't expected it to work." Steam began rising behind her.

Her fingers traced my jaw to my shirt collar. "Can I use it now?"

I nodded. "Sure."

Her fingers moved to the first button on my shirt and I felt it pop loose. "Want to use it with me?"

I nodded again. "Sure."

This wasn't the first time I'd had sex in this shower. During the winter when the lodge is closed, Ruth and I had many times stayed in the cabin. We both liked the romantic coziness of the place. It was like being somewhere else. Personally, I liked the kingsize bed. Compared to the narrow double in my room in the lodge, it was like a football field. Ruth loved the big, triangular tub with it's Jacuzzi jets, built-in seats and picture window view of Sweet Lake and, over the years, we'd both become quite adept at finding and maintaining sexual positions on the slippery surface.

Pam and I had a harder time. I'd like to say it was my damn cast, but it was more than that. "I think I'm going to drown, Max," she said, her skin squeaking on the porcelain bottom as she twisted out from under me. "Maybe we should just turn off the water." She stood, shielded her eyes from the beating spray and looked down at me.

I ran my hands up her legs to her hips and turned her toward the window. "Try sitting in the seat," I said, knee-walking behind her across the bottom of the tub and helping her sit in one of the built-in, butt-shaped recesses.

I leaned in, cupped her breasts in my hands and kissed her wet mouth. My belly pushed against her knees. "I can't open my legs, Max," she said. "This seat's too tight."

I sat back on my heels. I could barely see her through the water streaming down my face. I laughed. "I think it's safe to say that, although the shower's fixed, it doesn't work."

She laughed, squeaked out of the seat and kneeled on the bottom of the tub in front of me. "I'll bet the bed works," she said.

She was right. The bed worked fine and, although my cast was awkward here too and we were both still damp, the fire was warm and we rolled naked around the big mattress, playfully exploring each other's bodies through a variety of textbook positions. Finally, half on and half off the foot end of the bed, things became serious. Pam began to moan beneath me. I lifted her buttocks in my hands and, with her strong thighs pressing my hips, the sound of what I thought was the headboard rapping on the log wall filled the room.

It wasn't the headboard. It was Stormy pounding on the cabin door. "Max? Max, you in there?" she said. "Gordon Miller and The Sentinel's here to see the skull. Max, can you hear me?"

Pam tightened her legs around my back and put her hand over my mouth. "Don't answer," she whispered, breathing hard. "Not now." Her pelvis kept moving against my groin. "Not now."

"But . . ."

She pulled my face to hers and cut me off with a kiss.

"Max?" Stormy yelled, giving the door another series of raps with her hand. "I know you're in there, Max. Get yourself up to lodge. We got ourselves company."

I stole a look under Pam's knee at the door, half expecting Stormy to walk in.

Pam sighed and stopped moving beneath me. Her legs fell open at my sides. "Go ahead." She frowned, turned her head and looked toward the headboard. "Go."

I kissed her breasts and got to my knees on the tangle of sheets between her legs. "I'm sorry," I said, looking down at her. Her blond hair was a silken tangle around her face and firelight danced on her golden skin. I ran my finger from her sternum to the hollow of her navel. "Boy, am I sorry."

She turned back, reached out and touched my quickly fading erection. She smiled sadly.

I backed off the bed, went into the bathroom and began digging through my clothes for my underwear.

"Is it always this busy around here on a Tuesday?" I heard her say.

"Not usually." I wrestled my jeans over the cast.

"Stormy sounded mad," she said. "She must know what we were doing in here."

"She'll get over it." I pulled on my sweater and carried my sock and boot into the bedroom. Pam was sitting cross-legged on the sheets, a pillow in her lap. Rivulets of rain ran down the sliding glass doors in the wall behind her. Two, wet, fluffed up chickadees sat blinking on the back of one of the chairs out on the deck. I sat on the bed beside her and pulled on my boot.

She ran her hand under the back of my sweater as I leaned to tie the lace. "Asta's going to be mad, too," she said.

"Now what?"

"She'll think that now I've seduced her friend's father."

"You have." I gave her a kiss and, pulling on my barn coat, limped out the door and up the yard toward The Sentinel's black van parked in front of the lodge porch.

The dining room windows illuminated twice as what I assumed to be flash bulbs went off inside.

*   *   *

The Loon Sentinel is our only newspaper. When Gordon Miller Sr. was the editor and publisher, it only came out once or twice a week on Tuesdays and/or Thursdays. When the elder Gordon died in a hunting accident, his son Gordon Jr. left graduate school and took over. There were a few years where the citizens of Loon weren't sure whether young Gordon's new Sentinel was an up-country version of the NATIONAL ENQUIRER or a college prank. Eventually, however, Gordon Jr. reduced his consumption of Loon Lager, became involved in the community, got married and calmed down. Although still carrying the same masthead art and overall typeface of his father's original, today's Loon Sentinel regularly wins regional and national awards for journalism and photography and has grown from eight pages in one section to three sections, sometimes with as many as thirty-six pages.

All that, and I still don't like Gordon Miller Jr.

Ruth thinks I'm being unfair and has told me to forgive and forget. I can't. I can't forget how Gordon and his then sleazy little paper had mocked me as conservationist when I insisted on catch and release. Nor was I about to forget how he had trivialized my love affair with the mayor and been openly homophobic about my friends John Quinn and Bryce Hill when they were trying to buy the old Loon Hotel. Under his supervision, the paper has supported the crooked politicians, Elizabeth Ross and her nazis and our string of dishonest sheriffs. No, I thought, as I climbed the steps to the porch, little Gordon could get the Pulitzer and the Nobel Peace Prize and I'd still hate his guts.

"Hi, Max," Gordon said, as I limped to the dining room doorway. As always, he was wearing a tie, sportcoat and jeans. He came across the room and shook my hand. "How's that leg?" As he put his arm around my shoulders and walked me into the room, I remembered the other thing I didn't like about him; he was a space hog. He got too close. He always managed to violate that sacred 30 inches of private air they say we all unconsciously keep around us.

Stormy was at the sideboard pouring coffee into a line of cups and she gave me a dirty look over her shoulder. Sentinel photographer, Rusty Granger had Asta posed in one of the big chairs in front of the fireplace. She was smiling and holding the skull as he moved around her, snapping pictures and lighting the room with flashes from his flash gun.

Gordon accompanied me to the big table and when I sat down he sat directly across from me. He was short and boxy and, as far as I was concerned, used too much cologne. He had grown a thin moustache a couple years back to make himself look more "grown up". But like the friends of a man with a cheap toupee, no one had the heart to tell him it didn't work. "Stormy said you were fixing some plumbing in the cabin, Max," he said. "You finish?"

"Not exactly."

"Well, we'll be out of your hair in a few more minutes." He smiled. "It's not every day someone discovers what might be a one thousand year old skull."

"That's what I've heard."

Gordon waved his hand. "Rusty?" he yelled. "Get a couple of Ms. Singer and Stormy with the skull, huh?" He looked back at me. "What did you say, Max?"

"I said . . ." I shook my head. "What do you want from me, Gordon?"

He took a small tape recorder from his pocket and laid it on the table between us. A little red light blinked. "You found it, Max? What was it like? Could you see any other bones down there?"

"I didn't look for any other bones."

"Miss Singer here said you gave her permission to photograph it. That right?"

"I don't think it can hurt anything if she studies it," I said. "She is an expert of sorts. I think she's going to write a report."

"Are you aware of Sheriff Perkins' take on this thing?"

"He was out here this morning."

He smiled. "A pretty good angle for a story, wouldn't you say?" I frowned.

"You know. A sort of murder, but when? kind of thing. A thousand years ago as Ms. Singer and the Wabnakis say? Or the other day, as Simon Perkins says? A showdown. Who's right? Anthropology or criminology? It's great."

"Personally, Gordon," I said, "I don't really care which one's right. I just want the thing out of my lodge."

"Can't blame you there," he lowered his voice, "Question is, who's going to get it? The Wabnakis or the sheriff?"

"Right now, the Wabnakis have it," I said. "I'm just holding it for them. If Perkins gets his warrant, then it's his."

"So, you're not ready to take sides in this thing?"

I shook my head. "No sides worth taking. Like I said, I just want to get rid of it and get back to running a fishing lodge."

"You know what a Mexican standoff is, Max?" He clicked off the recorder.

I didn't answer.

"Two guys on different sides of a line in the dirt, holding their peckers and pissing at each other."

I still didn't say anything.

"You know what gets pissed on in something like that? The line." He pointed at me. "And that's going to be you, Max. This is going to turn into a pissing contest and Whitefork Lodge is going to be right in middle taking it all."

"I doubt it, Gordon."

"Don't doubt it, Max." He laughed. "This is an election year. Perkins hasn't got the balls to fuck with the Wabnakis. And Rachel? She wants the state's approval for her gambling casino so bad she can taste it. She doesn't need the bad publicity right now. She's not going to mess around with the law. You're in the middle. It's going to be up to you. You want to give it to the Wabnakis, fine. You want Perkins to have it first, fine too. It's your call because no matter what anybody says, it was found on your land. Sheriff may be able to get at it with a warrant if he's got the balls to go that far, but with Rachel and this NAGRA thing he can't touch it without a court fight. You own that skull, Max. The Federal Landowner's Act guarantees it."

"The what?"

"The Federal Landowner's Act. My research department dug it out of a couple old law books." He smiled. "It was written in the 1850's after the gold rush. Mostly it guarantees all mineral rights to the landowner." He rubbed the moustache again. "I guess they used to kill each other over stuff like that in California back then. But it's worded to include anything of value found on a piece of property. And I mean, anything."

"You know that for a fact?"

"Don't take my word for it, ask your lawyer."

I sighed and rubbed my eyes. He was giving me a headache. I dug a cigarette out of my pocket and lit it. I felt sorry for Danny. He was caught right in the middle too.

Gordon was about to say something else when Pam entered the dining room. Everything stopped. Asta turned and looked. I wasn't positive but, I think Rusty's mouth dropped open. She was beautiful. Almost regal. Her hair was up in a twist of spun gold behind her head and her pearl earrings matched the single strand around he long neck. Under the red sweater tied around her shoulders, a simple, collarless, pale denim shirt dress was unbuttoned from the hem to about mid-thigh and, as she walked across the room to the coffee machine, every step she took revealed a leg. A pair of delicate sandals were on her feet.

Stormy stood with her hands on her hips watching Pam approach and they said something to each other as Pam poured herself a cup of coffee. By now, Rusty had regained his composure and, cocking his camera, intercepted Pam as she started across the room to where I sat.

"Rusty?" Gordon's squeaky voice seemed loud in the silent room. "Get the van warmed up. We're leaving."

"But, Gordo . . ." Rusty had his hand on Pam's upper arm. "We haven't interviewed all the . . ."

"Rusty!"

Rusty whispered something to Pam and then headed for the door.

Asta stood and scowled. "Isn't this the story of my life lately." She held up the skull. "Where do you want to store this, Max?"

"Ask Stormy," I said, getting to my feet.

Asta looked at Stormy.

"Com'on, honey." Stormy took her by the arm and led her into the hallway. "Might as well put it right back where it's been," I heard her say as they went down the hall toward the kitchen.

I went with Gordon to the porch. It was raining again. Rusty was already out in the van revving the engine. He had the head-lights on.

"Thanks, Max," Gordon said, as he pulled his coat over his head and went down the steps to the van. "First installment will be in tomorrow's edition. Give me a call and let me know what you think, huh?" He opened the passenger door. "Who was that gorgeous thing who just walked in?"

"A guest."

"Fly fisher?"

I nodded.

He let a faint whistle leak through his teeth and smiled. "No wonder the sport's getting so popular."

When they were gone, I went back into the dining room. Pam and Asta were sitting on opposite sides of the room, glaring at each other. Stormy was no where in sight. "Where's Stormy," I asked.

Asta jerked her head toward the back of the lodge. "Cleaning up the coffee mess."

"Did you get your pictures taken of the skull?"

She nodded. "A whole roll." She dug in the pocket of her pants and produced an exposed roll of film. "I'm sending it to New York to my boss this afternoon by special messenger."

"Messenger?"

She nodded again. "Stormy said someplace called, Shady's Taxi will do deliveries seven days a week."

Shady's Taxi Company is owned and driven by Arab-American Abdul Nadim Shadid and consists of one dirty and dented 1988 Chevrolet station wagon with torn seats, a sagging headliner and bad shocks that, as far as I knew, only ferried the elderly or car-less from the supermarket or church to home. I didn't know he did out-of-state deliveries. "Is she sure Shady's will take something to New York City?"

"I guess. She says she knows the Arab who owns it from her AA meetings."

"Since when do Arab's drink?" Pam said.

"Who knows?" Asta frowned. "Maybe that's the problem."

I looked at Pam. She smiled and crossed her legs, taking her time covering her tan thigh with the dress.

Asta stood abruptly. "Stormy also said I can use your computer in the reading room to write the report I want to send with the film."

"You know how to work it?"

She gave me a frown and left the room.

I went to Pam's chair and sat on the arm. "What's her problem?" I said, sliding my hand under the denim fabric covering her knee.

"She's stressed about her job and the skull." She put her hand on mine and, uncrossing her legs, moved it along her thigh farther up under the dress. "And she thinks I'm a slut."

*   *   *

I pride myself in having a certain amount of self control. It's needed, not only when stalking trout in crystal clear water or waiting silently for hours for a hatch to come off, but it's essential in the business I'm in. You have to be able to look the other way when a guest gets obnoxious. You have to be able to quietly fix the broken china, rub out the water marks on the antiques, pour the drinks, look interested during boring stories, clean up the bathrooms and listen patiently to every complaint. I've learned that to make the business of running a fishing lodge work, I cannot let guests and their peculiarities get to me. So, as a rule, I try to be as accommodating as possible.

Accommodating Pam Fiore wasn't difficult. In fact, I guess I could say that yielding to her wishes was all a part of my job. Nevertheless, as we quickly ducked across the hallway and into my bedroom, I actually felt like I was breaking the rules. I felt guilty.

The feeling faded, however, as soon as I closed the door behind us.

Pam lifted her denim skirt, quickly peeled her panties over her hips and down her legs, and kicked them across the room. Then she sat on the edge of the bed, folded her skirt to her waist and laid back on the quilt.

I locked the door, kicked off the boot and struggled out of my jeans. I began unbuttoning my shirt.

"No, Max," she said, holding her hands out between her raised knees. "Leave the shirt. Come here."

I knelt on the squares of quilt between her legs and leaned over her. And as her mouth opened under mine, I felt her cool hand slide between our bellies and pull me into her.

It began as only a distant pinging and popping noise, but as it got closer and louder I recognized it as Danny's little VW. Then I heard tires crunching the gravel on the turnaround, the squeak of brakes and the noise stopped. But it was when I heard four car doors slam that I raised myself from Pam and, on out-stretched arms, peered out of the window above the bed.

It was Danny. It was also Rachel and two beefy young Indian guys who both looked a lot like pictures I've seen of a frowning Geronimo. One of them was chewing gum.

I looked down at Pam. She hadn't heard anything. Her eyes were still closed and a fine haze of perspiration dampened her upper lip. Her hair had come loose and one bare breast lay exposed in her unbuttoned bodice. It rose and fell with her quick, shallow breaths.

I heard the rubber soles of Stormy's Bean Boots squeak in the hallway outside the door. Then she knocked. "Max."

Pam stiffened and her eyes popped open.

"Max," Stormy said. "You better get out here." The door knob rattled. "Looks like we got ourselves a damn warparty comin' up onto the porch."

"No, Max." Pam grabbed my shirt front and pulled me to her. "Not again."

I peeled her fingers from my shirt, rolled off and stood at the side of the bed. "Take a look." I pointed to the window and began putting on my jeans.

Pam turned on her side, raised herself to an elbow and, craning her neck, peered out. "Oh, my God. Who are those nasty looking guys with Danny?" She tucked the breast into her dress and looked at me. "What do they want?" She looked back out the window. "They're all just standing out there in front of the steps in the rain."

I buttoned the jeans, zipped up and stepped into the boot. I'd tie it later. ·

"Max," it was Stormy again. "I ain't openin' this front door 'til you get out here."

I went to the bedroom door and looked at Pam lying there half naked on the quilt. "Sorry." I said, unlocking it.

She sighed, grabbed the edge of the quilt and pulled it over her bare legs. "You have an interesting technique, Mister Addams." She smiled and brushed a loose curl of hair from her face. "But there might be a bit too much foreplay."

I smiled back, slipped out into the hall and closed the door behind me. Stormy was peering out the door window. I opened the front door and went out onto the porch. "Kind of wet out there, isn't it, Chief?" I gave them all my best smile. "Why don't you come up here out of the rain?"

"We came for the skull," Rachel said from inside the dark hood.

Danny nodded. He looked uncomfortable and like he'd rather be up on the porch. "Would you get it for us, Max?" He smiled faintly. "Then we'll be on our way."

I heard the front door open and close as Stormy came out onto the porch behind me. "I thought you wanted the skull to stay here at the lodge," I said. "I thought you didn't want it to leave the company of your other ancestors." I looked down at Rachel. "Isn't that what you told me, Rachel?"

"I changed my mind, Max," she said. "I want the skull."

I looked back at Danny, laughed and gestured at the two Geronimos. "You need these guys to help you carry it, Chief?" They didn't even smile. The one with the gum blew a pink bubble, it popped and he expertly sucked it in and resumed chewing.

Danny looked at his feet. I think he was a little embarrassed.

Rachel took a step closer. I could see her eyes now. "Just go get it, Max."

"I thought next Wednesday we were having a big funeral out there on the lake," I said.

"Guess not." Danny shrugged and looked at the ground. "We'd rather have the skull now, Max." Something had happened to Danny. He reminded me of one of those American P.O.W.'s the North Vietnamese used put on TV. You could tell he didn't mean a word of what he was saying.

"Give us the skull, Max," Rachel said, jabbing a finger in my direction. "I want it now, dammit! Now! Or I swear you'll regret ever seeing that skull."

I slowly shook my head. "The way you're acting?" I pointed at the Geronimos. "You can't come in here and threaten me, Rachel. I'm not giving it to anyone. Not now anyway. And definitely not without a court order."

"You can't do that," Rachel sneered.

"Oh yes I can." I pointed back toward the access road. "Go talk to your lawyers. Ask them about the Federal Landowner's Act of 1850."

I could see that one got them. Rachel looked confused. She frowned at Danny. He shrugged.

The Geronimo with the gum stepped forward. "Don't make us come get it, buddy." His hands were clenched into fists. "Give the Shaman the ancient one's skull."

"Dammit, Max!" The hood fell from Rachel's head. "What are you trying to pull?" She looked around me at Stormy. "Go get the skull for me, Stormy," she enunciated slowly. "If you keep it, Stormy, I have no control over what might happen."

I felt Stormy back away and heard the door open and close again. I glanced quickly over my shoulder. She was gone. "I'm not going to let her give it to you," I said to Rachel. "You don't scare me with that stuff."

This time the other Geronimo took a couple steps forward. "I don't think you hear very well, Addams."

Behind me, the door opened again.

In front of me, their eyebrows going up in unison, Rachel, Danny and the two Geronimos took three quick, very big steps backwards.

Stormy stepped up beside me. She was holding the old lever action Winchester '94 we kept in the kitchen hanging above the back door. She uses it occasionally on the woodchucks who raid her garden. Right now, its long, blued, hexagonal barrel was pointed directly at Rachel. "Speakin' of hearin'," Stormy said, thumbing back the hammer, "are you deaf? Or don't you understand plain English?"

"Stormy . . ." I reached for the gun. " . . . I don't think that's necessary . . ."

She blocked my hand with her shoulder. "Hell it ain't." She narrowed her eyes at Rachel. "I ain't gonna to be threatened by no wacko and a coupla thug leg-breakers."

"Stormy . . ." Danny raised his hand and took a step back toward us.

"Get back there, Chief." She pointed the rifle at him. "I ain't through yet." She re-aimed at Rachel. "Why are you so all fired up to get that skull today? You wasn't last night. You told us to keep it and, by God, we're keepin' it. Like Max says, it's stayin' here 'til some court says we hafta give it up." She went down a step. "Now." She waved the rifle at them. "I'm only gonna say it once." She put the rifle to her shoulder and aimed at Rachel's head. "You can stay if you want, Chief. But the rest of you, git!"

They just stood there.

Danny extended his hand. "Com'on, Stormy. We just . . ."

The explosion from the rifle was deafening. "I said, git outta here." Stormy levered another cartridge into the chamber and the spent shell rattled across the porch floor.

My ears were ringing. "I think you'd better go, Chief," I said.

He nodded and started toward the VW. The Geronimos followed. A blue pickup with a yellow snowplow hitch and coated to the windows in red colored mud was parked beside the Beetle. They climbed in and gunned the engine.

Rachel didn't move. "You'd shoot me, Stormy?"

"You bet your ass, Rachel Arneau. And you don't believe me, just keep standin' there."

Rachel yanked the hood back up over head, turned and started after the others. "You're going to regret this," she growled over her shoulder. "You're really going to regret this."

Stormy didn't put the rifle down until they had disappeared up the access road and we couldn't hear the VW any longer. Then she let the hammer down slowly and handed the rifle to me. Her hands were shaking.

"I thought you'd gone to get the skull for her," I said, hefting the rifle. "I never imagined you'd . . ."

"Tired of that woman's bossin' everybody around." She stooped, picked up the spent cartridge and dropped it in the pocket of her caftan. "Tired of this whole thing, you wanta know the truth. Couldn't even eat breakfast. We've had the sheriff here. The newspaper. And now that wacko again." She frown at me. "And what's this about some Federal Landowner's law? Where'd you get that?"

"Gordon told me about it."

"So, now we gotta keep the damn thing?"

I shrugged. "Let's just say, we don't have to give it to anyone just because they tell us to."

"Oh Jesus. Sure hope you know what you're doin, Max Addams."

"Well," I held the door for her, "I was beginning to think I'd dug a hole for myself until you came out here with that rifle." I laughed. "You sure scared them. And that shot . . ."

"'Twas an accident," she said squeaking into the hallway. "My trigger finger slipped."

CHAPTER THIRTEEN

"Eyes as wide as a poisoned pig."

That's how Rayleen would have described the look on Pam's face peeking around the corner of my bedroom door as Stormy and I entered the lodge. "Are they gone?" she whispered.

I nodded and she followed us into the dining room. Asta was standing by one of the front windows. "Why didn't you just give it to them, Max?"

"I thought you were against putting the skull back in the lake," Pam said to her.

Asta shrugged, went the fireplace and stood looking down into the dead ashes.

"Yeah," Stormy said to Asta, "thought you was sure it was the missin' link. It should be saved for future generations to study." She dropped into one of the big leather chairs.

"I changed my mind," Asta said without turning.

Pam frowned. "You mean, you got what you want."

Asta turned slowly. "So what?" She tried unsuccessfully to hide a blush. "And it does belong to her, you know."

"Well," Stormy said, lighting a cigarette, "It ain't hers right now. And we ain't lettin' her bully us into givin' it to her neither"

"You looked kind of like Annie Oakley out there, Stormy." Pam smiled. "God. When I heard the shot I jumped so high . . ." She glanced at me " . . . I didn't know what was going to happen. At first I thought you'd actually shot her."

"Probably shoulda," Stormy said, studying her. "Ain't seen the last of that woman, I bet."

Pam smoothed at the front of her dress with her hands. We

had wrinkled it pretty badly. "Why is it so important to her she take the skull now? I thought she wanted us to keep it. What changed her mind?"

I lit a cigarette and sat on the edge of the dining room table. "Something scared her." I looked at Stormy. "Maybe Perkins went and threatened her . . ."

Stormy slowly shook her head.

"This whole thing's ridiculous," Pam said. "When the museum gets Asta's pictures and report, they'll confirm how old it is and Rachel will get it back." She looked at me. "Right, Max?"

I nodded and smiled at Asta. "Maybe I should just let you have it. That should impress your boss."

Pam had gone to the window and was peering through the rain-streaked glass. "Shouldn't you, at least, tell the sheriff Rachel was here and how she brought those two mean looking guys with her?"

"I don't know," I said.

Stormy snubbed her cigarette. "Poor Chief."

"Boy," Asta said, "and I thought I picked a loser to marry."

"You did," Pam said.

Asta's eyes narrowed. "And when did you decide this? Before or after you were with him?"

"I was never with him." Pam's face flushed. "I told you. I never even went out with him." It was the first time I'd seen her angry. "He called me a bunch of times, but that was all." She sat back at the table. "Why can't . . . why won't you believe that?" She glanced at me.

I started to say something but Stormy held up her hand. "I got a rule up here, ladies," She looked at me and then back at Pam and Asta "You ain't allowed to bring that kinda crap here. I don't care who you are, you come to Whitefork Lodge, then you leave your squabbles and the like up there on Route 16. Or just forget 'bout comin' down our access road." She pushed out of the chair and walked to the hall doorway. "Now, I don't wanta hear no more talk about who slept with who or who wrecked who's weddin'."

She pointed a stubby finger at Asta. "And I don't want no more of them nasty looks or snide little remarks you been tossin' around either. I'm real tired of all of it. Understand?"

Asta and Pam looked stunned.

"Understand?"

They nodded sheepishly.

Stormy nodded at Asta. "Now, you go finish that report. If you want someone to read it 'fore you send it, Pam and I'll be in the kitchen." She crooked her finger at Pam. "And you, young lady. Button up the front of that damn skirt and come with me. I got some potatoes you can help me peel." She grabbed the Winchester by the barrel, turned and was gone.

They looked at me.

"I'd do as she says," I said.

They did. I went into the hall and stood there looking at the phone trying to decide whether or not to call Perkins. I should, I thought. I don't need scenes like this morning. My daughter is here. I've got a business to run. There's an important group of fishermen coming in next weekend.

On the other hand, there was the Chief. I liked him and, quite frankly, wanted him around the lodge this summer. Asking the sheriff to keep his wife-to-be away would certainly end that. And, I had to consider the Wabnakis themselves. My relationship with the tribe had always been pretty good. They generously made the almost virgin trout-rich small streams and beaver ponds on their land available to me whenever I had special guests who liked that kind of thing. Even more than that, I felt an obligation to Ruth. She had worked hard to include the Wabnakis in the community. A complaint against Rachel I could easily screw up a lot of what Ruth had accomplished.

No, I thought. I'll let it go this time. If I ask Perkins to step in, I'll be exactly where Gordon Miller predicted I'd be; right in the middle of a pissing contest.

"What are you doing, Max?" Pam came down the hall. "You look lost."

I forced a smile. "Are you through with K.P. already?"

"Sort of, but Stormy says we should probably get going soon if we're to meet Sabrina at the Starlight at 12:30."

I looked at my watch. She was right. "Then go get Asta."

"I don't think Asta wants to go anymore."

I shrugged.

"Maybe we shouldn't go either," she said. "I mean, what if Rachel comes back while we're gone?"

"I don't think they'll be back," I said. "Everyone in Loon knows that if Stormy gets mad enough to pick up that Winchester, you don't push her."

* * *

Pam was right. Asta didn't want to go.

"I still have to spell-check my report," she said. "And I want to be here when the messenger comes. Tell Sabrina, I'm sorry. I'll see the Starlight some other time."

The Starlight is four miles north of Whitefork Lodge on Route 16. There's a circular sign high on a pole out by the road that stays lit day and night and reads, STARLIGHT in blue neon script. The "R" in Starlight has been missing for as long as I can remember, making it read pretty much the way a lot of the locals pronounce it. The establishment itself is a one-story building that sits perpendicular to the highway at the back of a large, unpaved parking lot carved out of the trees. Built initially during WWII to house a radar installation, the building has been just about everything from a body shop and used car dealership in the fifties to a topless disco in the sixties. Skip Willits and his Vietnamese wife, Lo Ming, bought it in the early eighties from the Vermont Department of Highways who were using it to store road salt and snow plows, and turned it into a bar and restaurant. Through good honest food, free pouring and fair prices, the Starlight quickly became the home away from home for just about every pickup owner in the area. In fact, on any Friday and Saturday night, no matter what the weather, the parking lot overflows and trucks crowd the shoulders of both sides of route 16 for a half mile in each direction.

Today, the muddy parking lot was only a little over a quarter full and just as Pam and I pulled in, a big Ford pickup with a load of wet cordwood in the bed pulled out and gave us a space only five feet from the front door. I pulled the Jeep forward so Pam could get out without getting her feet muddy and, once she was high and dry on the Starlight's little stoop, I backed into the deep, gooey tire ruts in the space, turned off the engine and, trying not to get my cast muddy, joined her inside.

Even with the drizzle and dark overcast outside it took me a few seconds to become accustomed to the comparative darkness inside the windowless Starlight. As we stepped into the long room, I was hit with the thick aroma of stale beer, people's bodies, wet wool, cigarette smoke and fried food.

"Phew." Pam wrinkled her nose. "It smells awful in here."

The Starlight is basically one long, deep room. Booths and tables run down the right side of the room to the raised stage against the back wall and a long bar comes up the length of the wall on the left. I looked for Sabrina at the bar among the dozen or so scowling faces that turned to look at us. Although I recognized a few of the men—Big Butch Kendall and his logging partner Gautier Raineau, taxidermist Dan Harrison, our mailman Doug Perilli and Frank Lombardi who delivered oil to the lodge . . . Sabrina wasn't at the bar. The men unabashedly hung their heads over their shoulders and inspected Pam.

I felt Pam's hand grip mine in the semi-darkness. "This feels just like a casting call," she whispered.

I was still searching the faces for Sabrina.

"There she is." Pam pointed toward the wall of booths. "Sitting with that woman."

I looked. Sabrina saw us and waved and the woman she was with turned and looked over her shoulder. It was Ruth. She smiled.

Pam started across the room. I held back.

"What's the matter, Max?" She still had my hand and was now trying to pull me into the room.

I shook my hand free of hers. "It's my former girlfriend."

Pam looked back at the table. "It is, huh?" She smoothed the front of the dress, threw back her head and with every eye at the bar following her swinging skirt, walked out into the room and across the linoleum dance floor. Someone whistled and I'm positive she threw more hip into her gate.

I sighed and slowly followed.

Pam slid in beside Sabrina. On the seat next to Ruth was the Coach briefcase I given her two Christmases ago. Ruth started to scrunch over to make room for me but I grabbed a chair and pulled it up to the end of the booth. One almost full Loon Lager and a Coke were on the table.

"I'm on my way out to Red Town to read childrens' stories, Max," Ruth said. "I hope you don't mind my joining you for a minute. I don't have time for lunch but Sabrina insisted I meet her friends."

I smiled and, fumbling slightly, lit a cigarette. "Of course not," I said as Pam quickly pushed the ashtray in front of me.

Sabrina looked beyond me toward the door. "Where's Asta?"

"Finishing her report," Pam said.

"Darn." Sabrina looked at Ruth. "I wanted you to meet her."

Ruth smiled and looked at Pam. "So, you're the dancer?"

Pam nodded. "I'm trying."

"And you also work at the Museum of Natural History with Sabrina's friend?"

"Well," Pam shrugged. "Not exactly with her. I'm a tour guide."

Ruth looked at me. "So what's this about pictures of the skull?"

"How did you know . . . ?"

"I told her," Sabrina said.

"I also heard that Simon Perkins paid you a visit this morning."

I frowned and nodded.

"That's not all," Pam said and proceeded to tell about the Sentinel being at the lodge and our confrontation with Rachel,

Danny and the Geronimos. I studied Ruth while she listened. I think she looked more beautiful today than I'd ever seen her. She wore a navy blazer over a pale green turtle neck. A Loon pin made of mother-of-pearl was on the lapel. The copper flecks in her short auburn hair were sprinkled with droplets of mist from the drizzle outside, her cheeks were flushed and her greenish eyes sparkled as she listened. When Asta got to the part about Stormy and the gun, Ruth laughed and her hand touched mine. I felt my stomach do a flip.

It was all news to Sabrina too. "Really, Daddy? Stormy shot at Rachel?"

"It was an accident," I said. "Things just got a little tense."

"I hope you were nicer to Gordon," Ruth said with a knowing smile.

I didn't say anything.

"It's always something out there at the lodge, isn't it, Max?" she said, touching my hand again.

I moved my hand and looked away. "It only seems that way."

Ruth was still looking at me. "Did you report this last incident with Rachel to Simon?"

I shook my head.

"We don't want to get Chief Shortsleeves in trouble," Pam said.

Ruth smiled slightly. "*We* don't?"

"No," I said, "*we* don't." I wanted to tell her my reluctance to call Perkins had been as much for her as me but instead turned, looked at the bar and caught Skip Willits' eye. I gestured that we wanted to order. He nodded and held up his forefinger.

When I turned back, Ruth said, "I got a call from Elisabeth Ross this morning."

I groaned. "I suppose she wants the skull too?"

"Of course." She smiled. "She wants it tested to make sure it's Native American."

"What else does she think it could be?" Sabrina said.

"Caucasian," Ruth said.

Sabrina frowned and I explained who Elisabeth Ross was.

"She sounds like she's a bigot," Sabrina said.

"So are a lot of people up here." Ruth smiled. "I've learned to take them seriously.

Skip came up to the table. "Hi ya, Max." He was a short, wiry man with carefully combed dirty blond hair and a long horsey-looking face. The top of his white apron was rolled down and tied around his narrow waist. The rest of it hung to his knees. His spaghetti sauce stained white tee shirt had a Marine emblem and the words, "LOOKING FOR FEW GOOD WOMEN" in big red letters on the front. He looked at Sabrina. "Thought there was going to be five of you."

"One couldn't make it," she said.

He looked back me. "Sorry to leave you sittin' here so long, Max, but Lo Ming's out today. Got the flu or some damn thing and I been as busy as ferret since ten this mornin'. Rain's got everybody drinkin'."

I ordered a Loon Lager. Pam wanted a Manhattan.

Skip blushed. "Lo Ming's the only one who knows how to do that fancy stuff, Miss. Sorry. Best I can do is give you some VO and the mixer of your choice."

Pam settled for a VO and ginger ale and, telling us he'd take our food orders when he returned with the drinks, Skip marched back to the bar. Pam excused herself. "I'm going to wash my hands." I watched her walk back across the room, this time with an even more distinct swing to her hips. All eyes at the bar, of course, followed again until the door marked, STA'LETS closed behind her. Then there was some mumbling, a couple giggles and several of the men tossed back shots.

When I turned back to the table, Sabrina said, "Kind of like the old days, huh?"

I frowned.

"The three of us, I mean." She smiled. "Sitting here in a booth at the Starlight."

I felt Ruth look at me. Sabrina was right. Except that I was sitting at the end of the table and not beside Ruth, it was like a lot of times in the past.

"You introduced us here, Daddy. Remember?"

I nodded and looked at Ruth. I had been so damn nervous that afternoon. Sabrina had been visiting for the weekend and when I'd suggested she meet Ruth—who I'd been dating for several months by then—at The Starlight for a couple drinks, Sabrina was skeptical. "Not another one, Daddy," she'd said. "I'm kind of tired of meeting all your girlfriends."

"This one is different," I'd said. "You'll see."

They hit it off like sisters and I distinctly remember sitting there watching and listening to them talk and thinking how much alike they actually were. Looking at them today was no different.

Ruth sipped her Coke. "So what's going to happen with this skull, Max?" she said. "It sounds like you've put yourself right in the middle."

I shrugged.

"It'll be interesting to see what kind of spin The Sentinel puts on the whole thing, won't it?"

"Yeah." I cleared my throat. "Have you ever heard of the Federal Landowner's Act?"

"It's been a while since I read my law books." She frowned and then slowly nodded. "Mineral rights belong to the owner? Something like that?"

"That's it. Gordon told me about it. I used it on Rachel when she came charging in today."

"You are in the middle."

"You told Rachel you're keeping the skull? Why Daddy?"

"They all piss me off, is why."

Ruth sighed. "Max . . ."

"Look, Ruth," I said. "I was keeping it for Rachel. I mean, she made sense. Besides, Perkins irks me. All he cares about are votes in November." I sighed. "But, then Rachel shows up with her war party." I shook my head. "As far as I'm concerned, that did it. I changed my mind. I don't understand her. One minute she's making me hold it for her and the next she's outside the lodge threatening me." I shrugged. "So, the hell with both of them. Each one of them has legal way to get it. They want it, they'll have to work for it." I lit another cigarette. "And that goes for Elisabeth Ross and her Hysterical Society, too."

Ruth laughed. "I never thought I'd hear myself say this but, I kind of agree with you." She put her hand on mine.

I laughed too and left it there. For a second it was like Doug Bolick had never existed. Then Sabrina said, "It's nice to see you guys laughing again."

We pulled our hands away. Ruth fiddled with her coaster.

Pam returned from the bathroom. She let her hand run over my shoulders as she went around my chair and slid into the booth.

Skip brought the drinks and, everyone except Ruth who wasn't eating, ordered Starburgers, fries, a big order of onion rings to share. At Sabrina's suggestion, we also requested a pile of napkins. "The burgers really drip," she said. "But, boy are they delicious."

Ruth drained her Coke, looked at her watch and, buttoning her blazer, stood. "It was very nice to meet you, Pam," she said, picking up the purse and arranging it over her shoulder. "I've got thirteen Wabnaki children waiting for me in Red Town," she said. "I've got to get going."

Sabrina stood.

"Send me that video of Elise," Ruth said to Sabrina as they hugged and then she looked at me. "Will you walk me to my car, Max?"

I shrugged, stood and followed her across the room. The guys at the bar, of course, turned and blatantly followed her every move. They were getting quite a show today.

Ruth waved to Skip as I held the door and we went outside. It had begun raining again. We stood under the peaked roof overhang on the shallow stoop while she unfolded a plastic rain hat from her purse, put it on and tied it under her chin. "I'm going to see if I can get Simon Perkins, Rachel and Elisabeth into my office tomorrow morning," she said. "Maybe I can arbitrate some sort of compromise. That skull, if it's really as old as Asta says, would be a marvelous addition in the Wabnaki exhibit at the library."

"That's what Chief thinks." I half smiled. "Although I doubt he'd say so around Rachel."

"I'll let you know if anything good happens." She pulled up her collar. "Meanwhile, I meant what I said. I actually agree with the way you've decided to handle this." She smiled. "And I appreciate it."

I didn't say anything.

She turned and looked toward her car. "Well, have fun. She's a beautiful young woman, Max." She looked back at me. She looked sad. "You should be pleased."

"Thanks." I smiled this time. "She looks more like her mother every time I see her."

"No." She shook her head. "I mean Pam, Max. And I'd say that from the way she never takes her eyes off of you that she . . ."

I sighed. "Oh, for Chrissake, Ruth. What do you expect me to do . . . ?"

"I'm not getting married, Max."

"What do you mean, you're not getting married?"

"I can't be any clearer than that. Doug asked me. I said, no." She looked down at her hands which were now fiddling with a button on her blazer. "In fact, it's over."

"Is that what was in the note?"

"No." She shook her head and sighed. "That was just ramblings. My uncertainties. You're the only person who understands me. Really knows me." She blushed. "I thought you'd help me decide what . . ." She smiled weakly. "It was stupid. I'm glad you didn't read it. I had to figure it all out for myself."

I was speechless.

"Don't worry." She touched my arm. "I don't expect you to do anything, Max. I just wanted you to know, is all." She turned, stepped from the stoop into the mud and went to her big, red Explorer. I didn't follow her and she didn't look back as she unlocked the door, climbed in and started the engine. I couldn't be sure with all the rain, but as she backed out of the parking space, it looked like she was crying.

The food had arrived while I was gone and my Starburger was luke warm, the fries were limp and the remaining onion rings were cold and soggy. As I struggled to eat the food, Pam put her hand on my thigh under the table and squeezed gently. I pushed it away.

We ordered one more round and Skip had just ducked back under the bar when the two toughs who'd been with Rachel and Danny this morning came in from the parking lot. They were laughing. Their shoulders, backs and long stringy black hair were drenched and they roughly pushed their way to the bar. Again, I was taken by how much they looked like old photos I'd seen of Geronimo.

There was some shouting and harmless pushing which Skip quickly put an end to by bringing out the axe handle he kept on the beer cooler. "Plenty of room for everybody," he said, tapping the business end on his open palm. "So figure it out and then quit the screwin' around. We got ladies in the room." He pointed the axe handle our way.

The Geronimos slid up on stools and looked over at us. When they saw me, their faces darkened.

"Those are the men Stormy shot at this morning," Pam whispered to Sabrina.

"No wonder," she said. "They look like assholes."

"Ignore them," I said.

"I wouldn't give them the time of day." Sabrina plucked an onion ring scrap from the dish and popped it in her mouth.

"They're still staring at us," Pam said.

They were. In fact, they'd turned completely around on their stools. The one on the right blew a pink bubble and grabbed his crotch with his hand, hefted it and winked.

Sabrina gave him the finger. "Ass-hole," she mouthed at him. "Ass-hole."

"Now you've done it, Sabrina," Pam said, looking quickly into her drink. "One of them is coming over."

I looked over my shoulder. Thumbs hooked in the waistband of his faded jeans, the bubblegum chewer was sauntering across the dance floor toward us.

"Ignore him," Pam said.

We all took sips of our drinks, pretending not to notice. My heart was beating so hard it made my beer bottle shake in my hand. He came up to the corner of the table at my right shoulder. I could almost chew on the sour smell of perspiration that clung to him. He put his hand on the back of my chair. "If Gerry 'n' me had known these babes were in the lodge this morning, Addams," he said. "we wouldn't've been so quick to leave." I heard a gum bubble pop.

I looked up at him. He scowled down at me. He was a lot bigger up close than he'd seemed across the room. He looked at the women. "Which one of you lookers is gonna join us for a drink?"

"Get lost," Sabrina said without looking at him.

"How 'bout you, legs?" He put his big, dirty hand on Pam's shoulder. "Wanna have a drink with some men your own age?"

Pam reached up and removed his hand like she was lifting a large bug from her shoulder. She didn't answer him.

There's a moment in every incident such as this where, as a man, you feel obligated to do something. It's weird. If Sabrina and Pam had been there alone, they would have been able to take care of him and his advances without my intervention. But, because I was there, I had to do or say something macho. As Sabrina would say, "It's a guy thing." And I guess it is. Albeit primal, there comes that time when, whether it's necessary or not, you have to stand up and lower yourself to the aggressor's level or you look like a wimp.

Now was that time.

I stood slowly and faced him. We were about the same height, but looking into his bloodshot brown eyes, I could see he was meaner. For me, suddenly standing there like that was awkward. For him, it was as natural as breathing. He blew a bubble. It slowly grew, popped and he chewed it back into his crooked mouth. "Sit down, old man," he growled. "Before you get knocked down."

There it was. The point of no return. Negotiations were off. A compromise was out of the question.

I didn't move. I glanced over his shoulder and saw Skip duck under the bar and start across the room. He was carrying the axe handle. I looked back at bubble gum just as he put a heavy hand on my chest and, like you would move to open a heavy door, pushed me aside. I staggered slightly, hitting my chair with my right leg. It fell with a clatter and skidded several feet out onto the dance floor. I grabbed the front of his shirt, more to keep my balance than anything else, and pulled him toward me. He grabbed my wrist with one hand and jammed the heel of his other hand into my mouth. I tasted blood. Then, like awkward dancers, we slowly spun struggling out onto the linoleum parquet. I kept my grip on his shirt and he pushed harder at my mouth. My head bent back. He grinned and another small pink bubble formed between his pursed lips.

I only saw the axe handle as a blur as it chopped down toward his head. There was a hollow clunk, his long hair jumped and the bubble gum popped from his mouth. His eyes went blank and we stopped spinning. His hand relaxed on my wrist. I let go of his shirt, stepped back and he dropped to his knees in front of me. Then, like a short, thick tree, he slowly fell forward onto his face. His head bounced twice and I distinctly heard a crunch as his nose broke on the scuffed linoleum.

Skip, his feet planted a yard apart, stood looking down at him. He tapped the axe handle in the palm of his free hand. "Goddam drunken Injuns," he muttered.

The other Geronimo came slowly across the room followed at a distance by everyone from the bar. "You fucker," he sneered at Skip as he knelt and rolled bubblegum to his back. Blood ran from a flattened nose. "Coulda killed him with that goddam thing."

"He'll live," Skip said, stooping a picking up the wad of gum. "Just get him out of here, Gerry." He extended his arms to hold back the crowd. "Give these jerks room."

I looked over at our table. Sabrina was standing. Pam, her eyes wide with fear, had her hand over her mouth. I put my hand to my mouth and it came away bloody.

"You better go put some cold water on that, Max," Skip said. "Looks like Willie split your lip." He turned to the crowd. "I said move back, dammit."

The crowd backed away toward the bar muttering. Doug Perilli looked at my cast. "Shoulda stepped on his foot with that thing, Max." He laughed. "Long as you two were dancin'."

The crowd laughed, grabbed their drinks, slid up on their barstools backwards and watched Willie dragged unceremoniously across the floor to the Men's Room. Gerry's burning dark eyes never left my face until the door closed behind them.

Skip accompanied me as I limped back to the table. "Sorry about this, ladies," he said, as I righted the chair and sat. "How 'bout another drink? On the house."

Sabrina declined the drinks and he went back to the bar. Pam never even heard him. She already was dabbing at my mouth with a napkin dripping with cold VO and water.

"Ouch," I said, as the alcohol burned into the cut.

"That was so brave, Max," she whispered as she gently dabbed at my lip. "You could have really been hurt."

Sabrina was silently watching.

Pam was still cooing and dabbing. "It was like in the movies." She looked at Sabrina. "Your father is wonderful."

"It was stupid, Daddy," Sabrina said, draining her beer. "He's half your age. God knows what he would've done to you if Skip hadn't stepped in."

"It's swelling up." Pam put the napkin of the table and slid out of the booth. "I'm going to get some ice wrapped in a cloth."

I watched Sabrina watch Pam walk toward the bar. "What choice did I have?" I said.

She shrugged and looked at her beer bottle. She didn't say anything.

There was laughter at the bar and we looked. Skip was filling a bar rag with ice. Pam was in the center of the group of men, her

foot up on a barstool rung. The denim skirt had fallen away revealing most of a tan leg.

"Ruth tell you?" Sabrina said,

I looked at her. She was peeling the label from her beer with
her thumb. "Yeah, she told me," I said.

"Ruth's hurting, Daddy. She made a mistake and she knows
it. And she doesn't know how to fix it."

"I don't know if it can be fixed."

"It can, if you want it to be."

I looked over toward the bar. Pam was slowly coming back to
the booth carrying a lumpy ball of white cloth. She smiled at me.
"Maybe, I'm not sure that's what I want anymore," I said, looking
back at Sabrina.

Sabrina was looking at Pam now. "Oh, my God." She quickly
looked at me. "Daddy. You and Pam?"

I sighed.

She leaned toward me and whispered, "I told you to have fun,
Daddy but I didn't mean . . ."

"You said, go with it. I'm going with it."

Pam slid into the booth. "Go with what?" she said. "What did
you go with, Max?"

I was still looking at Sabrina but she was now staring at her
beer bottle. The label was off and she began scraping angrily at the
chunks of glue still on the glass. "I'm going back to the lodge," she
muttered. "I need some air."

*   *   *

Sabrina left us sitting there.

"I think we should go too, Pam," I said, now holding the ice-
filled rag to my lip.

"In a minute." She peeked under the cloth. "Just let me make
sure it's not bleeding anymore."

It wasn't. In fact, except for a little sting, it was like it had
never happened.

Pam went ahead outside and I paid the bill, thanked Skip for his help and listened to a couple more dancing jokes from the guys at the bar. She was already in the passenger seat when I climbed in. Her white cotton panties were draped over the steering wheel.

"Heroes deserve rewards," she said, climbing over the shift lever and attempting to straddle me.

"Not here, Pam," I said, gently pushing her back into her seat. "Besides, I have to be able to shift."

She flopped back into he seat and, although I didn't look at her, I knew she was pouting.

We'd only gone a half mile up Route 16 when she grabbed my hand and stuffed it under the hem of her skirt. "Let's pull over, Max." She held it tightly between her warm thighs. "Isn't there some little road along here that goes back into the woods?"

I wrestled my hand free and laughed. "You want to get laid in this the Jeep? With my cast?"

She turned toward me, pulled her knees up on the seat and put her hand in my lap. "I just want to find someplace where we're not going to be interrupted all the time." She leaned and nuzzled my neck.

A tractor trailer truck with half a forest piled on it roared by going the other way, the wind in his slip-stream rocking the Jeep and making the canvas doors rattle. I removed her hand from my lap and placed it firmly on her knee. "Pam, stop it. I've got to drive."

She turned and faced forward, the heels of her sandals on the edge of the seat, bare knees at her chin. "It's her, isn't it, Max?"

"It isn't anything," I said, downshifting as we started up the grade. "I'm just trying to drive."

"I bet she told you she wants to come back." She looked at me. "I'm right aren't I? She told you she wants to get back together."

"She didn't tell me anything."

"Then why are you acting so strange?"

"I don't think I'm acting strange." I laughed again. "I just don't care for parking on lover's lanes."

"Then, will you come down to the cabin when we get back."

I was just about to shift up into fourth when an impact from behind snapped both of our heads violently back into the headrests. "Jesus!" I looked in the rearview mirror just as a big, blue Ford pickup with the yellow snowplow hitch rammed into us again. Our heads whipped and the Jeep tilted and the tires squealed. "Jesus Christ!"

Pam was wide-eyed and clutching the dash. She turned in her seat just as we were hit again. "Max! It's those guys from the bar!"

I looked in the rearview mirror again. The pickup fell back a few feet. I could see them. Gerry was driving and they were grinning. In the passenger seat Willie blew a bubble and then the truck lurched toward us again. "Hang on!" I yelled. "Here they come again."

This time we were ready for the impact. Still, when they hit us, Pam almost slid off the seat. I heard a crunch and the tinkle of glass. My tires shrieked. Then they backed off.

"What are they trying to do?" Pam screamed. "They'll knock us off the road."

"They're just trying to scare us," I said, hoping I was right. "Here they come again."

She dug her fingernails into the dash and ducked her head and I gripped the steering wheel but the big, blue pickup swerved and fishtailed and, now trailing a cloud of blue smoke, roared up beside us. I looked at Willie in the passenger window. He grinned. At the wheel, Gerry was watching me.

"Hold on!" I yelled at Pam. "They're going to try to run us off the road."

Gerry yanked the wheel our way and the pickup slammed into the side of the Jeep. Pam was thrown to the floor. With a squeal of tires, they swerved away.

"You all right?" I said, stomping the Jeep's accelerator to the floor.

She didn't answer.

As the old V8 kicked in, the little Jeep leapt forward and pulled away from the pickup. Pam wiped at a thin line of blood trickling from her nose. She started to climb back up into the seat.

"Stay down there," I said. "And hang on."

She hugged the seat bottom. She was trying valiantly not to cry. I looked at the speedometer. Sixty. Then sixty-five. At seventy, Gerry and Willie caught up and were beside us again. The passenger side window was down now and Willie was pointing at us and laughing. I didn't care about him. I was watching Gerry at the wheel.

Seventy-five. The Jeep was screaming. My tachometer showed 5500 rpm's. The pickup was right beside us, only a foot away. I watched Gerry and pressed the accelerator harder. At eighty miles an hour he yanked the wheel toward us. I stomped on my brakes almost putting my foot through the floor. Tires screeching, the Jeep skidded, fishtailed and smoke poured out behind us. Having nothing to hit, the pickup shot just ahead of us, swerved across the lane, hit the shoulder hump and was suddenly airborne. We skidded to a stop sideways in the road just as the pickup hit the ground, bounced and, trailing blue smoke, shards of chromium trim and wet leaves, plowed into the woods where, after flattening fifty feet of Hemlock saplings, it fishtailed again, cut left and, somehow missing several large oaks, bounced back up out onto the highway, where it sped away. I watched it careen precariously around the next curve and then it as gone.

The smell of burning rubber was strong. There was a haze of it over the wet road. Pam was now crying. The Jeep had stalled.

My hands were shaking on the wheel and my right leg was so rubbery, I had trouble holding it on the accelerator. I wanted to get the Jeep off the road but it wouldn't start, so I got out and limped around to her side where I opened the door and helped her out. "It's over," I said, taking her in my arms. "It's over."

"Oh, Max," she sobbed. "I thought we were going to die." I could feel the warm blood from her nose soaking into my shirt front. "What if they come back?"

"They won't be back," I said, reaching into the Jeep and picking the panties off the floor. I gave them to her. "Here, press this to your nose." I walked her to the shoulder and we stood under the thick, dark green boughs of a dripping spruce.

I don't know how long we stood there in the light drizzle but I was right. Willie and Gerry didn't come back. In fact, I was just beginning to wonder if anyone would come by when I finally heard a car. As it came around the curve toward us, I flagged it down.

His name was Robbie Elmes and he was a manufacturer's rep on his monthly swing through northern Vermont. He said he was on his way to The Starlight for lunch and insisted on staying until I'd called the sheriff on his cellular phone and help arrived. He tossed the mountain of newspapers, hamburger wrappers and styrofoam cups from the front seat to the floor in the back and Pam, now holding her panties to her bloody nose, got in.

I pulled up my collar and limped across the road to the Jeep. The left front fender was twisted down onto the tire which was flat. A greenish liquid that I assumed to be anti-freeze was puddling under the front. The driver's door was mangled and there was a diagonal crack in the windshield. Even though the rear end had taken the worst of it, other than broken tail lights, it looked all right.

I lit a cigarette. My leg ached inside the cast.

Enough already, I thought. When I get back to the lodge, I'm going to throw that damn skull back in the lake where we got it.

CHAPTER FOURTEEN

The five year old Loon Memorial Hospital is on the north side of town on landfill that years ago was the original town dump. Looking at the sprawling modern three story brick structure with its two acres of macadam parking lot, brick walkways and lush green grass, it's hard to believe there was ever a dump here at all. It's a good size facility considering the small population of Loon but, not only does it serve as an extension teaching hospital for the University of Vermont, it provides the medical needs for surrounding communities all the way to the Canadian border.

Pam and I were in the Emergency Room. Or, she was. She was inside having her broken nose reset by a doctor who looked young enough to be a grandson. I was sitting on a very uncomfortable plastic chair in the hallway outside wishing for a cigarette.

It hadn't taken long for Sheriff Perkins and Richie, a tow truck and an EMT van to arrive at the Jeep out on Route 16. Getting a little carried away with a neck brace and stretcher, the EMT's hustled Pam directly to the hospital while I stayed to answer questions.

Perkins was supervising the tow truck so, I guess as a part of his training, Richie got out his little pad and a stubby pencil and, taking a pose with his foot on the bumper of one squad car, began asking the questions. "Addams spelled with two D's, Max?"

"Hold on, Richie," I said and limped over toward Perkins.

"But, Max," Richie whined from behind me. "I have to do this. If you're going to press charges I need . . ."

Perkins saw me coming. "Watch yourself, Max," he said, as beeping in reverse, the tow truck backed toward the Jeep.

I backed up a step and pointed to the wrecked Jeep. "Those guys who did that have been giving us trouble all day, Simon."

"Willie and Gerry? I know who they are. We'll find them if the haven't lit out for Canada."

"This could have been my daughter and her car." I went and stood on the shoulder. "I've had just about enough."

He shook his head. "Don't blame you." He held up his hand to the tow truck driver. When the driver was close enough to my Jeep and had climbed from the truck cab to hook up, Perkins turned back to me. "I was you, Max, I'd give that skull to Rachel."

"Rachel? What happened to that big warrant you were going to get?"

He shrugged. "Your old girlfriend called Judge Emery about an hour ago. Talked him into arbitrating this thing. Old boy won't grant me the warrant until Rachel and I meet with him in his chambers."

"When's that?"

"Don't know yet."

"You hear that Rachel was out at the lodge this morning?" I gestured at the Jeep. "With Gerry and Willie?"

He nodded. "Stormy tried to shoot her, is what's going around."

"They threatened us."

"Rachel wants that skull."

"Just like you or Elisabeth Ross, Rachel's going to need a court order to get it now," I said.

"Elisabeth Ross?"

"Sure. The Historical Society's expressed an interest in it."

"You'd give it to them?"

"If Elisabeth Ross showed up with the proper legal documents first, you bet your ass I'll give it to her."

He frowned. "Now what're you trying to do, Max? Make money on this thing?"

"I don't care about money. I'm just not going to give away something that belongs to me to the person who yells the loudest. I'm tired of people trying to intimidate me. You included."

His frown got darker. "Since when does the skull belong to you?"

"Since 1850," I started back toward Richie and his note pad. "It's called the Federal Landowners' Act. Check it out if you don't believe me."

"Rachel know about this?"

"Damn right she does," I said over my shoulder. "And now you do too."

Richie was a good kid. He wasn't responsible for any of this. He was only trying to learn. So ignoring glares from Perkins, I answered Richie's questions and signed a description he'd made of the charges. Then, after the tow truck pulled away, I made him drive me to the hospital. I guess Perkins, meanwhile, had gotten tired of giving me dirty looks. Half way through my interrogation with Richie, he got in the other squad car and headed toward Robinson Mountain and, I assumed, Red Town.

As soon as Richie dropped me off at Loon Memorial, I called Sabrina and told her roughly what had happened.

When she was positive neither of Pam nor I were hurt badly, she said, "I'll be right there, Daddy. You should come back to the lodge and rest."

"No. Once we're out of here," I said. "I'm going to take a long walk. Last thing I want, is to be at the lodge right now. I'll call you when we're ready to be picked up. Okay?"

She reluctantly agreed, we hung up and I took a seat in the hallway waiting area among Loon's walking wounded with their gory cuts, broken limbs, chest pains, deep flu coughs and feverish crying babies. As one would be hustled into examination areas by a small group of very weary looking nurses and doctors, two more would enter through the automatic Emergency Room doors.

The last time I'd seen Pam out on Route 16, she had a bloody nose. When she finally joined me in the hallway, she had gained two rapidly swelling black eyes and a thick white bandage on her nose.

I tried unsuccessfully not to laugh.

There were tears in her eyes. "It's not funny, Max." She put her arm around my waist and her head on my shoulder as I led her outside. "As soon as the director sees me like this," she said, "I'll be fired."

Outside, the rain had stopped and the sun was just about to drop behind the western mountains. Patches of bright blue now showed through the pink scudding clouds over Robinson Mountain. The low sun felt good as we slowly walked into town. We cut across the square, under the big, dripping maples, around the white gingerbread bandstand and out the other side onto Main Street. The matinee at the movie theater on the corner was just letting out and dozens of squealing pre-teenage girls and posturing boys clogged the sidewalk. A small knot of Wabnaki children with big dark, frightened eyes watched from the doorway of Shady's Taxi which was next door.

Pam saw them too. "Kids can be so cruel," she said.

In the street in front of the theater, impatient parents in double parked cars honked horns and called out names. There was a lot of staring and some pointing and giggles as we pushed our way through the chest high crowd and once on the other side, Pam laughed. "I guess we really must look weird. You limping with that cast and me with this face."

Like a lot of river towns in New England, downtown Loon is made up of three and four story adjoining brick buildings built mostly in the mid-1800's. Although a few still carry the soot and grime of our industrial past, most of them, thanks to Ruth and her Loon Redevelopment Commission, have been sandblasted and now look quite gentrified, if not down right cutesy with their flowering windows boxes, pseudo early American signage and gas lamps. The buildings may look better, but every day at four, the traffic's just as bad as it always was; Loon has two traffic lights and when the loggers come off the mountains and the shifts at the Loon Lager brewery change, Main Street becomes a frustrating gridlock for half an hour. This late in the day, however, other than the clot of cars and pickups around the movie theater, the street was almost deserted.

Pam had two prescriptions to be filled . . . one for swelling and one for pain . . . and we followed four of the kids into Gray's Drug Store which is just beyond Shady's dispatch office. With a lot of pushing and shoving, the kids spun up onto stools at Gray's Original Old Fashioned Soda Fountain counter and began blowing the wrappers off of straws.

Pam and I continued to the prescription counter at the back of the store. Tom Gray, a silver-haired man in his seventies with thick glasses was behind the counter in a white jacket. He was counting pills into a small envelope and didn't look up until he'd finished. Tom is the third generation Gray to own the drug store. Like his mother and grandfather, he is also the pharmacist. Unlike them, he didn't like his first name and insists everyone simply call him what his wife had always called him, "T. Gray".

"Max Addams," he said over the thick glasses. "Don't see you in here very often. How's that leg?"

I told him the leg was fine while he eyed Pam's face. She handed him the prescriptions from the ER.

He glanced at the slips of paper and back at Pam. "And what happened to you, young lady?" He smiled. "This is pretty potent pain killer they prescribed here."

"Minor car accident, T. Gray," I said.

"No kidding? Was that the sirens I heard earlier?"

"Maybe," I said, pointing at the prescriptions. "Can we get these filled while we wait?"

"Heck," He turned and studied the large bottles on the shelves behind him. "I can fill these in a couple minutes."

I turned and leaned against the counter. The kids at the soda fountain had emptied the straw container and were now shredding napkins. A young woman behind the counter was making milkshakes and had one arm deep in the ice cream chest. She seemed oblivious to what they were doing.

T. Gray wasn't. "I know everyone of you kids' parents!" he yelled without turning around. "Knock it off or I'll call them!"

The kids quieted down and for a few seconds the only noise in the store was the grinding whine of the two blenders making milkshakes. Satisfied, T. Gray said, "So, what's happening with that skull you found, Max? I hear the sheriff thinks somebody was murdered out there."

"Somebody was," I said. "It's just a question of when."

"Heard that too." He poured some tiny white pills into a small amber plastic bottle, stuffed a ball of cotton in after them and snapped on a cap. "Also heard about how you have a lady from a big New York City museum here looking at it."

I sighed. "She's just a guest, T. Gray."

"Not the way I heard it." He set two small bottles on the counter in front of us. "Thelma Martin, Shady's weekend dispatcher came in here for a coffee and said that museum woman sent a roll of film, a lot of papers down to New York City today." He produced a small white paper bag from under the counter. "Probably there by now, the way Shady drives." He dropped the pill bottles into the bag and looked at Pam. "Prescription doesn't say so but, I was you, Miss, I'd take these only if you really need them. This is strong stuff."

She nodded and smiled.

I stuffed the bag in my jacket pocket and charged it to the Whitefork Lodge account.

"Heard the Sentinel's got a story in tonight's paper," he said after us as Pam and I walked through the straw wrappers to the front of the store. "Pictures of the skull too."

Back out on sidewalk, it was almost dark. A few stars were beginning to blink in the eastern sky. The wet street was steaming and the air smelled of a rich potpourri of balsam and woodsmoke from the surrounding mountains and frying food from Freddie's Lunch which was next door. Freddie's is open 24 hours a day, seven days a week and the closest thing Loon has to McDonald's. I could see Freddie Cosmopolis inside at the grill flipping burgers for booths full of rambunctious kids.

"Boy," Pam said as we started walking, "nothing stays private very long around here, does it?"

"You mean, T. Gray?"

She nodded and took my hand.

I shrugged but didn't answer. Her hand felt good.

We passed Loon Lanes Candle Pin Bowling Alley and even though the door was closed, we could hear the wooden rattle and thump of falling pins and balls in the five alleys inside.

At Judy's BookNook, Pam paused and looked at the display of best sellers in the window. I could see owner Judy Bowman, her big bosom and ample hips stretching the usual mismatch of pilled sweater and wrinkled wool skirt. She was on the telephone by the cash register but saw me, waved and then frowned questioningly when she saw I was with Pam. Judy is one of Ruth's staunchest supporters and, along with owning the bookstore, is president of the Loon City Council.

I waved back.

"Do you know everyone in town?" Pam asked.

"Most of the business people," I said. "I did date the mayor for quite a while, you know."

"I know," she said quietly. "I know."

We continued up the street to the corner and the front of Sam's Sporting Goods. There was a fly fishing display in the window. A sign propped in among the rods and waders read, CATCH THESE DEALS!

The Loon Hotel is across the street. It sits back behind an ornate white wrought iron fence. John and Bryce's perennial gardens, now a sea of yellow and white daffodils, flanks the cobble stone walk to the ornately trimmed, wrap around, Victorian porch. John and Bryce have done a masterful job of renovating the old building and everything you look at is impeccable. The red clapboards are freshly painted, the white trim sparkles and a dozen or more intricately woven white wicker rockers and matching chairs sit interspersed with plants in big red clay pots on the porch.

"This is beautiful, Max," Pam said. "Who would have thought a place like this existed way up here in the mountains?"

"More people than you think," I said, holding the stained

glass door for her. "You should see the crowd on this porch in June." The hotel's big business is retirees from southern Florida escaping the tropical summer heat. John more than once has joked that there are times he wonders whether he and Bryce are running a hotel or an old folks home.

I didn't see John or Bryce . . . I would have like Pam to meet them . . . so we went into the empty barroom.

It's called the Red Pump Room because the bar is built over the old well and the original red handle pump sits on a thick Plexiglas surface above it. The well is dry now but there are spotlights inside on the circular stone walls, and looking down the hundred foot hole is quite an experience after a few too many.

We sat by the pump. Pam ordered a dry sherry and I had a pint of draught Loon Lager. Ruth and I had cocktails here many times and the twenty-something bartender, a perpetually frowning Wabnaki with a shaved head named, Steuben took my ten dollar bill and, as he made change, studied Pam and, I assume, her dried blood on my jacket front.

I lit a cigarette and Steuben clunked an ashtray along with my change in front of me. "Looks painful," he said to Pam.

She touched her face and peered at her reflection in the mirror behind the bar. "It looks ugly, is what it looks." She suddenly looked like she might cry.

He looked at my bloody jacket. "What happened, Max?"

"A little mishap with my Jeep, Stu."

He seemed satisfied with my answer and returned to the limes he was slicing when we came in. Like all bartenders, however, I knew he was listening.

Pam sipped the sherry. "Yum. That helps."

I smiled and sipped the foam off the beer.

"It's still only Tuesday, isn't it?" she said.

I nodded.

"Boy, I've never in my life experienced two days like these. It's never stopped for a minute."

"It's usually a lot quieter up here. Believe me."

"It's been amazing." She exhaled and leaned on the bar, "Most people don't have half this stuff happen in their whole lives."

"I should have listened to you out there on the lake. I should have throw the damn thing back."

Stu scrapped his cutting board with the knife blade. "What's happening with the skull, Max?" he said without looking up.

"I'm going to let the law decide, Stu."

"It belongs to us."

"We'll see," I said, sipping the beer. I didn't want to get into it.

"You can't just keep it."

"Of course I can." I grit my teeth. I was getting tired of this. "It was found on my land, Stu."

"Your land?" He stuck the knife in the cutting board and came over to where we sat. His frown had deepened. "Long before Whitefork Lodge was your land, Max," he said bitterly, "it was English land and they took it from the French who murdered and stole it from the Wabnakis." He thumped his finger on the bar beside my beer. The coins in my change vibrated. "No whiteman has every paid Wabnakis to own that land. Not the English. Not the French. Not you, Max." He pointed the finger at me. "In fifteen days the Wabnakis will be rich. Then, we'll see who owns what." He turned on his heel, ducked under the bar and was gone.

Pam put a hand on my leg. "He's scary, Max," she whispered. "And what did he mean about the Wabnakis getting rich?"

"The Chief's first wife left him about ten million dollars," I said. "It finally becomes his and Rachel's in a couple weeks."

She dipped her finger in the sherry. "Boy," She licked it off, "if I was going to get that kind of money, I wouldn't be worrying about some stupid old skull."

I laughed. "What would you be doing?"

She smiled. "I'd be marking pages in the new Lord and Taylor catalog, for one thing."

*   *   *

When we'd finished our drinks, I called Sabrina from the phone in the lobby and Pam and I awaited her arrival in a couple of the elegant rockers on the porch.

Sabrina was stunned by Pam's face. "And you, Daddy? You sure you're all right?"

"I'm fine," I said, as I slid sideways into the cramped back seat.

She wanted a complete description of what had happened and, with only a little exaggeration, Pam gave it to her. I half listened and sat, watching the town thin to occasional mobile homes and shacks and finally just thick forest on both sides of the road as the big Cherokee's V8 carried us smoothly up along Gracey Gorge to the top of Morning Mountain.

"And I thought my days at home in The City were hectic," Sabrina finally said.

"It has been the day from hell," I said.

I could see her eyes looking at me in the rearview mirror. "Sorry about what I said earlier, Daddy. I was wrong. I should mind my own business."

"Don't worry about it." I smiled at her.

She glanced at Pam and then back at me in the mirror. Little lines crinkled around her eyes. I could tell she was smiling also.

*   *   *

It was seven thirty when we pulled up in front of the lodge. It looked like every light in the place was on. Stormy, Spotter and Asta came out the door and down the porch steps before we were even out of the car.

"Knew I shoulda aimed that rifle this mornin'," Stormy said, helping Pam from the passenger seat. "You look terrible, honey."

Spotter sniffed at my cast and I scratched his ears.

Stormy looked at me. "You all right, Max?"

I nodded and went up the steps.

"Want some supper?" she asked. "Asta 'n' me got sandwich fixin's and lentil soup all ready."

Pam declined and, saying she wanted to change out of the bloody dress, take her pills and lie down, started down to the cabin.

"Don't freak," Asta said after her, "but the skull's in the cabin's little refrigerator. Stormy wanted it out of hers."

Pam just waved indifferently and the cabin door closed behind her.

"Poor kid," Stormy said. "How's she gonna dance on a stage lookin' like that?"

"I know," Sabrina said. "I was afraid to even mention it."

"She knows," I said.

"Well, com'on back to the kitchen," Stormy said as she and Asta pushed by me and into the lodge. "We got some news you oughta hear." Side by side they went down the hall to the kitchen.

They were already sitting at the island when Sabrina, Spotter and I pushed through the swinging door. The ham-rich aroma of Stormy's lentil soup filled the room. A bottle of Champagne sat in front of them. There were three glasses.

"What's this?" I said, sitting on a stool.

"We're celebrating," Asta said, beaming. She poured Sabrina a glass and handed it to her. "It's a special occasion." She poured me a glass.

Stormy had a half cup of coffee and she raised it in a toast. "Here's to Asta," she said.

Sabrina and I tentatively raised our glasses. "What's going on?" she said.

Stormy reached out and clinked our glasses with her cup. "Damn skull's over a thousand years old," she said looking at Sabrina. "Them museum folks in New York called Asta just after you left to get Max and Pam."

We both looked at Asta.

She grinned. "That's right. It's, at least, a thousand years old. At least."

"How did they find out so quickly?" I asked, putting down my champagne. I hate the stuff. "How do they know just from photographs?"

Asta chugged her champagne. "They, of course, got excited as soon as they read my report. And they immediately developed the film. My pictures were good, Max. I took thirty-six different poses, many of them the exact angles the museum uses for its records. My boss and three staff anthropologists did comparisons with fifty other skulls in the museum's collection. They compared my notes to field notes from other Native American digs." She smiled proudly. "They stayed late to do them. Granted they're not conclusive, but these people are experts. I've never known them to be wrong." She poured more champagne. "The rough estimate right now is, our skull belonged to a man in his thirties, and he died somewhere between nine and eleven hundred AD."

"That's a thousand years in my book," Stormy said.

"Wow." I whistled through my teeth.

Sabrina hugged her. "That's great, Asta. You were right all along."

"Not only that," Asta sipped on the new glass of champagne, "my boss hinted that maybe I'll become a full curator.".

"All right!" Sabrina hugged her again.

Stormy laughed. "Sure answers this question, don't it?" She reached behind her and picked up a copy of the Loon Sentinel that had been lying on the counter above the dishwasher. She tossed it onto the island where it slid to my champagne glass. The front page banner headline above a photograph of a smiling Asta holding the skull, which read, "MURDER WHEN?"

Sabrina turned the paper so she could read it. "That's a terrible picture of you, Asta."

"I know," se said. "But they'll get a better one. Stormy and I already called the paper and told them about what the museum said."

Stormy nodded. "Gordon's comin' back out tomorrow to do a follow-up," she said. "After he gets the details from Asta's boss in New York City."

"I wonder if Rachel will change her mind about reburying it," Sabrina said, "once she finds out how old it really is?"

"Somehow, I think that's unlikely," I said.

"That's what I sort of told my boss," Asta said. "They wanted to send a team up here right away tomorrow. I told them to wait. I said it was becoming a political football. That I would let them know when and if the air clears."

"That was smart," I said, relieved she was keeping them away. All I needed was a bunch of foppish museum people hanging around when the guys from Trout Unlimited arrived this weekend.

*   *   *

The four of us ate at the butcherblock island. As usual, Stormy's lentil soup was rich and delicious, but for me, with my split lower lip, it was agony to eat. Sabrina told Asta and Stormy about the altercation at the Starlight and I replayed the details of the incident on Route 16.

When we finished, Sabrina and Asta put together a tray for Pam, and Asta took it down to the cabin to see if she was hungry.

"Tell her I'm coming down in while to look at that nose," Stormy said. "Wanna keep an eye on that swellin'." Stormy was a registered nurse.

Sabrina went to the hall phone to call New York. She wanted to say goodnight to Elise and David.

I took a cup of coffee and, with Spotter trailing behind, limped out into the cool night air and down to the canoe rack, where I sat on the Old Town under the star-filled sky. I lit a cigarette, sipped the steaming coffee and listen to the peepers and frogs, some of whom seemed almost at my feet.

Despite everything to do with Willie and Gerry, and the confrontations with Rachel and the sheriff, I felt pretty good. Asta had been vindicated, Pam would heal and, who knew, maybe with a little makeup, she wouldn't lose her dancing job. As far as the skull was concerned, it would now be between the Wabnakis and the Historical Society. I was no longer in the middle. Even if Asta's people got involved, it wasn't my problem. I took a long drag on the cigarette and watched the smoke from my exhale dissolve among the stars. I would give the skull to Ruth in the morning. She could hold it in the vault at City Hall until things were resolved. That's where it belonged. At the lodge, we could all go back to what we did best; eat, sleep and fly fish for trout.

Spotter leaned against my good leg.

Sabrina and Stormy's voices along with the clatter of dishes and running water floated down from the open window over the kitchen sink. I couldn't make out what they were saying, but I heard Sabrina's musical laugh.

From the cabin, I could hear Asta's voice and then Pam's. They were more distinct and it wasn't just because I was closer. They were arguing and Asta's voice increased in volume. " . . . he's old enough to be your father, for Chrissakes," I heard her say. "Stay away from him."

I couldn't make out Pam's answer.

Asta was even louder this time, "I mean it, Pam! He's off limits! They're my friends, not yours!"

Pam again said something I couldn't understand and I saw Asta's silhouette appear at the door. Her voice was very clear now. "I can't do anything about what happened in New York," she said. "But up here . . . you just keep your little ass to yourself." She shook her fist. "You hear me? You keep your filthy hands off that man. Or, I swear, I'll . . ." She shoved the screen door open and slammed it behind her. I watched her stomp up the yard and disappear into the lodge. She slammed that door too.

I sighed. I'll have to have a talk with that little hot head, I thought. And I think it should be now.

I stood to follow her but I'd only taken two steps when I heard Danny's VW clattering down the access road. A second later headlights appeared around the trees and I had to look away as the brightness flooded over me.

Spotter barked and trotted toward the car which pulled up

beside the lodge. The engine shut down and the lights went off. I heard the door open and close. "Hey, Spotter," I heard Danny say. "It's me. How are you boy?" Then he said. "Hello, Max."

I watched his dark shape come down across the lawn toward me. He stopped a few feet away. He looked troubled and ill at ease.

I extended my hand. "You missed a good supper, Chief."

The look faded and, his gold teeth flashing, the smile grew. "You ain't pissed at me, Max?" He grabbed my hand and shook it. "I heard what happened to your Jeep."

I smiled. "None of what's happened is your fault."

"It's not Rachel's either." He took a partially smoked cigar from his shirt pocket and relit it.

I didn't say anything and walked with him back toward the canoes.

He sat where I'd just been sitting. I stayed on my feet. "Hope they throw away the key on those two little dickheads for what they done," he said. The end of his cigar glowed orange.

"If they catch them."

"You didn't hear? They caught 'em out at Smitty's. Started a fight and Smitty called the sheriff. They're sitting in Simon Perkins' basement cell right now."

"You're right," I said. "I hope they never get out. The way Pam's face looks, she'll probably lose her job."

"Job, hell. They coulda killed you."

"Or themselves," I said, remembering how they'd plowed through the woods miraculously missing the big trees.

"I wouldn't miss 'em."

A bunch of ducks out on the lake started quacking frantically. Danny gestured toward the sound. "Bobcat gettin' his supper probably."

I nodded. "Or a fox."

He took a deep breath. "Sure like it here, Max."

I put my hand on his shoulder. "You coming back to work tomorrow?"

"Wish I could." He shook his head. "Don't think I should

though . . . not until this is all over anyway." He looked at me. "Nobody knows I'm here, right now as it is. I said I was going out for a coupla beers."

"It'll be over tomorrow," I said. "At least, for us it will."

He looked up at me questioningly and I told him about Asta's photographs, the report and what the Museum of Natural History had said.

His frown deepened. "They sure?"

"Asta says they're seldom wrong."

He looked out at the lake but didn't say anything. The end of his cigar pulsed. It was strange. I thought he'd be as happy about as I was. Finally he slowly stood and said, "Well, guess we'll see, huh?"

"Yeah, I guess."

He turned and looked at me. "At least I got to talk to you." He put his big hand on my arm. "You know, Max," he said. "Yesterday was one of the best days I've had in a long time." He smiled. "Really enjoyed myself. Kinda liked this guidin' stuff."

"I enjoyed yesterday too. Chief." I smiled back. "We'll have more days like it."

"Them girls are fun." He shrugged. "And when it was just you and me, you know? Even if I did get dunked."

I laughed.

He turned toward lodge, stopped and turned back. "So what're you gonna do with it now?"

"Give it to Ruth in the morning, I think. Let her hold it until everything's sorted out."

"It still up in the lodge 'frige?"

I shook my head and gestured to the cabin. "It's in that little refrigerator in there." I laughed. "I guess Stormy was tired of having it staring at her every time she opened the one in the lodge."

He dropped the cigar in the grass and ground it under his boot. "Well, I gotta go, Max." He started toward the lodge and his car. "I've been gone long enough to have ten beers. Say hello to Sabrina for me, huh?"

I watched his big bear shape lumber up through the yard and as he climbed into the VW and started the noisy engine, I smiled. The Chief and I were a lot alike. It was obvious he didn't want to lose our new found friendship anymore than I did.

CHAPTER FIFTEEN

The reading room is three walls of floor to ceiling books. The fourth wall is mostly fireplace and a small window that looks out on the dark spruce behind the lodge. There is no overhead light in the room but each of the two big recliners and the sofa have their own reading lamp. To the left of the fireplace the television and VCR are in the built-in cabinet under the three shelves which house my fly fishing library of books and instructional videos. An old oak rolltop desk converted by Rayleen to a fly-tying work area sits on the other side under the window.

Only one light was on and Asta was sitting beneath it at my fly tying table. She was using a pair of my expensive scissors to clip the article about her and the skull from the Sentinel. Another glass of champagne bubbled near her elbow and the bottle sat on floor beside the leg of the chair. She had one eye closed and didn't see me walk in.

"I wish you wouldn't use those scissors for that," I said, clicking on the light beside the couch.

She jumped. "Oh, Max. You scared me."

I gently lifted the scissors from her hand and put them back on the their hook above the table. "Those are for cutting feathers only." I pulled open one of the several drawers in the desk and took out a regular pair of scissors. "These are for paper."

"I'm sorry," she smiled sheepishly. "I didn't know." She looked a little drunk.

"That isn't what I wanted to talk about anyway."

"What's up?" She picked up the glass, crossed her legs and sat back in the chair.

"A little while ago, I was sitting out on the canoes," I said. "I couldn't help but hear the things you said to Pam in the cabin."

She blushed.

"I think what she and I think of each other or do together is really none of your business."

Her blush deepened. "I was just . . ."

"And, I am old enough to be her father." I clunked the scissors on the desk. "But, I'm not her father, Asta." I pointed at the newspaper article. "I've bent over backwards to help you get what you wanted. I expect the same consideration." I went back to the door. "Now, I'm going to walk out of here and I don't want ever again to hear or hear about you saying anything else like I heard tonight. Understood?"

"I was only trying to . . ."

"I asked if you understood."

She nodded and looked down at her champagne glass.

"I assume you'll apologize to Pam."

She sighed and nodded again. The phone began ringing in the hallway and I left her sitting there.

Sabrina came in from the porch and answered before I could get to it. "Whitefork, Lodge. Good evening." She listened and then looked at me, "Yes, of course. He's right here, Sheriff." She handed me the receiver. "It's Sheriff Perkins," she whispered.

I waited until she'd gone back out onto the porch and the screen door had swung closed. Then I said, "What do you want, Simon?"

"Gerald White Frog and William Creeksitter are out, Max."

"Who?"

"Gerry and Willie."

"What do you mean, they're out?"

"Someone made bail for them."

"Who was it?"

"I don't know," he said. "That Indian lawyer the tribe has, posted it."

"You just let them go?"

"I didn't have any choice. That's how bail works."

"When was this?"

"An hour ago."

I sighed. "Should Stormy get out the Winchester?"

"Be serious, Max."

"I am serious. They could have killed us today."

"I don't think you have anything to worry about," he said. "They know that if they do anything . . . even spit in public . . . they're back in here. I don't think they'll bother anyone." He laughed. "Who knows, I might see them back here before the night's over anyway. I'm sure they'll discover that it was nicer here than it'll be in Red Town. Mad as Rachel was this afternoon."

"You saw her?"

He didn't answer.

"Simon?"

"Yeah," he said. "I went out to see her."

"And . . . ?"

"What can I say, Max? Her mind's made up."

I considered telling him about what the Museum of Natural History told Asta, then thought the better of it. He'd find out soon enough. "Well, thanks for telling me about Gerry and Willie." I started to hang up.

"Max?"

"Yeah?"

"How's Miss Fiore?"

"A couple black eyes and a broken nose."

"That's too bad," he said. "She's a real nice looking woman. Hate to think of her all banged up like that."

"She'll be all right," I said. "She's got some pills that have knocked her out."

"Well, goodnight, Max. Just thought you'd want to know."

"Yeah, thanks." I hung up and went out on the porch.

Stormy and Sabrina were sitting in the rockers. "What was that all about?" Stormy asked.

"The leg-breakers are out." I leaned on the porch post. "Somebody put up bail."

"Somebody? Ain't no mystery who it was."

Sabrina was looking out into the darkness. "Do you think they'll come looking for us?"

I laughed. "Of course not. Sheriff Perkins assured me of that."

Stormy laughed too. I hoped I sounded more convincing than she did. "Those boys are probably out of the county by now," she said. "Maybe, the country. Hell, Canada's just up the road."

"Well then," Sabrina said, "I'm not going to lose any sleep over them." She stood and went to the screen door. "What scares me is finding out what quasi-disaster has struck my little family in New York."

"I thought you called," I said.

She shook her head. "Line's been busy all night." She went into the hallway, picked up the phone and began dialing.

"Say, hi to your mother for me," I said with a laugh.

She put her hand over the mouthpiece. "Oh great. That should be a big help."

I looked across the lawn at the cabin. There was a light on. I started down the porch steps. "I'm going to go see how the broken nose is doing."

Stormy lit a cigarette. I saw her smile in the flame. "Figured you might," she said.

With Spotter walking slowly beside me, I went down to the cabin and rapped softly on the door. "Max's twenty-four hour plumbing service," I said.

There was no answer.

"Hello?" I tried the door. It was unlocked. I opened it and peeked in. "Hello."

Pam, her golden hair in loops and coils on the pillow, a book open face down on her chest, was in the big bed under the covers. She was sound asleep. The beside lamp was on and a moth bashed around inside the shade. The tray with the soup bowl was on the floor. She hadn't eaten anything.

Spotter slipped in around my legs. I followed and quietly closed the door behind me. He trotted across the room and, before I could grab him, jumped up on the foot end of the bed and flopped on the quilt. He looked at me and laid his nose on his paws.

"Max?" Pam was awake.

"Sorry," I said. "Spotter just . . ."

"Come here."

"I'm sorry," I said, crossing the room. "I tried to stop him but I'm afraid he thinks I'm staying the night." I leaned in, kissed her and then sat on the edge of the bed. Her eyes were purple and almost swollen shut. "How do you feel?"

She pushed herself up slightly on the pillow. "Groggy." She looked a little like she was wearing a Halloween mask.

"They must be strong pills," I said, carefully brushing the hair from her face. "You've been down here since before supper."

She tried to squint at her watch. "What time is it?"

"Late."

"Brrr." She pulled the covers to her chin. "It's cold in here."

I looked at the sliding doors. "No wonder." They were open about six inches. "The sliders are open." I went around the bed, pushed them shut and latched them. I pulled the drapes closed. "You want me to make you a fire?"

"Would you?"

"One fire, coming up." I stooped at the fireplace and got a pile of kindling crackling. I put two logs on, set the screen in front and went to the closet where I took the extra pillow from the shelf and carried it to the bed.

"I don't like a lot of pillows, Max. I always think I'm going to suffocate."

I propped the pillow up against the headboard beside hers. "It's not for you." I lay down on top of the covers beside her. "It's for me."

"Come under the covers," she said with a smile. "I only have a nightgown on."

"Maybe later." I smiled back and slid my arm under the back of her neck. "Right now, this is nice."

She snuggled onto my shoulder and put her hand on my chest. "You're right. This is nice." She tilted her head and looked at me. "My face hurts too much for sex anyway."

I kissed her hairline. "You know about the museum calling?"

"Asta told me."

"I heard the other things she said. I was sitting out by the canoes."

"I told her about us." Pam sighed. "I thought she'd be happy for me like I was for her."

"I told her you and I were none of her business."

"My protector." She smiled and closed her eyes.

The fire snapped and popped. Spotter began to snore. My arm was starting to go to sleep. I peeked at her. She was staring at the firelight dancing on the ceiling. "I thought you were asleep," I said.

She shook her head. The fine golden curls tickled my nose. "Having Spotter down there on my feet made me remember when I was a little girl," she said. "My sister and I used to sleep in the same bed. She'd take one end and I'd take the other. Her legs on my feet in the night felt like Spotter does now."

"She older or younger?"

"Older."

"What's she do?"

"She's a single mom. Three kids."

"Where? New York City?"

"No, in L.A. But we see each other. I go out there. She lives in Sherman Oaks." She looked up at me. "You know where that is?"

I shook my head. "I've only been to L.A. once and then only to the Marina area."

"Sherman Oaks is real nice. Like New England, sort of. The trees lose their leaves."

"Any other siblings?"

"My brother Jack died when I was ten. He'd be forty now."

"You're the baby of the family."

"I guess. That's what my daddy calls me."

"He the one that they won't wash in the nursing home?"

"That's him." She chuckled. "Oh. Ow. Don't make me laugh, Max."

"Sorry." I kissed her forehead. "Where's the nursing home?"

"North Carolina."

"You get down there much?"

"I try but, it's so depressing. There are plenty of uncles and aunts and cousins who go see him."

"What about your mother?"

"She died last year."

"I'm sorry."

She was quiet for a while. Just when I thought she'd really gone to sleep this time, she turned and hugged herself closer to me and said, "So, maybe I have a chance?"

"A chance?"

"Against Ruth?"

I smiled. "I'm here, aren't I?"

She sighed. "That's a good answer, isn't it?"

"I'd say it is."

She kissed my beard. "Then it is." She closed her eyes.

I stared at the beamed ceiling.

"You know," Her eyes were still closed. "I don't think I've ever talked so much about myself. Not all at one time. And never with a guy I've only known for two days. These drugs must be something else, huh?"

I continued to stare at the ceiling. The moth from the lamp shade was now banging his head across the white plaster between the beams, heading for the fireplace. He swooped down toward the flickering firelight and disappeared. I looked down at Pam. She was asleep.

I slowly withdrew my now completely dead arm and slid off the bed. Then I leaned and kissed her forehead. The cinnamon aroma was faint. I tapped Spotter on the haunch and gave him a "get off the bed" nod. He slowly got to his feet, stretched and jumped to the floor.

Pam didn't stir. I covered her bare arm with a corner of the quilt, clicked off the light and Spotter and I went out into the night. I pulled the door quietly closed and looked up at the blur of stars above me. There were so many visible that they looked more liked clouds. Venus was just setting behind the dark mountains on the far side the lake and I stood there, smoking a cigarette until it was gone.

All the lights were out in the lodge and I assumed everyone had gone to bed. Then I saw the orange glow of Stormy's cigarette and, as I got closer, the faint outlines of her caftan in a rocker and the smell of the smoke. "What's the matter?" I said going up to the top step and sitting on it. "You're not tired?" Spotter sat between my legs and I lit a another cigarette.

"Just thinkin'," she said. "How's the little girl?"

"Sleeping. She really looks like hell."

"It hurt?"

"I guess so," I said. "Sabrina get through on the phone to New York?"

Stormy nodded.

"She say how things are going at home?"

Stormy chuckled. "Guess things are as good as they can be without her there."

"You know that Chief came by this evening?"

"What'd he want?"

"I think just to make sure we're still friends."

"I like that man," she said. "He wasn't marryin' that nut, think I might take a run at him myself."

I laughed. "That would be interesting."

A bright shooting star streaked diagonally across the sky. "You see that?"

She didn't answer for a minute. Then she said, "Guess Sabrina had quite a talk with Ruth this mornin'."

"They've become pretty close over the years."

"You know about her and Bolick bein' finished?"

"She told me."

A small dog, maybe a fox or eastern coyote, barked sharply several times in the woods over near the river. Spotter's ears went up and I slipped my hand in his collar.

"You gonna give Ruth a chance to patch things up between you?"

I blew smoke out into the darkness. "I don't know whether I'm ready for that."

"You mean, you don't want to."

"Maybe," I said. "Maybe I don't."

Her cigarette arched out over the yard like an orange shooting star and she stood. "Well, I'm goin' to bed." She walked slowly to the screen door. "Watch out if you go into the kitchen. I got a coupla mouse traps set around the counters on the floor in there." She opened the door and went inside. "See you in the mornin', Max."

I listened to her feet go up the stairs and then finished my cigarette.

Just as I locked the front door, the phone rang. I got to it before it rang again. "Whitefork Lodge," I said.

"You all right, Max?" It was Ruth. "I've been trying to get you all night but the phone's been busy."

"That was probably Sabrina talking to New York."

"Are you all right? How's Pam?"

"We're both fine."

"God, I've been worried. I almost drove out there when I couldn't get through."

"How did you find out?"

"Pauline called me." Pauline Tritch had worked for five Loon mayors and was now the head of Ruth's office staff. "She heard it on her scanner at home. You sure you're okay?"

"I'm fine."

"I heard from Gordon Miller what Asta's museum said about the skull," she said. "It's exciting isn't it? Something that old in Loon?"

"Yeah. I'm hoping you'll take it off my hands until it's decided who should get it. Put it in that vault of yours."

"I suppose I could do that."

"I'll bring it in to town tomorrow morning."

"Actually, I can pick it up," she said. "I'm reading again at the elementary school in Red Town tomorrow. How about I pick it up on my way back to town? Would that be all right?"

"Sure. We're not going anywhere."

She was silent for a minute. Then she said, "Maybe, we can get together for a cup of coffee or something after Sabrina leaves?"

"Maybe."

"Don't fall in love, Max. I didn't." And she hung up.

I returned the phone to it's cradle and took Spotter into my room. He jumped up onto the bed and, I think, was asleep before I opened the windows. There was a faint breeze from the lake and, as I slowly undressed, I could smell the water.

Before I crawled into bed and turned out the light, I peered through the window at the cabin. It was a dark, almost black, silhouette against the only slightly lighter, flat lake behind it.

I pulled the covers to my chin, stretched my cast and leg out under Spotter's warm weight.

The fox yipped again from the river.

*   *   *

There was a noise. My clock said 3:07 am. I leaned up on one elbow and listened. I heard it again. A thump.

Spotter's head came up. He barked twice.

As I shushed him and strained my ears, I heard it again.

I looked out the window and then back at Spotter. His attention was directed toward my bathroom door and the back of the lodge. He whined.

I flopped back onto my pillows. Damn raccoons at the garbage shed, I thought. "Go to sleep, boy," I whispered. "they can't get in."

Spotter sighed on my feet and I fell back to sleep.

In a minute, so did I.

CHAPTER SIXTEEN

A maddening, bone-deep itch inside my cast awoke me at six am.

Spotter, his rear end at my shoulder, lay stretched out on the covers beside me. I rolled my legs off the bed and pounded on the cast. Sometimes, if I hit it hard enough, the vibrations scratched the itch.

I looked out the window just as two blue jays, screaming their heads off in alarm, swooped across the yard between the lodge and the cabin. Their screeching had barely faded when a cow moose ambled slowly into sight. Her long legs were muddy and her wet hide steamed as she paused, bent her neck awkwardly and lipped a bunch of grass from the lawn. She stood there, fifteen feet from the porch, chewing slowly, big brown eyes alert, her ears twitching and scanning for sounds. She fed on the lush grass like this for a minute or more. I could hear her chewing. Then, something alarmed her. She took two big steps forward and stopped, her bulbulous wet nose testing the faint breeze. Her tail twitched nervously. Suddenly her ears went back, the whites of her eyes shown as they rolled in fear and she snorted. A second later she broke into a canter and she disappeared into the thick trees by the river. I could hear her breaking dead limps for a few seconds after that.

The jays, screaming louder than before, came swooping back across the yard going the opposite direction and disappeared into the stand of spruce down on the far side of the workshop.

Then it was quiet again.

I got up, pulled on a pair of jeans, a tee-shirt and an old, once dark brown, now tan, chamois cloth shirt. Spotter hadn't moved and I slipped on one moosehide moccasin, left him sleeping there with his butt on my guest pillow and went into the dining room where I put on a pot of coffee.

While the coffee dripped, I built a fire and when it was snapping up the dry white bark on two birch logs, I sneaked a cup of coffee from the unfinished pot and went out onto the porch to watch the misty morning lake wake up.

The lake, cabin, lawn and porch were still in shadow. The sun was still too low behind the mountain in back of the lodge and so far only the tops of the mountains out across the Sweet Lake were being skimmed by its rays. In the golden orangey light, the farthest mountain looked like the hip of reclining women. The air was crisp. My breath and the steam from the coffee cup at my mouth looked the same. I pulled up my collar and buttoned the top two buttons on the chamois shirt.

A translucent ribbon of smoke still rose from the cabin chimney, straight up, into the brightening sky. It was going to be a beautiful morning.

I hadn't closed the lodge front door tightly and Spotter nosed through and out onto the porch. He stretched, yawned wide and his jaws clicked together. He groaned appreciatively as I scratched him behind the ears, then trotted down the stairs and, nose to the ground, headed toward the blueberry bushes along the shore line between the canoe rack and the workshop, looking for this morning's bathroom.

From where I was standing, it looked like the door to the cabin was open. I took a couple steps sideways and looked again. I was right. It was open.

Pam must be up, I thought, going down the steps into the yard. After all that sleep yesterday, she'd probably awakened early and gone for a walk.

I crossed the cow moose's tracks in the lawn. Pam had probably been what startled it. On the chance that she hadn't left yet, I went to the cabin first. If she was gone, the least I could do was shut the door . . . already I'd noticed a few mosquitoes and there was no reason she had to have those in the cabin.

I stuck my head in open door. "Pam?"

There was no answer and as I pulled the door closed, I saw the soup bowl from last night overturned on the floor just inside, a long puddle of congealed lentil soup leading back into the dark room. The soup had been on the tray by bed on the other side of room when left last night.

I stepped inside. "Pam?"

Silence.

The wave of fear that swept over me was literally staggering. "Pam?" I took another step. "Pam . . ." I peered around the corner into the room. The coffee cup dropped from my fingers and, spraying coffee, shattered at my feet. I had to grip the door frame to keep from losing my balance.

Pam was on the bed face down in the pillows, her legs spread in an open "V" toward me. Her nightgown was pushed to her shoulders. The bedside lamp was on the floor, the sliding glass door to the deck, a spider web of cracks.

I barely remember crossing in the room, rolling her over and cradling her in my arms, but I'll never forget the cold, heavy limpness of her body and the wild, frightened look frozen in her eyes.

I shook her, screaming her name.

I knelt above her and pounded on her chest.

I put my mouth on hers and filled her lungs with air over and over and over again. Tears of my frustration dripped in her eyes and ran down her cheeks.

I knew it was useless. I knew Pam was dead.

*　*　*

There were squad cars everywhere. The sheriff's two were in the turnaround. Three Vermont State police cruisers were at angles on the lawn. An orange and white EMT van was backed up to the cabin, it's rear doors open. Another van, black and windowless, was parked beside it. The Vermont State Seal was on the door surrounded by the words, "CRIME SCENE—Montpelier Barracks". A uniformed state trooper and Richie Norville stood at the rear of the van talking quietly. Two more troopers, one with a metal detector, were slowly walking through the yard. Occasionally a flash bulb would go off in the cabin, momentarily lighting the windows. Smoke had stopped coming from the chimney.

Stormy and I were sitting on the front porch. Sabrina was still upstairs with Asta who'd become hysterical when she found out. Spotter sat on the steps watching the men and women go in and out of the cabin.

Lost in our own thoughts, Stormy and I hadn't spoken for almost an hour. Occasionally I'd look over at her and feeling me looking, she'd look back. Her eyes were red and swollen.

Finally, the State Police Captain, a black man named Hughes, emerged from the cabin and, pulling off a pair of rubber gloves, came up through the yard to the porch. "I'll take a cup of that coffee now, Mrs. Domini," he said coming up the steps. "If you're still offering." Hughes looked to be in his late thirties and perhaps a former college basketball player. At least six-six or seven, he towered over just about everyone in the yard and in the dark tan uniform and flat brimmed smokey hat, was quite an impressive figure.

Once Stormy had gone inside to get the coffee, Hughes sat up on the porch rail in front of me. "I don't really need anymore coffee, Mister Addams" he whispered, "but I wanted to tell you this so you could decide out how to handle it with the women."

I sighed. "What is it, captain?"

"I don't like telling anyone this kind of thing, but . . ." He looked toward the lodge and then back at me. He took a deep breath. "There's a chance she was sexually assaulted, Mister Addams. Although we haven't found any traces of semen yet, there is some blood and bruises on her . . ."

"I don't want to know any more." I grit my teeth and looked away. He had no way of knowing about Pam and me.

"I'm sorry," he said. "I just figured you'd know better how to tell the ladies. You know what I mean?" He gestured toward the cabin. "Even though a couple of those troopers are women, they can be a little rough when it comes to telling people things."

"I appreciate your thoughtfulness, Captain," I said. "I really do."

He shook his head. "Darn. I hate to see something like this happen. Long as I've been at this job, I still never get used to it."

"It was the skull, wasn't it?" I'd seen the little refrigerator open and empty.

"Looks that way. It's gone."

"You know who did it?"

He gave me a weak smile. "I'm not allowed to talk about that, you know that, Mister Addams." He stood and started for the steps. He stopped. "Almost forgot. I also wanted to tell you that the finger print people are going to need a full set of everyone's in the lodge. They'll be coming up here in a few minutes to do each one of you."

"Why?"

He shrugged. "Have to be able to sort the good guys from the bad guys." He went down the steps. "There are prints all over that cabin."

"Okay." I nodded. "But, hold them off as long as you can, huh? I've got one young lady upstairs who's still pretty upset."

"Sure. I'll see what I can do." He rubbed Spotter's head with his big brown hand.

I watched him go back down across the yard and disappear into the cabin. Another flashbulb illuminated the windows.

I looked out at the lake. I could see the tiny spikes of pale green beginning to poke through the surface of the water. They would soon sprout floating leaves and, by June, thousands of yellow water lilies would sparkle in the sun. A fish jumped out by the beaver dam. The mountains in distance had darkened one more shade of green since yesterday as summer dependably marched north on the warm breezes from the south. A flock of canvasbacks whistled in overhead, circled the lake and, quacking back and forth, continued on. The miracles of nature were all around me. Rebirth and life. But none of it could help Pam. There were no miracles up here in all this glory that could breathe life back into her. None.

*   *   *

Gordon Miller and Rusty Granger arrived shortly before noon and after taking what pictures the police would allow and interviewing me and Perkins, they showed surprising good taste and left.

Fortunately Asta was still up in her room when they brought Pam's body out of the cabin. It was in a black bag and, even though it appeared strapped to the gurney, it bounced and jiggled obscenely as the two EMT's rolled it the short distance across the uneven grass to their van. They roughly slid the whole thing inside, slammed the doors and, their lights flashing, jounced out of the yard and up the access road.

She was gone.

The contingent of Vermont State Police left shortly after, the crime scene department van loaded down with bed sheets, pillows, the lamp, the little refrigerator and every conceivable size plastic sandwich bag, each containing a fragment of this and a particle of that.

The cabin door and windows had been sealed with big X's of yellow crime scene tape.

Now only Perkins, Richie and Hughes were left and they were talking out by the hood of a squad car. Asta, Sabrina, Stormy and I were on the porch, plates of an uneaten and half eaten lunch on the floor by our chairs. Perkins had told us earlier that, as soon as everyone had gone, they would bring us up-to-date on what was known and what the next steps were to be. We were waiting.

Finally, leaving Richie at the car, Perkins and Hughes came up to the porch. "Why don't we all go inside," Hughes said, and we all filed silently inside to the dining room table where we sat around one end of the table. Perkins and Hughes stood at the other end. Both took off their hats. After rubbing the sepia hatband crease on his forehead, Hughes took a small notebook from his chest pocket, peeled it open and placed it on the table in front of him. His hands were enormous. "First of all," he said, "I want to introduce myself to those of you I didn't have a chance to meet this morning. I'm Dave Hughes. I'm with the Vermont State Police, Montpelier barracks and assigned to homicide. Although Loon County is Sheriff Perkins' jurisdiction, this has become my case so I, first of all, I want to tell you all how sorry I am this had to happen. By comparison to most towns in New England, Loon is a quiet, law-bidding community. When something like this happens, we don't take very kindly to it." He smiled at Asta. "I want to assure all of you that everything that can be done is being done to apprehend the person or persons responsible."

Asta stifled a sob and Sabrina took her hand.

"My main reason for this little meeting is to bring you up to date on our investigation and clarify some things. All right?"

Sabrina and Asta nodded.

"Now, I don't intend to go into any details other than to say that it's been determined that Miss Fiore died sometime between 2:30 and 3:30 this morning." He looked at me. "I mention that because it's about the time Mister Addams says he heard noises he thought were coming from the lodge garbage shed." He paused and studied his notes. "It also appears, as I'm sure you're aware, that stealing this ancient skull was the primary reason for the altercation. Since the lodge itself wasn't broken into, we also know that whoever did this knew that the skull was in the cabin refrigerator." He looked at Asta again. "Miss Singer here has told us it was put there only yesterday afternoon." He cleared his throat. "Unfortunately, this puts all of you in a, although temporary, difficult position . . ."

Stormy's fist hit the table. "You ain't sayin' you suspect one of us?"

He cleared his throat again. "I said, temporarily, Mrs. Domini. Once the fingerprints and other evidence gathered in the cabin has been analyzed, I'm sure that the restrictions on you will be lifted."

I frowned. "Restrictions? What restrictions?"

"You're not going to be allowed to leave the lodge property, Mister Addams."

"How long will that be?" Sabrina said. "I've got a husband and child in New York City," She looked at me. "Mother's flying back to Florida on Thursday, Daddy."

"Unfortunately, I can't say exactly," Hughes said. "It shouldn't be more than a day or two."

I looked at Perkins. "Com'on, Simon. That's ridiculous."

"I know, Max. I know. But that's the way it's done."

Hughes was looking at Asta. "Miss Singer? You told an investigator earlier that Miss Fiore was heavily sedated. That she was taking prescription medication for her facial injuries. Correct?"

Asta nodded and, fighting back tears, said, "But I didn't say she was heavily sedated. I said she was little goofy." She put her hand to her mouth and her eyes filled with tears.

He looked back at me. "And you were the last to see Miss Fiore alive, Mister Addams?"

I nodded.

"She seem sedated to you?"

"What's the point of this?" I said. "What's the difference?"

"Procedure, Max," Perkins said.

Hughes smiled and nodded. "Sheriff Perkins' right. If we establish now that, in your opinion, Miss Fiore was not sedated or partially unconscious, down the road some smart defense lawyer won't be able introduce the possibility of accidental death during rape." Asta sobbed. "There's a big difference between murder and manslaughter. And in today's world, the only way to make sure it stays that way, is cover all the bases up front."

Perkins cleared his throat and fiddled with his hat.

"Now, I know Miss Fiore has only been here a couple days," Hughes was studying his notes, "but is there any possibility that she might have made an enemy or enemies in that time."

"What the hell do you call what happened to her 'n' Max up on 16 yesterday?" Stormy grumbled.

"I mean besides that," he said.

I caught Asta's eye and stared at her until she looked down at the table. I looked at Hughes. "Do you know for sure that she was raped?" I said.

"No. Not in the ordinary sense, anyway. We won't know that until autopsy."

I looked back at Asta. She was still looking at the table.

Hughes saw the look on my face and looked at Asta. "Miss Singer? Were you and Miss Fiore close friends?"

Asta didn't reply. Tears dripped on the table.

"Miss Singer . . . ?"

"We argued, okay?" Asta cried. "I was mad at her for sleeping with my fiance and with Max. I yelled at her." She buried her face in her hands. "I'm sorry. I'm so sorry. I would never hurt Pam."

Stormy put her arm around Asta's shaking shoulders. "You're barkin' up the wrong tree, Captain," she said.

Hughes looked at me. "This true, Mister Addams?"

I looked at Sabrina and nodded.

"Do you generally have this kind of relationship with customers?"

I sighed but didn't answer.

"Look," he said. "I'm not trying to implicate anyone in this room. Far from it. You've all been under a lot of strain today. I know that." He looked over at Asta. "But to do my job, you have to tell me everything. You may not think it's important, but it could be." He looked back at me. "Mister Addams, if you were romantically involved with Miss Fiore then, for a reason as yet undiscovered, you could have wanted to kill her. Do you understand that?"

Stormy shook her head. "Oh, for Chrissakes . . ."

"Let me finish," he said. "And you, Miss Singer. Jealousy is a powerful motivator."

"Captain," Sabrina said, putting her hand on Asta's, "I've known this person all my life. And that's my father over there . . ."

"I know," he said. "And I'm not accusing anyone. My point is the importance of telling us everything." He sighed. "Now, is there anything else I should know?"

"Hell," Stormy said. "I didn't like her at first. Didn't like how she was stealin' Max away from any chance of gettin' back with Ruth."

"Ruth?"

"Mayor Pearlman," Perkins said to him. "She and Max were a couple until about a year ago."

He nodded and looked at me. "Did Mayor Pearlman know of your relationship with Miss Fiore, Mister Addams?"

I shrugged and nodded.

He took a pen from his breast pocket and made a note on the pad.

"This is stupid," Sabrina said. "Now you're suspecting Ruth?"

"Long as we're askin' stupid questions, Captain," Stormy said. "Instead of standing here tryin' to make all of us into murderers, why the hell aren't you over in Red Town arresting those two goons who drove Max off the road?" She glared at Perkins. "You know as well as I do, Simon, they done this."

Perkins' face reddened.

The criticism seemed to roll right off of Hughes. "Two of Sheriff Perkins' deputies," Hughes said, "and four members of the state police went out to Red Town over and hour ago, Mrs. Domini. So far, they've had no luck locating Willie Creeksitter and Gerald Whitefrog."

"Did your people talk to Rachel?" Stormy said.

Hughes looked at Perkins. "Rachel?"

"Rachel Arneau," Perkins said. "The Shaman."

Hughes looked back at Stormy. "Of course, they've talked to Miss Arneau. And she claims she hasn't seen either of them since Sunday morning here at the lodge."

Stormy made a face. "Yeah, sure. Who do you think bailed them out of Simon's jail?"

"We'll be determining out who bailed them out later this afternoon," Hughes said. "Deputy Norris is on the police radio right now arranging to subpoena that information."

Sabrina shook her head. "I just don't understand."

Perkins frowned at her. "Understand what, Sabrina?"

"I don't get it. What's so important about that skull? Why would someone want it so badly that they'd . . ." She couldn't say it.

"Someone?" Stormy was mad again. "Only one person I know of who wanted the skull that badly." She held out her index finger. "Only one."

"Rachel has an alibi for all night last night, Stormy," Perkins said.

"'Course she does." She stamped out her cigarette butt. "I ain't saying she did it, dammit. Might as well, though. I'm saying what we all know happened. Rachel sent them little hoodlums over to get that skull. And they killed Pam."

"We don't know that," Hughes said.

"That's the trouble with you cops today," Stormy said. "Everything's by the book. You gotta be so careful. You spend all your time walkin' on eggs so some fancy lawyer can't make a fool outta you in court and you forget to listen to your own gut." She shook her head in disgust. "That woman might not of done it herself but she made it happen. Sure as I'm sitting here, Rachel Arneau's your man."

Hughes sighed and glanced at Perkins. I don't think he'd ever been up against anyone like Stormy. "Look," he said finally. "Even if I were to agree with you, Mrs. Domini, Rachel Arneau has no motive."

"Hell. She wanted to have a Wabnaki burial. We wouldn't let her. She wanted the skull to go back in the lake. She became a freak about it. There's your motive."

Hughes looked at Asta. "You told us that your employers estimated the skull's age at around 1000 years? That right?"

Asta wiped at her wet cheeks and nodded.

"What would an artifact of that age be worth?"

She shrugged. "I don't know. It would depend upon its contribution."

He frowned. "Contribution?"

"If the skull contained information about the evolution of a race of people as yet unavailable," she said. "it would be worth a lot of money."

"Like?"

She shrugged again. "I don't know. Thousands. Millions, maybe. That's not my department. Besides, the skull is only part of something larger. You'd have to examine the entire skeleton to know."

He smiled. "Well, we're going to try to do just that, Miss Singer. A State Police underwater search and rescue team will be here at the lodge day after tomorrow. In the hopes that it will tell us something about why the skull was so important to someone, we're going to dive for the rest of that skeleton."

"You are?" Perkins looked genuinely surprised.

"Why?" Asta said, her eyes as wide as Perkins'.

"That's the smartest thing I heard you say this morning," Stormy said, lighting another cigarette.

"But why are you waiting until day after tomorrow?" Sabrina said.

"Unfortunately," Hughes said, "we've only got one team up this way and, right now, they're looking for a couple little boys who drowned down in Lake Willowby. It's a deep lake." Lake Willowby was near Burke Mountain over in what's called, the Northeast Kingdom. It's over 200 feet deep in places. "Of course, we could get lucky and they might find those boys right away." He smiled. "If that happens then, day or night, they'll be here diving."

Stormy blew a stream of smoke over the table. "Night?"

Hughes nodded. "Sometimes night dives are more productive, Mrs. Domini. Believe it or not. The divers are able to work better with one light source instead of the variables of sunlight." He smiled. "Besides, I've been told that usually in water like Sweet Lake, it's quite dark after about fifteen feet anyway."

"So, if you guys see a light out there after dark," Perkins said, "don't let it bother you. Before we leave today, I'll show Captain Hughes here how to get down to that side of the lake on that little Jeep road that runs around there. You won't even be bothered."

"That's correct." Hughes nodded. "And please, stay up here at the lodge if you do see us out there. The divers and their assistants are specialists. Handling skeletal remains is a delicate process. They don't need spectators."

They spent another fifteen minutes with us, verifying a few other things we'd told them earlier. Finally Hughes said, "We'll be notifying Miss Fiore's family." He squinted at his notes. "According to Miss Singer, there's a sister in Los Angeles and other relatives in North Carolina."

Asta nodded. "The sister lives in Sherman Oaks."

He closed the little notebook and returned it to his chest pocket. "Well, that's it," he said, looking mostly at Stormy. "Do you have any other questions?"

We shook our heads.

"Then, hang in there." He put on his smokey hat and adjusted the brim. "I'll keep you informed as things develop through Sheriff Perkins." They went to the front door and I followed. "He'll call as soon as you're all free to leave."

I walked them out onto the porch and shook Hughes hand. "If you or any of the others think of anything that you didn't tell us, Mister Addams," he said. "Anything at all. Call Sheriff Perkins. He knows where to find me."

I watched them go out to their respective squad cars and climb in. As they pulled away, I couldn't help but think that if I'd just given Perkins the skull yesterday morning, all of this would never have happened.

*   *   *

I went back into the lodge and found the dining room empty. As I passed the bottom of the stairs on my way to the kitchen to find and commiserate with Stormy, I heard Asta sobbing softly upstairs and Sabrina's voice consoling her. I felt sorry for Sabrina. Some relaxing vacation this had become and now, no matter what Hughes called it, she was under a form of house arrest when probably all she want to do is pack up her car and Asta and get the hell out of Loon, Vermont and back to New York City where assault, murder and robbery are the norm but don't disrupt daily life.

A cigarette stuck in the corner of her mouth, Stormy was in the laundry room folding towels. A big, thick stack stood on the dryer. I leaned on the door frame and watched her. The room was warm and sweet with the smell of fabric softener.

She looked at me from the corner of her eye. "Suppose, as usual, you're blamin' yourself, aren't you?"

I nodded. "All I had to do was give that damn skull to Simon yesterday morning."

"Only thing woulda prevented this, Max," she said, "is if you never pulled the damn thing out the lake in the first place." She gathered the towels in her arms and pushed by me into the kitchen.

I followed and sat on a stool. "Sometimes I think this place is jinxed," I said.

"No more 'n any other place where folks come in from the outside world." She set the towels on the island and snubbed her cigarette in the quahog ashtray.

"This trouble wasn't brought in by anyone," I said. "It was already here, waiting out there in that lake."

She went to the big eight burner stove, grabbed the tea kettle and took it to the sink. "Listen here, Max Addams," She turned on the faucet and began filling the kettle. "It's outta our hands now. That Hughes fella's gonna take care of it. I'm sorry 'bout Pam. Truly I am. She was a nice girl. But it's the livin' we gotta worry 'bout now." She returned to the stove and set the kettle on a front burner. "You got two little girls upstairs there that need you 'n me to set an example." She turned on the gas, adjusted the blue flame and looked at me. "They need us in a big way."

"What am I supposed to do?" I rubbed my eyes. "Pretend this

thing isn't tearing me apart?' I felt my eyes burn as fought back the tears. "I'm responsible, dammit. And you know it."

She came to the island and put her hands on my shoulders. "All you did is what you thought was right."

I put my forehead against her bosom.

"Nobody can be expected to do anymore 'n that." She stroked my head. "There was no way of knowin'."

We stayed like that, my head against her smokey smelling bosom, her hand stroking my hair for several minutes and then I felt the strength she seemed to always possess when I didn't, begin to seep through the fabric of her caftan into me.

*   *   *

I found Sabrina sitting on the porch steps with Spotter and I sat down beside. "You've been great through this," I said, putting my arm around her. "Really great."

"Oh, Daddy." She put her head on my shoulder. "I feel so terrible. I didn't treat Pam very nice. I made fun of her behind her back. I didn't think she was good enough for you. And now look."

"Don't think about it." I hugged her tighter. "The important thing is, you've been a friend to her friend. It's been hard on Asta."

She turned slightly and looked in my eyes. "How about you? Where do you find the strength to keep going?"

"In the kitchen." I smiled. "Stormy always manages to put things in the right perspective."

She wiped her eyes and sniffed. "God, I hope we never lose her."

The rest of the day was a blur. We talked. Sabrina, Asta and I took a walk around the lake. We tried to watch TV. But every time one of us looked out at the cabin and saw the police tape, it all came flooding back and conversation would turn to Pam and something she'd said or wore or had wished for. For me, it would be a long time before the look in Pam's dead eyes weren't there every time I shut mine.

We all knew that leaving the lodge for a while would be a good idea and each time the telephone rang, we'd scramble for it, hoping it was Hughes or Perkins with, if not news, at least notification that we could finally leave the property. It never was. In fact, one of the calls was vile. Fortunately, I answered it. "See what happens when you mess around with those woods niggers?" a woman's voice said and then hung up. The next was from one of Stormy's friends calling to make sure she was all right. I only heard a part of Stormy's side of the conversation; "No," Stormy said. "That's nice of you to offer, Pearl. But we can't leave." She paused, listened and them said, "No. I wouldn't leave these folks right now, even if I could."

The third time the phone rang, Stormy said, "Let it ring, Max, That thing ain't bringin' us nothin' but busy bodies and bad news."

I was already up. "Next time," I said, going into the hall.

It was Pauline Tritch from Ruth's office. "Ruth there, Max?"

"No. Is she supposed to be?"

"Well, she couldn't get through on the phone so she told me she was going to stop by the lodge after she did her reading thing at Red Town. Said she'd call me when she got there. She thought maybe you'd need some help."

"We haven't seen her, Pauline. When was she supposed to stop?"

"Well," I heard papers shuffling on her end, "her reading class with the children was at three. That lasts an hour. Usually. She should have been at the lodge by five, at the latest."

"You called Red Town, I assume."

"I will now."

"Let me know, Pauline, huh?" I said. "And if she shows up here, I'll have her call you right away."

"Thank you, Max. And, sorry about all your troubles out there."

"Thanks, Pauline. Are you at the office?"

She laughed. "Am I ever anywhere else?"

I gave her weak laugh and we hung up. I went back out onto the porch.

Stormy gave me a questioning look.

"Just Pauline looking for Ruth," I said. "I guess she's stopping by."

Stormy got to her feet. "In that case, maybe I better rustle up somethin' half way decent for supper." She went to the door. "Been a long time since we had Ruth out here." She looked at Asta and Sabrina. "You ladies wanta help?"

*   *   *

At seven o'clock, we were still waiting for Ruth. I was about to try her at home when Pauline called again. This time. she was worried. "I've called everywhere, Max," she said. "I so hoped she was there with you by now."

"What time did they say she left Red Town?"

"Last time they saw her was three fifteen, like I told you before."

"Have you tried Bolick?"

"No. I know for a fact she hasn't seen him for more than a week."

I didn't want to alarm her but I had to say it. "Perhaps you should call the sheriff. Maybe she's had car trouble. There's a lot of narrow dirt road between Red Town and Loon. She might have gone into the woods or . . ."

"Oh, don't say that. Max," she said.

"Call him, Pauline. If you don't, I will."

"I'll call him, Max. But, maybe you could go out there and look for her. I mean . . ."

"We're not supposed to leave the lodge," I said. "The State Police have us confined here because of the murder."

"They don't think that you did it, do they?"

"Of course not. It's just part of the procedure."

"Well," she said. "Procedure or no procedure, this is the mayor we're talking about."

"I know, Pauline. And a very good friend too. But let's give it another hour. If we still haven't heard from her or found her, then I'll go look myself."

"All right," she said. "I'll call the sheriff."

"And call Bolick, Pauline."

"Max . . ."

"Call him," I said and hung up. I stood there looking at the rogues gallery of pictures we have all along the hallway wall. In the chrome frame right in front of me was one of Ruth and I taken in Key West by my friend John Purcell. She was in a bikini. I was in shorts, holding a fly rod. She had asked to go along on that winter's fishing trip to the Keys and, stupidly, I'd consented. You could see it in our faces. I wanted to fish. She wanted to sightsee. We had a miserable time. It was the beginning of the end. Late the next summer she started seeing Doug Bolick.

I headed back to the kitchen. My bet was, she was with him.

Stormy, Asta and Sabrina, of course, wanted to know about the phone call. After I told them, Stormy sat hard on a stool. "Ain't like Ruth," she said. "One thing 'bout that woman. She says she's gonna be somewheres, she's there. And early to boot."

I wasn't going to say anything about what I really thought. "Probably had car trouble," I said instead. "She'll turn up."

"Hope she ain't gone back with that damn Bolick," Stormy mumbled.

*   *   *

We were sitting in the dining room waiting for the phone to ring. The sun had gone down and no one had bothered to turn on the lights. The flames from the fire in the fireplace were the only light in the room. Already, I'd nodded off twice in my chair.

It was Asta who saw it first. "Hey, look," she said, pointing out the window at the lake. "There's a light out there."

We all went out onto the porch.

It was actually several lights, bobbing and blinking out where Pam and I had found the skull. There were the shadows of people and voices. The clink of metal and splashing. Several times I could see the water in the area glow light green as a light shown under its surface. "They're diving for the rest of it," I said.

"Don't know whether to feel good or bad about it," Stormy said. "Must mean them little boys' bodies was found."

CHAPTER SEVENTEEN

The next day, Thursday, was more of the same; sitting and waiting to hear about Ruth.

Our only contact was Pauline and she told us that she had called the sheriff and he was doing what he could. She said he was notifying the state police. She also said she had called Doug Bolick and, as she had told me earlier, he hadn't seen Ruth for almost two weeks.

It was like she'd simply dropped off the face of the earth.

Twice I got up to leave and go look myself but Stormy and Sabrina talked me out of it. "Where you gonna go, Max, that the sheriff or his deputies or the state police ain't already checked?"

"Sit down, Daddy," Sabrina said. "They'll find her."

Perhaps it was because it was so soon after Pam's death but, terrible possibilities ran through my mind. Kidnapping. Rape. A shallow grave in the forest that someday would be found by hunters. And on and on.

It was an awful day.

We didn't eat. We didn't talk.

At six that night, Stormy was in the kitchen making tuna salad sandwiches for anyone who wanted them and I was in my bedroom, actually almost asleep. I might have made it if the phone hadn't started ringing. I was so tired of not receiving good news that I considered letting the phone just ring itself out and probably would have if Sabrina hadn't answered it. I could hear her through the wall. "Whitefork Lodge. Good evening." There was a pause while she listened. "No, this is his daughter. Whom can I say is calling, please?" Another pause and then she yelled, "Daddy! Get out here! Oh, my God, it's Ruth! Something's wrong!"

The speed with which I moved to intercept Rachel the other night on the porch was nothing compared to how fast I was out of bed, into the hall and reaching for the phone this time. Sabrina backed away, her hand over her mouth. Her eyes were as frightened as I'd ever seen them.

"Hello," I said into the receiver. "Ruth? What is it . . . ?"

"Oh, Max," I heard Ruth cry. "I'm . . . he's . . . they've . . .ummpff . . ." Her voice was cut off as if someone had put a hand over her mouth.

"Ruth?" I yelled. "Ruth?" She didn't answer but I could hear noises on the other end. "Ruth? What's . . . ?"

A man's voice, muffled like he was speaking through a piece of fabric covering the mouthpiece came on the line. "That was so you know she's alive, Addams," he said.

"What? Who is this?"

"Shut up, Addams and listen. Listen very carefully."

I waited. I looked at Sabrina. Stormy was coming down the hall, frowning at me. "Ruth's in trouble," Sabrina whispered to her.

Finally the voice came back onto the phone. "You still there, Addams?"

"I'm still here. What have you done with Ruth? Who is this?"

"I told you to listen carefully, Addams."

"I am listening."

"No more questions."

"I'm listening," I said.

"What did you do with the tooth?"

"The tooth? What do you mean the tooth?"

"Answer the question! Where is the tooth that was in the skull when you found it?"

I took a deep breath. "I don't know."

"Addams?! Don't fuck with me."

I didn't want to say we'd lost it. Obviously, whoever this was didn't know. "What have you done to Ruth?" I tried to stall.

"I told you, Addams. I'm asking the questions. If you care about your girlfriend here, you'll answer mine. Where's the tooth?"

"I'm not sure . . ."

"Find it. We'll call you back in five minutes." He hung up.

I stood there looking at the phone. Sabrina and Stormy were looking at me. Asta was slowly coming down the stairs in her stocking feet.

"What is it, Max?" Stormy asked. "What happenin'?"

"Oh, Daddy, Ruth sounded so afraid."

"Max! Dammit!" Stormy grabbed my arm and shook it. "What's goin' on?"

I put the phone down and looked at them. "Someone's got Ruth and they think we've got the tooth from the skull." I sighed. "They want it."

"Got her?" Stormy gripped my arm. "Got her how?"

"I don't know," I said. "Prisoner. Hostage. Captive. But they want the tooth."

"We ain't got it."

Sabrina put her hands over her mouth. "Oh, God, Daddy. They want to trade Ruth for the tooth? What are we going to do?"

I shook my head. "I don't know. He's calling back in five minutes."

"Well, just tell 'im we ain't got it," Stormy said. "Tell 'im to let Ruth go 'cause we ain't got no damn tooth. It was lost long time ago."

I sighed.

"The tooth isn't lost," Asta said from the stairs in a voice so quiet I almost didn't hear her. "I have it upstairs."

We all looked at her.

"You have the tooth?" I said. "What do you mean, you have the tooth?"

"The tooth from the skull?" Sabrina said.

Asta nodded, turned and went back up the stairs.

Sabrina, Stormy and I looked at each other.

Crying again, Asta came slowly back down the stairs. She held her fist out to me and opened it. The molar from the skull was in the palm of her hand.

I grabbed it. "What the hell are you doing with it?" I said. "Where did you get it? Why haven't you said something . . . ?"

The phone was ringing again. Asta sat on a step and began sobbing. I reached for the phone. "Quiet!" I said to Asta. "Just be quiet!"

"Let me get it," Stormy said, reaching for the phone. "I'll get to the bottom of this."

"No," I said, pulling her back. "I think Ruth's really in trouble. Let me handle this." I picked up the receiver. "Hello?"

It was the same muffled man's voice. "You have it?"

"Yes."

"You're not fucking with me are you, Addams?"

"I said, I have it."

"Good. Now listen to me carefully. I want no sheriffs. No State Police. Understand?"

"Yes."

"You're to call no one. No one. Understand?"

"You want the tooth? It's your's for Chrissake. Just don't hurt Ruth."

"Call no one. I'll get back to you in a few minutes." I think he started to hang up but he added, "If I call back and your phone's busy, I kill her." Then he hung up.

I hung up and looked at Sabrina. "Go out to your car quick and call the sheriff on your car phone," I said. "Tell him someone has Ruth and is threatening to kill her if we don't give them this tooth. Tell him to get out as fast as he can. Tell him to come alone and not tell anyone." I took the tooth from Stormy. "Jesus, I hope including the sheriff in this is the right thing."

"'Course it's right, Max," Stormy said. "Why wouldn't it be?"

"The guy on the phone said he'd kill Ruth if I did."

Sabrina went out the front door. We had parked her Jeep Cherokee out by the workshop to get out of the way when the all the police were here and it was still there. I couldn't see her and only hoped she was getting through to the sheriff. I looked at the tooth in my hand and then at Asta still sitting on the stairs. "What the hell were you thinking? What did you want, a souvenir?"

"I just wanted to keep my job." Her lower lip trembled.

I stood there staring at her. I felt like hitting her.

"Oh, God. What have I done?" she groaned.

Stormy sat on the step below her and gently took her hand. "What have you done, honey?"

She just shook her head.

I looked at my watch. What if the guy on the phone knew we were calling the sheriff, I thought. What if somehow he was monitoring? No. That wasn't possible. But why hadn't he called back? It had now been eleven minutes since I hung up.

At twenty-two minutes, thirty-three seconds, Sabrina came trotting up the lawn from the workshop. As she started up the porch steps, the phone rang.

I grabbed it before it stopped vibrating.

"Okay, Addams," the muffled voice said. "Here's how you can be a hero and save your little girlfriend's life."

"Sheriff's on his way," Sabrina whispered.

"What do you want me to do?" I said into the phone.

"I told you before, Addams. You don't ask questions. You're to listen. Understand?"

I sighed and looked at Sabrina who stood against the opposite wall still breathing hard from her run up the hill.

"I said, do you understand?!?" the voice yelled.

"I understand," I said.

"It's now almost six-thirty. I'm going to call you at eight o'clock sharp and tell you what I want you to do."

"What's wrong with right now?" I yelled into the phone. "I've got your damned tooth. You want it or not? Tell me where to go. I'll be there."

"Eight o'clock, Addams." And he hung up.

I threw the receiver against the log wall. "Dammit!" It bounced, but didn't break.

"Now what, Max?" Stormy stooped and picked up the phone.

She put it to her ear and, satisfied it still worked, returned it to its cradle.

"We have to wait again." I looked at Asta. "I want you to tell me what you were doing with this tooth!" I grabbed her buy the arm and led her into the dining room. I pushed her into one of the big chairs. "And I want you to tell me now."

"Max . . ." Stormy was right behind me.

"Goddammit, Stormy. If this thing . . .," I held the tooth out at Asta, " . . . if they hurt Ruth, I'll . . ."

"Daddy, the sheriff said he'd be here." Sabrina sat on the arm of Asta's chair.

I sat on the couch. "You got through okay? I was worried the car phone wouldn't work."

"Works fine," Stormy said. "It's that sheriff's office that don't work so fine. Had to patch us through to Simon."

"Where was he?"

"Up near Red Town, I think the dispatch said."

I looked at Asta. I was calmer. "Just tell us, Asta." I held up the tooth again. "What were you doing with this?"

She looked at Sabrina, then Stormy, then back at me. "I'm so sorry . . ."

"Tell us."

"The skull isn't a thousand years old," she said. "I doubt if it's a dozen years old."

"What?" I stood. "What the hell are you . . . ?"

"Sit down, Max," Stormy said. "Let her tell it." She looked at Asta. "Go on, honey."

I sat.

Asta swallowed hard and continued. "The first time I saw the skull I knew it wasn't old. I mean, it was obvious. But, everybody else thought it was," she sighed, "so, I kind of went with it." She looked at Sabrina. "You know?"

Sabrina nodded.

"I mean, it was fun. I was sort of the big shot expert. And Rachel thought it was old too. So, I played along. I knew I could take pictures of it in a way that would make it look old and, if I wrote my report right and lied a little about the kind of lake bottom it was found in and stuff like that, my boss would believe I'd discovered something cool." She looked at Sabrina again. "I didn't want to be fired, 'Brina."

"I know," Sabrina whispered.

"Why did you steal the tooth?" I said.

She sighed. "I was afraid one of you would see the filling in it. Then you'd know I was lying."

I looked at the molar in my hand. I turned it with a finger. A shiny silver filling glinted in the lamp light. I handed it to Stormy and she squinted at it. "I'll be damned," she said and passed it to Sabrina.

Asta continued, "The filling started to show as soon as I began soaking the skull that first night so," she smiled sheepishly, "I pried it out and hid it."

"Yeah, but," Sabrina handed the tooth back to me, "weren't you worried your boss might send someone up here to see the skull first hand? They'd know you lied right away, wouldn't they?"

"I figured it would be back in the lake by the time they got up here. Besides," she blushed, "I sent them pieces of this," she pulled her bone and topaz necklace from inside her blouse, "to keep them occupied. It carbon dates at 1200 years."

"You mean, it wasn't just the pictures and your report?" I said. "It was pieces of the necklace that led them to believe it was so old?"

She nodded. "They did a rough scan on the bone chips in the museum lab late yesterday."

"Jesus," I said, lighting a cigarette.

"I was sure you knew, Max." She sniffed. "When you saw me in the workshop? I wasn't fixing my necklace. I was chipping pieces off of it. And I put the pieces in the envelope and said they were from the skull." She ripped the necklace from her neck and tossed it on the floor at Stormy's feet. "I'm a liar. I should be the one dead. Not Pam."

Stormy leaned and picked up the necklace. She looked at me.

I simply shook my head, stood and walked out onto the porch. I waited and smoked and paced and looked at my watch. Where was Perkins?

Stormy joined me. "Little girl's pretty upset," she said.

"I am too."

"What's done is done."

I didn't comment.

"One thing let's not do," she said. "Let's not mention this lying about the age thing to Perkins."

"Why the hell not?"

"Wanta keep him focused, is why not. Focused on gettin' Ruth back safe and sound."

Perkins arrived fifteen minutes later. He was in his personal car, an old, rusting, Suburu wagon. No sirens. No flashing lights. No one with him. He parked in the turn around and got out. No uniform either. He was wearing a pair of jeans, sneakers and a white tee shirt under a rust colored windbreaker. When it flapped open, I could see the grip of his revolver in a shoulder holster under his arm. I met him at the top of the porch stairs and, as thoroughly as I could, told him everything the man on the phone had said.

"Let's see the tooth," he said.

I dug it out of my pocket and handed it to him.

He turned it in his fingers. "Rather unremarkable, if you ask me." If he saw the filling, he didn't show it.

"Someone doesn't think so," I said, a little irritated at his non-chalance. "He's going to kill Ruth if he doesn't get it."

"How do you know it's a he?" Perkins narrowed his eyes at me.

I shrugged.

"Sabrina said the voice was muffled like a cloth was over the mouthpiece, right?"

I nodded.

"Well? Could it have been a woman?"

"Jesus Christ, Simon, who gives a shit? I heard Ruth's voice.

He's got her. I believe him when he says he'll kill her. What should we do?"

He put his hand on my shoulder and turned me toward the lodge. "First, let's go inside," he said. "Maybe you can have a Loon and calm down." He opened the door for me. "I need you to relax before we can do anything." I swear I saw him actually smile as he tucked the tooth in his jacket pocket.

Stormy was standing by the fireplace and Sabrina was sitting with Asta on the couch. Asta saw Perkins come in and said, "Oh God. This just keeps getting worse." She pulled Sabrina to her. "It's a nightmare."

I declined having the beer and Perkins and I sat at the big table. The sun was setting out over the lake and trout were rising everywhere. I didn't care. "What are we going to do, Simon?"

"You call that Hughes fella, Simon?" Stormy sat with us.

"Whoa." Perkins held up his hands. "One question at a time." He looked at Stormy. "Yes, Stormy, I called Captain Hughes. As soon as I got off the phone with Sabrina." He looked at me. "What we're going to do to get Ruth back." He took the tooth from his pocket and laid it on the table, turning it with his finger tip.

"Well?" I said.

"Yeah." Stormy picked up the tooth. "How we gonna get Ruth?"

"As you know, I spent many years in Burlington with the State Police. Part of my lieutenant's exam was hostage negotiation. I was good at it. Top of my class. In fact, I was so good, I was called out on special assignment all over the state." He looked at Stormy. "You remember the VanDine kidnapping, Stormy?"

She nodded. "That gas station girl? I remember her but I don't recall you bein' no hostage negotiator."

He looked at me. "This was maybe two years before you moved up here, Max. Two drugged up kids robbed a Texaco station down in Bennington and when they found out the young woman . . . Nancy VanDine was her name . . . who was on duty that night couldn't open the safe, they called the cops and demanded a million dollars or they were going to blow her and the place up." He looked over at Sabrina and Asta. "I negotiated that incident. Got the girl out. Sharp shooters took care of the rest of it."

"You think you're going to negotiate with this guy?" I said.

"Don't think," he said. "I am."

"Now, wait a minute, Simon . . ."

"No, you wait a minute, Max. Hughes agrees with me. Once this person calls you again, we're going to take over. I assume the kidnapper'll give you instructions where to take that tooth." He pointed to the molar. "I'm going to call Hughes after we find out, and he and a special hostage team will meet me at the place."

I slowly shook my head.

"I understand how helpless this makes you feel, Max. Believe me, I do. But, if anyone can make this turn out right, we can."

I sighed. "I just picture guns blazing and Ruth caught in the middle of it."

He put his hand on my forearm. "One thing you have to face, Max. Ruth might be gone already."

"Oh, Jesus," Stormy said.

He didn't look at her. "So, the first thing we have to do when we get to wherever this drop off point will be, Max, is attempt to determine how Ruth is. And where she is." He narrowed his eyes. "Because, whoever this is, he's not getting the tooth until I get Ruth. Now," he looked at his watch, "it's almost seven. We've got an hour." He looked at Stormy. "You don't suppose I could get a cup of coffee, do you?"

"Comin' up." Stormy went to the sideboard.

I picked up the molar and held it in the light. Stormy's fingernails had chipped more of the black film from the tooth and now a part of the uneven chewing surface showed yellowish white. I dropped it in my shirt pocket.

While the coffee was brewing, Perkins used our phone to call Hughes and set up a tracer to be put on the line. "We're going to try for a fix on where the call is coming from," he said, when he came back into the room. "Just in case whoever this is just wants the tooth thrown out a window somewhere."

"But doesn't that mean I've got to keep him on the line?"

He nodded. "Two minutes, minimum." He shrugged. "It's worth a try."

*   *   *

Eight o'clock came and went. At eight forty-five, Perkins went out to his car to call Hughes from his car phone. "He'll wonder why he hasn't heard from me," he said, going to the door. "But I better use the my phone outside, just in case your guy tries to call."

I watched him go to his car and, as he climbed in, I went back into the dining room. "I wish there was some other way to do this."

The phone rang at eight-fifty-one. Perkins was still out in his car. "Should I answer it?" I said to Stormy.

"I'll get Perkins." She said. "You get the phone. And remember what he said about two minutes, Max."

I watched her go out the door and down the porch steps and then picked up the phone. I cleared my throat. "Whitefork Lodge."

It was Rayleen. "Lordy, lordy, Max," he said. There was a lot of static in the call. "I can't believe it. I just heard 'bout Pam."

"It's true, Rayleen. Listen I have to . . ."

"We said prayers for her soon as we heard." His voice echoed and faded in and out. "More'n two hundred of us."

"Where are you, Rayleen?" I said, covering my other ear with my palm. "I can barely hear you. You sound liked you're in a metal drum."

"Kinda am," he said. "I'm in the Workers' van on their car phone. I just dumped a bunch of Wabnakis at Red Town."

"Red Town?"

"Yeah. Had us a big mass baptism today. Boy, was that water cold. I volunteered to bring 'em all home."

"Rayleen, I have to get off the . . ."

"How's Stormy holdin' up?"

"Better than the rest of us." I had to get him off the phone.

"Listen, Rayleen. We have a sort of problem here right now and I need the phone line clear. Do you mind?" I felt terrible not telling him what was going on but, it was too complicated.

"Oh," he said. "What's goin' on?"

"Nothing you should worry about," I said. "It's just that I've got to hang up and free this line."

"You need me there, Max?"

"No, Rayleen. Go back out to Monday Lake. Call back in an hour or so. I'll explain everything then."

"You sure everythin's okay?"

"It's fine, Rayleen. Fine." I started to hang up.

"Oh yeah," he said. "Just seen Ruth up there at Red Town."

"You what? When?"

"Dunno. Maybe fifteen minutes ago. She didn't see me. Was ridin' in a big blue pickup goin' the other way up the main street there."

"A blue pickup? With a yellow plow hitch?"

"Yep. Didn't see who was drivin', was so surprised to see her, you know?"

"You sure it was Ruth?"

"'Course I'm sure, Max. Know her anywheres."

I hung up on him, grabbed my barn coat and quickly went out onto the porch. Stormy and Perkins were coming up through the yard.

"Where you going, Max?" Stormy said.

"I know where Ruth is," I said. "Rayleen just saw her fifteen minutes ago in Red Town."

Perkins frowned. "Who saw her?"

"Rayleen," I said and told them both what Rayleen had told me. "I'm going up there and get her. I've had enough of this."

"Hold on, Max." Perkins grabbed my sleeve. "Think about what you're doing."

I shook his hand off. "I know what I'm doing."

"No you don't, Max," he said. "You're just going to drive around hoping you'll see her?"

I shrugged.

"This guy on the phone's no dummy, Max" he said, taking my arm again and turning me toward the lodge. "We know where she is. That's good. But, this changes everything."

I didn't understand. "What do you mean, it changes everything? Now we know where she is. The guy on the phone doesn't know we know. We've got the advantage, Simon. We can go get her."

"No," he said. "You stay put. I have to call Hughes." He headed back to his car. "This changes everything. He's going to have to move in on Red Town." He pushed me toward Stormy. "Don't let Max go anywhere, Stormy. You both go in the lodge and wait for that phone call. The wrong move now and Ruth will be dead for sure."

"I hope the guy didn't try to call while Rayleen was on the phone," I said after him.

"Don't worry, Max," he said over his shoulder. "He wants this over as much as you do. He'll call back."

Perkins was right. Stormy and I had barely stepped into the hallway when the phone rang.

"You want me to go get Simon?" Stormy said, starting back for the door.

"No, wait." I picked up the phone.

"I've been trying to call you Addams and your line has been busy. You talking to the police?"

"No," I said. "I wasn't talking to the police, dammit. This is a fishing lodge, you know. We get phone . . ."

"Shut up, Addams and listen. I want this over and done with."

"I'm listening."

"You have a car phone?"

"In my daughter's . . ."

"Good. Your housekeeper there with you?"

"What do you want with her?"

"Addams, I told you to listen."

I sighed and looked at Stormy.

"I want you to get in your daughter's car and drive west on Route 16. Don't turn off or stop until your housekeeper calls you on that car phone."

"What the hell . . . ?"

"I'll be calling her Addams and giving her instructions that she'll relay to you and that you'll follow. Understand?"

"Why all the bullshit?" I said. "Just tell me where you want the tooth and I'll take it there. All I want is Ruth."

He laughed. "I don't trust you, Addams. You do it this way, or it doesn't happen."

"You want me to get in the car and drive west on 16 until Stormy calls me and gives me the rest of your instructions?"

"If you want to see this woman alive. Now, do it." He hung up.

I looked at Stormy.

"Well?"

"Get Perkins," I said.

Back in the dining room I told everyone what the caller had told me.

"Oh, Daddy, I don't want you going."

"Don't worry, Sabrina," Perkins said. "He isn't going anywhere. I'm taking it from here."

"No you're not, Simon." I stood. "I listened to you once and stayed here but this is different. He wants me and he's going to get me."

Stormy sighed. "Max . . ."

"I started this thing, Stormy. I'm going to see it through to the end. If it hadn't been for me, the skull, much less that goddam tooth, wouldn't exist. Pam wouldn't be dead. The Chief would probably be sitting on the porch smoking a cigar right now and Ruth would probably be sitting right over there in that chair having a martini with Sabrina."

"Max," Stormy said. "Don't be a fool. Let the professionals handle this now."

I shook my head. "I've let too many things be handled by other people, Stormy. I haven't ever been there for Ruth. I'm not going to let her down this time."

"You're going to get her killed, Max." Perkins stood and glared at me. "That's what you're going to do."

"Daddy . . ."

"Whatever you're gonna do," Stormy said, looking at her watch. "Think you better be doin' it quick. You're supposed to be drivin' west on 16 right now."

Perkins was still glaring at me and I glared right back. "I'm going, Simon." I patted the tooth in my shirt pocket. "I've got what he wants." I went to the peg by the door, grabbed my barn coat and pulled it on again. "Come if you want."

Perkins sighed. "Alright, Max. Alright." He joined me at the door. "I'll follow you in my car. And I'll call Hughes and tell him what we're doing." He went out the door, down the steps and across the lawn to his car.

I started out the door after him.

"Max?" Stormy was going down the hall toward the kitchen. "Pull up to the front of the lodge before you go. I wanta give you somethin'."

Once I figured out which key was for what and got the Cherokee started, I pulled up to the front of the lodge. I could just see Perkins' taillights as he waited in the trees part way up the access road.

Stormy came out the door with the Winchester. It had one of the lodge towels wrapped around it. She opened the back door and tossed it on the seat. "Just in case," she said, giving me a wink. "There's five cartridges in the magazine. Be careful though. I already levered one into the chamber. Baby's ready to fire."

"Jesus, Stormy," I said. "I don't want that thing . . ." But she'd already slammed the door and gone back up the steps. She waved.

As I pulled away from the light of the lodge, I could see Venus.

And like the night I'd left Pam sleeping in the cabin, it was blinking coldly in the dark sky out over the mountains.

This time, I thought, as I pulled past Perkins and he fell in behind me, at least I'm not going to stand around and watch it disappear.

CHAPTER EIGHTEEN

Except during the fall when the leaves are turning, Route 16 doesn't see much traffic other than lumber trucks on their way to the big paper mill over in New Hampshire or pickups on their way to Skip's bar at The Starlight.

Tonight was no exception. Other that Perkins' headlights in my rearview mirror, I had yet to see a car. I had passed the place where Pam and I had been attacked by Gerald and Willie and, about a mile ahead, could see the blue and red lights blinking on the Starlight sign.

Sabrina's car phone hadn't rung either.

We passed the Starlight's parking lot and plunged back into the dark, now only my headlights and Perkins' illuminating the broken yellow line on the roadway and the white dots reflecting from the guardrail posts along the sides.

The big Jeep was an automatic and, obviously, the top of the line. It still smelled like new leather. The cluster of instrumentation on the plastic wood grain dash glowed green. The odometer read only 2600 some odd miles. Brand new. I wondered vaguely where Sabrina and David kept this thing in the city. And even more vaguely, why they'd own it. It seemed to me that, if you lived in a place like New York City, you used public transportation. When you needed a car, you rented one.

I lit a cigarette. The ashtray was full of quarters and dimes so I found the correct button and cracked the window. The telephone, it's keys lit green like the dash, was mounted on the center console at my right elbow.

Perkins stayed about two car lengths behind me. His brights weren't on but his right headlight was slightly askew and I had to tilt the rearview mirror to keep it out of my eyes.

I wondered whether I was being foolish by insisting on going along.

About four miles beyond The Starlight, the phone rang. The sound was so shrill and foreign to me in an automobile that I swerved and almost drove off the road. Tires squealed and, behind me, Perkins ate some gravel dust from the shoulder but, once I was back in the correct lane, I stuck the cigarette in with the coins and picked up the handset. "Hello?"

"He called, Max," It was Stormy.

"Where's he want me to go?"

"Where else?" she said. "Red Town."

"What do I do when I get there?"

"He says to drive through on the main street until you see the red mobile home on the left. It has a . . . damn, I can't read my writing . . . a . . . white fence in front. Turn left just past it, This is called, Creek Road. It goes up a hill and . . ."

"I know where it is."

"Dammit, Max. Will you just listen?"

"Sorry."

"At the top of the hill . . . he says you'll know it's the top 'cause it flattens out . . ."

"Stormy, I've been up there. There's a swamp up there on the right where the creek starts."

"Well, that's where he wants you to go. Drive right back to the edge of that swamp. You know the little dirt track that takes you in there?"

"I know it," I said. "Finding it at night might be a little tricky."

"Hope you do. Sounds like that's where Ruth'll be. You're supposed to park at the end of the track. At the edge of the swamp. He'll bring Ruth and you can swop."

"That's it?"

"That's it," she said. "'Course who knows what's gonna happen after. You're gonna tell Simon what you're gonna do, I hope."

"Right now." I flicked on my blinker and pulled off the road onto the shoulder. Perkins put on his blinker and followed. "Stormy?" I said.

"Yeah, I'm still here."

"Wish me luck."

"Already been wishin' so hard, Max, feel like one of Rayleen's God botherers."

I looked in the rearview. Perkins wasn't getting out so I figured he wanted me to come back to him. "Gotta go, Stormy. See you in a while."

We hung up and, leaving the Cherokee's engine running, I limped back to Perkins' car. He rolled the window down. "Get your instructions?"

I leaned on the Suburu's roof and told him what Stormy had told me. He had a big, full, tan canvas duffle bag in the back that took up the entire the seat. His telephone was a portable and a wire ran from the cigarette lighter to the unit which was lying on what looked like and old tee-shirt on the passenger seat.

"I know the place," he said, when I'd finished with the instructions.

I pointed to the phone on the seat. "Hughes going to be in Red Town?"

He nodded. "They're there now. We won't see them, but they're already there."

"You going to tell him about the meeting at the swamp?"

"Of course." He nodded toward the idling Cherokee. "Get in your car and let's get going. I'll call him on the way."

"Where are you going to be once I go up to the swamp to make the exchange?"

"I'll see what Hughes thinks I should do."

I nodded and started for the car.

"If he wants us to do anything special," he yelled to me, "I'll flash my headlights. Pull over, if I do."

I waved and got into the Cherokee.

*   *   *

In a straight line, Red Town is two miles back off of Route 16. Unfortunately, that only works if you're a bird. In a car, Red Town is eight and a half hemorrhoid-popping miles of bumpy, rock-strewn dirt road that, in some places, is barely wide enough for one car to negotiate, much less two trying pass each other going opposite directions. During Mud Time in the spring after the snow melts, if you don't have four wheel drive, you don't even think about going to Red Town on this road. Or about getting out.

Of course, there is another road into Red Town . . . and a paved road at that . . . but Perkins and I would have had to drive north all the way around Robinson Mountain and come in at it from the Graniteville side. An hour trip at best.

Tonight, we didn't have the luxury of that kind of time and I took the eight and one half miles of jolts and thumps as fast as I dared push Sabrina's big Jeep. Perkins' headlights bounced behind me.

Red Town itself is the exact opposite of it's violent, unpredict-able access road; Neat frame houses, mobile homes and a few shops sit up on a raised wooden plank sidewalk along the packed dirt main street. Dead end side streets with names like "Winoma", "Waterlily", "Tupi", "Talking Cross" and "Crow Walk" run per-pendicular to the main street and small, well maintained neigh-borhoods of more trailers and little houses sit under big oaks and maples behind mowed lawns.

Tonight, the streets were relatively quiet and in the few houses or trailers I looked into as I drove slowly by, the blue light of television sets flickered on walls and ceilings.

On the corner outside the still busy and lit up Red Town Superette, a sullen group of long haired young men and laughing women with quarts of beer and cigarettes watched Perkins and I go by. In my rearview mirror, I saw two of the young men give us the finger.

The two story, wood-frame, Red Town Elementary school, where Ruth donated time to the reading program, was on the left. In my headlights just ahead, was the red mobile home with the white fence.

I looked in my rearview mirror again. Although Perkins was right on my rear bumper, he hadn't flashed his high beams so I hung a left onto Creek Road and started up the steep hill.

Creek Road is nothing more than a little used old logging road; two muddy tracks separated by a grassy ridge of exposed granite that climbs steeply up to and then along the spine of Robinson Mountain. On the left, the creek from which the road gets it's name, tumbles noisily back down the mountainside, through Red Town and on down the hill where it eventually joins the Whitefork River about fifteen miles below my lodge.

The road itself finally tops out in a section of lightning scarred and stunted alpine-like spruce and scrubby oak clinging to massive glacier-shaped and rounded granite boulders. It is here in this semi-barren and unlikely place that the creek begins as a boggy, ten acre swamp the Wabnaki call, "Grass Mole". Rayleen has told me that every mosquito we have in Loon County comes from Grass Mole. I doubt it but, I've fished up here on many hot summer evenings and the clouds of mosquitoes have more than once forced me from the water and back into my car. Once, they even drove me back down the mountain.

Tonight, however, it was too early in the year for mosquitoes and I lowered the window as the Cherokee crawled up over the lip and onto the granite flat to the left of Grass Mole. The stars were like you see aboard ship and the chirps, honks, burps and peeps of a million unseen frogs filled the cool night air making it seem as if it were the stars I was listening to.

It was only another quarter mile to where I was supposed to turn toward the swamp and park, and Perkins' headlights suddenly flashed behind me. I stopped, turned off my headlights and watched him in my outside mirror shut off his own lights, climb out and come toward me.

He came up to the window. "Hughes told me his people are all over this mountain," he whispered. "You see them?"

I shook my head and peered out into the darkness.

"They're here." He smiled.

"Now what?" I said.

"You drive on ahead, park where you're supposed to and wait. I'll see if I can find Hughes."

I put the Cherokee in Drive and looked back at him but he was gone. I drove slowly the next quarter mile looking for the faint opening in the trees that would mark the little road that went down to the edge of the Grass Mole. When fishing up here, I had parked my Jeep on it many times. Of course, that was in the daytime. At night, everything looked different and, quite frankly, tonight it was just plain spooky.

I would have driven right by the opening in the low knarled trees if it hadn't been for the tire tracks of another car in the mud indicating where it was. Someone had turned in ahead of me. I turned and, with branches scraping the Cherokee along both sides and the roof, slowly drove in. I was close enough to the swamp to see water through the trees in my headlights and I felt the big tires slide and spin in the soft mud. Sunday's rain had obviously raised the level of Grass Mole and I could only hope that the mud I was in was sitting on rock.

I stopped and took the tooth from my shirt pocket. I stuffed it down inside the front of my jeans and into the pouch of my Jockey briefs. I twisted in the bucket seat. It wasn't very comfortable in there and dug into my testicles but, from here on, who knew what might happen? And right now, the fact that I had the molar was the only thing keeping Ruth from being harmed.

The narrow road turned slightly to the right just ahead and, as I steered around the corner, my headlights illuminated the blue pickup. It was parked fifty feet farther down the road, facing away from me, in about six inches of oily looking water. Only an empty gunrack showed through the back window.

I gunned the engine and, spraying mud, bounced and slid the

big car up behind the blue truck. I jammed it into Park, left the headlights on and jumped out, water instantly filling my shoe and running up inside my cast. "Ruth?" I called out as I slogged to the truck's cab. "Ruth?" I yanked open the passenger door.

The acrid aroma of stale urine hit me first. Then I saw Ruth. She was lying on the long seat on her back, her arms behind her. Her skirt was up around her thighs, her ankles duct-taped together. Another wide strip of duct tape was across her mouth. Her eyes rolled and her nostrils flared. She struggled and twisted.

"I'm here now," I said, lifting her into a sitting position. "Everything's going to be all right."

She strained against the tape and her eyes rolled even more frantically. She moaned and nodded her head. She was looking at something behind me.

I turned.

I didn't jump because I wasn't surprised. It was Rachel in her hooded cape. Beside her stood Willie, chewing gum and holding a blue-black revolver with a very long barrel. It was pointed at my chest. He smiled and blew a pinkish bubble and, just as it popped, I felt something hard hit the back of my head, heard a loud crash, saw a flash of light and fell sideways into the dirty water. Just as I blacked out, I looked up at Rachel. I thought I saw Chief Danny Shortsleeves standing in the shadows just behind her.

*   *   *

I regained consciousness on my back on a very hard surface. I didn't open my eyes at first. I listened. All I could hear were frogs. I smelled pine and, faintly, the same urine odor as there had been in the blue truck. I was wet and cold. I tried to move. My hands were bound behind me. I felt something bump my shoulder. I opened my eyes. It was Ruth. She was lying on her back beside me. She appeared still to be bound. The tape was still on her mouth. We seemed to be on a very large bare outcropping of smooth granite. the black bowl of starry sky above us like a planetarium show.

Everything else seemed to be below us. By raising my shoulders slightly, I could see only the twisted tops of spruce interspersed with bare dead tree limbs. Mostly, we seemed to be alone.

I looked down my body. My coat was gone, shirt pockets were ripped off and hanging and my pants pockets were inside out. My left pant leg was ripped to my crotch. My broken leg was bare. The cast was gone.

I looked at Ruth. She was watching me.

My mouth wasn't taped and I leaned toward her and put lips on her face and using my teeth, picked up the edge of the duct tape. She immediately understood what I was doing and, when I had a good grip on the tape, slowly pulled her head away from mine. There was a ripping sound and her eyes teared as the tape pulled away from her lips. Although it didn't come completely off, her mouth was uncovered. The strip of tape hung from her cheek.

"Oh, God, Max!" She took a deep breath. "Thank you. Thank you. Thank you." He voice was hoarse. "I thought I was going to suffocate. Those bastards." She studied my face. "Are you all right? He hit you pretty hard."

"Probably not," I said. "What's going on? Where are we?"

"Not far from where they hit you," she said. "We're on a big flat boulder right next to Creek Road."

"Where are they?"

"Trying to find the tooth. Look at your clothes. They couldn't find it on you. They cut off your cast. I think they're tearing Sabrina's car apart."

I wiggled my thighs and felt the tooth in my underwear dig into my groin. The pain made me wince which made my head throb.

"You look like you hurt," she said.

I rolled onto my side and faced her. "Are you all right? Did they hurt you?"

She grimaced. "Other than getting felt up on a regular basis by those two pigs Rachel has with her, I'm okay." She twisted slightly. "I can't feel my hands or feet, though."

"They didn't ...?"

She frowned. "I said, felt up, Max. Like in, they put their filthy hands all over me." She sighed. "But that's all. I don't think either one of them has the guts to do anything else."

"They murdered Pam."

"I know. I'm so sorry, Max. I tried to call you all morning Monday but the state police had your line shut down. Then this happened and . . ."

"I thought I saw the Chief before I blacked out."

She nodded. "I've seen him watching." She sighed. "I guess I should be glad. He pulled one of those filthy pigs off of me this morning."

"I thought he was my friend . . ."

"I know," she said. "I'm so disappointed . . ."

I lowered my voice. "There are state police all over this mountain right now."

"What? What do you mean?"

"Shhh. They know all about this. You. The tooth. Everything. Perkins followed me up here. His car is just back down the road. He had the state police come in first. They're probably watching us right now."

"Then why aren't they helping us?" she whispered back.

"I don't know. They're probably waiting until everyone gets back out here."

"Well, I wish they'd hurry. I'm tired of peeing in my pants."

"Stormy's been right all along," I said, laying my head back on the rock and looking up at the stars. "Rachel has been behind everything. The skull is Danny's wife's isn't it??"

"I'll tell you what it is about that skull, Max Addams," It was Rachel's voice shrill and directly behind my head. "It's the only thing that stands between us and ten million dollars." I felt her hand slap the top of my head and a pain shot down my spine to my hips.

"Rachel. Don't." It was Danny's voice. Then there was the sound of several feet on loose stones, a couple grunts that also sounded like Danny and suddenly five dark people shapes climbed up onto the big boulder and loomed above us. They stood in a half circle at our feet. I couldn't see faces or details, but I assumed they were looking down at us. I could identify Rachel by her hood. She was in the center. Danny's bulk gave him away a little behind her to her left. What I guessed to be Gerald and Willie because of all the hair silhouetted against the starry sky, were on Rachel's other side. One of them had what looked like Stormy's Winchester in his hands. I squinted at the fifth figure and, as was trying to make out the face, it spoke. "Where's the tooth, Max?"

It was Perkins.

It took a few seconds for it to register. And when it did, the realization of how I'd been duped created a feeling of hopelessness so intense I sagged back onto the rock. "Oh, Jesus, Simon," I said. "Not you Simon . . . not you . . ."

"Yes, me, Max." He squatted near my thighs and I could see him now. "Where is it, Max?" He took the revolver from his shoulder holster and rapped the shin of my broken leg with the butt. It hurt and I tried to pull it away. "Where's that tooth? You're holding things up, Max. You got your girl. Now Rachel wants the tooth."

"Hughes isn't here, is he?" I could barely speak.

He laughed. "That dumb boy scout? He's probably sitting down in Montpelier watching the hockey play-offs on TV." He whacked me on the shin again. Harder this time. I heard the clunk and the pain shot to my ankle. "The tooth, Max."

"Knock it off, Simon!" I yelled and kicked him onto his ass. "You touch that leg one more time and you'll never know where the tooth is."

He started to get up.

"Back off, Simon," Danny growled.

Breathing hard, Perkins got to his feet. His revolver was still in his hand at his side.

Danny reached across in front of Rachel. "And give me that gun, Simon."

"No, Danny," Rachel pushed the big man's hand back. "Sheriff Perkins agreed to do three things for me before he gets paid. He's done only one. He got me the skull . . ."

I closed my eyes and took a deep breath. "You killed Pam?" I said to him. "Why? How could you . . . you . . ."

He shrugged. "It happened."

"Shut up, Simon," Danny said. "You didn't have to kill her."

"You bastard." I hissed at Perkins. "I'll . . . if I ever get . . ." I tried to get up but one of the Geronimos stepped across the rock and pressed his foot onto my chest. I fell back onto the boulder.

"Please, Max," Rachel said. "No profanity." She turned to Perkins. "As I was saying, Sheriff Perkins, you've got a long way to go yet before you've earned that money you want so badly. Now, I know you're going to get Max to tell us where the tooth is, but, until then, wasn't there a third thing you were going to take care of for me when the time came?" I couldn't see it but I could feel her evil smile in the hood. "Do you know what I'm talking about, Sheriff Perkins?"

"Now, wait a minute," Danny said to them. "What are you . . . ?"

"I'm talking to the sheriff, Danny," Rachel said, still looking at Perkins. "Do you know what I'm talking about, Sheriff Perkins?"

Perkins took a deep breath. "Yeah," he said. "I know."

"And do you remember how much money it's worth to you?" He nodded.

"Well, Sheriff Perkins." Rachel stepped back away from us and turned her back. "That time we talked about has come."

I looked at Perkins. He stood there for a second looking down at Ruth and me and then, without saying a word or really even aiming, he raised his revolver and, holding it at arm's length, pointed it at Gerald's face and shot him. He then swung the gun at Willie and did the same thing. Two flashes from the muzzle. Two explosions. Boom. Boom. Just like that. And that fast. Gerald staggered backward, grabbed at Rachel, missed and fell off the rock. Willie, who was still standing with his foot on my chest, just disappeared out of sight over my head like he'd suddenly learned to fly.

Ruth screamed and curled into a fetal position against me.

"This is goin' too far," I heard Danny say. "When did we decide to do that?"

No one answered him. I could hear what I assumed to be Willie's spasmodic kicking in the bushes somewhere behind me, but that was it. The raw smell of cordite hung in the still air over the rock.

"You're crazy!" Ruth yelled.

"Tape her mouth back up," Rachel said.

Perkins started for Ruth.

"No," I yelled. "Leave her mouth alone, asshole. You want the tooth, I'll give you the tooth. Just keep your hands off of her."

"Leave her alone," Danny said, yanking Perkins away by the back of the shirt and shoving him to the other side of the rock. "And put that Goddam gun away."

Perkins just stood there. "What's with you, Chief?"

"Do as Danny says," Rachel said. "Put it away, Sheriff."

"Fuck," Perkins said and shoved the revolver inside his jacket.

I struggled to a sitting position. I looked up at Danny. "Let Ruth go, Chief. I'm asking you as a friend, let her go."

He looked away.

"Don't think we can do that, Max," Perkins said. "If we let her go . . . if we let either of you go . . . then all this will have been for nothing."

"All of what?" Ruth said. She was angry now. "All of what?"

Perkins laughed, pulled the front of his tee-shirt up over his face and spoke through the fabric. "Hello, Addams," his voice was muffled. "You ever want to see your girlfriend alive again, listen carefully." He dropped the tee-shirt and laughed again. "Sound familiar, Max?"

I sighed. It was familiar. "What did you do, Simon? Call me from your car in our my front yard?"

"It was working pretty good too. Until that damn Rayleen called you."

"You've never negotiated anything, have you?" I said.

"Guess not." He shook his head. "Sure couldn't get you to give up the skull the easy way." He looked at Rachel. "Neither of us could."

"Dammit!" Ruth yelled. "Will someone tell me what's happening?"

I looked at Rachel.

She looked at Danny. "Tell her," she said.

"I can't," he said and hung his head.

"How about you Max?" she said. "You seemed to have figured most of it out. Why don't you enlighten your girlfriend."

I looked at Ruth and smiled. "Don't worry," I said. "We'll get out of this somehow."

"You going to do as Rachel says?" Perkins kicked me in the lower back. "Or you going to lay there making eyes at each other?"

I took a deep breath, rolled to my back and looked up at Danny. "You guys killed your wife, didn't you?"

Danny looked away.

"Close," Rachel said. "But no cigar. I killed her." She paused either to let it sink in or to get better control of herself. I could see she was shaking. "Winnie was no wife to Danny. She was a drunk. She didn't deserve him." She spit out into the night. "I hated her. All the times we had to go find her. Covered with vomit and shit. Her hair filthy." She paused again and I could hear her breathing. "Winnie didn't deserve that money her father left her either. She would have just spent it all on booze. She was useless. So, I gave Danny what he needed in a woman. And things were fine for a while."

"And she found out," I said.

"Yes, she found out." She nodded. "She yelled at Danny. Wanted a divorce. Then she got drunk and disappeared. Three whole days. I found her lying in the garbage behind the Starlight." She sighed. "Certainly you can understand how I felt, Max. All that money. Going to a drunk like that."

"Oh sure," I said, facetiously. "I understand perfectly. She needed killing."

Perkins raised his foot as though he was going to kick me again.

"Simon!" Danny growled.

Perkins lowered his foot. "Do you want to hear this, Max?" he said. "Or do you want your other leg broken?"

I really didn't want either. I wanted somehow to stall for time. "Go on," I said to Rachel. "So you found her drunk. Then what? Is that when you killed her?"

"I put her in the back of Danny's car and took her down that little road on the north side of your lake and I shot her. It was no different than shooting a dog gone bad. Or shooting these two." She gestured in the direction of Willie and Gerry. "Then, I filled her body with stones and pushed her in." She actually smiled. "That was ten years ago and I'd almost forgotten she ever existed."

"Until we pulled her out of the lake," I said.

She didn't answer.

I looked at Danny. "You didn't know, did you, Chief?" I said. "When did you find out? Yesterday? Today?" I looked at his face. "You just found out tonight, didn't you? Jesus, Chief."

He didn't answer and just hung his head.

She put an arm around Danny's back. "Poor Danny never knew."

Rachel stepped up to my feet and looked down at me. "It was perfect. Then you had to find her skull . . ."

"There's a lot more than just a skull now, Rachel," I said. "A state police dive team pulled up her skeleton last night."

"No, Max. You're wrong," she said.

"I saw them."

Danny shook his head sadly. "No, Max."

"What you saw was us, Max," Perkins said.

"You don't think I intended to let the police have the rest of those bones do you?" Rachel said.

"Borrowed the scuba gear from that kid, Kevin," Perkins said.

I tried to get up. "If you hurt that boy, Simon . . ."

"We borrowed it Max," Danny said. "Kevin even wanted to help but I wouldn't let him."

"That what's in the duffle in the back of you car." I said.

He nodded. "Going to return it to him as soon as we're done

here." He patted his wallet pocket. "Gonna pay him handsomely for it too."

"Where are the bones?" Ruth asked.

Rachel pushed the hood back off her head. Her eyes flashed. "In the Grass Mole. The skull too. All that's left is the tooth, Max, and I want it. Now."

"Why?" Ruth struggled to a sitting position. "What good is one tooth?"

"It has a filling in it," I said.

"Now where is it?" Rachel snarled.

"Let Ruth go, Chief," I said. "Let her go."

"No, Max," Ruth said. "I'm not going without you."

Danny came across the rock and stood between Ruth and I. I've never seen anyone look so troubled. Not even at a funeral for a child. He lowered his big body and sat cross-legged between us. "I don't know what to do, Max," he said softly. "You gotta tell 'em where that tooth is." He put his hand on my chest and gripped my shirt front.

"You don't like this, do you Chief?" I whispered.

He sighed and leaned closer. "I don't like anything, right now," he whispered back. Then louder, "You put it in Willie's truck, didn't you?" His face had become blank but his dark, wet eyes were pleading with me. "Didn't you, Max?" His grip tightened and he yelled, "Didn't you?!"

I tried to read what his eyes were saying.

He shook me and yelled again, "It's in the truck, ain't it? Max? Dammit! Ain't it?"

I frowned. I didn't know exactly what he was doing but I nodded. "Yeah. Yeah. It's under the seat. On the passenger side. Now what are you going to do? Kill me?"

"Yes," Perkins said, as he jumped from the rock to the ground. "As soon as I have that tooth."

I could hear his footsteps fade away toward the Grass Mole and then the sound of twigs snapping as he entered the low trees. Danny didn't get up. "It's over, Max," he whispered, digging in his jacket pocket and pulling out a large folding knife. "I'm so sorry about all of this. It's just plain gone too far." He opened the knife, rolled me onto my stomach and cut the tape around my wrists. Then he turned to Ruth and quickly did the same thing to her ankles and wrists.

Rachel had been watching the woods where Perkins entered and when she saw me start to get to my feet, peeling the tape from my wrists, her eyes widened. "What the hell are you doing? Danny?"

"It's over Rachel," he said, getting slowly to his feet. "Over. I can't do this. Winnie was a long time ago. She was a sick and dyin' woman. I understand. I guess I forgive you for that. You loved me." He shook his head and pointed toward the bodies of Willie and Gerald. "But these boys? What'd they do?" He looked at Ruth. "They were bad boys, but did they deserve to be killed like that, Ruth?"

Ruth was rubbing her wrists. She shook her head. "No one deserves that."

"I know," he said, sadly. "Where's it gonna end, Rachel?"

"It ends here, Danny." She reached for him. "The money's ours now."

He pushed her hands away. "Don't want the money."

"Get hold of yourself," she said. Suddenly her eyes looked frightened. "We've got the tooth, Danny. What about the casino? Our plans? Our . . . ?"

"Your plans," he said, climbing off the boulder and helping Ruth to the ground beside him. "I'm sorry, Rachel. We shouldn't have let it get to this. Winnie was one thing." He helped me slide off the boulder. "But now . . ." He shook his head, stooped and pulled the pistol with the long barrel from the waistband of Willie's jeans. "I can't let us kill anyone else." He sighed and looked at me. "Take Stormy's rifle, Max, and go. Before Perkins gets back." He roughly put his arm around me and hugged me to him. "Don't forget that Saturday, huh? It was sure a good day." Then he pushed me away. "Now go." He pointed down over the hill into the thick dark forest. "Down that way. Perkins might think you went the other way toward his car."

I stood there looking at his big catcher's mitt of a face. He had tears running down his cheeks.

"Go, Max," he said. "Before you can't."

I grabbed the Winchester with one hand and Ruth's hand with the other and, with my newly exposed leg sending shockwaves of pain up and down my side, we scurried between the boulders, slid down a short drop and were suddenly in the thick stunted trees. It was as dark as if we were inside a windowless room.

Downhill was easiest, so, after pausing a minute to let our eyes become accustomed to the blackness, we kept moving that direction. Tree limbs reached out of the dark and tore at our faces and clothes. Low bushes grabbed at our legs and loose stones cut and bruised our bare feet. I stopped and held a branch so Ruth could duck through. As I turned to follow her, I heard a gunshot from behind and above us and we stopped, breathing hard.

"Who's shooting, Max?" Ruth whispered.

"I don't know," I whispered back.

We strained our ears and listened. Then there was another gunshot from above us. We both jumped. I felt Ruth's hand find mine. We waited. I could hear both our hearts pounding.

Then we heard Perkins' voice above us. "Danny?" There was a pause, then, "Jesus Christ! Oh Christ, Rachel! No!" His voice had started low and quickly built until he was screaming on the rocks above us. "Danny, you dumb shit! How could you? Why? Why?"

Ruth squeezed my hand in the darkness and whispered. "What do you suppose happened, Max?"

I shook my head and pushed her ahead a me. "I don't know," I said, a branch whipping me in the chest. "And, right now, I don't care."

We continued climbing down over boulders and trees for about ten more yards when we heard Perkins again. This time he was closer. "I hear you down there, Max." There was the sound of breaking branches and stones rolling from above us. "Maybe the Chief can let you go, but not me."

"He's coming after us, Max," Ruth screamed.

"You got that right, Mayor," Perkins yelled. He wasn't very far away.

Ruth started to run. I grabbed her arm and sitting on the downhill side of a boulder the size of a car, pulled her roughly down with me. "You can't run," I said. "It's too dark."

"Oh, Max . . ." She pushed herself against me. "He's crazy."

I heard another big branch break and looked up hill. There was a hole of starlit sky about three feet in diameter at the top of the boulder. It was framed by the silhouettes of shaggy spruce limbs.

I heard another limb break and then it was still for a full minute. He was listening and we held our breath.

Finally he spoke, "Com'on, Max. You're making me angry." His voice was surprisingly close, just above us to the left. "Com'on, Max. Think of Ruth."

"He's right over there," Ruth whispered.

I laid the barrel of Stormy's Winchester on the rock and aimed it at the dark hole full of stars. "You can have me, Simon," I said loudly. "But you have to let Ruth go."

He didn't answer and, instead, there was sound of twigs snapping as he started down at angle toward my voice.

"Did you hear me, Simon?" I pressed my cheek to the stock of the rifle and aimed at the hole full of stars. "Simon, I said, did you hear me?"

More stones rolled and twigs snapped.

A rock about the size of a baseball rolled directly by us and at the end of the Winchester's hexagonal barrel, the stars in the hole disappeared.

I pulled the trigger and the old rifle barked fire. I quickly levered in another cartridge and pulled the trigger again. Another explosion. I cocked and shot again. Ruth was screaming now and the shape blocking the hole above us tumbled in over the boulder and Perkins slid face first down the smooth granite into my lap.

Screaming loud now, Ruth dove to her right. I heard her roll away in the darkness.

I was pinned under Perkins' body and expected any second to have him rear up and kill me.

He groaned. I felt warm liquid on my bare leg.

"Max?" Ruth's voice was weak. "Max?"

I pushed Perkins off of me and, with another groan, his body rolled away downhill in the darkness. When I couldn't hear it crashing through the trees anymore, I crabbed over the loose shale to Ruth's side.

She grabbed at me, her hands finding and holding my face in the darkness. "Max? Did you . . . ? Is he . . . is he dead?"

"Maybe. I don't know. I'm not sure." I took her hand and helped her up. "Let's just get out of here." As fast as we could manage, we started downhill at an angle away from Perkins and toward, I hoped, level ground and Route 16.

CHAPTER NINETEEN

The 28th of December is the annual Whitefork Lodge Sleighride and Holiday Dinner.

Once a simple affair with one horse-drawn sleigh to ferry a few close friends from where they would park their cars up on Route 16 through the snow and down to the lodge, now almost two dozen people attend and, weather permitting, the sleighride alone takes most of the afternoon.

This year the caravan of sleek, horse-drawn sleighs began all the way up in the village of North Stoneboat. From there, with harness bells jingling in the cold clear air, the eight sleighs traveled south down the center the full length of frozen Monday Lake, around the dam and through the unplowed side streets Loon where we stopped at the Loon Hotel to pick up John Quinn and Bryce Hill. We warmed ourselves with coffee and mulled hard cider in the hotel's Red Pump Room and then it was back into the sleighs and under the blankets and bearskins and up over Morning Mountain on Hooker Hill Road to an old logging trail that terminates just across Route 16 from the Whitefork Lodge access road. After that, as usual, it was a race down the access road to the lodge for our traditional hearty dinner of venison, wild duck and turkey. This year we were lucky and had several grilled brook trout and three poached landlocked salmon that were accidentally killed by guests during the fishing season.

The lodge was lit up like a wooden cruise ship. Small electric candles sparkled in every window. A big wreath covered the front door. White smoke from the birch logs crackling in our two fireplaces trailed from the big chimney on the snow covered roof. Our

Christmas tree, a thick, blue spruce Rayleen and I cut up on Robinson Mountain, stood in the front hall stairwell, the only place in the building that would accommodate it's ten foot height. It blinked with white lights, red glass balls and, this Christmas, several dozen miniature ginger bread cookie snowmen that Sabrina, Elise and Stormy had made in the big ovens of the Wolff Range in the lodge kitchen.

Typical of Stormy, most of the baking was done several days before the party and several mince, apple and pumpkin pies had been arranged on the sideboard in the dining room by the evening of the 27th, with more being brought by guests next day. Skip and Lo Ming Willits usually brought a banana bread, carrot cake and a 10-gallon hat-size plum pudding from the Starlight's kitchen. John and Bryce contributed big wooden bowls of the Loon Hotel's famous spinach and bacon salad, and Lyle Martin's widow, Merriam and her two little girls carried in strawberry-rhubarb pie made from fruit frozen during the summer, as well as, my favorite, mountains of sweet, golden yams baked in butter and maple syrup. Judy Bowman and her husband, Bill don't cook and, instead, brought a box full of beautifully illustrated story books for Elise, and Gary LaFontaine's thick book on the Caddis Fly for me.

Actually, no one's required to bring anything. And some people don't. God knows, Stormy has enough of everything already.

Rayleen and I are in charge of major decorating. Always trying for something beyond just wreaths and kissing balls, this Christmas we had stapled looping garlands of thick, fragrant balsam boughs to the peeled log beams around the perimeter of the lodge's giant dining room. Ruth was in charge of the decorations and place settings on the two fifteen foot long tables we set perpendicular to the fireplace just for the occasion and by dark on the 28th, eight sleighs were parked in front of the lodge and eleven tethered horses, albeit a bit crowded, munched warm dry hay inside the Workshop.

Inside the lodge there were twenty-four green and white checked cloth napkins with red bows around the two long tables and the dining room, reading room, kitchen and hallway were alive with red-faced people and the din of conversation, tinkling glasses, childrens' voices, Christmas music, snapping fires, laughter, the scent of pine and pies, woodsmoke and roasting turkey.

At nine, Stormy lifted the hem of her holiday red caftan, waded out into the snow by the back door and rang the big black iron dinner bell. Everyone filed into the dining room and, for a few minutes, milled around the tables of steaming food reading the little name cards Ruth had put at each place.

Stormy and I were at the heads of the two tables. As a favor to me, Ruth had put my son-in-law, David at Stormy's table. She knew how his constant lectures about my need for better financial planning drove me nuts. I also noticed that this year Ruth had made sure that Skip and Lo Ming's doe-eyed twenty-eight year old daughter Kate was at Stormy's table also. John Purcell, my bachelor friend who had flown in from Colorado just for the occasion had managed a seat next to her. Ruth placed herself at my left. John Quinn was to my right. Just beyond John, Sabrina was in an animated conversation with the youngest sheriff ever elected in Loon history, Richie Norville and his date, a very pretty brunette named, Jennifer TealEye. Rayleen, thinking no one could see him picking at the bowl of stuffing near his elbow, faced me from the other end of the table. A row of candles stretched the length of the table between us broken only by a large wicker basket of white mums and overflowing, steaming platters and covered bowls.

Stormy tapped her salad fork on her water glass and stood. She hadn't taken off her apron. "I want to make a toast," she said, lifting her glass of non-alcoholic beer. "To another year and those old friends who are here," She smiled at the familiar faces around the room, "and those friends who ain't, namely Lyle," She looked at Merriam Martin, "Chief Danny Shortsleeves, Pam Fiore and my husband, Bendel, rest their souls." She smiled. "Also, wanta say hello and welcome to the friends that's new this year." She looked at Asta and her date, a Columbia University photography professor, who had arrived late and almost missed the sleighride. She also looked at Richie. "Thanks for comin' Asta and Bill, and Richie and Jennifer. And thanks everybody." She held the glass out at arm's length. "And, 'course, peace." She chugged the beer. "Now, let's eat 'fore this mess get's cold." She sat.

There was applause and someone whistled and some people attempted to clink wine glasses between the candle flames and then for the next forty-five minutes plates and platters, pitchers, bowls and wine bottles crossed and re-crossed the long tables as most of us ate too much, much too fast.

After eating, Ruth, the consummate politician, got up and I watched her begin to work the other table. I envied the ease with which she seemed to fold herself into the conversation already in progress. Besides the more obvious things like figure, face and eyes, it was one of the first things I'd noticed about her when we originally met.

As Ruth laughed and was engulfed in the big arms of Bill Bowman, I collected a stack of dessert plates and, with Spotter stepping on my crutches, took them to the kitchen. Unlike Ruth, I'm not much for social events, even if it is Christmas. I don't know whether it's the small talk or what seems to happen when so many people get a bunch of drinks in them but, by the time coffee is served I'm ready to get up and go do something else.

Tonight had been especially hard. I hadn't thought about Chief Danny Shortsleeves or Pam in a long time. Seeing Richie and Asta and hearing Stormy mention their names brought those awful three days in April back to me.

Spotter went to the back door and I let him out. Then I opened the refrigerator and took out a cold Loon Lager. I snapped the cap, sat on a stool at the island and, after a sip, lit a cigarette and blew the smoke up toward Stormy's Winchester hanging on it's rack above the door.

The front sight is still bent from where it had banged along the rocks as I used it as a crutch that night Ruth and worked our way down Robinson Mountain and away from the death and dying above us.

By the time we got to Route 16, a half inch long piece of bone was protruding from a bloody tear in my ankle. Ruth's dress and sweater were shreds and I had to give her my shirt before she would go out into the road and try to flag down a car.

It's actually a wonder anyone stopped to help us at all, the way we looked. But someone did and once we were up inside the warm cab of the big eighteen wheel lumber truck, Ruth put her face in her hands and cried. The driver, a French Canadian named, David Vanasse, took us directly to Loon Memorial Hospital. This time, I needed the facilities of the ER as much as my companion.

My ankle had rebroken and this time the fracture had compounded. I was back to where I'd started in the cast department. Not only did they refit me with the original heavy, hot and itchy plaster number, this one didn't stop just below my knee. Because it was important that my leg not move, it went all the way up to mid-thigh.

Ruth was treated for exposure and they cleaned and bandaged her various cuts and bruises. Of all her injuries, however, the area where the duct tape had covered her lips gave her the most trouble for the longest time and it was weeks before we could kiss without her wincing.

State Police Captain Dave Hughes and an entire squad of Vermont's finest swarmed over Robinson Mountain. Not only did they find the bodies of Willie and Gerald but that of Rachel with Danny lying over her. They had both been shot at close range.

I don't like guns and wouldn't hunt if someone paid me to do it. And I don't like killing. When I was told Perkins was found dead a hundred yards down the side of the mountain with two holes in his chest, I threw up.

After the inquest and hearings, Hughes was pursued by the Loon City Council for month or so. Their hope was that they could entice him into taking the job vacated by Perkins. He wasn't interested. As it turned out, Richie was, and his fresh approach to the job, his youthful enthusiasm and an advertising campaign paid for with Jennifer TealEye's father's money were enough to convince

Loon voters to give him a chance. It still seems strange when I hear someone call him, "Sheriff". To me, he's still the kid who forgot to lock the squad car.

Asta left the lodge as soon as the police said she could, and she flew back to New York alone to resign, clean out her desk at the Museum of Natural History and begin circling employment opportunities in the New York Times' Job Mart. After a month of unsuccessful interviews and form rejection letters, she borrowed money from her father and went back to school. On a lark and, because she'd actually enjoyed photographing the skull with Bendel's equipment when she was at the lodge, she took a course in still life photography. She claims she loves it, but Sabrina only laughs and says, "She doesn't know an f-stop from subway stop. It's the professor, Bill Schmidt, she can't get enough of."

Needing two crutches, I joined Sabrina and Asta in Fullersburg, North Carolina for Pam's funeral. It was held in a shady little cemetery on the side of a Kudzu covered hill looking west out over the mountains of Tennessee. Pam's father, her sister, the sister's children and several carloads of Fiores were there. Her sister and the children were beautiful and it was easy to see what Pam might have looked like had she lived long enough to marry and have children. Pam's father, a severely bent little man with yellow skin and a white uniformed nurse pushing his wheelchair, ran his hand up Sabrina's leg under her dress during the silent prayer.

Ruth overheard more than she thought while she was being held by Rachel, Willie and Gerald. Her testimony and from what we've been able to piece together from other sources over the past several months, indicates that Rachel knew the skull was Winnie's from the moment she saw it that first night. She also new that Danny would suspect something if she took it off the lodge property or just threw it back in the lake. So, late that same night, she approached Perkins who was helping organize the night shift at the Red Town Police Department. She promised him total Wabnaki support in the November election if he would go to lodge and using legal means, get her the skull.

Perkins, of course, wasn't successful that first morning and he reported his failure to Rachel immediately afterward. Evidently, she thought she could intimidate us into giving it to her and, telling Danny she'd changed her mind, returned to the lodge with Gerald and Willie.

Everyone in town knows how that turned out. And they also know about the threat she made as they left empty handed.

Rachel made good on her threat and called Perkins again. This time she offered him big money if he'd get the skull. A neighbor who heard Rachel talking on her portable telephone, testified that Rachel said, "I don't care what you have to do, sheriff. Just get it."

Perkins, as we already know, agreed.

We're not sure but, somehow Danny must have let it slip as to where the skull was being kept that night. As far as we know, he was the only one besides ourselves who knew where it was.

The complete circumstances surrounding Pam's death will probably always be a mystery. Obviously, seeing Pam lying there completely unconscious was more than Perkins could resist. And it's possible he didn't even know he'd smothered her until I called him to report the murder the next day.

He did give the skull to Rachel who instantly saw the tooth was missing. She demanded he go back and get it. By then he knew he'd killed Pam and sensing Rachel's panic demanded 100 thousand dollars. She had no where to go, but agree.

He enlisted the aid of Willie and Gerald to kidnap Ruth and, disguising his voice as the kidnapper, did the rest.

It was assumed that Perkins had killed Rachel and Danny, when he discovered Danny had released Ruth and me. However, further study of their wounds, the bullet entry angles and attendant powder burns by state police pathologists in Montpelier changed that. And, disturbing as it is, to me at least, it is now known that shortly after Ruth and I went over the hill, Danny shot Rachel and then turned the gun on himself.

I snubbed the cigarette in the ashtray and drained the beer just as Ruth backed into the kitchen carrying a stack of plates and bowls. "Max?" She smiled and put the bowls on the counter by the sink. "What are you doing in here by yourself?" She turned on the water.

"Taking a breather," I said. "You know me and parties."

"I guess that's something else I have to re-learn." She was letting her auburn hair grow out and she tucked the coppery ends in the collar of her green blouse as she began rinsing and stacking the plates in the dishwasher. "You look a little sad. Everything all right?"

"Yeah," I got up and took the empty bottle to the recycling bin in the pantry. When I came out, she was wiping her hands on a dish towel. "I guess I get a little depressed this time of year," I said. "So many people who should be here, aren't."

"Come back into the dining room, Max." She stepped up to me and put her arms around my waist. "Most of these people are here because of you. They're your friends."

"I know." I pushed my nose in her hair and kissed her on the forehead. I could smell cinnamon. "New shampoo to go with the new hair?"

"No." Ruth looked up at me. "I found it in your bathroom." She laughed. "I hope you don't mind. I kind of like it."

— THE END —

About The Author

David Leitz grew up on a farm in Indiana and his love for the outdoors began in the woodlots and small ponds that surrounded his home. His love for writing began at about the same time and flourished along with painting at Syracuse University. An advertising agency copywriter and creative director in New York City, San Francisco and Boston for over thirty years, David has written and directed many famous award-winning ads and television commercials.

He and his wife Frances live in a 250 year old farm house near the ocean on Massachusetts' north coast although David does much of his writing in a rustic little cabin a roll cast away from a trout stream in southern Vermont. He is the author of five Max Addams' novels as well as numerous award winning short stories.

David is working on Max Addams novel number six. It is due out in the fall of 2000.

You can contact him at dfleitz@mediaone.net